Wolcott Balestier

Benefits Forgot

A novel

Wolcott Balestier

Benefits Forgot
A novel

ISBN/EAN: 9783337028732

Printed in Europe, USA, Canada, Australia, Japan

Cover: Foto ©Andreas Hilbeck / pixelio.de

More available books at **www.hansebooks.com**

Benefits Forgot

A Novel

BY

Wolcott Balestier

Author of
" The Average Woman"
Joint-Author with Rudyard Kipling of
" The Naulahka"

London

William Heinemann

1895

BENEFITS FORGOT.

CHAPTER I.

IT was James Deed's wedding morning, and the town knew it. Deed himself was so full of the knowledge of it, that his face would break from time to time, without his will, into a fond and incommunicable smile of happiness as he rode alone toward Maverick on his horse. His eye measured the crisp and sparkling Colorado morning; and he took the sun upon his large, wholesome, likeable face, with the pleasant feeling that its shining was for him. The agreeable world seemed to have him in thought, and to be minded to do the handsome thing by his wedding-day. And the evil things—the blizzards and sand-storms, and the winds that will be howling at all hours in Colorado, shunned the face of this thrice blessed day.

The cattle pony which Deed was riding had got the news of the kindling morning air, though he lacked word of the wedding; but it was enough that he also knew what it was to be happy. Deed patted his flank affectionately, as they swung into town together; and he was of a mind to give good morrow to the herd that came to the barbed wire fence to observe his happiness with impassive eyes. It was too

B

early to see Margaret; but when he had waked at the ranch-
house on his cattle range, where he had spent the past few
days, he had found it impossible to remain quietly within
doors, and since he must ride it was the nearest thing to
seeing her to ride in her direction.

The curtains were still down at the windows of the house
where Margaret had been staying with Beatrice Vertner for
a month.   The Vertners occupied the largest dwelling in
Maverick, except the brick house which Snell had built since
he had made his strike at Aspen ; its architecture was in the
journeyman-carpenter Queen Anne manner common to
Western towns which have reached their second stage.   The
pony, accustomed to stopping, swerved in toward the gate,
and Deed was obliged to restrain him, unwillingly.   There was
no one in sight to mind that he should kiss his hand to a certain
curtain in the second story; but he was obliged to content
himself with this.   He gave the pony the rein, and went
swinging into Maverick by way of Mesa Street.

His eye roved anxiously, with another thought, as he galloped along, over the circle of snow-peaks that separated
Lone Creek Valley from the world outside, and rested on a
cleft in the white hills, through which his youngest son,
Philip, should at the moment be making his way from
Piñon, on horseback, to be present at the wedding in the
afternoon.

Zacatecas Pass, which found its way through this breach in
the Sangre de Christo range, led down, at a point thirty miles
above Maverick, to the railway, by which Philip should be
taking a train within a few hours.   A dusty cloud hung
above the trail, of which Deed feared he knew the meaning.   It seemed probable that it was snowing in the mountains.   If it was, Philip would almost certainly fail to arrive
in time : it was equally certain that he would be in danger.

There had been a thaw, succeeded by freezing weather,

and the crusted snow clung upon the huge mountain shapes with an effect of being moulded on them.

It was charming to follow the modelling of their mighty bulks under the conforming vesture of white, swelling and dying away in divine suggestions of hidden grace, with the effect of a maiden's raiment. The edged lines by which the hills mounted to the summits lay crumpled on one another, buried in softness. The snow plumped the hollows; and pursued their climbing sides to the secretest fold. The angles were curves, and the curves glistering reaches of satin; for, at every point the sunlight meshed itself in a gleam of white, and the whole field of snow shone with a blinding glitter.

The polished radiance of the hills gave off, in fact, a glare which the eye could not meet with patience, and Deed, withdrawing his glance from the mountains, fixed it on the scattered town into which he was coming. He knew every building in it: he had seen most of them go up. He remembered when the general supply store of Maverick had stood—if a tent may be said to stand—where the post-office now reared its ugly splendour of brick, stone-trimmed and mansard-roofed. In the road over which he was riding there was a familiar spot where an embattled squatter had held his own against the town for a twelvemonth, refusing to move the log cabin which he had built in the centre of Mesa Street before there was a Mesa Street. Deed had contributed to the building of the Episcopal church, past which he was riding at the moment; and, as he glanced at its roof and front, he was sorry that he had not put aside more profitable business long enough to get himself appointed a member of the committee on its architecture. He tried to excuse himself by remembering that he had insisted on the simple and genuine Gothic interior, carried out in pine, which made it a very tolerable little church within.

He had had nothing to do with the roller skating rink ;
nor with the Grand Opera House, which depressed the
observer by its resemblance to Libby Prison, though it was
an achievement of wood, and clapboarded up to the summit
of its false front.   The ingenuousness of the pretence with
which the false front faces down the spectator in the new
towns of the West would be almost a thing to disarm criticism
if the front were, in itself, more beautiful : certainly if the
aspect of the front on the side intended for the audience
were less hideous one could hardly like to humiliate it by
going around behind and spying out the nakedness of the
device.   As it is, nothing could be pleasanter.

As Deed's eye ranged over the roofs of the main street behind the fronts, he smiled at the disproportion between the
height of the actual squat buildings, and the height which
the fronts alleged for them.   His happiness gave an edge
to his observation ; he saw familiar things as if for the
first time.   On the treeless plain over which Maverick
was dispersed nothing obstructed the vision for miles,
and from so slight an elevation as that along which
Deed was cantering, one commanded a panoramic view
of the entire place.   The hotel at the station, the public
school, with its high central tower, the post-office, and the
railway hospital, were the only structures, besides the church,
which lifted themselves above the level of the prevailing one-
and two-storied buildings.   Except in the main street, the
dwelling houses lay isolated from one another in archipela-
goes, marking the push of the real estate boom to one and
another corner of the young city.

As Deed came into the business centre of the place
(distinguished as such by the board sidewalk that went loftily
along the thoroughfare on either side the way, and by
the blazonries in red, black, and chrome yellow, on the
muslin signs tacked upon the fronts of the shops, and the

tethered cattle ponies, burros, and Studebaker wagons of the ranchmen who began to come into town), he was hailed by a loitering group gathered about a telegraph pole in front of the post-office.

"Goin' the wrong way round, ain't you, Mayor?" inquired one of the group.

Deed had served the unexpired term of a Mayor of Maverick who had suffered the inconvenience of being shot in the early days of the town ; and the usual military titles refusing to fasten themselves readily to a certain dignity which the town recognized in him, it had compromised upon "Mayor," as being a fortunate combination of the respectful and the jocular.

Deed's answering smile owned the impeachment of the humorous reference ; but the etiquette of Western chaff is not to sanction such an understanding with speech. It is, rather, *de rigueur* to meet such references with a heavenly unconsciousness of innocence—and to own them only deep within the understanding eye, which admits both parties to such amenities into the open secret of the no-secret.

"Well, yes ; for Aspen and some places up Eagle River way I'm going a good ways around, Burke," said Deed with twinkling eyes, as he checked the pony ; "but I'm headed right for the telegraph office, I think, unless I've taken my observations wrong."

He was giving his pony the rein, as some one said, "There was some tell about town here, Mr. Mayor, of your having asked unanimous consent to make another matter a special order of business for to-day." The postmaster, who had served a term in the legislature, was fond of the phrases he had learned at Denver.

"Yes ; anything we can do for you, you know.....," darkly intimated the young fellow on whom the town's repute

for the possession of the hardest drinker in the county depended. On Sundays Sandy was the sexton of the Episcopal Church; other days he divided between Ira's and
certain odd jobs.

"To be sure : that reminds me—there *is* something you
can do for me, Sandy. Ira has my orders. Call on him this
evening and take the camp."

"Make it a dozen, Mayor," wheedled Sandy.

"Could n't," responded Deed. "I've made it two." He
smiled at the group. Sandy guffawed his enjoyment of the
prospect. The rest coiled their tongues deep in their
cheeks, shifted the pain of sustaining their bodies from one
leg to the other, and gazed at the "Mayor" with a broad
smile.

"Denver ?" asked some one.

Deed shook his head. "Anheuser & Busch."

"Bottles?"

"Kegs."

He surveyed the grinning group with a smile, as he caught
up the reins. The points at which he differed from them
were perhaps rather more obvious at the moment than those
by which he was allied to the life of the place, and of the West.
In spite of eight years spent in the West, broken only by occasional visits to his old home in New York, and, (while Margaret was still in question), by a single visit to Europe, his
bearing retained a sort of distinction, which no measure of
consent to a civilization that surveys life with its hands in its
pockets and its trousers in its boots was likely to vitiate.

In being unaggressive this bearing escaped the condemnation under which all forms of aloofness from the common
lot properly lie in the West; and, in being on humorous
terms with itself, it rather commended itself than otherwise
to a people who must see life as a joke if they would escape
seeing it as a tragedy. It was far from being his manner

of distinction that gave Deed his place in the regard of
Maverick, and of Lone Creek county, of course; and it was
scarcely by it that he prevailed in his practice before the
Supreme Court at Denver, or in his fights for mineral claims
at Leadville. He counted, as every one does in the West, who
counts at all, by pure force.

Deed liked the West as men like what serves their ends,
and for something more. There was a kind of obligation
of gratitude upon him to like it, for it had been his rescue
from lethargy after the death of his wife in New York ten
years before. He had had no wish to live when he came
West, and his friends were surprised to hear after six months
that he was still alive. He was what is called "a very sick
man" when he reached Maverick; and, as he was also a
very miserable one, the chances that he would presently be
borne to the desolate little graveyard on the *mesa* just outside the limits of Maverick were rather better than the
chances of his pulling through to find a new strength with his
reviving interest in life. In the event he not only "came
around," as the neighbours said; but, in laying hold upon
the practice of his profession again, discovered a pleasure
in pursuing the application of ·its principles to new
conditions.

He chaffed the West, now, when he met a man who, like
himself, had once been a New Yorker or a Bostonian; but
this was by way of reminding himself to remember how
absurd the whole affair was, after all. The real fact was,
that, absorbed in his work, in creating a future for his boys,
and finally in accumulating the fortune which he had seen
one day, might be his for the use of the needful energy,
he had forgotten to philosophize the West, as he had been
used to do while he lay staring idly from his sick-bed on a
range of mountains which he remembered thinking too big.
Consciously, or unconsciously, he had cast in his lot with

this huge, crudely prosperous, blundering, untutored land; and if he had still reserves, there was never time left from his mines, his cattle and his law to think of them.

He was putting spurs to his horse, as Snell, the leading merchant of the place, who had just joined the group, inquired suggestively, "The young men will hardly arrive in time for the ceremony, I take it, Mr. Deed?"

"I don't know, Mr. Snell," said Deed, restraining the pony which was chafing to be off again. "I hope to see Philip. He's dropped his mining experiment up at Piñon, at my suggestion, and he will get through by the two-thirty train, I hope, if he gets over the Pass all right. I don't know whether to hope that he has left Laughing Valley City or not. I'm just on my way to the telegraph office to inquire." He cast a doubtful look toward Zacatecas Pass.

"Looks some like snow, up around the Pass," commented one of those young men of middle age who, in the West, somehow keep the sap of youth jogging lustily in their veins, at an age when it has dried out, or soaked down into the roots of New England men. It is possible that the speculative fancy of man does not engender a new scheme with every moon for nothing. The habit seems to keep the juices alive and fluent; and, at least, it makes an open mind, which is itself, no doubt, the better part of youth.

"It does look like snow," owned Deed, as he glanced anxiously again toward the mountains; and some one ventured to ask him about Jasper. He was detained by business in New York, he said, at which Snell exchanged a significant glance with his neighbour. He hardly expected him for the wedding, he added. It was pretty well known in Maverick that Jasper wasted no approval on his father's second marriage; and there were persons who saw dubious things beneath the peremptory summons which he had given out a fortnight ago as calling him to New York.

As Deed, to cut short the embarrassment of this line of questioning, definitively caught up the reins and gave the pony a cut with the quirt, the group gathered about him lifted their sombreros, or such rakish or merely slovenly caps as they wore, and swung them about their heads in the burlesque by which Western manners express their condescension to the customs of a superseded civilization. It was not a bow, nor precisely a ceremony of farewell, but a mixed expression of thanks for the "irrigation" to be offered at Ira's in the evening, and of an embarrassed sentiment of congratulation on the event of the day, which did not quite know the smartest way of conveying itself.

When some one inquired "What's the matter with James Deed, Esquire?" and the crowd gave the foreordained answer, with a single voice, they had really done for him all that one sovereign can do for another in the way of expression of good-will : it was frankincense and myrrh, and oil and wine and precious stones offered him on a tray of gold, if you liked. It was meant for the same thing; and Deed did not like it less. He turned in his saddle, and waved his own wide-brimmed hat to them in acknowledgement, his fine smile on his lips.

The Colorado sunshine was flooding the room in which Margaret awaited his coming, without let from blinds or shades. She stood in the big patch of radiance flung upon a rag carpet past fear of fading, and looked wistfully out of the window. The house stood a little apart, at the head of Mesa Street, the chief thoroughfare of Maverick, near the outskirts of the town; and, in the clear mountain air she could see for a long distance down the road.

Breakfast was over; and Beatrice Vertner had left her after it to attend to some household duties, which weddings apparently do not make less important in their process of dwarfing all other concerns.

A quarrel between father and son, Margaret was saying to herself, as she stood by the window—it had not come to that yet, but Jasper's opposition to his father's second marriage had only been saved from that by the moderation and temperance of her husband who was to be : she felt sure of that—seemed, at best, a wretched business; but this was, she felt, unbearably sad. In the foolish days when she was saying Deed nay, because she did not yet know herself,—and he was following her from New York to Paris, and from Paris to Geneva, and from Geneva to Naples, patient, decently doubtful of himself, but persistent,—she had seen what it cost him merely to be separated from his sons. Later, she had come to understand how the obligation he had felt to find something within himself to replace the tender care of the mother his boys had lost before they were old enough to know the meaning of such a loss, must have reacted upon, and enriched his feeling for them. She remembered how, seeing that his concern for their welfare was the substance and texture of his life, she had warned him—it was at Naples—that such affection as his played with high stakes; and how his face had darkened almost angrily at her hint of the possibility that sons might disappoint one's faith in them.

Just before their first meeting Deed had bought and stocked for his boys the cattle range from which she hoped he was riding in at this hour, and Jasper was established there in undivided charge until Philip—then in the first year of one of his foolish boy's experiments in Chili—should be ready to come back and take his share in the management. She recalled well enough how she had rallied their father's unwitting boasts of Jasper's success, how she had assisted with inward amusement at the pretence that he kept his fatherly fondness covert by bantering it with her, and how, when that was his mood, she had seemed to consent to his transparent vainglory in the shrewdness of his clever young men of twenty-four as a natural enthusiasm about a successful venture of his own. But constantly she had the sense of his loving pride in both his boys; and she liked it.

Deed could not have told her, even if his knowledge of it had got out of the region of half-perceptions in which we keep our reluctances about the faults of those we love, that Jasper belonged to the Race of the Magnificent, who have their own way—a happy provision arranging that no one shall find it worth quite what it costs to oppose such ways. When Margaret discovered it for herself, she had only to put it with familiar characteristics of Deed to understand how the partnership papers in the range, which were the origin of the present difficulty, had got themselves signed.

When Deed, in good-humoured recognition of Jasper's successful management of the range, had offered him a half-share in the profits from it until Philip should be ready to claim the third already belonging in all but form to each of the boys, it was like Jasper to say that it was very good of his father, and that they ought to " put the thing on a business basis." But it was rather more like Deed—whose pride in Jasper's business shrewdness commonly took shape before the young man himself in a habit of ridiculing him indulgently about it—to have laughed at him and consented. And it was not less of a tenor with their usual relation that he should have let Jasper have his way about giving this profit-sharing, for a limited term, the form of a partnership.

About his own way Margaret knew he would have no conceit, while regarding the symmetry of his act in giving Jasper something like the reward his faithfulness and sagacity in the management of the ranch had earned, he would have a certain pride. For Margaret, who, for her own part, had

ever frugalities and cautions to be satisfied before she could
be about a matter, both understood and admired the reck-
lessness with which Deed was accustomed to do a nice thing
thoroughly.   To her it was an inevitable touch of character
that he should have glanced over the papers of partnership
which Jasper had drawn up, should have signed with a smile
for his gratification in doing an entirely gratifying thing; and
then should have had the boy to supper with him at the only
restaurant in town, where they drank to the success of the
range in the champagne left over from the previous night's
supper of the Order of the Occidental Star.

Deed had not meant to marry again, then, of course, and
the cattle range was then an incident of his fortune, instead
of one of the main facts of it, as it presently became.

When he first thought of Margaret he congratulated himself
that there was still the ranch, for, at a little past forty, he
found himself, through the scoundrelly trick of a man he had
trusted, almost as entirely on his own hands as he had been
at twenty—with a fortune to be won again, and with life to be
begun pretty much afresh. When this trouble came on him he
thought of the boys; remembered with satisfaction that they
were provided for, whatever came ; shrugged his shoulders ;
took a look at himself in the glass, measured himself thoughtfully against the future, brushed the black lock down over the
fringe of grey in front; smiled; went out and had a good
dinner, and began again that afternoon.   A year later, when
he first offered himself to Margaret, it was pleasant to know
that the ranch was now not quite all (some of his mining
stocks were doing better); but the third interest, which
would still remain to him when Philip should have claimed
his share in the range, had not lost its importance to him.
And Jasper had done wonderful things with the enterprise
since they had pledged each other in the bad wine of the
" Delmonico of the West."

It was a little later that there began to be discoverable in Jasper's manner the hints of opposition to his father's second marriage, which had lately come near ending in an estrangement between father and son. The difference between them was, after all, but scantily patched up: and on the head of it Jasper had set out for New York, knowing that he could not be back in time for the wedding, and leaving word that he would write his father regarding another matter which Deed had broached to him just before his departure. The other matter was the re-organization of the arrangement at the ranch to include Philip, who had given over mining, after a twelvemonth in the mountains.

He had gone to Piñon on his return from Chili, with his young man's interest in anything rather than the usual and appointed thing lying ready to his hand; but he was now willing enough to accept his father's advice of a year before and join Jasper in looking after the ranch, where an assured income awaited him. Deed had wished to see this wandering, impulsive, hot-blooded, unsettled son of his actually established on the range before his marriage to Margaret. Unexpected events at Piñon had prevented this; but when he should come down for the wedding it was arranged that he was not to return, but was to take up his residence at the ranch immediately.

If this provision for Philip's future had not already been made when Margaret first began to be in question, Deed could not have asked her to marry him. He felt, in a degree which it would be difficult to represent, his responsibilities to his boys; and the long habit of making them the first concern of his life must have prevailed with him, whatever his feeling for Margaret, if they had needed anything done for them. But the ranch was a property which, conducted with any skill, must yield them both a handsome revenue, when both should be established on it.

Margaret liked the faithfulness to the future of his sons, which would not suffer him to put even her, or their common happiness, before it. He was determined to leave nothing at loose ends; and he was even awaiting the formality of Jasper's assent to the new arrangement at the ranch, as if it were an assent which he was free to withhold—as if all property of his boys in the ranch were not derived from his generosity, and as if Jasper's present tenure were not peculiarly by grace of his father's good humour. It was only a form; but Margaret knew that Deed characteristically regarded it as a sacred preliminary to their marriage; and when she saw him riding up to the door, waving a letter in his hand, she knew what letter it must be.

She ran out into the frosty air to meet him. Standing on the porch, under the shadow of the scroll-saw work, which was as much in the Queen Anne manner as anything about the house, she waited for him to tie his horse, cuddling her arms about her waist. The air had an edge. She gathered herself together: there was the cold to keep out; and there was a soft, interior content which she was willing to keep in.

It was hard not to be afraid of some of her feelings lately.

"Watch your horse!" she adjured, with a little nervous shiver. He was trying to tie the pony while he kept his eyes on her; and the tying was on the way to failure. He had taken the letter into his mouth for greater convenience. They both began to laugh, so that he had to take it out.

"Dearest!" he whispered, as he caught her to him in the porch. But she would not give him his kiss until they were in the hallway.

"It's come!" she said, with a joyous nod toward the letter in his hand, as they went into the sitting-room, which was as discreetly empty as the whole house seemed suddenly to have become in the hush of their happiness.

"Yes," he said, alternately offering and refusing it to her, as he held her away to make certain that she was the same Margaret with whom he had parted the night before for the last time, and who was to give herself to him in a few hours.

She sniffed at the flowers he had slipped into her hand in the hallway; and to make sure she did not cry, laughed at the smile of love on his face, which often oppressed her with the obligation it seemed to lay on her to keep it always there. And then she clapped her hands and laughed again to perceive in herself a kind of young girlish pride in his being handsome and manly and altogether very fine and impressive this morning.

It was true that he was a striking figure as he stood holding her at arm's length; and not less so when he left her side and went over to the mantel, where he leaned his head upon his hand and watched her for a moment in silence, as he struck at his riding boots with the quirt he had brought in with him. His hair was a bit grey where his large round head had begun to grow bald on either brow; but this, with his grizzling eyebrows, and the strongly-marked lines about his mouth which, in a younger man, would have seemed merely the outward sign of resolution, were the only tokens by which one would have known him to be more than thirty-five. His hair, like the moustache, which was the only adornment of his face, was worn clipped quite short; and this gave him, coupled with his rather careful habit of dress, a certain effect of trimness and well-being uncommon in the West. He had the habit of resting his weight firmly upon the ground; and the dignity and ease of his bearing was not lost in the most impetuous of his habitually rapid movements. His eyes had a tinge of blue in some lights, but it was the indefinable grey in them which gave the look of power and firmness to his face. It is doubtful if these eyes were really

more blue in his kindly moments; but it is not doubtful that
they seemed so. That which distinguished his look and his
manner, however, after the force which no one could fail to
feel in him, was an effect of unconquerable youthfulness and
buoyancy. His eager, mildly searching glance, his manner
of unceasing alertness and energy gave one the sense of a
man much alive.

He glanced with keen liking about a room which he had
known for a long time; but which, somehow, had never been
as interesting a room as it was this morning. He was
almost in a mood to forgive the wall-paper, which insulted
the remnant of Eastern taste in him; and, as he turned and
stared, with his hands in his pockets, into the fire, not knowing what to say in his happiness, it gave him a warm feeling
about the heart to see what a gay time the combustible piñon
wood of the mountains was having of it in the little grate.
There was even a certain light-heartedness about the "what-
not" in the corner, on which the collection of mineral
specimens,—part of the religion of Colorado housekeeping,
—was reflecting the Colorado sunshine from unexpected
facets of ore; while the iron pyrites winked in the sun at
some possible tenderfoot mistaking it for gold.

Beatrice Vertner's taste had contrived to give a home-like
expression to such furniture as there was; but the room was
rather bare. The big photograph of Veta Pass, in which a
train had stopped to be "taken," hung in frameless, fly-spotted
solitude above the tennis racquets and riding crops in one
corner. There was a good engraving above the fireplace,
framed in unplaned scantling, and a couple of clever oil-
paintings, by some of Beatrice's Eastern friends, brightened
one corner of the room, which was further lighted up by a
brilliant-hued Navajo blanket, hung as a *portière* at one of
the doorways. The home-made rag carpet, in its modest
propriety of colouring, caused the Western villainy in wall

paper to wear a self-conscious smirk. At the side-window there was a burst of colour, where the lower sash pretended, not very seriously, to be stained glass.

"Such a spick-span conscience as I've got this morning, Margaret," he said, coming over to her and taking her hands again, while he looked down into her eyes, which she straightway dropped. "There is n't an unswept corner nor an undusted piece of furniture in it. I've had out all the couches, and had down all the pictures, and gone in for a general house cleaning. The boys are safe and settled, both of them, and in seven hours——"

"Seven - and - a - half," she corrected, smilingly, with the precision which seems never to leave a woman who has once taught school.

"Half is it? To be sure—half past four. But everything must be whole this morning, Margaret, like our happiness. Have you noticed how every one feels responsible, and —interested about this affair? They were all at the windows as I rode up the street; or rather they were behind the curtains—and I had to try to look the disinterested morning caller on my way to pay a sort of duty call. But they saw through me. My foolish joy leaks through my eyes, I suppose. Margaret, dear," he asked, taking her doubtful and feebly reluctant form in his arms—for even on the eve of her wedding, the indomitable Puritan in her must have its shamefaced way with her will—"tell me, does it distress you that I can't conceal it? You are so much better at it. Let me see your eyes. Come, you are not fair. Look up!" And then, as she tremulously took his glance for a moment he put back his big head, and laughed monstrously. "I see: you *were* thinking it: that it is unbecoming that they should be laughing over our happiness—indecorous—um—unseemly. Oh, Margaret, you are great fun!"

"Am I?" she asked, with a shy smile, keeping her eyes on the button she was twisting on his coat.

"Yes, yes," he cried, through his laughter, as he drew her to the sofa, "you don't know what you miss in not being able to enjoy yourself." He caught her to him, and she hid her head on his broad breast for happiness.

And with his arm about her he opened the letter. "Isn't it fine, dear, to know that Philip is settled down and done for, before we begin with each other, and that we need not fear for him? I should have felt as if I were running away from him otherwise. I like to get this letter from Jasper, just at this time. It's only a form, but it makes everything quite sure. I'm afraid we're too happy," he sighed, as he glanced over the first lines of the letter, and, as he turned the page he looked up in a daze, and could not believe there had ever been such a thing as happiness in the world. He bit his lips, not to cry out.

Margaret watched him in silent fright as he read on. A pallor deepened over his face. It went, and he appeared to regain himself. But the thought—whatever it was—seemed to clutch him, of a sudden, at the throat, and he buried his face in his hands with a groan.

Margaret's arms, for the first time of their own motion, stole gently about him. And so they sat for a long time, in silence.

Once she said softly, "I'm so sorry, dearest!" Questions she saw, could not help him, and she did not know how to say her sympathy. She understood without words that Jasper had in some way played his father false, and she yearned over the man who, in a few hours, was to be her husband with an awed sense of what such a falsity must mean to him.

The letter shocked her when she read it; but it could not . sharpen her pain for him.

Jasper explained that he could not hold himself bound by the understanding under which his father apparently supposed him to have taken a half-share in the profits of the range, and that he must decline to surrender to Philip any share in it. He "stood upon the articles of partnership, giving him the rights of an equal partner, for a term of years." The rest was phrases. He should be very glad to offer his brother employment on the range ; should be "most happy to afford him every" . . . . . trusted that "such an arrangement might be mutually" . . . . . hoped that this "would be accepted in the spirit in which " . . . . . ; was sure that his father must feel that "Business is always business ": and, disclaiming any motive of greed or animosity, begged him to believe that he remained his "most affectionate son."

Margaret did not dare look at the stricken man beside her when she had finished this.

"If he had only died !" he moaned.

"Oh, I know, James, I know !" she murmured, with an uncertain caress.

"Do you, dear?" He looked up dully. Something vital seemed to have gone out of him. His haggard look appalled her. She shrank from it with a fluttering glance. "No, no," he said, " you don't know. You should be glad you can't. You must have cared for a child in sickness and health and done things for his sake, and been through all sorts of weather with him, and scolded his badness and loved his lovableness to know."

"Of course, of course !" whispered Margaret mechanically because she could not find the right words, if, in truth, there were any.

"You can guess, dear," he said, "and it's good of you ; but to really know you ought to have watched his growth, with its touching likeness to your own growth ; and have seen the little armful of flesh, with the tiny beating heart, that you were once afraid you should stop with a rough clasp, grow to be a man, with a man's comfortable power over the world into which he came so unknowingly——and with a man's awful capacity for right and wrong." He sighed. "Yes, yes," he went on with a note of bitterness, "you must have done what you could to help him to a place in the world"——his voice broke——"and perhaps you ought really to have been both father and mother to him," he added with the ghost of his smile : "his friend, as you stood in the place of his mother ; his comrade, as you were in fact his father, to honestly know. Thank Heaven you don't know, Margaret !"

The patient desolation of his tone touched her inexpressibly. She took his hand in both hers, studying it absently a moment ; and one might have thought she meant to raise it to her lips ; but, struggling against the tears in her voice, she said, "Ingratitude, though, James—is n't it much of a piece wherever you find it, and—and suffer from it ? I can understand that, I think." She paused, biting her lip for self-control. "Oh, it is cowardly !" she broke out. "Does n't it seem so, dear ? Cowardly and brutal !" Her arm slipped about him again, as she searched for these blundering words of helpfulness. She would have given the world to reach and soothe the pang which she seemed to herself to be merely moving about in a helpless circle. The unyielding tradition in which she had been nurtured, and which possessed her less since she had let herself love him, but which still was mistress of her, had never been so irksome to her.

At the moment she longed to recreate herself, for him, the creature of some sunnier land, whose women do not have to wonder how they shall comfort those they love : who have a natural language for affection. But the honesty in her would not suffer her to express more than she could feel instinctively. "Who,—who but a coward," she went on chokingly, "could wrong so unanswerably as ingratitude wrongs——so far past help, so deep beyond protest : so deep, deep down that the mere thought of lifting a voice against it is a misery, a nausea, a degradation ! "

He leaped up. "Yes, yes," he cried, with impatient energy. "But one can act—*must* act when the thing's past talk. Where did I leave my hat, Margaret?" He took her by both shoulders, with a sudden impulse, and looked for a moment into her eyes. She took fright at his set face in which, save the tenderness for her, there was scarce anything of sanity.

"What—what are you going to do?" she asked, under her breath.

He clenched his hands, as he turned from her, and caught up his hat, which lay on the sofa. "Oh, I don't know, my girl! I don't know! My worst, I suppose."

He was flinging himself out of the door; but, "James !" she murmured reproachfully. He turned and kissed her. "In an hour," he whispered; and was gone, before she could utter one of all the pleadings that hung upon her lips. She tremblingly watched him untie his horse. Every movement of his hands was charged with an angry energy that terrified her. Her heart leaped in fear at the wrathful twitch with which he loosed the knot they had been laughing at together twenty minutes back; and she cowered at the ugly cut under which the pony shrank, as Deed set off at a gallop.

Was this the good, the gentle man she loved? She put her hands to her eyes to shield them from the memory of the look on his face, as he parted with her. It was like the look of unreason—such a look as one recalls in explanation of a terrible event, after it has befallen.

CHAPTER II.

It was rather more than an hour before he returned, and Margaret had time to think of many things. She trembled at the thought of what he might be doing at any moment of her watching and waiting and poking of the fire. She recalled all that she knew of his hot and reckless temper; she told over to herself all that she had ever heard from others of the relentless fixity with which he carried out a thing on which he was resolved.

She knew sadly the quality of his temper of course; her experiences of it could hardly have failed to be numerous and bitter, in the time which had elapsed since she had known him. It was the chief flaw in his character. In accounting for it to herself she said, when she was not fresh from suffering from some manifestation of it, that no doubt it went along inevitably with his generous and impulsive heart. She was ignorant about such things, and about men in general, but she had never known any one so entirely good and kind and open-hearted, and she told herself it was not for her to measure or question the correlative fault that must always go with a great virtue like that. She had moments of grave doubt about this, of course, and her doubt had been a minor reason among the controlling ones which had caused her to refuse him at first. When she finally discovered that she loved him, it did n't matter; nothing seemed to matter, then. She now thought of his

temper as one of the things she should set herself to modify
—or, rather, to help him about—when they were married.
What was marriage for if not for some such mutual strength-
ening and improvement?

Something Vertner had told her when she first came, and
at which she had laughed, at the time, recurred to her. It
made her smile, still, but in a frightened way. Vertner had
heard it in Leadville. It was *à propos* of the grim strength of
purpose which every one felt in Deed. Some one had come
to a young lawyer, there, to offer him a case, in which Deed
was engaged on the other side, and had been asked to
'Come off!' "Ain't you got more sense," inquired the
practitioner, expressively, "than to take half a day out
of a ten-dollar-a-day job to come and set me on to
Deed, in a case where he's got the ghost of a show?
Never saw him grip his fist, like that, in a court of
law, did you? Thought not. Must is *must* about that time,
young man! There ain't no two ways to a burro's kick.
I've been there. In fact I was there day before yesterday.
Beaten? No, sir, I was n't beaten. I was cyclonized. I was
taken up by the toes of my boots and swung round and round
with one of the prettiest rotary motions you ever saw ; and
banged against the top of Uncompaghre peak, out there.
No one but myself would have thought it worth while to pick
up what was left of me, I suppose. But I did it; and I
picked up too much sense at the same time to try it again.
Why, that man's got more knowledge of the law and more
raw grit, and hang on and stick to 'n——." He questioned
the air with uplifted arm for a comparison. "Well,——!"
he ended hopelessly. "I'll tell you what it is," he went on,
with renewed grip of language, "for them that likes monkeying with the buzz-saw, there ain't nothin' like it, short of
breaking a faro-bank. It's strawberries and cream to that
sort. But to peaceably disposed citizens, like you and me,

Charlie, there ain't nothin' at all, anywhere, like stayin' pleasantly, and sociably to home, and lettin' the saw hum its merry little way through the other fellow's fingers."

From time to time Margaret would go to the window, and look wistfully down the road. The expression on her round, shrewd, suggestive, wise little face at these times would have helped an observer to understand the look which made her seem older than her twenty-nine years : it was the authoritative look of experience. The look of over-experience that sometimes fixes itself, to the sadness of the beholder, on the face of a woman who has been down into the fight for bread, with men, had passed by Margaret's inextinguishable womanliness ; but she had not led an easy life ; and one saw it in her face—a face proportioned with a harmony that strangely failed to make it beautiful.

Her eyes, which were small and bright, were deeply set under a high and well-modelled brow, from which the hair was brushed straight back, in a way that must have been unbecoming to another type of face, but which was admirably suited to her own. In falling over her shapely little ears, the silky brown hair waved in a fashion pleasant to see. Her mouth, which was small and daintily made, wore an expression of unusual firmness.

In conversation she would fix her animated hazel eyes on the face of the person with whom she spoke in absorbed attention, and when the talk was of serious things, a deep, far away look would suddenly possess these eyes. She had an extraordinarily sweet smile ; and there was a gentle and kindly soberness in her expression. She was well and compactly made. Yet her effect was unimposing. She seemed short and slight. She had a well-kept little effect in her dress and the appointments of her person ; but no one would have accused Margaret of knowing anything about dress. She was rather discreetly clothed than dressed in the sense of adornment. She wore white cuffs at her wrists and a narrow collar at her throat, fastened by a brooch of gold, wrought in an old-fashioned pattern.

Margaret was not smiling when Beatrice came in some time after Deed had gone, and found her with her head pressed against the pane. She turned her tearful face away as Beatrice drew her to her.

Mrs. Vertner, one saw, had been quite recently a pretty woman and she was still young—a year or two younger than Margaret. The brilliant expression, which had distinguished her among all her acquaintance in her young girl days in Newton, (the Boston Newton),—where she was still remembered as a clever girl who had made an inexplicable marriage, —was overlaid, for the most part by a look of anxiety and harassment, due to the conditions of her life. She made her housekeeping as little a sordid, crude, and ugly business as she could, and took its difficulties light-heartedly ; but housekeeping in a Western town which has still to " get its growth " is at best a soul-wearing affair. Just now she suffered under the rule of a Swedish maid-servant who knew no English, and whose knowledge of cooking was limited to a fine skill in broiling steak insupportably, and a vain address in the brewing of undrinkable coffee.

"Crying, little one?" she asked, affectionately. "Won't you do something a wee bit like some one else, dear, one of these days, and let me be by to see it? That's a good girl." She kissed her, with a laugh. "But stay odd all the rest of the time, Margaret. I should n't like you if you were n't odd, you know—not even if you were ever so little less odd. If I want you to be conventional it is only for a moment, to see how it would seem. Come ! Other brides smile. Try one smile !" she pleaded. And at Margaret's helpless amusement, she snatched her from

the window, and humming a vague air, which defined itself
in a moment as one of the Waldteufel waltzes, she beat time
for a second, laughing in Margaret's bewildered, tear-stained
face, and caught her away into a romping dance.

"There!" she cried, as she sank upon the sofa, breathless with laughing and dancing. "I've shaken you into
sorts, I hope; and you're ready for the ceremony; or will
be if you'll ever get yourself dressed. Not that I call it
dressed, to wear that grey—— Oh, I don't mean that,
Maggie dear," she exclaimed at a pained look on Margaret's
face. She crushed her to her in a devouring embrace. "Or,
rather, I do," she added, honestly; "but I did n't mean to
say it. No: you'd better wear it," she went on at some
sign of hesitation from Margaret. "It will go beautifully
with all the rest of it. Margaret Derwenter," she cried,
with an affectation of seriousness, "shall I tell you something? You will never be married." She retired for the
effect; but fell upon her with all the armoury of woman's
peacemaking at Margaret's start. "Literal!" she cried.
"Will you never take things less hard? As if I meant it!
What I did mean sounds foolish after you've taken it like
that. But I may as well say it. I don't believe the marriage ceremony is going to marry you, as it does other
women, Margaret; and you need n't tell me it is. If you
are ever married it will be by yourself: yes, I mean it—
by a kind of slow process of consent to the affair. Of
course you will have a proper respect for the ceremony;
and you will think it has married you. But women like
you, Maggie—not that there are any—are not married in
that way. Now, I was married when I left the church, and
everybody knew it."

Margaret laughed,—not on compulsion this time, and
catching her arm about Beatrice's waist drew her to the
window to look down the road with her for Deed's coming.

Almost any part of Margaret's history, before the time when she began to teach, and, by a curious arrangement of her own, to see the world, must wrong, or at least mis-speak, in the telling, the gentle and sweet-natured woman she had become.

She had been accustomed to hear in her childhood that she had inherited her father's energy, and her mother's face. This did not strike her as going very deep. She was aware, herself, of several unmanageable drifts in her that she might have understood better, perhaps, as derivations from her parents, if they had lived long enough for her to know them. Her father, who had gone to the Isle of Martinique as a young man, and had made a fortune in business there, had married, rather late in life, a Frenchwoman, a native of the island, and the daughter of one of its chief officials. Margaret supposed that she must attribute the unmanageableness that she perceived in herself to this French mother : that, at least, was the theory of her New Hampshire grandmother, with whom she had gone to live after the death of her father and mother.

Her grandmother did not care for foreigners, as she called them ; but she loved the child, and during all the years that Margaret lived with her was particularly good to her. This was the more to her credit, since Margaret had, from the first, ideas. The habit of mind which she had inherited from her mother, had sometimes a hard time of it with the New England austerity; though the romance bestowed on her from the same source made friends in a curious way with the Puritan capacity for self-abnegation. Her conscience—perhaps one should say her indomitable conscience—was altogether Puritan ; while it would be hard to say what we must call the ambition which gave purpose and meaning to all her young days. The abandoned pursuit of Culture for Culture's sake is at least not 'French ; and, as it is perhaps followed with the most pathetic sincerity in the Middle West, it cannot be called altogether a New England foible—though it must have been in its beginnings a New England idea. One suspects it of having been engendered in the bleak farm-houses on the New England hills, where the Winter is hardly less long than our American joke avers; from which the dwellers emerge only for "socials," "mite societies" and lectures, and where the snow-bound solitude turns the limited diversion of apples, hard cider and hickory nuts rather wan before the Spring comes.

It would be a quarrelsome person who would not suffer any one to get what fun he might out of the idea of Culture for Culture's angular dear sake, no doubt; and as an alternative to the apples and cider, the mite societies and the lectures, it has, certainly, advantages. But if it should be urged that the theory of life which it implies lacks ease, lacks curves, lacks atmosphere, lacks even—to say the worst of it, and have done—the sense of humour, only one who had a great many such New England Winters in him ought to say a word. The Winters, though, would palliate worse things—things mistaken in fact as well as in spirit.

Margaret, in her pursuit of this mystic Culture, since it must be said, conceived of education, until her education was done, as an affair possessing length, breadth and thickness. It is to be feared that she even "improved" her opportunities. They were not many, poor girl, until she left the New Hampshire village for her first stay in New York, where she studied at a school in which she spent a year learning that she was the only pupil who regarded its advantages as precious privileges. Then she left it for Vassar, which was, at least, not touched with sham. She found here other girls with her thought about education; and she went about the erection of her structure of intelligence with an energy which presently sent her home to her grandmother ill. The structure remained her point after her return, however; and the reader who knows anything of this habit of thought should not need to be told that she looked upon it, not as a dwelling that she should one day inhabit, much less as a temple which should one day inhabit her; but as a shrine whose graceful proportions it was the final privilege to set for ever within one's blessed sight. 'At nineteen Margaret was more in the way to becoming that distressing product of our felicitous new ways of thinking about women and about education—the female prig—than a friendly biographer would like to record.

Her escape from such a fate was due to circumstances outside her control. In the midst of one of the Summer vacations she took up a copy of the *Springfield Republican*, to learn that the little competence left her by her father had been embezzled, with more important trust funds, by an unscrupulous executor. And, soon after, her grandmother died. Every Sunday morning, from the time when Margaret had come to her as a child, she had lain in bed— this estimable lady—thinking how she would change on Monday in Margaret's favour, the will which bequeathed all she had to a charity. On Sunday morning a late breakfast gave time for reflection on such subjects; but on Monday there was never any time at all. And on one of the Mondays which was to have witnessed the fulfilment of her resolve, she died in Margaret's arms.

The double catastrophe had many lessons for Margaret. She sorrowed for her grandmother bitterly out of the simple and loving heart which no system of cultivation could have educated out of her; and she never thought of blaming the neglect which had left her with the problem of earning her living close upon her. The money lost through the executor's rascality troubled her solely as an educated girl: a girl with duties, with responsibilities to her self-

development. It would be putting it too crudely to say
that she grieved for the loss of the money, because one
might have bought such a lot of Culture with it : travel,
that is, and the leisure for study, and the sight of good pic
tures, and the knowledge of all the "cultivated" things.
But it is only the expression that is at fault : her idea
hovered very near this thought. And, as she could not
have the thing in one shape, she determined to buy it for
herself in another.

It was necessary that she should provide for herself;
and she conceived the enterprising notion of making this
necessity serve her purpose. She "taught"; but she gave
the heavy-hearted word a meaning of her own by procuring,
through a friend of her father, in Boston (after a year spent
in school teaching), a position as travelling governess with a
family which put several of her favourite novels to shame by
treating her as one of the species.

She made the tour of Europe with these people, with
what she called, in her letters to one of her college-friends,
" most satisfying results." She did not mean to the business
man's children whom she was teaching ; but to what she
might have called her own "mental progress." The business
man, when he called the results " satisfactory," meant something separated by the distance between any two of the
planets from the idea contained in Margaret's word ; but his
word was at least as much reward as she had expected,
outside her salary, for her faithful efforts to decant some of
her knowledge into the minds of the business man's
children.

When she was back in America again, she recklessly sat
down and waited for another engagement looking to the
same ends. This time she wanted to go to Japan, and she
kept the advertisement in which her wishes were succinctly
stated in the *Nation* and in the *Tribune* until a family dis-

covered itself intending toward Japan, and desiring a governess of Margaret's capacity, temperament and terms.

It will be seen that this was a woman of energy, of independence and of original ideas; but so much lies on the surface. To make it at all clear how she contrived to reconcile these rather aggressive qualities to the softest and gentlest womanhood there need be, one must have known her. To be sweetly firm, to be gifted with the kind of lucidity that does not roil one's own commonplace muddle of a mind by its mere existence, to know, and not to know you know, to hold immoderate opinions in a moderate way, to be transfigured by energy and yet consent to the propriety of your neighbour lying on his sofa; to perceive that the boundaries of the State of New York, or even—though this is asking a good deal—the confines of the British Isles, do not limit the imaginable, not to say lady-like regions of our globe; in a word to be tolerant—these are great matters. It can hardly discredit Margaret with any reasonable soul to own that she failed, for the most part, to realize all these excellences; but they had become the torment-ing measure of her ideal some time before she met Deed, on a visit to Beatrice Vertner (the one friend she had made at her New York school) at her home in Colorado.

It was mainly the travel which she had sought as gratifying her aspirations toward Culture, which disabused her of her young feeling about that *ignis fatuus;* the sight of the various, the populous, the instructive world furnished her with an altogether new point of view from which she grew to pity the provincial Diana who had set out with such a fine courage to hunt down Culture with her little bow and arrow. And yet the Diana remained; and the Margaret of ten years after the Vassar days was at least as remarkable for her likeness—in remote, illusive ways—to the Margaret who had one and the same conscience for

the Temple of Culture, and for the Temple of Pure Right,
as she was remarkable for her exquisite, her admirable and
surprising difference.

The new notions of life begotten of going about and
seeing things had led the way; but no one who knew her
well could have been at a loss to perceive the moulding
force which had done the real work of change. It was
her womanliness coming in upon her, at the same time,
with its incomparable enrichment, which had taught her old
vagaries the way to the graces of the new Margaret; it was
what one might almost have called her natural gift for
womanliness which finally chastened her edges, and which,
in shaping her young strenuousness to softer lines, lost for
it none of the validity and justness and simple strength
which had gone with her maidenly ways of thinking.

And yet it is certain that one is not reared in New
Hampshire for nothing; that one does not spend four
years at Vassar without bearing the Vassar mark; above all,
it is clear that no one can teach for ten years—it may be
that no one can teach for an hour—and live to hide the fact.

It was Beatrice who first caught sight of the familiar
figures of the pony and his rider, coming up the road at a
gallop, pursued by a swirl of dust. She could not be persuaded that she did not hear the baby crying; and descended
upon the sound before Deed could reach the porch.

Margaret would rather he had not tried to find a smile
for her. He looked a year older than when he had left
her side. They stood for a moment when she opened
the door to him, looking into each other's eyes. Then she
cast her arms about him, and drew him to her with an impulse of protection—the kind of refuge against the vexations
of the world that a woman offers to the man who is dear to
her, as if he were the sole sufferer from them on the planet,
—and whispered some words in his ear.

" I am so sorry," she said simply, as she took his arm, and led him into the room, where she had made up a brighter fire against his return.

He sat heavily on the sofa, and stared at the blazing piñon sticks, with the look of a man whose fight is done.

He looked away from her. "We must n't talk of it," he said, after a moment. "It's no stuff to make wedding days of. I don't know," he went on, biting his lip, "how I am going to get my forgiveness that this should have happened as it has."

She came and stood by his side. "Do you begrudge my sharing your trouble, James?" she asked. "Would you rather have borne it alone? I thought that was what it meant to be——"

"What, dear?" he asked tenderly. He drew her down to him, and put his arm about her. She sank on the floor beside him.

"——A wife," she said, blushing faintly, and looking down.

Their romance was not less dear to them than if they had been younger: it was more sober, but not less valiant.

"Um" . . . . . commented Deed, with a wan smile, patting her hand affectionately. She sat, for a moment, in a reverie that took no account of their trouble, and was almost happy. But catching sight of his tense and stricken face, "Something has happened," she said tremulously.

"Yes: I thought the law could help me," he answered wearily. "It can't. If there were nothing else, I must have let him go with his plunder, and have found heart, somehow, to tell Philip that I had let myself be done out of his future, with a fool's trust."

" Nothing but the law? Then there is something else? There *is* a remedy? "

He did not respond to the joy in her tone. "Yes," he answered gravely.

D

She started back and rose from his side, all her fears alive
in her face.

"James!" she cried incriminatingly.   He sat silent, with
his head in his hands.   She regarded him for a moment in
anxious perplexity.   Then she reached forth her hand, and
laid it softly on his shoulder.   "You—you are quite sure you
are doing right?" she asked gently.

He withdrew himself.   "Margaret!" he cried reproachfully.   "How could I do a wrong to him?"

"You can do a wrong to yourself.   You can let a longing
to right yourself carry you too far," she said bravely.

"Don't talk in that way, Margaret.   There was but one
right and one wrong in the world.   I had to have that right.
What I have done is just."

"Oh, I hope so!" she cried.

He was silent for a moment.   He was thinking of many
things.   Suddenly he turned his eyes to hers, and regarded
her piercingly.   He took her hands in an eager pressure.
"What would you do for me?" he asked at last abruptly.

"My dear James, I——" began Margaret, startled.

"Would you give up all that I have meant to make yours
for—for me?"

His intense gaze was unbearable. She turned away. "You
know I would," she murmured.

"Don't think that because I am giving, I have the right
to take away.   It's not so."

"Rights, dear——?   Must we talk of them?   Don't you
think . . . . ?"

"Well——?" he asked, trying to be gentle ; but his restless anxiety got into his voice.

"That they stop, I was going to say, where love begins.
But, James, you seem so far off—so strange."   She laid a
hand doubtfully upon him, and looked into his face with a
questioning glance.   "Would it reach you, if I said a thing

like that?" she asked. Her smile was pitiful. "Oh, my dearest, of course I don't care. How should I? Did I ever care? And now if it would make you happy——"

"Must it make me happy?" he asked.

"Would it be worth while to you if it did not?"

"Ah, well——!" he exclaimed inconclusively. And for some minutes they did not speak. Margaret watched his absorbed face and knitted brows with a thousand rising doubts.

He may have seen the pained look of inquiry on her face, for he took her clasped hands, and stroked her hair thoughtfully. With her elbow on the sofa, and her head in her upturned hand, she coiled herself on the floor, and regarded the crackling fire for a long time, in wistful absence.

She was glad when he spoke, though all her fears cried out against what he might say. As he bent over her, speaking in a low voice, she kept her eyes on the fire, " Tell me again it would not pain you to lose it all, Margaret. It is not merely money. It has many sides, and meanings. It is all worldly comfort, advantage, leisure, of course, but besides it is freedom—freedom to do the things you have wished to do, Margaret; the things you have not been able to do. It's not fair to ask you until you have tested it. You don't know how much you would be giving up."

She smiled where she sat. "I know how much I should be gaining if—if it can serve you," she said softly, her head turned from him.

He observed her with keen, grave eyes, which, as he looked, filled with tenderness. He rose and took her in his arms.

"Is this my reserved Margaret?" he asked. "Is this the quiet little woman who, a few months since, would scarcely own she loved me, and only the other day was protesting that her training had not taught her the language of affection?"

She hid her face. " What is it that you wish to do, James ? " she asked anxiously, when she could raise it again.

He released her without answering. After a moment he took a turn up and down the room.

"You won't believe it ! " he said suddenly. He went back, and flung himself upon the sofa, with a half groan. The fire had blazed up, and in its play upon his face Margaret read the torture that was going on in him. She was beside him again in a moment. " Margaret," he said, as he caught her hand once more, " do you remember the story of Samson ? "

" Surely," she answered in wonder. " Why ? "

" His locks were traitorously shaven. His strength, which was all his riches, was basely taken from him by one he trusted. Then his enemies believed they had conquered him, for his power was gone, and they had put out his two eyes. But in Gaza—do you remember, dear ?—when they were gathered to see his shame, he put forth one last, mighty effort, and pulled down the temple over their heads, and his. The story has always had a noble ring to me,—I don't know why. To day it comes back with special meaning. Would you mind reading it over to me, dear ? "

Margaret gazed at him in trouble and uncertainty ; but she went for the Bible which was her single inheritance from her mother. At home she always kept it on the table near her bed. Just now it was in the trunk, up stairs. When she had it, she brought the volume to him ; and kneeling down with her arm on his knee and face to the blaze, where she could see him by turning her head, opened quickly to the place.

" ' But the Philistines took him, and put out his eyes,' " she began, " ' and brought him down to Gaza, and bound him with fetters of brass——' "

" No, a little further on, please," said he, keeping his eyes closed.

"'And it came to pass,'" she began again, toward the end of the chapter, "'when their hearts were merry, that they said, Call for Samson, that he may make us sport. And they called for Samson out of the prison house; and he made them sport; and they set him between the pillars.

"'And Samson said unto the lad that held him by the hand, Suffer me that I may feel the pillars whereupon the house standeth, that I may lean upon them. . . . .

"'And Samson called unto the Lord, and said, O Lord God, remember me, I pray thee, and strengthen me, I pray thee, only this once, O God, that I may be at once avenged of the Philistines for my two eyes.'"

Deed rose abruptly, and paced the floor. Margaret read on, fearful of she knew not what.

"'And Samson took hold of the two middle pillars upon which the house stood, and on which it was borne up, of the one with his right hand, and of the other with his left.

"'And Samson said, Let me die with the Philistines. And he bowed himself with all his might; and the house fell upon the lords, and upon all the people that were therein.'"

Margaret dropped the book, and looked at Deed. He was standing quite still, listening in absorption.

"Was it not great? Was it not well done, Margaret?"

"I don't know," she said, with the touch of preciseness which, without her will, would often make its way into her tone when matters of propriety or morality were in question. She reflected a moment. "Was it right to kill so many for revenge only?"

"It was just. His loss was not a common one. It was his two eyes."

"But barbarous justice—don't you think so, dear? It would be better to suffer under the sense of the worst wrong."

"No, no," said he, earnestly, almost eagerly. "To me

it seems nobly done. He did not try to save himself. He perished of his own will in the general ruin."

Margaret had long been watching him anxiously; but now, terrified beyond control, she burst forth, "Oh, James, what has Samson's story to do with you or me?"

"Everything! Everything!" he cried. "Has not Jasper taken my strength in teaching me to know him? Has he not taken my eyes in robbing me of himself, and of Philip's future, at a stroke?"

He paced the floor impatiently. She put forth her hand with an instinctive gesture of deprecation. His haggard face, with its look of determination, awed her. When she tried to cry out her voice failed her.

"Margaret!" he cried, pausing suddenly in his walk at some look in her face. "You would not have me bear it?"

"Oh, James!" she answered. "It is hard, very hard, I know. But, yes: I would bear it. What else is there for it?"

"What else?" he cried. "All else! Why, Margaret! Can you ask? Do you think I could live, and not strike back? Am I so weak a thing? Am I cheated of *all* my power, even in your eyes? Why, dearest——" He drew her to him, as she rose, with a tremulous motion, and surveyed her face. "Why, dearest," he repeated, "I have still Samson's power."

"Still Samson's power?" She repeated the words helplessly.

"The power to make him suffer with me," he said sternly. "The power to pull down the temple over his head."

"And yours?"

"Surely. Did you think I could not find Samson's courage for Samson's remedy?"

"But you will not! Surely you will not!"

"I have," he said, as he turned away.

Margaret bowed her head. "Oh," she cried, "you said well that I could not believe it." She kept her face in her hands, catching her breath with the sobs that shook her.

"Margaret! Margaret!" he besought her. But she did not heed. He turned away in desperation.

"Is it—is it irrevocable?" she asked, when she could command herself.

"Could Samson have built the temple again?"

"There must be some retreat."

"I have given my word."

"You can buy it back again."

His face hardened. "So Jasper might say," returned he. "Listen, Margaret!" he entreated. "I am within my rights —my legal rights. What would you have? May I not do what I will with my own? In his letter he says that he reckons his 'half interest,' as he calls it, at $75,000, and that he 'can't be expected to give up a thing like that.' An hour ago I sold the entire range and cattle for $25,000, without inquiring his preferences. He *has* given it up," he said grimly.

She looked into his eyes for a moment in silence. At last she said, "Is this sale completed?"

"No, but I am morally bound to complete it."

"You shall not."

"What?"

"My dear James, you shall not. Oh, how can I argue such a thing, if you don't see it? It is cruel, it is wrong, it is wicked."

"You must let me be the judge of that, Margaret," said Deed gravely.

"Oh, James, why am I what I am to you, if I may not be your conscience, when yours—under frightful trial, I know— has left you? You have no right to do this thing." She came close to his side.

"Oh, there comes your teacher's theory of life," he cried in unbearable irritation—"your hide-bound New England conscience that will not see circumstances, that refuses the idea of palliation as if it were a snare, that finds the same wrong in an act under all conditions, as if killing were always murder."

"James, James!" begged Margaret, quite calm and brave now, "don't talk of me.   I am anything you say. Think of yourself!   Consider the life of remorse you are condemning yourself to.   Distrust the false passion and pride that tells you you are right now.   You are wrong. Listen to me, who have nothing to gain by telling you so. You are wrong."   She spoke the words that came to her.

" Have I not the right to make him suffer as I suffer?" he asked coldly.

"I don't know.   You have not the right to use all your rights.   I am sure of that.   It is what they are always telling us, but is it the less true—the world would be intolerable if every one demanded all he is entitled to.   You must feel that.   Self-surrender, self-denial : all that—are they only phrases in the books?   Are they too big and fine for our every-day world ? "

She paused for a thoughtful moment, and with a glance of infinite tenderness regarded him, where he stood restlessly gnawing at his moustache, and snapping his fingers.

" As if I need ask!" she exclaimed.   "As if you had ever needed anything better than just ordinary Thursday Friday and Saturday for your goodness, dear!   Don't I know it?   Who ever used more every-day generosity and kindli——"

"Hush, hush, Margaret," he insisted.   "The thing's done, I tell you."

The fire, which had been dying down, leaped up, and glowed upon his face.   The look she saw on it taught her patience. "Listen, James," she begged, fighting back the sudden tears, which, somehow, had slipped by her guard.

He shook himself free from her hand with a kind of courteous impatience, and walked to the other side of the room.

"Don't preach, Margaret, of all things."

She gazed at him sadly. "Suppose we wait until to-morrow morning to speak of this, dear," she said gently. "I can talk to James Deed; but his evil spirit I don't know." She tried to smile.

"I am quite myself," he said, almost stiffly. "Was it not I who was wounded,—and in the best part of me : my love for him? Why should it not be the best part which answers it?" He spoke with a kind of fierce calmness, as if he were endeavouring to be gentle and reasonable with her, and found it hard.

"Is it the best part which tempts to vengeance?" she asked wearily.

"I fancied you were calling it that in your heart," he said, with bitterness. "And if it were? Did not Samson call on Heaven for vengeance—that was his word—'vengeance on the Philistines,' and was he not richly answered? Was he not given strength for it?"

"Oh, James," she cried in despair, "how can I argue against such frightful sophistries?"

They were both in the tense mood in which the added word snaps the bond of friendship, of blood, of love itself.

"You need not," he said, as he turned from her. "We have had more than enough of argument. It does not change my intention. I shall complete the sale in the morning."

He was about to leave the room, but she called,

"James!"

"Well?"

"You must not." She caught her breath, and sat hastily upon the sofa.

" Pshaw !"

"I tell you you must not. I—I will not have it. I have my—my rights, as well as you, my rights as your wife who is to be. I will not have your property—*my* property, thrown away for a whim."

He came toward her quickly. She shrank involuntarily. Her face was white : she set her teeth.

" Do you mean that ? "

She nodded painfully.

"It would have been simpler to say so in the beginning— not to say honester," he said with slow bitterness. "You might have spared me the pain of knowing that you could promise to give it all up, when you thought yourself secure from being held to your word. You might have saved your sermons."

It was like the agony of death to hear these things from him ; but she shut her lips and bore it. If she spoke now, she knew that her tone must belie her words.

"A moment ago you said," he went on coldly, " that you had nothing to gain. Pardon me if I say that you seem to have had much. It may make your sleep easier to-night, if I tell you that you have gained it."

He put his hands to his head in bewilderment, caught up his hat, and without a glance at her, left the room.

Margaret rose, and closed the door behind him. She stood a long time at the window, trying not to cry.

CHAPTER III.

ELEVEN thousand feet above sea-level the dry air reaches the point of saturation with a kind of gasp and shiver. Philip Deed was sure of the storm in the air half an hour before the clouds began to gather. It was the day on which he was to meet his father, at Maverick; and he had set forth in the morning from Piñon, where he had spent his unprofitable year in mining, planning to reach Bayles' Park by one o'clock, and to take the railway there for Maverick, where he expected to arrive in time for the wedding. Cutter, who had failed in the mountains also, and whose arrangements for the future were indefinite, was going to the wedding with Philip. His family had always known the Deeds in New York and he and Philip were friends.

The air grew moist, and the sky darkened as they put their horses at the ascent out of Laughing Valley, into which they had just come down from the other side. A mile up the trail they stopped on an eminence commanding the valley, to look about. A ray of sunshine shot a half-hearted glance from behind the clouds brooding above the way they were to take. The ray was instantly swallowed up; but the valley was swept by a momentary radiance, under which it started dazzlingly fresh and green, and took the sudden gold on its face with a dancing quiver which almost excused its foolish name.

The range of hills over which they had just come rose

behind Laughing Valley City to the North. To the South
the exit from the valley was through Red Rock Cañon, between whose narrow walls the Chepita fled roaring. The
sound reached them where they stood on their height at the
edge of the cañon, above the scattered noises of the town,
which, at this hour (just before the three o'clock shift at the
mines) was as peaceful, and almost as noiseless, as if it had
not been a city on all the maps.

Where the Chepita cast itself down out of the hills over
Moshier's Rock, at the other end of the valley, they could
vaguely see its white leap ; and then could follow its serene
course through the town.   Down at their feet they watched
it go brawling into the cañon.   Quietly as it slipped through
Laughing Valley City, the river gave a certain effect of life
to the valley, which spread a vast green lawn at their feet,
unbroken save by the huddle of buildings at its centre, and
by the " dumps " of green or grey or red, which marked the
mines outside the town. The close-ranked mountains looked
down from every side upon the young city ; and the only
apparent points of egress to the world without were those by
which the river entered and left the valley—the cleft in the
hills through which the Chepita hurled itself upon the fall,
and the cañon by which it swept away.

Philip Deed was giving up his mining at Piñon because
his father wished it, not because he liked the easy prospect
of a home and a bank-account held out to him from
Maverick. The thing for which he actually cared was a life
not responsible to its next minute—a life that should leave
him altogether free to speculate with himself. At twenty-
three Philip Deed was an interesting subject for prophesy.
It would surprise no one who knew him if he should turn
out to be a great success,—and this was Cutter's faith,—but
the betting was against it. He had a fine, straggling army
of talents, and for commander of them a gusty temper. The

sound sense that would often bless him was for the most part present in the hours when he did not need it, and when he would not have been anything but sensible, upon any temptation. He was wise upon impulse, and the propriety of his sentiments in his best hours merely served to shame him when he was less wise : they did not establish a permanent state of wisdom in him. He made mistakes as other men are respectable : from instinct. He often had occasion to denounce himself passionately. He had a noble and unthinking generosity, a warm heart and a habit of taking people at their own valuation, and of owing more than he could pay.

There was a generous touch even in Philip's incapacity—for it amounted to that—to perceive the delicate moment at which *meum* melts into *tuum*. It was a kind of incapacity to infect an entire character, and it infected Philip's ; at strange times and upon odd occasion the fibre for which one instinctively looked as the accompaniment of other fine traits in him was missing : it was like a lacking sense, rather than a vice, as excellent people are absent-minded. It might nevertheless have been odious—Jasper said it *was*—if it had not been seen to be merely the obverse side, of his generosity : what was his was yours, if you were his friend ; and it followed as the kind of corollary to which no open-handed man would give a thought, that what was yours was his. Good fellowship was like that ; it was one of the things that one did n't question. One did n't compel one's friend to ask for one's second coat, when one's friend was shivering ; one gave it and asked no questions when the friend forgot to return it : that was the way of coats and friends. And when the need for a coat was one's own it was a poor compliment to one's friend if one could not trust him for as good an understanding of the transaction as one's own.

Philip had never reasoned it out—it was not the sort of

thing to reason about—but this was, in general terms, his instinct about the whole business of give and take. He had an entirely good conscience about his money dealings, and obligations of every sort. He knew that he borrowed more than he lent, but that was because the borrowers did not come to him early enough. When he received a sum of money there were always a dozen tedious people who wanted it—people to whom he owed it : they got hold of it often before he could lend it to any of the half dozen borrowers who usually hang about such a man. About certain obligations of honour he had as sensitive a pride as that of his father, who never owed anybody a penny; but he would have postponed any ordinary debt to lend a friend in need ten dollars, and he would have had no more scruple in putting the gratification of some wish of his own before it. It was, in fact, often a race between the wish and the creditor : the kind of wish that it took some time and trouble to gratify was an advantage to the creditor. When the conditions were favourable he would often arrive first. Philip was, in fine, upon principle and in practice, always generous before he was just.

He would have found it difficult to explain his theory about the propriety of being generous to himself. It was involved in the foolish pride, not unlike a sense of caste, which had given him a belief, cherished in a careless way from his boyhood and now become an instinctive feeling in him, like a religion, that certain things were proper to him. Reduced to its obvious terms it would have become, like a number of our more obstinate inner religions, an absurdity. Philip got along with his religion by not reducing it—by not so much as thinking of it. He acted upon it. Was it that certain insignia, a certain ceremonial, a peculiar dignity were an hereditary appanage of his station? But what was his station? If he had been brought to this, he would have urged that his station was to be Philip Deed, which might not be much, but was what it was. He could n't pretend to explain.

One of the more immediate results of this theory of the pre-eminence of the debt he owed permanently to himself over the accidental obligations incurred in paying it, was that his unpaid bills in Piñon, over and above the money his father sent him regularly to run his mine amounted to a trifle over $400. The several small debts making up this sum began to be pressing; and he was glad to be leaving Piñon, not merely because the mines he had been working for himself and Jasper offered no prospect of yielding ore in paying quantities, but because he saw no present means of paying these debts by his own exertions, and they had reached a point where it was inconvenient, and occasionally a little humiliating to add to them. He meant to ask his father to lend him the money. He would be able to pay him in six months; he knew where he could make twice $400 by that time; and meanwhile he would pay him interest. He disliked to be borrowing from his father in the loose way he had used hitherto. They would make it a business transaction, and he should have his note.

" Is n't that Piñon Mountain to the right of the big dome of Ute Chief?" he asked, as they stood on their height, looking out over the hills.

" Yes; I make it out so," said Cutter. ." Melancholy sight."

" Yes—oh, yes," agreed Philip heavily. " I've been thinking of our year up there : what an ass I made of myself dropping three or four hundred days into those holes in the ground on Mineral Hill."

" Ugh ! " grunted Cutter.

" They were n't much as days, of course ; but they were the best I had at the time. They might have brought me in a clear ten thousand or so if I had set them to work bank-presidenting, or something. Why think of it—a fellow might have married on the earnings of those days. And there they lie at the bottom of the 'Little Cipher' and the 'Pay Ore.' 'Pay Ore'!" he exclaimed scornfully. "Happy thought of its fairy godmother—that name."

"Well, I'm not banking heavily on the 'Little Cipher.' But it was luck enough for one day to locate the 'Pay Ore.' The Ryan outfit are going to have those days out of the 'Pay Ore,' you know, Deed. There's stuff in that claim."

"Yes, I know," assented Philip indifferently, "low-grade stuff. I don't see how it helps me that it would pay to ship if it assayed three dollars better. It might as well be a thousand."

"Wait awhile. It *will* be a thousand—a thousand better than pay dirt."

Philip made a contemptuous sound; but his contempt was outward only. He believed in the future of the "Pay Ore," now that money enough was to be put into it to sink the shaft to the proper depth, as men believe in the woman of their secret ideal—the woman whom they shall one day meet and love, but whose virtues it is unprofitable to discuss meanwhile.

"That's all right," returned Cutter unshakenly. "I've been down in the mine. Ryan's going to make a big stake out of his lease of the 'Pay Ore.' Watch him and see. He might even take something out of the 'Little Cipher.' He and Buckham know what they are about. Who supposed there was anything in the 'Celestina' until they took hold of it on a lease? And now look at it. Why, they were saying in Piñon yesterday that the last assay gave $1,000 to the ton."

"Pshaw, Cutter! I am ashamed of that bargain with Ryan."

His companion permitted himself a smile. "Well, you ought to be—the other way. You did n't get enough. Man alive, you don't suppose he and Buckham are here for their health. How many pairs of eyes do you think they need to see that you are next the 'Celestina;' and that the 'Pay Ore,' anyway—and perhaps the 'Little Cipher'—is a straight continuation of their lead?" He had raised his voice, but he lowered it to say, "Why, look here, Deed, I'll tell you what I'll do: I'll stake my reputation as a mining engineer that they have struck a true fissure vein in the 'Celestina,' and that it dips your way."

Philip laughed. "Your confidence is charming, Cutter—charming. If you will give me a note of introduction to the person you have in mind who is prepared to furnish me with board and lodging in exchange for such confidence as that, I don't see what more I can ask."

The silence that fell between them recognized the existence of the subject they were shying away from. It was an hour since Philip had been handed his father's long telegram as they passed through Laughing Valley City. He had bit his lip and turned it over to Cutter. They had found no words for it since, and were still trying to talk of other things.

"I wonder if you'd mind, Deed, if I were to say what an awful cad that brother of yours seems to be," Cutter broke forth at last, while they still stood looking down into the valley from their eminence.

Philip ground his teeth.

"Hardly! It saves me the trouble. Oh!" he cried, venting the feeling he had been choking back in a helpless shout of rage, "to think of his coming it over father and me like that! Confound it, I believe I could have stood being swindled out of my whole future and have managed to pull a decent face about it if he had done it like a gentleman. But this . . . . ! The thing's so dirty, so small, so sneaking !

E

Why, Cutter, it's the grade of midnight assassination. Fancy
father! The favourite son!" He gave a scornful little laugh
and dashed his hand to his eyes. "Damn the fellow, any
way!" he cried. "I swear when I think of it, it seems
too low a thing for any one who has a drop of my father's
blood in him to have done. I was n't old enough when
my mother died to know her intimately; but I don't
believe she was like that. And to think that I have spent
a year in those cursed mountains up at Piñon, working
that mine for him right alongside my own—rising early and
going to bed late; giving up every Christian habit; denying
myself every kind of decency of living—yes, forgetting how
it might feel to live like a gentleman; and all of it just as
much—every ounce as much—for his infernal mine as for
my own; and I get this for it. I tell you, Cutter, some
things turn you sour. The beastly ingratitude of the thing
makes me so sick that I can't kick against it. I have n't
any kick left in me. I believe some day, when I am cooler
about it, I shall be sorry for the fellow for being such a
devil of a cad. And to think that he is my brother—yes,
and my father's son!"

"Pshaw! He'll never stick to that point, Deed. It's
too indecent."

"Won't he!" cried Philip bitterly. "You've got a lot to
learn about Jasper. He'll not only stick to it, but he'll
prove that he's right. And what's more he will think so
himself. Jasper would n't do anything he didn't think right.
He'll think it right if it chokes him. He has done the right
thing, and done it at the right time ever since I can remember; and I've always admired it in him. A man can't help
admiring a quality so remote from himself as that, you
know," he said bitterly. "Jasper is n't the kind of fool to
chuck away a year in a place like Piñon. He knows better,
and I respect him for it. His discretion and propriety, that

habit of his of doing the wise and sensible thing while I was lucklessly going to some new style of dogs every six months or so, and disappointing my father—you can't think, Cutter, what an impression that makes on a younger brother. Jasper's very schoolmasters used to praise him, and even then I knew they were right, and that I had earned my stool in a corner for shirked lessons. As early as that he had a sort of instinct for the buttered side of life, and you see he has n't forgotten it. You ought to have played marbles with a boy for 'keeps' to really understand a man, you know, Cutter."

"Oh, come!" said Cutter. "His habit of being right is n't going to help him to hold that ranch against your claim. Your father will have him out of that before we get to Maverick. Jasper is n't the only man who knows law."

"Humph! Poor father!" sighed Philip. He lighted a cigarette. "He won't have much heart left for law, I'm afraid. His way is a quicker way. I can't think what would have happened to Jasper if he had told that to father instead of writing it. Like him to use a letter for it! Father does n't bear things well, you know. They make him wild, just at first. It's part of Jasper's discretion that he knew better than to stand up and tell him such a thing. I believe father would have had to kill him."

"And that is the kind of man you think likely to sit down under such an injury and twirl his thumbs?"

"Hardly. He won't be sitting down. He will be raging about. But it won't do him any good. We've only got the barest facts; but you can figure out a good deal if one of your known quantities is character, and if you know Jasper's character you may be sure that he's behind the strongest kind of fortress, if it comes to that. The law can't touch him, I'll wager. Jasper always knows what he is about; he's got his earthworks piled sky high. You might

as well try to storm that cliff over there." He pointed to
the sheer lift of rock opposite them. "It would be a pity,
I'm sure, if a man's going to abuse a trust, if he should n't
make a good job of it. Poor father! That's what cuts him
up, I know. He trusted the fellow, you see. Trusted him!
Heavens! He loved him! Pshaw! Let's talk of something
else, Cutter. What's become of *your* trouble? Come, I
don't want to monopolize all the fun. Tell me, old fellow,"
he said, laying his hand on the other's shoulder; "do you
hear anything?"

Cutter bit an end off the cigarette he had just lighted, and
nibbled at the tendrils of tobacco nervously. He glanced
with a vengeful look at the stony wall opposite, as he cast
the cigarette out into the air, and watched it fall in a waver-
ing line into the cañon, a thousand feet beneath them. "No,
nothing!" he answered at last.

"And you want to?"

"Want to? You don't suppose I have any will about
it, do you? A man in love, as you may find out some day,
Deed, is away past 'want' and 'not want.' It's all 'must.'"

"Yes," admitted Philip sententiously, "it's been described
to me that way. But one would say——"

"Of course they would; and awfully easy it is to say,
when it's somebody else; and the girl does n't happen to be
the archetype of girlhood, and the one maiden arranged for
you from the beginning of time, and possessed of the only
smile and the only droop of eyelid you have any use at all
for, and all the rest of it. They babble about the happiness
of love until a man has to try it, as he tries smoking,
because it seems at the time about the most interesting
experience one can buy; but it is a good deal like the
smoking when you have taken a puff or two at it: your
cigar *has* a Havana wrapper, 'as advertised'; it's the
Hoboken filler that breaks you up."

Philip roared at the gloomy face with which Cutter said this; but his companion's countenance kept its ruefulness.

It was a year since Cutter's easy life had been given a violently new twist by Elsa Berrian's refusal of him. He had left New York immediately after in a passion of rage, humiliation and love; and his hurt was still fresh in him.

The day on which she refused him held more instruction for Cutter about the constitution of human society than he had gathered in the entire preceding twenty-four years. Perhaps most men can look back to such days, when life closed about them with a kind of rigour, and they fought their way through the desperate view of the excessive and useless hardness of things (which suggested suicide as a natural, and not unpicturesque remedy), to the mixed doggedness and pluck that enabled them to rise next morning, and have a try, at least, at the inexorability of Fate. Cutter, when he had tasted the dregs of this species of learning, was, to his own sense, a stalking repository of melancholy wisdom.

He had thought his misery must make all things indifferent. But, when he snatched at Philip's suggestion that he should go West with him, he had not supposed it would be so unlike New York. He had what he called his "profession"—he had studied mining engineering for two years at Columbia—but the demand for his inexperience at Piñon left him plenty of time to wish he had not been in such a hurry to leave a life which was arranged for him, and which he understood, for the crude West. His dissatisfaction may not have been altogether unconnected with the fact that at home he had been a young man about town with a rich father who did not object to his idling until he should have found the thing he wanted to do; while at Piñon every one was a worker, and was grossly, even brutally, intolerant of any one who was not.

He was going to stay a year, though. He was resolved

upon that. He would have felt it to be a confession that
he lacked "sand" to give it up earlier; and he was really
too heart-sick about Elsa to be able to think with patience
of revisiting New York for a long time to come. It ended
in his forcing his habit of laziness into regular application to
such business as found its way to him, and, for the first time,
he began to study mining engineering in earnest.

He felt after a few months of life in Piñon as if he had
"had a great deal of nonsense knocked out of him." He
liked the outdoor life, and, when he could keep the old
Cutter under, he got along fairly well with the men with
whom his business brought him in contact. But it was
perhaps because, after all, he could not help letting them
see that he could imagine nobler, not to say more interesting, examples of the race than they, that he was a failure
at Piñon, when all was said.

It was not quite his fault. It was not to be expected that
he should at once be able to rid himself of the New York
theory of life; and that, other things being equal (though
other things had a hard time of it to be equal under such
conditions), a man should not seem somehow a better man
to whom such words as Wallack's, Daly's, Del's, the Union
League, the Academy, Brown's, suggested the same host of
associations that they suggested to him. This was of course
no more than the deathless and invincible New York conceit
which amuses the country at all times; but it was perhaps
dearer to him than to the usual New Yorker, because he
had for a number of years had nothing better to do than to
foster it. It was his misfortune that he had somewhat less
than the usual tact, which helps other New Yorkers to cloak
their sense of an obvious superiority; but it was happily his
luck not to be a snob in any sense or degree.

Philip, who had long since accepted the West, and
whose direct habit of thought removed him from the tempta-

tion of remaining the critical outsider who analyzes the
situation it is his main duty to be living, was never tired
of making game of Cutter's crude struggles to be crude, and
of his habit of pettifogging with his temporary Western lot.
He had been accustomed to defend him when he was ridiculed
in Piñon ; but in the privacy of the cabin which the two
occupied together on Mineral Hill he guyed Cutter's amusing
fopperies as much as the camp could have desired.   Cutter
continued to apply his daintiness to the coarse exigencies
of Western life with a smile ; and good-humouredly went on
being in his dress the most elegant rowdy that ever was.
He was a picturesque figure when in full regalia, with his
fire-new chapereros, his nickel-plated spurs, his spotless sombrero, on which he kept a fresh leather band at all times, his
English riding boots, and his crop.   His revolver was of
the latest make, and his cartridge-belt looked as if he never
used it.

Cutter's faults, like this little foible of his, were for the
most part on the surface.   Beneath them all he was as
simple, honest and manly as any one need be ; and men who
had need of a loyal friend sought Lenox Cutter.   The self-
confidence, which was not quite conceit, and the touch of
selfishness which went with it, were of that not too insistent
sort which women are accustomed to the need of condoning
in the men of their acquaintance daily, and which men—
because they know how much of both qualities a man needs
to earn a living—are accustomed to tolerate so long as the
like qualities in themselves are not trodden upon.

The clouds had been gathering while they talked and
hung a threatening black bank in the West as Cutter,
turning away from Philip's laugh, glanced at them.

" We are going to catch it," he said.   " Shall we go
on ? "

Philip put out his hand from his pony to test the air·

The harsh damp that had fallen on the day made itself felt between his interrogating thumb and forefinger.

"I must, you know. They will be looking for me at Maverick to-day. I couldn't risk being snowed up down there in Laughing Valley City for a week or two. But you must wait, Cutter. There's nothing to hurry you."

"Pshaw, we shall get to Bayles' Park before the fun begins. Anyway, we'll see it out together, unless you want to get rid of me."

"You're a brick, Cutter; but you'd better stay. I am going to have company whether or no, I think." He nodded, toward the town. "Down the trail there—do you see?"

Cutter, following the direction of his nod, saw a large crowd of men on horseback issuing from the town, which, a few moments earlier, had seemed depopulated. They had just passed the last group of cabins, on the outskirts of the settlement, and were riding at a canter up the first rise of the long hill which the young men had climbed half way. In the still air the talk of the company rose loudly. It was plain that an unusual event had called them forth.

"Let's have the glass," said Cutter suddenly. "Fact!" he exclaimed, after a moment. "There's a young girl among them—riding alongside the tall fellow in front. See?"

Philip took the glass Cutter handed him, and scanned the party. "By Jove!" He studied the shouting throng anxiously for a moment. "I don't more than half like the look of that crowd, Cutter. The girl—why, man, she's——"

"Rather! See how she bears herself at the head of that crazy lot. A lady? She's a queen."

"Yes," assented Deed musingly, while he kept the glass upon the moving group. "But the man in the centre—what do you make of him?"

" Which ? " asked Cutter, taking the glass. " The clerical-looking chap ? "

" Yes, I thought he looked like a clergyman."

" He is too, by George. See here, Deed, there's going to be a circus here of some sort. We'll have to see this thing out."

Philip nodded. " Do you notice how all the gestures point his way ; and how they seem to be shouting at him, and keeping him in the centre while he sits his horse without a word. Do you know, I believe *he's* the row."

Cutter's restless pony would not stand while he turned the glass on the crowd again. He got off, and putting an arm through the rein, made an attentive observation.

" It can't be," he said at length.

" What ? "

" That they are running him out of town."

" Why, my dear fellow, it fits in perfectly with all you 're in the habit of pretending you believe about the cloth."

" Stuff ! I never said they were rascals," said Cutter, keeping the glass to his eyes. He put the glass down, and remounted.

" What do you make of the girl's relation to him ? " asked Philip after a moment.

" Oh, daughter, I suppose. She does n't look as if she belonged to any of the rest of the mob."

" Careful there, Cutter ; careful ! " He was straining his eyes through the glass. " Some of them may be Englishmen. In fact, I think I see a Viscount. That's no way to speak of the imported article."

The group was coming within easy eye-shot. A shout that went up at the moment sounded close by.

" The imported article has a domestic howl," said Cutter.

" Yes ; and it's getting precious near. We must n't let them find us studying them."

\With one of the silent twitches of the rein understood by cattle ponies, they put their horses into a canter, and passed out of sight of the crowd by a turn in the trail, which writhed about the hill until, near the summit, it pushed forth in the direction of their journey, and began to find its way loftily along the walls of Red Rock Cañon. The winding trail brought them in a moment to a point just above that which they had left, and looking down from behind a pile of rocks shielding them from observation, they saw the party halted there. It was a shaggy mob, not carrying out in its dress its suggested English birth and breeding.

It seemed to be made up of all classes of the town's population. Those in the group at the left, with clay-grimed trousers stuffed in their boots, were from the mines, and, in one or two instances, the candles which they had apparently neglected to put down in their haste were carried by the steel hooks upon their fingers. The two wearing white shirts, (the rest were clothed in the flannel of the West) had a hard look, and might be gamblers. The shopkeepers, who had come along to see the fun, were to be distinguished by the eccentricity of allowing their trousers to drape themselves outside their boots. There were a couple of cowboys, with chapereros, spurs, and sombreros; and with lariats coiled about their saddle pommels. Most of the crowd carried their weapons in sight. Some of the revolvers were to be seen peeping from saddle holsters. The cowboys wore their "guns" in cartridge belts about their waists. It was a threatening-looking lot; yet, when the leader drew his fat black revolver from his belt, and began to toy with it, his playful use of it seemed merely a waggish substitute for the hems and haws of other public speakers.

The crowd, grouping itself about him, arraigned the clergyman before them, and somewhat apart (still on his horse), with that eye for the scenic and dramatic which plays its uncon-

scious share in all the extra-legal functions assumed by the
people in the country beyond the Mississippi. The tone in
which the leader addressed the clergyman was peremptory,
certainly ; but his address had its humorous moments, and
once,—when, from the pitch of his voice, the listeners above
guessed that he was burlesquing the hortatory clerical manner,
—the guffaw greeting the bit of farce showed how the sovereign people may find rewards even in the solemn and pain
ful duty of administering justice.

Philip watched the scene intently. " We shall have to
take a hand in this," he whispered at last. " They mean to
lynch him."

" No, no," answered Cutter, under his breath. " The
leader is beginning on a set of resolutions. They don't
resolve at lynching bees. They act. Besides, what would
they be doing with the girl ? They're running him out."

Philip said nothing, but glanced thoughtfully at the clouds,
which had been folding hill after hill while they waited, and
had now totally obscured the mountains which, in fair weather,
seemed so near Laughing Valley City that it appeared at
times as if one might touch them by stretching out his hand.
The vapour scurried close above them. They knew that
their own hill must be out of sight from the town. The air
grew chillier.

" Perhaps they might better lynch him," said Philip, at
length. " Do you remember when they ran that tin-horn
gambling outfit out of Piñon ? It was just such a day as
this has been—all sun until ten o'clock. You surveyed the
' Little Cipher ' and the ' Pay Ore ' for me that morning ;
and the weather could n't have been fairer. But how it got
its back up after they were escorted out of camp ! It was n't
an hour before the town was trying to find itself."

" Yes," admitted Cutter. " It snowed."

" Snowed ? You could n't see the electric lights until you

ran against the poles. And those fellows, wandering toward shelter in that storm, without a horse, and with no telegraph poles to guide them to Castaway Springs . . . . I know, you always say the Vigilance Committee could n't suppose it was going to snow. But when they brought the bodies in the week after—do you remember?—it was awful to see the camp find its conscience. Absolutions would have had a livelier sale than whiskey in Piñon that day, I've often thought."

"The wind is n't right for an old-fashioned blizzard to-day," said Cutter, divining his thought. "You and I and the minister will get through all right if they'll only start him. But they'll have to get a move on soon."

"I was n't thinking of him," said Philip.

"Why, great heaven, Deed, you don't suppose they are going to send her along?"

"Send her? No. But she'll do what she likes, I think ; and you don't believe she'll desert her father, do you?"

Deed took the glass from its case again, and directed it to where she stood withdrawn at a considerable distance, out of earshot, gazing on the scene with a face of anxious misery. He had not seen her closely before. She seemed a quite young girl. She might be twenty or twenty-one ; not more.

"By Jove!" he exclaimed, in a low tone.

Cutter took the glass he offered. "She *is* pretty," he admitted.

"Pretty!" cried Philip.

Cutter smiled. "Well, do you want to go down and rescue her? I'm with you."

"From what? Don't you see what delicate consideration and courtesy they use toward her? See the tall óne standing guard over her privacy with averted eyes. And did n't you notice, as they came up the hill, how first one and then another would ride forward to see if there was anything he could do for her? Why, those fellows are knights, you know, Cutter, when it comes to regard for a woman—especially a woman above them. By George, she has an air!" He spent a long moment watching her through the glass. "She is the Princess they treat her like : and she can unbend, too. See the gracious smile she gives her subject-captor—the tall fellow. He's been offering to fetch her an ice from the North Pole, and she has declined, with the sort of grace that makes denial a favour."

The leader folded the paper from which he had been reading the resolutions, and stuck it in his belt. Philip, turning his glass on the minister, caught the glance of uneasy scorn with which he awaited the next movement of his persecutors. It was violent only in its sarcasm : they lifted their wide-brimmed hats as one man, and made way for him to pass. The unanimity and silence with which this was accomplished would have been impressive, if it had not been rather laughable. The minister winced, but straightened himself immediately on his horse, and rode by the ordeal of the row of eyes, fixed contemptuously upon him, with proudly lifted head. Jake Devine, the leading saloon-keeper of the town, bridled in imitation of his haughty carriage, and a smile ran about. Maurice continued to look before him, implying his indifference as well as he might by the walk out of which he scorned to press his horse. The crowd seemed under the spell of its own silence, and no jeer broke from it until the minister had passed the last man, and was on his way up the hill.

A jocose stone or two pursued him amid the derisive yells that now rose, and one of the group, creeping nimbly up behind, smote the horse resoundingly with a cudgel. The beast gave a snorting bound, and leaped forward up the steep at a gallop. The clergymen's hat—an English parson's wideawake—was blown from his head by the sudden movement, and his dignity was scattered upon the wind which wafted it from him toward the crowd, and which blew his thin locks out behind as the horse scampered up the uneven ascent, reckless of rocks and turns.

Philip had seen the girl's streaming eyes as she started to follow him and was gently withheld ; and now he saw her dry her tears with a start of indignation, and point imperiously to the flying hat. The tall young man beside her made after it, and returned it humbly to her. She nodded her thanks, and at the same moment, with a dexterous hand, wheeled her horse, and with a smart touch of the whip set off at a run after her father.

The thing was so quickly done, that no one had time to interfere, and they all stood gazing stupidly after her for a moment. Then the tall young man gave his pony the spur, and followed her. His animal's clattering hoofs on the rocks urged her horse on, and he did not overtake her until she was rounding the summit on which the young men awaited, unseen, the issue of the scene below. He appeared to entreat her ; she shook her head vigorously, and put his hand down from her rein with a firm, but not unkind briskness. She gave him a smile through her tears ; and he rode on with her.

The young men followed. It had begun to snow.

CHAPTER IV.

The Rev. George Maurice's difficulty with the Vigilance Committee at Laughing Valley City was the climax of the ill-will which began to show itself against him in the town a month or two after his arrival there from his last parish, in Dakota. He had failed with these people not merely because he lacked the cardinal virtue of the West—adaptability; though certainly he was tactless enough, and would often rasp the sensibilities of those whom he would willingly have pleased. Nor had he failed altogether because he was arbitrary, and dictatorial; his congregation could no doubt have borne that cheerfully from a man they respected : indeed it is not certain that they might not have liked him the better for being a bit of a bully.

If they had been asked to lay a finger on the source of their dissatisfaction with him they would probably have had to own that they could n't. That was not a thing to make them less dissatisfied, however. He was, in fact, one of the men to whom it would be a pleasure to attribute something forgivable—like a definite sin. It was perhaps his indefinite weakness that was unpardonable.

One might say, for example,—as certain people did— that he was not too scrupulous about money matters ; but it could not truthfully be said that he was unscrupulous. It might be alleged that he did light things, unbecoming his cloth ; but his behaviour was never clearly unseemly. He could easily be proved lacking in consideration for others, or, if one liked—and there were usually several who liked—for his daughter ; yet when one would say "selfish," the remembrance of a reckless act of generosity would recall itself, or the recollection of the strain of self-sacrifice in him, declaring itself in acts that enslaved to him those whom they helped, and endeared him to a following among the young of all his parishes ; and condemnation was laid by the heels.

Maurice did not pretend to be perfect. If he had made any such pretence he would, for instance, have felt bound to bury Carstarphen and Telfner when they died of small-pox, brought to Laughing Valley City by a party of China-men. The men had lived, like other miners, in disregard of every sanitary precaution ; no measures had been taken for disinfecting the cabin in which they had died, and to go to it to read the burial service over them, and then to accompany their bodies to the grave, on the side of Car-bonate Mountain, two miles from town, was, as a matter of fact, a serious risk. It was unfortunate that those duties of a minister of the Gospel, which, in personal experience of them, one must, of course, qualify a trifle, should be so simply conceived by the friends of the dead men. His refusal to perform the last office for the men, though made with the proper reluctance and regret, and reasoned cogently, was taken extremely ill.

The miners who had come to ask his services as the only minister in town, " cursed him out," as they afterwards told the indignation meeting. It was at this meeting that the resolutions were adopted, in which the word " coward " occurred six times—exclusive of the indignant preamble.

The resolutions, which, after the received custom, gave him twenty-four hours to leave town, expressly excepted his daughter ; and the ladies of the place had arranged among themselves to keep her by them, and look after her, with the purpose of sending her after her father, if she should desire to go, when he should be settled somewhere. This plan had, carelessly enough, reckoned without Dorothy's energetic will, it was found, when the time came ; and they let her go with the band that escorted him to the edge of the town because she very quietly would have it so, not imagining it necessary to extract a promise from her to go no further.

Dick Messiter (a young man whom the ladies knew to have a mill-owning father somewhere in Massachusetts, and whose occupation at Laughing Valley City was that of Super-intendent of Cincinnati Mining Co. No. 3) had offered to go along and look after her ; and, in spite of the lamentable occasion of the association of the two young people under these conditions, the circumstance gratified that dumb novel-ist, or perhaps it is merely romancer, which seems to lurk in every woman's breast. It struck the ladies of the town, as a beautiful situation ; and they would have been the last to interpose an obstacle to the crisis which is somewhere toward the top of every situation.

They trembled appropriately for the clergyman, when he was led out in the midst of the shouting mob, and they exchanged the observation that they ought not to have thought of such a thing as letting her go, when they saw her riding among the noisiest of them. It would have been hard if they could not assuage their remorse by the suggestive spectacle of Dick and the girl riding side by side up the hill. If one looked at the matter from this standpoint it was clear that the mob could not be too noisy, and, in a harmless way, it was even to be hoped that it might prove obstreperous : it would be a pretty opportunity for Dick.

The trail over which Philip and Cutter followed the

F

three riders clambered difficultly along the walls of Red
Rock Cañon; or sometimes it would dip into it, or
wander quite out of it, and take its way along the table
land above. Bayles' Park, where they were to find the
train for Maverick, and where the railway terminated for the
present, lay in one of those green and sheltered hollows, in
the penetralia of the hills, known to Colorado vocabularies
as a Park. For a good part of the year, the parks—which
are a kind of small paradise to the traveller who comes
down into them out of the mountains—keep a Spring
festival, and if anyone supposes that there are hill-gnomes,
he must be sure that it is on these fresh and flower-starred
lawns that they hold their revels. At all events, the hills
water and refresh them, as if they would keep their ball-
room bright—or perhaps it is with the hospitable thought of
maintaining one guest chamber among their unfriendly
rocks; and every mountain traveller knows how to praise
the shelter it offers.

Bayles' Park was still well nigh a two hours' journey
forward, however, and the snow had begun to fly more
thickly. The noiseless coming of the storms in which
men and beasts are lost in these mountains is their most awful
effect : one could die more easily, one feels, in the worst riot
of tempest. The snow fell silently about them as they rode,
piling the folds of their great-coats, and their ponies' flanks,
with its stealthy increase. The wind, which blew the flakes
in their faces blindingly, was smitten soundless by the solid
curtain of white through which it passed to reach them.
The world was filled with snow and silence. It had grown
very cold.

There are often such snow flurries in the mountains; and
then in a few moments, sunshine again. Philip and Cutter
consulted with each other, and did not believe it would last.
But they agreed that it should make no difference if it did.

They could not turn back and leave those in advance to take their chances, even if Philip was ready to give up the wedding. So people will agree while their feet are still warm; and they pushed on doggedly, as the fall grew heavier.

The telegraph line followed the trail, save when, at rare times (led on stubby iron poles), it would go forward, for the sake of a short cut, in a dizzy run over the rocks jutting from the cliff above them. Where the poles were set along their path they were higher, and when the snow was most blinding it was still easy to make out the road by them. But the poles were presently less plain; and the sullen murmur of the Chepita rising steadily from the chasm which opened at the outer edge of the trail, a measureless void, warned them to use their eyes before they used the reins by which they would sometimes guide the horses.

"Look sharp, there, Deed!" shouted Cutter, suddenly; and Philip withheld his pony in time to save himself from the gulf.

The pony backed in terror, and when Philip got him started forward again, Cutter's horse refused to budge. Cutter alighted, and led him. The animal came forward reluctantly, cowering before each step, and eyeing the way before him doubtfully. The snow-fall appeared suddenly to grow more dense, and the river, down at the bottom of the cañon, which had marched with them until now to a soothing melody, seemed suddenly to shake itself free from the silence of which it had been part, and to give forth a muffled roar and shout.

Cutter looked back for a sight of Philip's face. He could touch his pony's nose; but the rider was a vague spectre. Cutter gave a prolonged shout.

"Helo-o-o-o-o."

They were not three paces from each other; but he

could not be sure whether the answer was an echo, or
Philip's voice.   He pressed his pony back against Philip's.
They caught at each other's hands as the animals came
together.

"I was afraid of this," said Cutter hoarsely, with the fear
which we find after the event.

"Yes," answered Philip.

The frightful huddle and scurry of the big flakes came
between them, as they peered in each other's faces; and
their voices reached each other dully out of the pall of
snow.

"Think of those people!" said Philip, after a moment, in
which they let their horses stand.   "Think of that girl!"

"Hellish!" muttered Cutter, who had had no comment
for the business while they watched it.

"Come on!" said Philip briefly; and Cutter understood.
It was true: they must find them.   And at the moment
they heard a vague sound like voices, in advance.

Philip's pony would not move quickly enough, and he
threw himself off, and jerked him forward.

"You heard?" he asked.

"Yes."

They pressed forward, and presently came upon the group
halted in the middle of the trail, bending over the girl, who
had been taken from her horse, and was being plied with
brandy by the tall young man.   Her father, who was rubbing
her ears with snow, would raise his eyes from time to time
desperately, frowning and blinking at the storm.

She had not fainted.   She was merely exhausted by the
storm, and numbed by the cold.   The spirits seemed to restore her.   She looked up at sound of the shout of greeting
with which Philip and Cutter made their presence known,
and descried their figures.

"My horse——" she murmured to Messiter, who was

stooping over her ; and he and her father raised her up, and set her on her pony, while Philip put himself at the animal's head.

Philip shouted something in Messiter's ear, as he came around in front of her animal to take his own by the rein.

"To be sure !" answered the girl's cavalier. "Had n't thought of it."

Messiter did .not catch what Philip added ; but he replied to the question he guessed in his voice, "Yes ; near here. I know the place well enough when the weather has n't got the blind staggers. Blast the snow !" he shouted, rubbing his eyebrows and moustache, and mopping the little segment of face which showed between his high muffler and low fitting cap. "Brown's Cañon, don't they call it ?"

He was near enough to see Philip's nod.

"A cut in the rock, and the cave just inside of it ? Beyond the Fifth Cascade ?"

"That's the place," said Philip.

They set forward for it without delay, each leading his own horse, except that Philip took Messiter's besides his own, while Messiter led the girl's. Cutter, who did not know the cave, brought up the rear with the clergyman, who made no attempt to hide from him his disapproval of the storm and of the entire situation. Cutter had never heard such pleasant-hearted, even mellow, grumbling. The man had a charm of manner which one felt through the snow itself. In front, the two young men discussed the whereabouts of the cleft in the rocks (which was known as a cañon, for no very good reason), and of the cave. About the place itself, Philip knew best, having bunked in the cave for a night, when he had come over the Pass the year before, on his way to Piñon ; but his companion was much more familiar with the trail.

They went peeringly forward, dragging the trembling

horses. There was always an uncertain moment after they
had lost sight of one telegraph pole, and before they could
make out the next; and at these times they felt cautiously
along the rocky wall that soared into the air on the inside
of the trail, and did not venture toward the outer edge.
The horses tried each step inquiringly before taking it;
and the two men in the lead, advancing into the unknown
with such courage as they might, would often pause to take
counsel with each other's ignorance and helplessness. It was
impossible to say where anything was in this night of snow :
all of their world was that next step which they could see;
and that step might always plunge them into the world
which no man has seen at any time. The cold seemed
somehow to numb the thought, by sympathy with the
bodily pain and bewilderment which intense cold brings.
The girl, who had not their resource of motion, was crying in
silent agony from it, Philip saw, when he made way at a turn
in the path for the young man to lead her horse by him;
and he pressed his flask of whiskey into her hands. They
were so cold, and the men's mittens she had drawn over her
gloves so clumsy, that she had almost dropped it; Philip
caught it up as it slipped from her, and shouting to his
companion to hold on, asked her by a motion to raise her
veil, and pulling himself by a jutting boulder to her level,
put the flask to her lips. She was very pale; and the smile
she extorted from herself for thanks was pitiful.

Sometimes the trail turned sharp corners; and once they
found themselves at the edge of the precipice, and the cry
of the river leaped up to them through the storm with a
sudden loudness. The two in advance shuddered back
from the sound, clutching at each other and feeling blindly
through the swirl toward the cliff on which their lives hung.
Shouldered firmly against the wall once more they paused
for a weary and discouraged moment to shake off the snow,

and to take heart for another venture into the awful mystery of white.

The death which might lie before them was certain where they stood, from snow and cold; and at last they dared question the wall again with advancing hands. Philip was sure the cañon and its cave could not be far. But the storm created its own far and near. Ten paces were far—one might have to lie down and give up the fight at the end of them—the second step was not near; one might never take it. The wind had risen to a gale; the cold searched their veins, and their limbs began to answer their wills uncertainly. It was time they found shelter. One of the horses stumbled, and could not rise until Cutter felt his way back along the bridle rein and helped him up. But when he tugged at the reins again the pony would not move.

"We shall have to give the poor beast up, I'm afraid," he said. Philip went back and spoke a heartening word to the pony—it had belonged to him in the mountains —and the animal came along for a few paces, and stopped again, when it became necessary to repeat the action.

It was all done in silence. For half an hour no one had spoken, when Philip shouted, "The cascade!"; and there reached their ears as they halted to listen, remotely, as if from a great distance, the steady, down-beating pour of a waterfall. The sound triumphed over the clamouring river, and the loud-breathing wind, though it seemed so far away; and hope blessed them again.

When the wall opened at last to their weary hands, and discovered the cañon, and, a moment later, the cave, they had just strength enough left among them to get the girl from her horse, and set her within the cavern. They sank about her exhausted when they saw her safe; and for a long time lay powerless to help her or one another.

Philip was the first to find his feet.

"Here, Cutter! Stop that! Wake up!" he cried. Cutter was dozing in the dangerous sleep in which men die from cold. He shook him violently.

"Let me alone," grunted Cutter; but Philip caught him up, and seated him against one of the walls of the cave.

"Wake up! Do you hear?"

"Oh, come off!" exclaimed Cutter drowsily.

"See here, do you want your head banged against these rocks? They're sharp, I warn you."

Cutter started awake. He cast a listless glance over the cavern which was high and spacious, with boulders scattered about the floor. The roof and sides were toothed and rutted, and showed everywhere sharp points of rock, at sight of which Cutter rubbed his head ruefully, and having found a smile, knew himself again. "Got a match?" he asked.

"No: but I think you have."

"Fact." He fumbled for the silver match-case, with the figure of the humorous young demon atop, which was one of the relics of his Eastern career as a young man about town.

"Good!" said Philip, energetically. "Then we'll have a fire! There's a sort of room just back round the curve in the rock there, unless I am out of my bearings, and a thing Hicks and Baxter used to call a fireplace when they were living here on a grub-stake. You'll find some wood. Get up a fire if you can, while I look after this poor girl. Sing out when you're ready, and I'll fetch her back."

He spoke rapidly and urgently, and Cutter got himself on his feet and made his way with stumbling steps in the direction of the rear of the cavern. Philip watched him anxiously a moment: he had asked him to go, to give him a reason for bestirring himself; but he feared he would drop asleep again, while he went about the kindling of the fire. But there was no time for concern about Cutter. He stood upon his own stiff legs with a groan, and made his way over to where the girl sat propped against the wall of the cave.

Her head was drooped upon her breast; but she was not asleep, and she looked up with a lifeless smile as Philip bent over her. He made her take another long pull at his flask, and then snatched off the heavy mittens which Messiter had given up to her, and peeling off the thin gloves underneath, fell to chafing her hands as briskly as his own benumbed arms would let him.

After a moment, when she began to look about her, he ran over to the prostrate figure of the clergyman, and shook him alive, and then punched up Messiter. When they had found their feet, they came over and helped him; and the girl was able after a time to reward their common efforts with a look into which the heart and courage had a little returned. She began to seem again something like the girl who had cast off the restraining hand on her rein and galloped up the slope above Laughing Valley City after her father; and, when they judged it safe, they bore her in among them to the fire which Cutter had cried out awaited them. The ears of one or two of them had been nipped; but none of their limbs had been frozen, and, with the fire in sight, the men began to dance about, flinging their arms wildly, and beating their hands upon their legs in search of their lost circulation, and suppleness of joint.

She laughed at their crazy motions, where she sat cuddled in all the wraps they could muster for her in front of Cutter's roaring fire; and they smiled back at her amusement.

"Whew!" shouted her tall cavalier, taking off his heavy gloves and blowing on his fingers. "We forgot to shut the front door after us. Don't you people feel a draught?"

She gave him a mirthful nod. "That's the etiquette of cave-mouths," she said. "You must always leave them on the latch! It's in case we should have visitors. Oh, think," she cried, in sudden terror, "if there should be any one else out in this storm!"

"Heaven help them!" said Philip, "or show them the way to something like this."

"Yes," said Cutter, drawing a musing sigh, as he settled himself by the fire. "I don't know how it was with you, Deed, but there were n't many minutes of stand up and take it left in me, when we found this."

"Yes; it's very nice we're here," she said thoughtfully to Philip, who had come over to her corner, and was standing above her, asking if there was anything that could be done to make her more comfortable. "It was awful!" She paused for a long moment, in thought of it. "How did you happen to know this place? Only think if you had n't come up with us!"

Philip perceived that she did not know that he knew —that they knew. He pulled himself up, with an inward start. He saw that what he had been about to say would have presumed on their common acquaintance with the scene on the hillside above Laughing Valley. It was evident that she had not seen them, as she swept by their post of observation on her flight to join her father.

"Oh, your friend would have remembered it. It was he who piloted us here?——Mr.——."

"——Messiter: Mr. Richard Messiter to the minister who baptized him: to everybody else, just Dick."

"I should never have found it without Mr. Messiter."

"And we should never have found it without Mr. ——?" She hesitated, in her turn, as she looked up into his face.

"Deed," supplied Philip.

"—— Deed?" she repeated. "Oh!" she added thought-

fully. "I wonder if you know a Mr. Deed who——."
Philip waited for her to finish. "Why, he once took me
quite informally out of a burning building. Our school was
on fire. It was in a village—a Pennsylvania village—and
there were no engines. The boys from the other boarding
school across the way formed lines and passed buckets. It
was at night. He happened to see me first at a window
from his place in the line, and ran in and carried me down
stairs. The fire, just for that one frightful moment at the window, was worse even than the storm we've escaped, I think.
Wasn't it fine of—of that other Mr. Deed, Mr. Deed?"

"It *was* fine," said Philip, looking down into her glowing
face. "I'm hoping I can prove kinship with him. What
was his Christian name?"

"A rather odd name—Jasper."

Philip started. "Did all that happen in a village called
Aylesford?"

"Yes. How do you know?"

"Oh!" laughed Philip uncertainly. He bit his lip.

"Is it some one you know, then? How very nice!"

"Yes," said Philip, "it is some one I know—my brother."

Dorothy exclaimed her surprise. "Then you must have
heard my story long ago. I thought I was telling you something new."

"It was new," returned Philip, without animation.

"Of course. I ought to know that he would n't say how
he had done an heroic thing. It would n't be like him."

"No," assented Philip, "it would n't be like him." It
was true that Jasper was not a man to exploit himself. He
recognized the trait in him, on reflection, without cordiality.
It was part of his propriety. He would long ago have said
to himself that to boast was crude.

"But how very odd that you should be his brother!"
cried Dorothy, returning to her original surprise. She drew

the saddle blanket with which Philip had covered her feet closer about her.

Philip burlesqued his thanks, and, with a little " Oh ! " of appreciation, her face melted into a smile. " I did n't mean——," she began imploringly. She joined in his laugh. " Do you call that fair ? " she asked.

" What ? " inquired he.

" Entrapping me, like that."

" Have I said anything ? " retorted Philip unblushingly.

" No, but you've made me. Or perhaps I said it myself, but the meaning is yours."

" Must I mean what you say ? "

She pretended to muse. " You must n't say what I mean," she answered, looking up at him with a smile that enchanted him. The name, Maurice, suddenly detached itself as he met her glance from the haze of memory in which it had been floating since he had heard it. Since she had mentioned Jasper he had been casting back for the origin of this memory. He recognized it now with a start. It was from Jasper himself that he had heard it. A myriad memories went buzzing in his head. Was it possible ? He recalled a school-boy passion of Jasper's of which he had known a very little—as little as younger brothers, just learning to smoke, are thought fitted to hear of an elder brother's love affairs—and had guessed a great deal : as much as such brothers commonly guess from slender premises. He had never seen the girl : it had all happened while Jasper was away at school. But he remembered the name now. It was Maurice.

A pang without meaning or reason passed through him as he glanced at her again. She and Jasper had once been lovers, then. She had permitted him to know her in the intimacy—the sacred intimacy, the intimate strangeness, of betrothal. The thought gave him something like a physical shock. With his knowledge of his brother's falsity fresh in his mind the idea filled him with an empty, retrospective anger for her. He felt as if she had been profaned, and he believed his pang to be wholly for her.

In the silence that had fallen between them while he pursued these thoughts, he discovered himself to be studying the face which she turned, now, half toward him and half toward the fire-light. There was certainly a nameless expression in it which made the thought of any homage to it lower than the finest peculiarly intolerable. Philip fancied that he liked the sweet seriousness of her face even better than its prettiness; but he was not sure, a moment later, that he did not like its unconsciousness better than either. She had less than the usual American pallor; and in her cheeks two bright spots of colour, which had fled before the exposure through which she had passed, began to show themselves unassertively.

Her gaze had a certain charming freedom, and in all her motions she was singularly unafraid; but this consisted with a remote touch of reserve which never left her; and which was constantly causing one to rejoice the more in a confidence that was in every expression of itself a new gift to the observer, because, in its openest moments, it seemed always to withhold a part of itself. In the same way the sober look, which slept upon the verge of her lightest glances, enriched and gave a special value to the dancing light which would come into her eyes at any challenge of her attention. The eyes themselves had been meant to be grey, apparently; but one of them had rather agreeably failed on the way to greyness, and had a fleeting tinge of brown, in some lights. A little more pronounced and it might have been a blemish: as it was, it was a part of her indescribable charm. Something in the modelling of her cheeks left the full view of her face a trifle disappointing, perhaps ; but this was because her clear, and almost perfect profile promised so much.

As she sat in the half-darkness, her face thrown into relief by the fire, she was certainly extraordinarily pretty. Her shapely chin was well in the air, her little mouth—she was in all ways made upon a little pattern—was pursed in meditation, and her straight, sensitive nose was cut with particular clearness against the light. It was not her nose which disappointed in her full face; it was incontrovertibly very good. Her hair, which had taken several tumbles under the late stress, showed that shade of brown which you felt like thanking her for combining with her eyes and complexion, and had, as well, that pretty crinkliness, and excellent habit of waving or curling at unexpected moments, which one knows.

The pained thought which had drawn Philip's musing glance to her was being replaced by an untroubled pleasure in her beauty as he was roused from his preoccupation by Cutter's voice, inquiring of her from across the fire, " Cosy ? " Their common plight seemed to beget a species of respectful intimacy among them ; and they all spoke as if they had always known one another.

" Very ! " assented she. Dorothy Maurice had been born in the South, of a Southern mother, and her voice had the melody and vibrant sweetness of the voice of Southern women, without the accent and pronunciation which it would be difficult to prove altogether desirable, but which is pretty, too, if you like. " We might almost be happy here for a week, if we could keep warm so long, and if we could find something to eat. Don't you think, Mr.——"

" Cutter," he said ; and her eyes met Philip's with another smile.

" Don't you think we might find a larder somewhere about, if we looked ? It is n't possible that the miners who left this wood for our fire would stop at that."

Cutter glanced at Philip interrogatively; and at her hint they explored. Houses wander dissolutely from street to street in Colorado towns, in wheeled pursuit of the real estate market; but provisions which have once found their way on the backs of burros to a prospector's home in the mountains are less vagrant. After a Summer's work a prospector would be in a poor way who had not something more valuable to load on his pack animals than the jerked beef, coffee, and canned fruits and vegetables upon which the young men presently came.

"Uncommonly white of them to leave so much canned hospitality on a shelf for us, was n't it?" said Cutter, exhibiting their discoveries.

"Dear me! All that!" she said. "I should think so! They must be very nice fellows. Did you say you knew them, Mr. Deed?"

"Yes; as one knows men who take you in for the night, and do the handsome thing for the wayworn traveller. I spent a night here when I first came over the Pass. They were working a claim a little way on down the trail, as I passed them on horseback. It was rather late in the afternoon, and when I asked my way of them they told me I'd better let them bunk me for the night. I'm afraid they did n't leave these good things here with us in view, quite; but if they had known we were coming along it would have been like them. They will be back in the Spring, I suppose, to begin work again. I hope they won't miss what we shall have to borrow from them."

"Oh, I dare say they won't mind," said the clergyman, who had been silent for some time, while he thawed himself out by the fire. "Politeness is rather wasted on the rough people one meets in this region, I find."

"I don't know that, sir," said Messiter. And Philip, who was about to protest, conceived in time that the clergyman was not without reason for his feeling, and forbore.

"Ah, well, *I* do, you know!" returned Maurice courteously. "An odd business, that, Dick, was n't it?" he said, with an uneasy humour. "Were you by chance in the place they call Laughing Valley City this morning?" he asked suddenly of Philip. The intention to ascertain, if possible, how much these two strangers knew of the affair on the hillside was obvious; but Philip responded, as if he had not perceived it.

"We came through Laughing Valley City in the morning from Piñon," he said.

"Ah!" said Maurice. "Then we passed you very likely on the road without observing you."

"I think very likely," answered Philip, d'singenuously. "We stopped for a while once a little out of the road." He saw her rising flush; and wished to spare her even if the clergyman did not care to be spared.

Philip saw Miss Maurice draw a sigh of relief as he made this reply; and she rose at once, and set about making the coffee—or such coffee as was possible without milk. The sugar they had.

"Any tobacco?" asked Cutter, as Philip came over his way.

Philip offered him a bag from which the best of the contents had been spilled in fighting the storm; and knelt beside him to strike a match. He seated himself near him, next the fire. "Mighty poor business, this," he said as the tobacco began to glow in their pipe-bowls, and the smoke made a home like fragrance in the air. "I shall never get to Maverick in time for my father's little affair."

Cutter smiled. "Why, you monstrous ingrate!"

"Oh, of course I'm thankful it's no worse, but when a thing's no worse, who would be so stingy with his wishes as not to want it better? Plain luck is n't enough for a man. He's got to have luck *glacé.*"

Cutter roared until the echoes answered him; and they all looked his way. " Man ! Man ! " he shouted. " You don't want luck any more *glacé* than to-day's I hope."

" What amuses Mr. Cutter? " asked Dorothy, coming towards them unfolding a ragged red table cloth which she had found, and which she was about to spread for them on a square of rock.

" One on me," said Philip. " He wants to know if it's cold enough for me. May n't I help you, Miss Maurice? "

She let him endeavour as much as he would in the helpless helping which young men are accustomed to offer young women in such things; and which is doubtless so much better for being so little effective.

As they spread the cloth between them on the rock, Dorothy used the opportunity of her position opposite him to observe him attentively, for the first time. She thought him less handsome than Jasper after a moment's inventory. She immediately added that he was better looking than she had fancied in her casual glances. His broad-shouldered vigour had its own value, and she did it justice in recalling Jasper's effect of shapeliness. Philip's robust build wanted symmetry, and his strong face, tanned by exposure to the weather, and undeniably a little freckled, had the look of force rather than beauty. It was not upon a pattern and failed at important points; but it was in no danger of confusion with other faces of equally simple and rugged cast. His grey blue eyes, derived from his father, had the quiet look of power: they fronted her squarely when he caught her look, in an amused and kindly twinkle. Less gentle things looked out of their depths unaggressively. With his wide, full forehead, the large mould of his face, the sensitive

nostrils and firm under-jaw, he had the look, Dorothy thought
to herself, of a man who can do and make do.

She reflected that he seemed, much less than Jasper, to
have himself on his conscience.   One could hardly use his
long stride to whom it had ever occurred to wonder how he
might look in walking ; and he would certainly have made
sure, after their fight with the storm, of his hair and the
sailor knot straying out of sight under the collar of his
flannel shirt, if he had felt the responsibility about his appearance which she remembered in the Mr. Deed she had
known.   The gods playing at bowls would be a sight valued
out of proportion to the consideration in which the game is
held, and Dorothy found a peculiar entertainment for her
thoughts in the spectacle of all this lustiness and vigour
spreading a table cloth with her.

She smiled when the idea occurred to her, and as they
failed for the third time to lay the cloth true between them,
she caught the ragged thing out of his hands, with a righteous
hesitation about her enjoyment, and began asking him questions about Jasper, as she went on to lay the cloth and set
the table herself. Philip answered mechanically. The thought
that this sweet girl had once been Jasper's affianced wife
became more tormenting, more shameful, as he perceived
her charm.   He caught himself staring almost rudely at her
in the frequent pauses of their talk—abandoning himself to
speculation about the affair.   How could she ever have
cared for him ?   He had saved her life ; had she not just
said it ?   That would be a permanent fact for such a girl—
a reason for a life-long gratitude.   But besides : everybody
liked Jasper until they knew him very well.   Some of them
liked him afterward.   It was one of his talents—making
himself liked. She seemed still to like him herself; all that
she said implied it.   Was it a lover's quarrel that had parted
them, perhaps ?   Did she still love him ?   He smiled to

himself at his concern. All human contingencies were absurdly remote. He knew very well that they might never leave the cave alive.

They hung shawls and some tattered blankets, found in the bunks, at the crevices and angles of the rocks, for her, when they were seated at last around the flat bulk of rock which she had divined to have served as the miners' table; and they spent themselves in entreaty of her to discover or invent another draught which they might shield her from, until Philip suddenly bethought him of the horses, which they had been obliged to abandon at the cave mouth. In the mortal exhaustion which had overcome them all when they found shelter, they had known nothing better to do for them. It occurred to Philip that perhaps they could be got into the cave.

They thought it a joke when he proposed it. But when they saw him serious, Cutter and Messiter volunteered to venture out with him; and, after what seemed a long time, they returned covered with snow, having found all but one of the ponies, and got them into the outer cave. Their whinnies came to them from there piteously; and Dorothy was for trying if they would eat jerked beef or dried peaches. She went out with Philip when their little picnic meal was done, and brushed the snow from their flanks with a clothes-brush she produced from the bag that was strapped on the saddle of her own pony.

"What would be the horse for coffee?" she asked; and at Philip's, "Water, I'm afraid," she drew a sigh. "And we have n't any more than what we found in that little cup of a spring. You see, Mr. Deed, we must get away from here as soon as we can for the horses' sake, if not for our own. I'm afraid they would n't care for the week I was proposing, even if we should. Poor fellows!" she murmured, as they set up their long-drawn moan again.

They all rose when she returned to the inner cavern, and made a soft seat for her with blankets on the flat rock next the fire. Dick Messiter and Cutter were clearing away the traces of the meal they had just eaten on it. They took turns in fanning from her face the smoke which would sometimes be driven back down the chimney into her face, by the wind still whirling at its worst, without; and they piled the wood lavishly on the fire for her comfort, until, with a practical instinct, she went over to the corner in which the wood was, and pronounced against the reckless use of their scanty store.

When she was seated again on the daïs of rock, which raised her a little above her court (who, ready to do her bidding, sat or lay about her, coiled into such ease as they could manage on the rocky floor), she looked a smallish sort of monarch; and, humouring their attribution of despotic power to her, she queened it with a gentle gaiety among them, issuing her commands in the royal plural, and admonishing our good Earl of Deed, and our right worthy servant, Sir Lenox Cutter, with benignant severity. When Dick was beckoned imperiously to her side, he knelt in humbleness, and, with a tap of her riding crop on his shoulders, she said, with an air she knew, "Sir, I dub thee Knight," and cried, "Rise, Sir Knight Dick!"

Her unconsciousness of Messiter's devotion was a pretty thing to see. Her unconsciousness, as I have said, was one of her charms: it was pleasant to observe her modest diffi_ dence of all that touched the thought of self-valuation, and to perceive the impossibility of her ever coming to feel the world's thought of her. But it was especially nice to see how she would not know the love that followed all her motions with pursuing eyes; and yet how she could give herself so unthinkingly to him in every word.

Philip, because he would occasionally catch the familiar

glances that often passed between them, judged them lovers, with a man's haste. But a more instructed eye would perhaps have seen how the divine unconstraint of her attitude towards him might very well be a secret pain to Messiter ; for sometimes a light would come into his eyes by which one might almost guess how he might be hating her for liking him so well.

CHAPTER V

MARGARET had not seen Deed since the morning he had flung himself from the house. She knew nothing of him save what she had lately learned : that he had been called to Leadville the same afternoon to argue a case, and that he had gone. The information of the town regarding the sudden abandonment of the wedding was equally scanty.

All that day, until far into the afternoon, Margaret sat waiting his return with patient certainty in Beatrice's little parlour. Tears were easy while he was in trouble ; but she could not weep for herself. She sat watching the long stretch of road leading from the house down past the church in which the wedding was set to take place at half past four. A desolate, hunted look crept gradually into her stony gaze, as the cuckoo-clock in the hall told off the half-hours, and he did not come. She rose quickly, biting her lip to repress the tears that began to flow readily enough, as Beatrice came in at four o'clock. Beatrice's face trembled with her own emotion ; her eyes were wet and red, as if she had been crying ever since Margaret had last seen her, when she had looked in, at the slamming of the door behind Deed, to ask what had happened. Margaret caught Beatrice's caressing arm away.

"Let me go," she said hoarsely. "You can't help me," she added in a hard, uneven tone. "No one can help me !" She choked back a sob. "Oh, can't you see

that——" A surge of heart-sickness rose in her throat.
She turned from Beatrice's pitying face, and ran up the stair.

There were very few wedding garments to put away; but
one may drop as many or as scalding tears as one could
wish on a quite small spray of orange blossoms.

It all seemed so strange, so impossible, so trivially outside
reason and experience. The orange rind on which one slips
and breaks a limb, the elevator that happened to be here and
not there, the train that was on the other track—how motive-
less, how needless, what a littleness of fortuity! She could
not explain how it had happened. It was like a great grief
which simply comes upon one; which befalls without our
agency. She had spoken—had lied to him, if anyone liked
the word better—in the irresistible utterance of a feeling
stronger than herself. That he should do what he proposed
was unthinkable, intolerable : she could not let him blight
his life like that. For good or ill she had to speak; and
now, though the event itself was much the most anguishing
thing she had known, the only part of it she would have
done otherwise, if it had been to do again, would have been
to avoid the lie, somehow.

She would not allow Beatrice to blame him when she let
her into her bed-chamber next morning. The shock had
affected her physically, and she had yielded to Beatrice's
earlier insistence from outside the door at half-past seven
and remained in bed. It might have been possible to listen
to accusations of him, if her own heart had gone out yearn-
ingly to him in forgiveness. But she was frightened by the
hardness against him which she felt to be growing in her.
Something almost like rancour began to prosper side by side
with her love : it seemed to have warrant in the tenderness
which no event could really diminish—perhaps it grew out
of it. .

If he would, no one could venture to say what the

desecration of a woman's inmost life must be through the intimacies, the familiarities, the endearments of a betrothal which comes to naught. The exchanged amenities, so infinitely right and sweet because marriage follows, become each a separate indignity and horror when it does not. To Margaret, who took all matters over-seriously, whose training had erected barriers against these things, each of which had been broken down with a pleasant pain of its own; who cherished, who almost loved her reserves, there was a new and subtler misery behind every pain which could have tormented other women in like trouble. To cast a glance, the most doubtful and fleeting, back upon this one romance of a life curiously lacking, hitherto, in all emollient experience of this sort, tore her with nameless pains. She felt as if she should like never to see a man again.

She had given up all thought of his return the day before, she fancied. But when Beatrice entered with the morning mail she stretched forth her hand with the impulsive certainty that there must be a letter from him. She perceived when Beatrice reluctantly shook her head, that she had secretly believed that he must still come back. It was because the thing was still too incredible. Did men, then, belong to a different race? Was there one loyalty for them, and another for women? Was there another tenderness, another forbearance, another love? She had never had a brother: Deed was the only man she had ever imagined qualities for; she did not know about men—were they like this? Could it be that they knew how to justify such things to themselves—that there might be cruelties indigenous to the conscience of men, which women must not blame because men could not know them to be such? Perhaps to know all the wrong there may be in a wrong, one must have the gift to guess all the poignancy of its consequences; and she saw that no man could really understand her humiliation.

It was the lot of a woman to be chosen, distinguished, called apart,—made to believe that for one man she was different from all the rest : it was only the extremity of that distinction that could measure the shame of the credulity cast back in the face, the innocent faith become a thing to bite the lip and flush with pain at thought of. She did not lessen her own offence. Coming hard upon Jasper's perfidy she saw how it must have maddened him. She loved him, and, imagining his suffering, pitied him from her heart. But all her smarting pride, the selfhood wounded to death, cried out against the cruelty of this desertion on their wedding-day. Cowering under the indignity which seemed to have stripped her of self-respect, she could not be sure of the validity of any judgment of the miserable woman she had become. His act had beaten her down. She was sickly, unsure of herself, of life, of what she must think. But she knew the dumb resentment that grew slowly in her for the helpless bitterness against him that it was. She loved him. She supposed that she must always love him. But the injuriousness of the thing he had done stifled in these first hours every gentle thought. When the memory of it was hottest in her she would set her teeth in still wrath.

There was another thing. It would seem as if the most straightforward of women must have, somewhere in their depths, a kind of sense for indirection, which they can never quite forgive men for not understanding in them. Margaret had wished him to believe her : she felt that his whole future and hers had hung upon his crediting her lie. But this was, unexplainably, a very different thing from liking it in him that he should have believed her. Deed had not closed the door behind him before she had said to herself indignantly that he should have known her better.

There were moments when it all seemed different,—when she compassionated his situation, condemned herself as the

cause of it, and accused herself passionately for accusing
him. He would be suffering as well—not in her way at all,
but worse, perhaps, because it was impossible to know how
bad suffering might be which was outside one's comprehension. He must be thinking what she had said the final
faithlessness. At these times she would say to herself that
she could not wish him to think it less. If it had been
what it seemed it was as bad as possible, and she would
have liked to have him hate her.

But when echoes of the scandal stirred up in the town by
his abandonment of her began to come to her ears, the springs
of tenderness dried in her. The two daily papers published
at Maverick—having the fear of Deed before them—had
reported the barren facts with what they meant for a picturesque reserve, and speculated about the affair with what
seemed to them a self-denying decency. Beatrice kept the
papers from Margaret of course; but her boy turned innocent busybody and brought a copy of one of them to her
in furtherance of an enterprise of make-believe which Margaret had joined him in. Her eye caught the audacious
headline ; and before she knew it she had read a dozen lines.

She buried her face in her hands in shame : alone with
the child she blushed as hotly as if all the world looked
on. In fact it did see her : that was her feeling.

She shed no tears then ; but when Beatrice came in at
twilight to light the lamp, she saw that she had been crying.
It was not precisely for the comments of the newspaper.
She had been thinking of the lines of a poem :

"Be good to me ! Though all the world united
Should bend its powers to gird my youth with pain,
Still might I fly to thee—Dear !—and be righted—
But if thou wrongst me, where shall I complain ?

"I am the dove a random shot surprises,
That from her flight she droppeth quivering,
And, in the deadly arrow recognizes
A blood-wet feather—once in her own wing."

After Beatrice, Margaret found it easiest in these first days to see Dr. Ernfield, whom Mrs. Vertner had called in immediately. Margaret had liked Dr. Ernfield long before; and she liked him still better in observing gratefully the devices of kindness by which he referred her prostration solely to physical causes, and the delicacy with which he implied that she had had no history previous to the moment of any of his calls. They had been on almost intimate terms before her wedding day; and she was grateful for his attitude in proportion as she perceived the difficulty to which he must be put to maintain it.

He had been interesting to her, during the month she had passed in Maverick before her wedding day, not merely as a man—though he was an unusually interesting man—but because of his situation. He had left a prosperous practice in Boston to come West in search of health. He was still under thirty, and had won his success very young by mak-ing a speciality of diseases of the nervous system; but he had paid for it, so to say, with himself; and he was in consumption. Beatrice, who had known him in Boston, was very fond of him, and in the first month of Margaret's stay he had been often at the house. It was the only house where he felt at home; he was practising his profession in Maverick to avoid the stagnation of idleness, but he really knew no other family, and he had found that to have known people even slightly in the East is a tie when one comes to meet them unexpectedly under the shadow of the Continen-tal Divide. Beatrice, on her part, was accustomed to say that he was very nice. She perhaps meant by this that he had the gift of helpfulness, of sympathy, which, perhaps, is not especi-ally common among men. Margaret had thought she saw how this faculty, comfortable as it may be to a physician's patients —not to go into the question of his friends—might be ruinous to a sensitively made physician; she had perceived that the excess of his sympathy with the work he had done before he came to Maverick had been merely by way of devouring him.

It was pitiful to remark how his disease had him in its clutch. The sinewy lines of his big body, designed plainly for the use of a strong man, had begun to waste before the attacks of his malady. It was observable, however, that he was still strong of limb ; and the look of his face—kept alive by his ardent and commanding glance, and hidden, for the most part, by a thick brown beard—was scarcely the look of a sick man.

It had been a pleasure to Margaret to see this sturdy fellow —who had the effect, in spite of his weakness, of confident strength—ramp up and down Beatrice's little parlour, with his hands in his pockets, expounding his theories of health and disease—theories which fascinated Margaret by sinking instinctively for the moral spring underlying all large theories of health ; or anathematizing the whole system of living which gives us the damsel known to discussion as the " American Girl "—a creature whose tenseness might not be half bad, Ernfield owned, for the spectator, but was death to the girl. And then it had been still pleasanter to hear him counter this with the story of nervously wrecked young lives, which Margaret saw, around the corners of his modesty, he had won back to the normal way of life. He never spoke of having cured anybody. He would sometimes own that he had taught a person here and there how to live. It had seemed to Margaret that he had accomplished this by transfusing a portion of his own life into each of these persons : for it was obvious that such patients as these must always have drawn their new life, in great degree, from his life : that—a cure being in such cases so much an affair of sympathetic understanding, of a brisk, urgent, imperious individuality—they had lived at his expense.

The thought of this strong, fine fellow, who had given

his young manhood to the business of reinstating others in life, doomed to a death against the halting wretchedness of which no hindrance could be opposed, unless it existed in the air of Lone Creek County, had been too painful to Margaret for endurance.

Margaret's frank liking for him and the gentleness of her manner toward him, springing from the compassion for his situation to which she could not give other expression, were perhaps part of her charm for him ; but that which had really drawn him to her was the constant charm residing in her sincerity, her simplicity and directness ; in her goodness ; in the irresistible need in her to front all questions in their highest phase—above all in her gentle womanliness. In the three weeks that had passed after her arrival, before Deed and she were ready to lay themselves open to the town's comment, by announcing their approaching wedding, Ernfield had had time—in ignorance of her betrothal, and wholly without Margaret's suspicion of what was happening—to fall deeply, miserably in love with her.

It was not precisely his fault ; but his position, when he ascertained it, gave him the sense of moral turpitude he would have experienced if he had allowed himself to become enamoured of a married woman.

It was just as well, he said to himself : he had deserved it. A man who, in his condition, indulged the thought of connecting his future with another's for longer than one of those radiant moments of monstrous and baseless hope that must visit even the hopeless, was properly condemned to such an awakening. This reflection should have made it easy to think of Margaret's wedding with equanimity ; and certainly should have silenced the thrill with which he heard of Deed's desertion of her on their wedding day. Its effect, however, was to fill him, before the day, with a gloomy reluctance in her presence and a fear of meeting her honest eyes ; and after it to shame and daunt him with a clear vision of the meanness of the hope that began to live tremblingly in him.

He writhed under her approval of what he saw she took for his tact and delicacy, when he was forced, after the event, to visit her in his professional capacity. He felt like a scoundrel when he heard from Beatrice that she could bring herself to see no one but him and her, for the present : that she could not bear that any eyes less friendly and familiar should look upon her grief in these first days. Her trust humiliated and abased him. He wanted to tell her what a scamp he was. He could have blushed at sight of the humble light of thankfulness she turned on him from her weary eyes, as he constructed a theory about her indisposition which referred it to purely physical causes. To see how her pride smarted under this blow in every fibre ; to see how she was ashamed of being ashamed, and yet not abashed to let him perceive it, became intolerable. On the second day, in the mere necessity of putting an end to it, he ordered fresh air for her : he told her that she must go about.

Beatrice went over the house on her daily duties, with a grieving face. Margaret's position pained her to the heart. She could understand how she might have partly brought it on herself, with the noblest motives ; but nothing could even shadowily justify what Deed had done. She called his act by the hardest names to herself, when Margaret would not hear her denunciations. It was small comfort to talk to her husband.

" What are you worrying about ? " he would say. " You ought to be throwing up your cap on any reasonable theory of friendship. It's an escape for both of them. You don't think they would have been happy, do you ? "

"I don't know," returned his wife frankly. " Don't you ? "

" I think," said Vertner ambiguously, " if they had not been—especially Deed—it would not have been for lack of hard trying—especially Miss Derwenter's."

"You think she might have tried too hard," suggested Beatrice quickly. "Yes," she owned, after a moment's meditation ; " Margaret has that way. Perhaps she rather—insists."

"She *does n't* know quite when to let up," said Vertner in the tone of admission. His wife had to smile. " It's a virtue—knowing when to spare."

"And you think Margaret has n't it ?" asked Beatrice, as anxiously as if she did not feel that she entirely understood Margaret's sweetly-intentioned severity, and as if she had not reasoned with herself, and with Margaret about it.

"Well," owned Vertner, "I think she might consider it not quite moral."

"No," said Beatrice vaguely, as she helped him on with his coat. She had followed him out into the hallway to see him off for the day. "Perhaps not."

" And Deed would n't really enjoy that after a bit," said Vertner as he adjusted the fur collar of his coat. "He can take things hard himself, and he does, but not in her way, and he does n't take *everything* hard. There's a sort of sense of perspective about Deed : that's his humour. He has his varioloid moments."

" Yes," rejoined Beatrice in sad musing, "and Margaret has n't. I know that. All her moments are acute. She goes conscientiously through the whole disease, whether it's a question of a pin or an elephant."

" Well, perhaps you can see then, if you've got to that point, how Miss Derwenter would be the very best wife in the world for a man who takes things in bulk—in Deed's whole-souled, passionate, hearty way. There's nothing equal to a gingerly, conscious, penny-wise way of looking at things for a wife for such a man."

" Ned, you sha'n't say such things of Margaret ! "

" Oh, Margaret's all right," said Vertner in a tone of con-viction as he put his hand on the knob. He really liked her when she would let him. " It is n't her fault that Deed is n't built to appreciate her. She could make plenty of men ecstatically happy."

" What kind of men ? "

" Well, my kind," returned her husband, audaciously. " I should always be ecstatically happy anyway, you know ; and all that she could do for me would be so much clear gain."

After these talks with her husband nothing but a long conversation with Margaret could put Beatrice right again. She enjoyed the play of her husband's mind of course, but there were occasions for seriousness, and this was one of them. She found Margaret serious enough, yet even she would smile dismally sometimes at the thought of certain contrasts. The concern which she had given herself during the month preceding her wedding-day (the month in which she had made acquaintance with Maverick) as to whether she should be able to like the West struck her, for example, in her present forlorn case as food for a sad amusement. She had not been afraid she should not get along, as the phrase is : she was accustomed to managing so much as that for herself in all sorts of queer places. But it had occurred to her that, even with Deed, the West, as a permanent place of residence, would leave a great many needs in her unsatisfied. She had not dared use adjectives about Maverick ; she might have to live in it, and she had the forethought to avoid attaching labels to the place by which even her own thought of it might finally discover itself to be bound. But it was at least undeniable that Maverick lacked a Public Library. She had thought she should induce Deed to return to the East when he had won back the fortune he had, lost the year before he had offered himself to her. Her ideal was a suburb just out of Boston.

Nothing had taught her so incontrovertibly the force of her love for him as the willingness she had found in herself to face for him the contrary prospect: for her heart had sometimes sunk grievously during her first fortnight at Maverick; and once, when she thought she perceived from something he said that he was really fond of the West, that it suited something in him—his sense of humour, perhaps; she did not know—her heart had gone coweringly down into her boots. It was at the thought of this terror that she now indulged a smile. One troubled one's self about such things when one was happy: it had become pitifully indifferent to her whether Deed lived in Colorado or Patagonia.

One of the pangs which reached Margaret from the outside during the first days of her misery was that which she felt when she learned that Philip was at last arrived in Maverick. She had heard, in a kind of dream, that there were fears for his safety; and, finally, that he was given up for lost; and it had seemed at the time only one of the thousand sides there appear to be to even physical pains. Now that she had come out of the stupor of suffering which had followed Deed's going, and began to be sensible to exterior measures of her trouble, she was surprised to find a fleeting wretchedness in the knowledge that Philip lived, and that his father, who must have been down into the bitterest depths of grief for his imagined loss, rejoiced without her. For a moment she thought of Deed with untroubled tenderness. The other feeling followed, but the loving impulse taught her freshly the unbearable reach of her loss. It went too far. It cut too deep.

Vertner met the snow-bound party at the station. He usually went to the trains when he was in town. Men he knew were often passing through on their way to Denver or

to the mountain towns. They gave him the last word about
the outlook at the newest mining camp ; they kept him wise
about the ups and downs of older places. When they would
stay over night at Maverick he would often spend the evening
at the hotel losing a little to them at poker, and getting
on the inside as he said, of good things in mines and real
estate. He brought Margaret word of the arrival of Philip.

"Mighty close shave those fellows had!" he said. "It
could n't be done once in a dozen times. I would n't back
Charlie Cozzens to do it, and he knows every foot of the
Pass as if it were his Addition." The retired stage-driver's
investment in Maverick real estate was known as "Cozzens's
Addition." "But they are badly done up after it. The
young lady went to bed."

"Young lady ! Ned !" exclaimed Beatrice.

"Certainly ! Young lady. Young lady and father, in
fact. Maiden slender, fair, good-looking—very. Father a
clergyman ; large, clever, manners until you can't rest : not
here purely as a sanitary measure. The young lady really
bore it pretty well. You can see that she was prettier three
days ago, but she will pick up her prettiness again at the
Centropolis House."

"A clergyman, Ned ! "

" Well, not too much of a clergyman—not the kind that
would worry the clerical Inspector of Weights and Measures with overweight. A good, practical, every-day, earthly
Christian, with a soul away above the unrighteous nickel,
—shaped to nobler ends, like thousand dollar bills : could
make arrangements with soul to overlook some things.
Good fellow ! I took a kind of shine to him."

It was one of Ned Vertner's own sayings that he
was a composite. He would not have been anything but
the "rustler" he was,—dependent on the friendliness of
fortune to this month's scheme for his next month's house

rent—on any account; but he liked to remember how easily and naturally he might once have been the conventional gentleman whom he hated.

The Vertners had memories of the revolutionary hero with an honest grandfather, and the three succeeding generations of Unitarian ministers which makes a good family in Berkshire. There were no better than they in their village; and though Ned Vertner, before he was sixteen, disliked the people his family knew in Boston, as he disliked the propriety of the white picket fence in front of their white frame house with green blinds, it was a gratification to him at times to recall that the good social form of his family had existed for him to refuse. He went to Chili instead of to Harvard at seventeen, and remained there three years, helping a little to build the railway which his party went out to build; and learning to live hard, to drink hard, and to gamble more than he could afford.

It was in his third year—when he was coming down with a fever which went near to finishing him—that Philip Deed joined the party. Philip would have said to anyone who had challenged his liking for Ned Vertner, that he liked him because he had contributed what effect there might be in three months' nursing to saving his life. At all events when Vertner was well enough to sail for home they parted in the relation of good comradeship often existing in new countries between men who are of no spiritual kindred.

It was Deed who, at Philip's suggestion, put Vertner in the way of coming West when he had found Berkshire more impossible than he had left it; and it was Deed whose professional relations to various adventurous enterprises opened the way to Vertner's first "scheme," and showed him his natural calling.

The impartial spectator would scarcely have supposed it a calling justifying marriage; but in Colorado rustling has the recognition of one of the liberal professions, and when Vertner had been engaged in it a year he worked a pass as far as Chicago through a friend, and returned from Boston, ten days later, married. It was an incredible marriage; it was the one thing, Philip told him, when he met Beatrice, that he should never forgive him for. Vertner admitted that he was ashamed of himself; no one was more conscious than he that he was an undeservedly lucky dog.

"But what could I do?" he would say. "I told her it was a shame and a fraud; I gave her a full *résumé* of my worthlessness; I told her that if I had ever been good for anything I'd got over it; I told her that my doings out here would turn a Public Gardens swan red with pure shock, and would keep her conscience working on horse-car drivers' hours every day. She said she liked it. Then I went for the country, and gave this section down the banks. I told her that she would have to breakfast on climate and dine on scenery; that in this altitude it takes ten minutes to boil an egg soft, and that they put on beets the day before; that chickens can't live, and cow's milk is twelve cents a quart; that pneumonia rides around on a mowing machine; that she would n't find a library in Maverick, that the church was closed and the lecture bureau in the dry dock, and that you could take up all the civilization in the place on a fork. She said that none of these things mattered, and that something else did. I gave her up."

"Hush, Ned!" she was saying now, in response to his profession of liking for Maurice. "Perhaps we can get him to stay with us here for next Sunday. It is months since we had a service. An Episcopal clergyman did you say?"

Vertner nodded, as he cut a little more steak for himself (they were at their one o'clock dinner). "I did n't say; but that's his rating. Don't count me in, though, Trix, on any scheme for supplying the pulpit of St. John's in the Wilderness. You remember I took a hand in the last Gospel boom in Maverick. Invite him here, if you like, and get him to preach for you next Sunday. I've no objection, and he won't kick if you make it worth his while. But leave me out. I would n't undertake the contract of furnishing a clergyman to that congregation again for a commission of fifty per cent. on his salary. If I knew a recipe for a durable angel-wash it would be a different thing : I should know where to look for a market, though the angel-market rules rather low in Maverick. At $700 a year it might n't be worth my while to put on more than one coat."

"Shame, Ned ! Stop it ! "

Vertner laughed with enjoyment. Margaret, who had found no way of taking Vertner in the month she had spent in the house with him, was silent. She was thinking of Philip, and wondering how to frame a question which should inform her about him without seeming to seek the information.

Beatrice saved her the need. " We might go and call on Miss Maurice at the hotel," she said, doubtfully, looking toward Margaret. " That would commit us to nothing. We could see Mr. Maurice and judge for ourselves. Do you think she would see us, Ned ? "

" Why she was going to bed, when I saw her, to stay until she was rested. But she would see St. John's in the Wilderness on her father's account, I should think, if you made it plain who you were. Write under your name on your card : ' Mrs. Vertner—representing St. John's in the Wilderness.' You'll get the consideration of a commercial man travelling for a big house."

Beatrice did not smile, but looked at Margaret questioningly. " I think she might be willing to see us," Margaret answered to Beatrice's enquiring look. " After such an experience she might be glad of the sight of friendly faces, even if they were strange."

They found this to be true when they went next day. They both made friends at once with Dorothy, who was sitting up, and who told the story of what had befallen them in the mountains, gaining for the first time, in seeing its effect upon her hearers, a sense of the danger through which she had passed. She did not need a reminder to make her shudder at the journey through the storm; but the time in the cave had not seemed unhappy. She had not felt that they were in danger—perhaps she had not been allowed to feel it. It occurred to her now to wonder what might have happened if the storm had not ceased the morning after they had taken refuge there; if the wind had not fallen, the snow had not begun to melt; and a party of miners, on their way from Bayles' Park, had not found them on the second day, weak and exhausted of course, but able to ride to Bayles' Park where they took the train.

It was the hope of seeing Philip that had helped Margaret to come out for the first time since the day that was to have been her wedding day. The event had left her spiritually sore : she could not bear to see anyone, much less listen to the questions which must be asked if she went out. Yet there was nothing she liked so little as what she called, in her plain speech, "dodging": it seemed cowardly not to take the world as it came; and she was glad of a strong reason for going out. She wanted to see Philip, whom she did not know: it would be the next thing to seeing his father. But it seemed that Philip had left Maverick within a few hours of his arrival. Philip, in fact, had taken the evening train the night before for Leadville, leaving Cutter to go on to Denver, where he had friends who might find something for him to do in connection with the smelting works there. Margaret knew that he must have gone to see his father at Leadville, and she flushed as she thought of one of the probable subjects of conversation between them.

CHAPTER VI.

As Philip asked for his father at the hotel which Deed was accustomed to make his home during his frequent visits to Leadville, it was in his heart to wish that he had not always been the unsatisfactory son. The day before he might have wished it in a spasm of contrition for the necessity of asking his father for more money; but he was wishing it now because the things they were saying about Deed at Maverick pained and angered him; he was sure his father was in trouble, and he had come up to Leadville with an impulsive desire to help him if he might. He had telegraphed him from Bayles' Park of their safety, and from Maverick, as soon as the rumours reached him, that he was coming up to Leadville.

He wanted to help his father in the trouble he merely guessed—he had not stayed to hear the story—; but to speak to him as he would like to speak, their relation should be more equal: it ought to depend less for its harmony on his father's forbearance. He wished heartily that he had never done anything in particular; or, lacking that, that his failures had cost his father less. In these moods he always denounced his failures to himself as the result of crude and silly experiments which he should have known enough to avoid; but when he was so sensible as this he was usually a little more sensible, and perceived that the whole fruitless drama of his life, thus far, was inevitable—a fellow like him, he supposed, had to make an appointed degree of fool of himself.

In this light the restless longing of his boyhood to possess himself, to lay hands on the charter of his life on his own account ; his refusal to please his father by going to Columbia; the unquiet wish for a different, a freer life, another set of conditions—say a man's— ; his aimless and resultless year in Chili as a civil engineer, his six months of orange-growing in Florida, his other six months, in which he saw a fortune in evaporating peaches in the Southern States—it was the fortune which had evaporated—and this last empty-headed folly at Piñon seemed foolish, indeed, but necessary, like the stages of a disease. He always said to himself in these contemptuous reflections on his doings that he knew better now ; had learned a lesson. And this was in so far true that he seldom made the same kind of fool of himself twice.

He was thinking how glad he should be to see his father again, as he followed the bell boy out of the crowded hotel office along the creaking hallways, and up the swaying stairs (the hotel had been built of unseasoned timber, when saw-mills were fifty miles away, and money was worth four per cent. a month, and the structure began to fall apart) ; and was adding to himself that since it was in his blood to do undesirable things, it was trebly undesirable that they should be destined to be the disappointment and trouble of so good a fellow as his father. He treated him so hand-somely, always, that his disappointment was seldom in evidence ; but Philip knew that it existed, and knew—he recalled the fact now with a bitter smile—that it had been left for Jasper to realize his father's ideals.

Jasper had been a cautious and conservative investor at ten ; a patient, thorough-going man of business at seventeen. He sold foreign stamps at school while he was in the First Reader, and drove hard bargains in decalcomanie and marbles before he knew his Latin paradigms. He was eight when it occurred to him that he might as well turn a penny by serving the morning paper to his father, and the gentlemen whom he knew on the block (it was in New York), as to let the regular carrier earn it. He rose at five o'clock in the morning to look after his papers, and he had been getting up early ever since.

Philip never got up early unless to go hunting, or birds' nesting, or fishing, or to catch the train at the end of the term when he came home from boarding school. He was glad to be going home then, and did n't mind : it was always a happiness to see his father again. He was not merely his father, but a kind of a hero to him. Jasper often got home rather later; there were trades to be settled with the boys at school. As the elder brother (he used his advantage of a year for all it was worth) he was properly reserved in his feeling about the home-coming. And when the time came Jasper went into business, liked it, stuck to it, succeeded in it; and then took charge of the ranch and made a success of that.

Jasper had known what he wanted to do from the beginning; and was entirely capable of doing it. Philip had known clearly only what he did not want to do; and thus far he had not done much. It was this that made him hesitate as he came to the door of his father's room. He wished again that he could feel that he stood near his father; that the invariable kindness which he remembered in him from boyhood had nothing to forgive in him; that he had not disappointed him.

But he turned the knob and went in. His father was sitting under the ineffective light of a huge bronze chandelier, wound about with a brambly wreath of gilt, absorbed in work upon a heap of legal documents scattered over the table, and did not hear Philip's entrance.

When his son touched him on the shoulder, he turned hastily, and for a moment did not perceive who it was. When he saw he rose hastily, stretching both hands out to him. "Why, Phil! Phil!" he cried, and stopped, choking and not knowing how to go on. "I—the fact is—I thought we should n't be seeing you—should n't—. Oh, Phil," he broke off, dashing his hands to his eyes, "what luck—what blessed luck! I had given you up. I—find a seat, will you?"

Deed sat down hastily and buried himself in his papers. His lip shook.

Philip found a seat on the bed. He was himself much agitated. He had not counted on this at all. He had allowed for his father's anxiety; and had telegraphed him as soon as they reached Bayles' Park; but that he would think him lost in the storm was outside all his thoughts. Yet no one knew better how near they had all actually been to death in the snow. "Dear father!" he said to himself, as he watched him making his poor feint of going on with his work. "It's awfully good of him to care!"

Deed glanced up at him once, venturing a smile; and looked down again forthwith. When he was done with the last practicable pretence, he folded his papers slowly. Philip had never seen him so careful about adjusting them.

He rose at last, clapping the bundled documents on the table briskly, and came over to where Philip was sitting on the bed. Deed dropped down beside him, laying his arm lightly about his shoulders.

"Well, boy, how goes it?"

Philip dropped his eyes. "Why, that was what I came up to ask you, father. How does it go?"

A spark lighted in Deed's eye. He drew in his breath sharply. He came back and stood before Philip after a nervous turn across the floor.

" Phil ! "

" Father ! "

" You got my wire at Laughing Valley ? "

Philip nodded. His father regarded him for a moment in pained question of his face. He thought he read his condemnation in it.

"Say it, Phil ! Say it ! " he cried hoarsely. " Don't sit there dumb ! I know what you think. You're right. I sold you out. I signed away your rights. I did you out of your future with a foolish, amiable stroke of the pen. I trusted a scoundrel, and you've to pay for it. I wanted to do the handsome thing by Jasper, and I did it—at your expense. It's been your treat, all along, Phil," he said, with a miserable smile, " though you did n't know it."

Philip leaped up. " Great heaven, father, you have n't been thinking that I was shouting around about my miserable little share in that business. Surely you don't think that I could name it beside your trouble, much less be fooling with the poor question of blame. I should think Jasper was enough to blame for half-a-dozen."

His father smiled sadly. " What Jasper has done can't excuse me. He could n't have done it if I had n't thrown the way open to him. If I had n't trusted him—"

"And you expect me to accuse you of having trusted him? Would n't a father trust his own son, I should like to know? Is it a thing he must answer for ? "

" My God, Phil, has n't he answered for it, is n't he answering for it, will he ever get to the end of answering for it ? " He covered his eyes.

"I know, father," said Philip, taking a turn across the room. " Ingratitude is like that. It hurts—it keeps on hurting."

" Yes," owned Deed grimly ; " it hurts."

" Surely it's enough then. Pray don't bother about me.

You would have done it for me in the same situation. Do you think I don't know that, or that I don't know that I never gave you the chance? I 've not been doing the approved thing. I never have. When I do it will be time enough for me to trot out a grievance."

"Oh, Phil, I 've not been fair to you." It was the expression of his sense of his whole course toward him from boyhood; but Philip took it to refer to the contract.

"Pshaw, father, I shall rub along for the few years left of the partnership. What difference can it make? I shall be all the better for having to make my own way for a while."

"Few years?" exclaimed his father.

"The partnership—it's five years, is n't it?" said Philip, dropping on the bed again, and curling his legs up comfortably. "You won't mind my smoking?" he asked, producing a cigarette.

His father did not speak, as he drew a match across his boot. "You have n't given Jasper anything. I could understand your feeling that unfair. He has nothing permanently that is mine. At worst you've lost me nothing, father—merely postponed it. It's only five years, and if it were ten or fifteen, it's not your act. It's Jasper's. Don't talk of my loss. There is none. And if there were, what would it be to yours? I could only lose money by him. I'm—well, I'm not his father. I have n't protected him, and worked for him, and kept him from every sort of harm, and done all I knew for him since he was a child. I never gave him a father's love and trust to wound me with!"

Deed groaned. "Oh, stop it, Phil! Stop it! You make it impossible to tell you." He rose and wandered about the room aimlessly, picking up the rose-flushed vases on the mantel and studying their red and gilt flowers, turning up the gas and leaving it hissing, detaching the loop that caught back the window curtain, and returning it to its bracket again. Philip watched him wonderingly. His cigarette went out.

"Oh, come father!" he said at last, smiling. "One would think you had been putting up some infernal job on me."

His father looked up, eyeing him haggardly. "You 've said it."

"Said what, father? I don't understand."

Deed paused with the poker in his hand to say over his shoulder, as he stooped to the fire, "They did n't tell you at Maverick, then?"

"I gathered you were in your trouble. I heard that your marriage was postponed. I thought you would rather tell me?"

"Oh, so I would! So I would!" exclaimed his father absently, as he turned from the fire. He looked remorsefully into the eyes that met his. "Why did n't somebody tell you!" he cried. Philip made a place for him by his side as he came meditatively toward him, with his head down. Deed guessed the grease spot on the carpet, clouding one of the fruit-bearing boys in their ovals, to be kerosene, as he paused a moment in study of it.

He had decided it was champagne, as he looked up and faced his son again.

His voice melted. "How the deuce am I going to tell you, Phil?"

"What's the use, father?"

"Oh, use!" exclaimed Deed impatiently. He tapped his foot above the curly head of one of the dove-coloured boys. "You've got to know. Pshaw! Why did n't some one tell you!" He strode away to the other corner of the room, snapping his fingers noiselessly.

"Tell me, father——" began Philip.

"You won't believe it! She did n't." He breathed a heavy sigh. "I suppose it is n't very credible," he said, staring into the air. "I don't understand it myself all the time."

"But———"

"It's infamous, I tell you. You don't want me to tell it. Better go hear it from the gossips, Phil. I supposed they knew about it by this time—I trusted to your having heard it from them. They will know what to think about it. I don't. I think it magnificently right one minute, and the other thing the next. It's cost me enough to be right: it's cost every. one else enough to be wrong."

"Tell me, father," insisted Philip, "what coil has Jasper got you into?"

"Ah, now you have it, Phil! That's something like! Stick to that! That's what I say to myself when I've accused my-self black and blue. I say it was Jasper. It *was* Jasper; and it was Adam, too, in the same way. Things have got to have a beginning. It would be a poor sin that had n't some sort of provocation to its back."

"You forget who you're talking to, father. You don't think you can make me believe you have done anything wrong."

"I don't know what I can make you believe. Suppose, Phil, you are fool enough to trust a man to wear a diamond. He is n't only wearing your diamond, you see, but your trust. One day he simplifies things by pocketing the stone. In a wrestle for it, you snatch it from him and throw it into the river. You are not strong enough to get it back for yourself and keep it: only just strong enough to keep it from him by losing it yourself. You see how you could n't let him have it, don't you, Phil?"

"Yes, I see," said Philip thoughtfully.

"It's not the stone, you know."

Philip stroked his moustache thoughtfully. "No, it is n't the stone."

"You could bear that. The other you can't. I've sold the range for $25,000," he said abruptly.

Philip started. "But it was worth $150,000."

"Yes," said his father, drily, "that's the point."

Philip stared at him. "And what does Jasper say?" he asked in a voice which he seemed to hear speaking in the tones of some one else from a distance.

His father glanced up at him doubtfully. He caught his hands behind his big head as he crossed his legs and threw himself back in the deep sleepy-hollow chair. "Jasper? Why, that's just the pity of it. We have n't heard what Jasper thinks. It's too bad, because that's where all the fun comes in—what he thinks. The fun has been rather slow so far in other quarters."

"Do you mean that you have ruined yourself to even things up with Jasper?" demanded his son, making no answer.

Deed glanced at his nails. "I should n't put it that way," he said huskily; "but that's what it comes to."

"And Miss Derwenter—Mrs. Deed, my mother who is to be!"

His father looked steadily into his eyes a moment "I meant to ruin her, too, but she objected."

"And that is what—— ?"

"What parted us. Yes," said his father.

Philip turned suddenly upon his heel and strode away to the window, brushing aside the lace curtains and vanishing within the embrasure. The street was alight with the night gaiety of Leadville. He bent an unseeing eye on the spectacle.

As his father gazed after him a look of desolation settled on his face. The lightness he had forced fell away from him and he fixed a glance upon the spot where his son had disappeared—bitter, doubting, wistful.

He saw suddenly how the self-accusations of his loneliness —the miserable loneliness which had overtaken him since he had broken with Margaret—had instinctively looked to Philip for contradiction all along: how he had relied on Philip's comprehension. At his lowest he had said to himself that Philip, cruelly injured as he was by his act, must see how he had come to do it—must recognize its inevitableness. Jasper had always had his admiration, his approval: Philip was right about that. But he had always understood Philip better. He was more like himself. And now he trusted him to understand him—to make allowances for a thing which he had known quite well, even in his passion, must need some allowance from anybody, and would never be understood at all by more than one or two. One of these he had supposed confidently would be Margaret. To repeat his disappointment in her with Philip would be merely killing: he could not bear it. Why, he began to ask himself, had he done this thing?

"Oh, come out of that, Philip!" he cried, at last, in an irresistible burst of impatience. "Come out, and say what you've got to say. I can stand it, I guess."

Philip obeyed slowly. He paused just outside the curtains, fastening his eyes on the floor.

"There's nothing to say, father. You've done it, have n't you?"

"Do you wish I had n't?" asked his father quickly.

"Why, it's hardly my part, is it father, to question what you do?"

"Pshaw!" exclaimed his father, contemptuously. "I'm not asking for criticism. I ask about your feelings. You know about them, I suppose. You understand, I dare say, how it feels to lose $50,000?"

Poor Deed! Why should the wrong which he was conscious of having done Philip and Margaret, make him hard toward both of them, where he most wished to be gentle?

Philip winced, but controlled himself to say, "What has my feeling to do with it, father? It's the thing itself that matters, is n't it?"

"You mean on high moral grounds?" asked Deed, the colour rising in his face threateningly. Philip knew the approaches of one of his father's bursts of passion too well to feel guiltless in provoking one of them, however remotely.

"Do you want me to say I like it, father? I don't. But would my liking better it? Surely you see, father, that the thing is wrong in itself."

"Oh, I don't know what I see," cried Deed, gnawing at his bristly moustache as he paced the floor. "I know it seemed the only right thing there was when I did it. I know I had to do it. That's my safest ground, perhaps I had to do it. Good God, Phil! you see that! You would n't have had me leave him with his plunder?" He sat down, and instantly leaped up again. Philip wandered restlessly about. "I have n't it, it's true; but he has n't. It's cost the whole subject of dispute to beat him; but I *have* beaten him. I have rounded on his devilish falsity. And I would do it again. Yes, rather than have to think that he had done such a thing and prospered in it, I would do it twice over. Why, Phil, I 've beaten him! Could I pay too much for that?"

Philip bit his lip. "Why, since you ask me, father, I'm bound to say that I think you could. I think you have. His being a blackguard does n't help it. It makes it worse."

Deed's face darkened. "You mean that *you* have paid too much. You mean that I let you in for enough in making you pay for my whim of pleasing Jasper without making you pay for my squaring of accounts with him?"

"No," said Philip, looking in his father's face, "I don't

1

mean that. They are my accounts, too. It's against me
that Jasper has done this as much as against you. Heaven
knows," he said, as his face darkened, and he doubled his
fist under his sleeve, " I'd be glad to square my account
with Jasper. If there is going to be a settlement I'm ready
to pay my share. But, father, there must n't be a squaring
of accounts on this basis. The thing's wrong, it's indefensible, it's impossible."

Deed drove his clenched hand into his open palm.
"Impossible? For whom? For you? For Margaret?" he
demanded. "Or perhaps you mean for Jasper?" he asked,
mockingly.

"I do mean for Jasper. It's a wrong to him."

"A wrong to Jasper!" cried Deed in scornful amusement,
kicking a chair out of his path as he walked back and forth.
"T—s—s—s!"

"See here, father, I've no love for Jasper. You must
know that. But I can't be part of a scheme for burking
him like this."

"Burking him?"

" Well, selling him out, wiping out his share while he's
away. You don't want me to help you do a wrong like
that to yourself, father?"

"Did I ask for your help?" inquired Deed, in a tone of
offence.

Philip flushed. "Why, I should have said that you had
used it."

" In wiping out *your* share?" said his father with threatening calmness. " Do you object to that?"

" I suppose I must say that I object to the purpose you
are wiping it out for. Why, father, you see it yourself. You 've
as much as owned it. The thing's not fair!"

Deed's mouth fell. He stared at him in an amazement
that gave way to a look of inexpressible grief, as he came

and stood before Philip and laid a doubting hand on his shoulder. " Phil ! *Phil !* " he cried, miserably interrogating the eyes which his son let fall. " *You're* not going back on me ? "

" Going back on you, father ? " Philip snatched the hand hanging by his side. " I'm trying to save you. You're letting yourself in for a life time of remorse. You'll kick yourself for this thing before you are a week older. Think, father ! Can you afford to do a wrong like this to Jasper ? "

His father gave an inarticulate grunt of contempt, and bit his lip as if he feared what he might be tempted to say. It had been in his mind to tell him that he had done his best to buy his word back about the range, in order to keep his word with Margaret, and that he had had his trouble for his pains. But he would not give him so much satisfaction, now. It had not been done for Jasper's sake, at all events, he said to himself scornfully.

" Drop it, Phil ! " he said suddenly, at last. " This isn't a safe subject between us. I know what I've done. I've never had a doubt—not one single moment's doubt, mind you—about this as far as Jasper is concerned. He's done me the cruellest wrong that a son can do a father. Do you think it's a time to be nice about what I do to him ? "

" Why, father, is n't it the time of times ? If he had never wronged you, one might afford a luxury like that. One can do it with best friends. But to do an indefensible thing —you own that, father : it *is* indefensible—and to choose Jasper for the object of it !—you see, yourself, it won't work. When you put him in the right by putting yourself in the wrong with him you' re simply taking a permanent lease of torment ! There's no end to the mess, this way ! Don't you see it ? Aggression of some sort becomes his right. It will be almost a virtue in him. Where will there ever be an end to it ? It will make you unhappy, father. That is what

I'm thinking of. And the unhappiest part of the whole business will be when you see that, after all, it *was n't* fair."

"Fair!" cried his father hoarsely. "Fair! Oh, the devil!" He sat down clenching his hands. The blood rose in his face.

" Did you wish to be unfair ? "

"Yes!" shouted Deed. "Yes! I wished to be all that you imply! I wished to be unfair to both of you!"

" Both of us!" exclaimed Philip, turning pale.

"Oh, I know what you think! I wished to be unfair to Jasper, and to do it I must be doubly unfair to you, and I did n't care. You don't say it. You talk of Jasper."

" Father, can you think—? "

"Yes—more than you say."

Philip grew white about the nostrils. "I have said all that I mean. I say it's shabby to freeze Jasper out in his absence. I say that you are free to use whatever share I may claim in the range as you like. But not for that. I won't be a party to it. I won't stand by and see you do such a wrong to yourself."

"Say what you mean!" cried his father with an implication in his voice which maddened Philip beyond control.

" Father!" he cried warningly.

Deed thrust his hands into his pockets, and facing him with deliberate bitterness, looked into his eyes. " I will pay you every penny of your damned fifty thousand dollars before you are twenty-four hours older."

For a moment Philip stared at his father in speechless anger. Then with a cry of rage he burst from the room.

CHAPTER VII.

THE clerk in the office spared a single gleam of the eye which was busy challenging the new-comers by the evening express from Denver,—looking them into the earth and pardoning them into existence again long enough to send them aloft in the care of " Front,"—to observe Philip's quick push through the office. The crowd parted before his blind look and determined arm, and in a moment he was in the air, reeling up the street, with his veins aflame and his tongue hot upon his lips.

His anger bore him on through the mob that commonly fills the sidewalk to its edge at night in Leadville. They gave way before his white face and set look. He did not know where he was going until a sharp ascent on the outskirts of the town took his breath in the manner of lesser elevations at the altitude of Leadville. He paused on the summit and, snatching off his hat, bared his moist forehead and beating head.

The sweet, strong, uplifting keenness of the mountain air swept through his brain. He pushed back the thick hair about his brow and stared up at the stars, shining down upon him through an atmosphere fined to an ethereal rarity. The intolerable exaltation of the air played upon his fevered spirit.

Standing there, he said to himself that he could never forgive his father : the affront was too deep, the misconception too gross. That he should think him capable of such meanness; that he should be ready on the suggestion of an instant to class him with Jasper; above all that he should asperse him with the thought that he could use a pretended impulse of fairness to a man who had done him a wrong— an impulse of generosity if one liked (standing out there in the air Philip said to himself that, after all, it was generous) to cloak a low appeal for himself,—it was too much! It was not what any man could be expected to forgive another. He repeated to himself often that he did not care that he was his father. No human relationship could give a man the right to insult another like that.

And then, in a moment, he laughed at the boyish self-assertion; and could have wept for his father. The air was really too tense: he could not think in it.

He recalled inconsequently that he had meant to ask his father to lend him $400. The recollection was a fresh pain. It seemed to him that his father could not have suspected him in just that way, if he had not given him good cause to know that he was always in want of money—that the whole question of money ruled him, at times, in a way which he could not, himself, reconcile with better things in his nature. No wonder his father had thought his urgency interested. Had he ever shown himself disinterested where money was involved?

As he went back through the town he thought he would go straight to his father and make it right with him. But the low instinct of pride which Philip was disposed in heated moments to take for the noblest thing in himself withheld him. He could not do it. Finally, perhaps he would do it—indeed, the subtle second consciousness knew very well that in the end he must do it, for he could not live unreconciled to his father: the amiable need, mixed of generosity and selfishness, to live at one with those nearest him would force him to it at last; and he knew that he could never let

his father make the advance : that would be too shameful—
yet he must refuse himself the happiness of going to bed
with it righted.

He knew for a folly the honour that he did the shallow
conceit of dignity, in waiting ; but he could not get himself
into the door of the hotel and up the stairs to his father's
room when the time came. He crossed over to the other
side of the street when he reached the hotel ; and then he
saw that his father's light was out. He told himself, now,
that he had probably meant to do it to-night, after all ; that
he had been postponing it until he should have had a glass
of something at Pop Wyman's to clear his head ; and he
believed that he was sorry his father had gone to bed. But
when he found him playing at the faro table where he paused
for a moment, after his glass at the bar, he sheered away
hastily, avoiding his eye ; and went unhappily down Chest-
nut Street, plunging into the first dance hall he passed, and
suffering one of the "beer jerkers" to wheedle him into
treating her to a mint julep. She said she never took anything but mint juleps. He saw again remorsefully the look
on his father's face as he bent over the faro table (he was
losing heavily) while he chaffed the girl vaguely, from some
exterior nimbus of intelligence, on her fad for mint juleps.
When she would have dragged him upon the floor, however,
to join the quadrille that was forming, he broke away without
ceremony and made for the door.

The miners in their blue shirts and brown, copper-riveted
trousers stuck in their boots, and with their armories belted
around their waists, beat time to the music which was just
beginning in the hot and reeking hall, dimly lighted by
kerosene lamps. One of them shouted after him by name
to come back. Philip recognized the speaker for a man he
had known at Piñon, as he turned for a moment at the door.
It was young Hafferton, the tutor who had given up his post

at Dartmouth to come West for consumption, and, recovering, had not yet found enough money to get back with. He had been the single reporter of the daily paper at Piñon. He had a long nose and a thin straggling beard and wore glasses. Philip supposed he was working the mine he used to talk to him about taking with half a dozen other impecunious young men of his own sort, on a lease.

"Oh! hello, Hafferton!" he said in listless recognition. He went back for a moment to shake hands with him over the rail dividing the dancing floor from the drinking bar. Hafferton told him, that, as he had supposed, he was working the "Come to me Quickly," on a lease. They were hiring no labour; but putting in their own. They had found good pay dirt he said, and were doing well. He hoped to start for home in the Spring, and to have a little left when he got back to keep him going until he could find something to do again. He was tired of mining. He had given up all the brave hopes with which he had begun. He was content to take a fair day's wages out of their leased claim day by day, if he might.

" I suppose we shall think of this as a stereopticon view we've seen, rather than as a real experience a year or two hence, when we're back East," said Hafferton, glancing about the dingy room. "But we must take what fun's moving. 'Everything goes in Colorado,'" he said, repeating the current slang phrase.

Philip refused the inclusion of himself in this point of view with a glance which should have explained to Hafferton what an ass he was. But Hafferton went on, undisquieted.

"You're down on your ranch, now, I suppose?" Philip's plans for leaving Piñon had been known before Hafferton left for Leadville.

" I've no ranch!" growled Philip, ungraciously.

" Why, but I thought——" began Hafferton, doubtfully, beginning to feel the distance in Philip's manner.

" I know you did. So did I."

"Somebody jumped your claim?"

Philip surveyed him for a moment, wondering if he could have heard anything. "No," said he, truculently, as if Hafferton was likely to dispute it, " I sold it."

" Oh !" exclaimed Hafferton. He had a chirpy manner, and a polite little voice which twisted every nerve in Philip. " I hope you got a good price for it."

"Yes," said Philip, ambiguously, " I got my price."

Hafferton glanced at him uncertainly. " I think they're waiting for me," he said, glancing behind him, where the three sets on the floor were making the preliminary bows to their partners. His own young lady was beckoning to him. " So long !" he said, waving his hand lightly as he disappeared.

At the theatre across the way Philip made out, through the cloud of tobacco smoke hovering between him and the stage, an elderly woman in a ball dress, the skirt of which reached to her knees. She was describing to the audience from the footlights in song how she met her "Harry" on Carbonate Hill every pleasant afternoon at the change of shifts. The burden of the matter was that Harry was "such a *nice* young man !" Philip found himself waiting for the wriggle by which the cracked voice attacked this phrase, at the end of each stanza ; and came to wonder dully, as she would begin the amorous tale afresh, how she was going to manage to connect the sense of this stanza at the end with her central truth, while the thought went buzzing in his head, " He means to raise that money to-morrow. How?"

The epithets which he would use against himself on ordinary occasions of remorse did not enough blacken his act. How could he have allowed the talk with his father, which he had meant should console him with the knowledge that he, at least, remained faithful to him, to issue in an estrangement between them, and in this miserable resolve of his father's to pay him a foolish debt of pride? His father had been trying. Oh, of course! But might he not have guessed that he must be trying? He knew his temper. Knowing the fine, the good, the generous man behind it, had he ever cared for that before? And remembering the trial through which he had just passed, recalling that he had found him still trembling from the hurt that Jasper had dealt him, should he not have forborne; should he not, at all events and at all costs, have avoided losing his second son to him? But what he had implied was intolerable : he turned hot at thought of it. Yet if to be imagined so base was maddening, what must it not be to his father to think him so? He rose with the determination to hunt up his father and make him know his thought before he slept. They could settle the Jasper question another time. Just now his only anxiety was for reconciliation.

He refused the return check offered him by the frowsy being who guarded the exit to the theatre. The assurance that Harry was " such a *nice* young man " followed him, with a dying quaver and simper into the street.

On the sidewalk he encountered Vertner. It appeared that he had come up to Leadville from Maverick to see Deed about a mine they were interested in together—to speak accurately, a mine which Vertner had induced Deed to join him in purchasing. The mine was filling with water, and it was a question between putting in expensive machinery to pump it out, and abandoning it. Vertner had in his pocket an assay of the vein they were working.

" Your father says we can't afford to go on with it : says *he* has n't got any money (I believe him, for he was just trying to borrow $25,000 when I struck him); but I say we can't afford to give it up. Taber might: we can't. It's a chance in a lifetime. With dirt like that in sight it's only the rich who can afford to economise. You don't happen to have $10,000 in your clothes, do you?"

"No," said Philip, "I was just going to ask you if you knew where I could borrow $50,000."

Vertner stopped short (they were walking together toward Harrison Avenue), taking Philip unceremoniously by the arm. "See here! Put me on to this thing! What are you and your father up to? Is there a dollar in it?"

"Are n't you in schemes enough, Vertner?" he asked to turn the subject.

"No, my boy. There are not schemes enough in the cosmos for the energy I feel in myself when I get up any of these fine mornings. And the mints don't manufacture the money that I feel I could use. What's the use of living if you have n't a new idea for the new day, as it comes along? These fellows that get an idea when they are eighteen, and spread it thin over the rest of their lives, to make it last, give me a pain. Come! Whisper it to your uncle! What are you up to—you and your father?"

"Oh, drop it, Vertner!" cried Philip wearily.

Vertner's quick ear caught the accent of pain in his voice. "Oh, well, *now* you've *got* to tell me, or own up that you won't let a fellow help you. The scheme is dropped with pleasure. I'm starting a popular subscription that's worth two of it. I call it 'Vertner's Grand Popular Subscription for the Presentation to Philip Deed, Esq., of a Nickel Plated Derrick to be employed in elevating him from some Confounded Muss.'" He wrote the words on the air with a fluent hand as they walked up Harrison Avenue toward the hotel. The crowd had begun to disperse: the shops were dark, and the gambling houses cast the only light, save that of the electric lamps, upon the street from behind their glass fronts. "There's going to be one subscriber to my fund—just one. If you want $50,000 you've got to have it, and I'm going to get it for you."

"It's deuced white of you, Vertner," said Philip with gloomy gratitude ; "but you can't do it. I want it to-morrow." He threw away his cigarette and began rolling another. "Try something possible. Prevent my father from borrowing $25,000. It will do me the same service."

"Oh, come ! I call for a show-down !" cried Vertner. "*I* don't know what you are driving at."

"My father has a crazy notion of paying me $50,000 to-morrow. Other men would threaten it. He will do it. He fancies—he thinks—" Philip gulped down the lump in his throat. "He has an idea that I am kicking about that business with Jasper. You know about that ? "

"No," said Vertner, a quickening glance of curiosity passing over his shrewd face, "I don't. What was it ? "

Philip told him fully, as they paused under an electric lamp, whose knife-edge glare showed them each other's faces and would have tempted an observer to note the contrast between them—to remark how Philip's sinewy bulk made more than its impression by the side of Vertner's slight, wiry build, thin, alert little face, and medium stature ; and how Vertner, who, in his own way, was as sufficient as the driving-wheel of an engine, took an aspect of ineffectiveness from the power expressing itself in every line of Philip's frame.

The deceptive outward look of ineffectiveness which was accented by contrast with Philip was always what impressed those who met Vertner for the first time ; and, (coupled with the still, sleepy gaze habitually dwelling in his eyes while he was engaged in the approaches to "talking business,") it had often encouraged men with whom he dealt in his early Colorado days, to trade on the unsophistication of an under-endowed young innocent. As Vertner said, with a twinkling eye, in the Western slang that often displaced the inadequacies of his Massachusetts English, " It was the kind of case where a man picks you up for a sucker, and lays you down for a shark."

To the casual eye Vertner looked about Philip's age, not because he was not seven years older, but because Philip's superior height and weight, his tanned cheek, heavy moustache, high-growing hair, the lips closed firmly on each other from habit, and a certain look of manly self-command in his quiet eyes, added five or six years to his twenty-three summers; while Vertner, who went always clean shaven, whose hair was fair and thin, whose smooth, clever, keen, good-humoured face had that incurable boyish look through all its shrewdness, which every one will remember in some man-boy he knows—Vertner, I say, procured a diminution of his thirty years by six or seven in the eyes of the casual observer. The observer, when he came to know him better, would have perceived the shrewd lines beginning to gather at the corners of his mouth. By this time he would have liked Vertner, or he might have gone on to add that it was a sophisticated, even a calculating mouth; and might have found something hard in those shrewd lines.

" Father imagines," concluded Philip, as they moved on— "something I said gave him the idea—that I feel myself swindled by what he did : selling Jasper out. You know my father. He does n't need facts for his anger; and what I said was easily misunderstood. It was in the nature of the thing. One word for Jasper looked like two for myself. It ended in his swearing that he would pay me my third share in the ranch within twenty-four hours. That was to-night. He has the $25,coo by him from the sale of the ranch.

That's plain enough from his trying to borrow only $25,000. But he can no more raise $25,000 more by to-morrow, as things are with him, than you can, Vertner. He'll do it though. You know that. And he'll do it at a cost that he will pay for with every moment of his life afterward."

" Um. You would n't need the—the trifle you mention very long, would you ? "

" Long enough to lend it to my father, take it from him and pay it back."

"You're not thinking of lending it to him yourself, I take it. There is to be somebody in between ? "

" Certainly. I suppose it would n't be hard to find a man generous enough to lend father $25,000 of my money without security if I could get the $25,000."

They were at the door of a saloon. Philip said he had just been drinking and wanted nothing ; but he went in with Vertner, who ordered vermouth and insisted on his taking something with him. Vertner had learned to drink vermouth in the fast set into which he had fallen at the preparatory school from which there had once been an intention of sending him to Harvard.

"No, no more," said Philip, shaking his head in answer to Vertner's urgence, after their one glass together.

"Well then, take my good advice," said Vertner, as they went out into the street together. " Take *something* with me. If I were in your shoes, I'd skip."

"Oh, no you would n't Vertner. You'd know my father if you'd lived in my shoes as long as I have, and you'd see the folly of it. He'll pay that money over to me just the same, you know, whether I am here to take it in person or not. It's not difficult to deposit a cheque to my credit at his bank, and notify me by wire. If I am going to attempt refusing it I can do it better by staying. The other

way I should be helpless. If I stay, though I can't really
refuse it, perhaps I can manage what will come to the same
thing."

"Oh, all right!" exclaimed Vertner, good-naturedly
abandoning the point. "Count on me!"

They walked Harrison Avenue for an hour or more, discussing plans for preventing Deed from borrowing the money.
Philip could not have given a name to his fears. He merely
knew that since his father had stripped himself of the ranch
he could not lay hands at such notice on $25,000 of his own;
and he knew no less well that somewhere, in some way, he
would lay hands on it and would pay it over to him, if he
would let him, next day, together with $25,000 more. He
was haunted by a strange dread.

They went into one saloon and another. Philip was
restless. At several places they overheard talk about Deed.
It was one o'clock and they had dropped into St. Anne's
Rest, when Philip, as he put his glass to his lips (he was
drinking too much and was conscious of it, but was incapable of stopping), heard a red-faced man standing next
him at the bar, say, with an oath :—

"Just my luck! Deed and I are on this here Church
Building Fund together: our committee subscribed the
square thing, and now Deed'll shirk his share when the
time comes, and the committee'll have to make up his
subscription among themselves. I always said we ought to
have subscribed it separately 'stid of as a committee, but
Hank Jackson wanted to keep his subscription dark. He
was n't ponying up as much as usual. Should n't wonder if
he was going same way as Deed. 'Iron Silver' or 'Morning
Star,' did you say?"

His companion, whose florid face was supported upon a
bull neck, and whose moustache had been trained to wanton
in a grandiose curve and to hang its spreading boughs within

easy twirling distance of his collar, said that it was the "Iron Silver" he had spoken of.

"He *must* be hard up! Men in this town ain't putting up 'Iron Silver' stock even when they want to borrow $25,000 pretty bad—not very brash!"

Philip had put down his glass. His muscles grew rigid. The impulse to seize the bull neck, and choke the man until he denied it was a mastering need; but he forbore. Perhaps the man spoke the truth. He turned pale, and pinched his eyes with his fingers and beat his head to clear his brain of the fumes of the liquor he had drunk. "Come!" he cried to Vertner, clutching his arm. Vertner stood still, listening. "Come!" he repeated hoarsely.

"You heard?" he said, when they were outside, in the cold, strong air.

"Yes. The thing's got to be stopped! I'm with you."

"Stopped!" exclaimed Philip. "Stopped! My God, man, do you know whose 'Iron Silver' shares those are?"

"Your father's."

"Humph! Listen!" He whispered in his ear.

Vertner started. Under the ghostly glare of the electric light, his face paled. He repeated Philip's word in the same whisper. He caught his arm vehemently, inquiringly.

Philip nodded. "Come!" he said.

"Where?"

"To the telegraph office."

"It's closed."

"They'll open it for a thing like this."

"What are you going to do?"

"*Do?* I'm going to get that money."

Vertner went with him.

CHAPTER VIII.

BEATRICE did not wholly respect her fancy that she occasionally saw a look of dogged repression or patient pain in Dr. Ernfield's eyes lately. She had fallen into the wifely habit of seeing things a little qualified by her husband's probable comments on her observations; and she knew that Vertner would make fun of her if she told him of this fancy. But the listless step, which had replaced the briskness prevailing through the worst of his former weakness, and the growing haggardness of his whole outward aspect were things which any one must see, she said to herself after a day or two. She wondered that Margaret, who saw so much of him, appeared to be blind to them; but then, Margaret *was* blind. For her part she resolved to say nothing. It was not her affair.

Fred Kelfner, his stable boy and factotum, the warmth of whose affection for his employer was one of the jokes of the town, noticed the change at all events, immediately, and told at home that, " Doc. was growin' peak-ed agin, and losin' all he'd gained." Fred drove Ernfield about, and was frequently at the house. Beatrice and Margaret often exchanged a word with him: his loyal adoration of the doctor, taking no account of the derision it won him among boys of his own age, touched them.

"It don't make no difference to a feller what he does for a *brick!*" he had said at some intimation from Beatrice on

K

one occasion that his fealty might lose him caste among the boys. He said it with the exaltation of a noble of King Henry's at Ivry, chanting,

"And be our oriflamme to-day, King Henry of Navarre!"

And Beatrice gladly abandoned him to the consequences of his faith to his liege.

His talk about Ernfield's health, reaching Beatrice at last through her kitchen, suffused her prophetic soul with a glow of confirmation not all pain. When it finally reached Margaret, through Beatrice, she took shame to herself for having leaned on him so much. She recognized that, in the week since Deed's departure, she had fallen into a habit of dependence upon him for part of her daily support—a habit which she could not help seeing was growing upon her. A perception of the way in which others must have leaned on his generous strength, if she, so entirely accustomed to stand alone, could fall in a few days into the habit, overwhelmed her at the same moment. In the light of this she seemed to understand how he had come to his present condition.

When Margaret had worked so much out in her own mind, she had a conscience about suffering him in any way to help her to bear the weight of her own misery. But her resolve to deny herself the support of his strength was found to be less easily carried out by a mere exertion of will than some of her other resolves. If she was to see him at all she discovered that he must constantly lend her a part of himself unconsciously : it was not a question whether she could feel free to accept the beneficent sturdiness that walled her about from the poignant world that she dared not yet take a look at, and sustained her from day to day in her own sense of the Duty that remains, though Pleasure goes. It existed for her, as the sun exists : if she put herself in the way of its rays she could not be less than warm if she would.

When, at length, she took this scruple to Beatrice, she was openly scorned for it.

"But what a girl it is!" cried Beatrice. "Poke, poke poke at a fire that even *your* conscience could n't prod into burning a fly; and let a regular conflagration—a Chicago fire—kindle under your very nose! Oh, Margaret!" she exclaimed with an indescribable accent of despair.

"Why, what in the world have I done?" asked Margaret.

"I don't know whether you *have* done it yet; but if you have n't it's his character rather than your carefulness that's to be thanked for it. You remember what I used to tell you before—before the other day. You would n't believe it then. You would n't tell him, or let *him* tell him of your engagement. But I've seen it going on this five weeks. A week ago it might n't have been plain to a girl whose modesty won't let her believe that she can matter to anybody. But even to her it must be plain now. Maggie! Surely you've seen!"

They were seated in the room above the parlour in Beatrice's little two-story house. Beatrice was running a long seam on a pinafore of green gingham for her baby, and, bent over the sewing-machine, in this motherly occupation, and delivering herself of these sagacities, the air of matronly wisdom seemed to have descended upon her.

When Margaret took her meaning, after a moment, the shame of it seemed as bad as the newspaper article—worse indeed, for of that she had only read a dozen lines, which it was possible to forget; but of this she tasted the entire ignominy. She did not know what to say. She wanted to fall on Deed's shoulder, and beg his protection from such thoughts. Why was he not here to shield her from them? But her next reflection was for Ernfield.

"Beatrice!" she cried. "I wonder at you!"

"I thought you would," she answered calmly. "But

it is really time, dear, I made you wonder.   I often try to
fancy what such people as I can be made for, you know,
Maggie.   But I never wonder when I am with you.   It's
our business to cut a path for the feet of people like you,
who are made to walk with their heads in the clouds."

" It's an insult to him ! " breathed Margaret irrelevantly.

" Of course ; and an indignity to you ; and an open affront
to Mr. Deed.   Don't imagine I don't know that.   But it's
necessary to say it, all the same."

" How can you think such a thing of him ? " cried Margaret
indignantly.   She was scarlet.   She put back the lock
that habitually strayed into her eyes with a gesture of self-
control, and went on with the crocheting on which she was
engaged.

" Dear Maggie, he is only a man," returned Beatrice con-
vincingly.   " What makes you think him so different from
other men ? "

" Because he is, I think, for one reason," Margaret returned,
studying attentively the baby sack she was making for Beatrice,
for a lost stitch.   " But if he were ever so like, it would not
be cause to suppose him capable of such—— " She paused,
inconclusively ; and bent her eyes upon the work again.   It
had been a fortunate resource since she had been unable to
fix her mind on reading, or any of her usual occupations.
One could think, one could even be as miserable as one liked,
or as one must, while one crocheted.   " You seem to forget,
Beatrice," she went on, quietly, after a moment, " that he is
very ill—dying perhaps ; and that I am,—— " She did not
know how to say what she was.

" Why, you dear, crazy, heavenly-minded, impractical
thing ! " cried Beatrice, trying not to laugh.   " Since when
did men love women less when they were ill ?   The people
who are most against woman—who won't have her on any
terms—agree that she is a famous nurse !   Oh, Maggie ! "

she exclaimed, at a look of deep pain on Margaret's face,
" I don't mean that. I mean only that men are just as
capable of falling in love with a woman on a death-bed as on
horseback, or on a front piazza, in the bloom of health.
What has that to do with it? And as to your other objection, it's just no objection at all. He can't know that
you hold yourself no less bound to—to *him* because—
because of things. He can't be expected to imagine that
you are abhorring him and being loyal to him in a breath.
Come! Be fair, Margaret! You must own that there is
no reason why the man should n't have tumbled into love
with you. The next thing is to rescue him."

" If you mean that I am to show him by my manner that
I know him to have such a feeling; if you mean that I am
to insult him, I'm sure you must know I could never do it.
To think it would be bad enough; and I don't think it.
To give an idea like that the sanction of a word, a silence, a
look. . . . . . Beatrice!" she cried, in a tone of injury
which almost frightened her companion, who remained silent
a moment.

Beatrice pondered the prospect from the bay window in
which her sewing machine was set, and from which she could
look over her geraniums, fuchsias, roses, lilies, Wandering
Jew, and sweet alyssum, up and down the road, and far out
to the mountains, flushed just now with the pink of sunset.
The flowers ranked in pots on the shelf which followed the
bow of the window, caught the gilding light on their greens
and let a little filter through upon her head, as she sat
before her unfinished seam, thinking.

" Margaret, dear, you know I can't like to wound you. I
have to be so terribly frank to produce any impression on
you : I don't wonder that it hurts you. But you must be
hurt ; it's a duty to hurt you—to sting you. What century
do you suppose you are living in ; in what country ; in what

state of society? I'm sure I never said or thought that it was nice to be such complicated people as we are, or as our ancestors have made us after spending nineteen or twenty centuries tying bow-knots in themselves. I've not the least doubt—goose—" (she gave her an affectionate smile) "that Corydon and Phyllis managed such things a deal better : they would have been stupid if they had n't, with nothing to do but mind the sheep. But we have travelled a frightful distance from such a state of things. Dr. Ernfield and you know sheep only as mutton and lamb : it's impossible that people who have arrived at that should treat each other as simply as if they were still wandering around with crooks under their arms."

"What makes you think I was born yesterday, Beatrice?" asked Margaret, fixing her eyes on her. "I know all that. I know it; but it does n't avail with me. There are other considerations—considerations infinitely above those ; and which you are just as capable of understanding, if you would only let yourself."

"Maggie, look at me !" said Beatrice seriously. Margaret observed her obediently. "*I can understand what people say.* The fear of that is anything you like : I don't respect the fear of it ; but I do respect the idea. The wisdom of the ages is in that phrase."

"You mean the folly," answered Margaret quietly. "You must know quite well, Beatrice, that I could never let the thought which people use in such matters weigh with me. If I should give up my individuality, my life, to conformity, and serve, with all the cowardice I could find the heart for, before the world's notions of things, I should only have lost the realest thing I own, and gained not so much as my master's thanks. I learned that long ago. And one must prick one's fingers on one's own brambles about these things, anyway, I suppose. No one can be a guide for another."

" But, Maggie," urged Beatrice concretely, "the man's in love with you."

"So says Beatrice Vertner," returned her companion, gravely. "But if she should be mistaken—which she is—can she suffer for me the shame which I must feel if I did anything which presumed upon that idea ? And who is there to bear his hurt for him ? "

To which Beatrice, who, when she was serious was tremendously serious, answered, "And who, I should like to know, is going to restore to him his present feeling, from which you might turn him back, while there is still time ; who is going to re-create for him the peace of mind you are encouraging him to lose for your sake, without the faintest chance of giving him anything in return ; and what in the world can you say in common honesty when he accuses you, as he will, of having led him on ? "

" Beatrice, dear," returned Margaret, patiently, "there are things which even you must not say." She went on with her crocheting for a moment in silence ; and the quiet, steady little push of her forefinger as it ran along the needle, and caught the stitch, seemed, for the moment, the embodiment of her sober view of life. " Don't you think it would be very unworthy for us to assume that a man like Dr. Ernfield could have anything less than the highest, the most delicate regard for a position like mine ? Whatever you say, I believe he must have some guess about my feelings. If he has any such—such feeling as you say, he may be trusted, I think, to find wisdom of his own for it : I'm sure he does not expect me to control it for him. And if he did, or if I should wish it a thousand times over, pray how should I set about it ? "

" But, Maggie dear, you could n't be reckless enough to let a man go on ! "

"I suppose I must have heard that question discussed in

twenty different cases," returned Margaret a little wearily, "and I could never believe that the remedies proposed could be felt by the man for whom they were to be employed as anything better than cruel and insulting. Letting a man go on, as you call it, is, at worst, postponing a question which you may never have to answer—which, in half the cases to which women apply what they take for a considerate and unselfish kindness, would never be asked."

"Oh, dear !" sighed Beatrice. "Men are such stupids. You talk as if they were wise—like us. As if they would n't all get themselves into the most dreadful puddles, like a duck's chickens, who think they can swim, if we were n't by to look after them !"

"A woman is certainly bound not to allow a man to believe she cares for him when she does n't," owned Margaret ; "but it's hard to see why she must keep a scouting party of foolish ideas about men's feelings in the field every moment of her girlhood. Surely the aggressive attitude that everybody sees in young girls, which implies that every man who comes near you is on the eve of proposing marriage, is not maidenly. I'm not sure, though it means so well, that it is not gross. For me to imagine such an intention in Dr. Ernfield (who, if there were no other reason, is too ill to think of marriage with any one,) would be simply unspeakable, Beatrice. You must see it. Come !" She left her work, and going over to her, stooped and kissed her cheek. "Come, Beatrice, you *must* see it ! "

All this judiciousness could not keep a certain change out of her manner toward him, of course, when he came again. Beatrice, though she had retired from the contest defeated, had contrived to poison Margaret's thought of him with consciousness. But it was pleasant to see that he seemed to have no sense of the change.

Ernfield continued to come ; and Margaret allowed herself without a prick of conscience to look forward more and more to the cheer he brought into the desolate days on which she had fallen. It was certainly true that Margaret always saw her own point of view so plainly and was so simply faithful to it, that she was in danger of reckoning too confidently upon the counterpart of her own feeling in another. It was at least a faith that anyone understanding it must have abused with reluctance ; and in so far she was protected by her very rashness. But Beatrice was probably on unassailable ground in thinking it the reverse of worldly wise.

Yet, if Margaret had been bothered by two consciences about him, instead of feeling quite free with her one, her need for distraction from the gnawing of her thoughts must have been equally real and equally irresistible. She could not turn over in her mind the scene with Deed on that morning quite every moment in the day. She must have gone mad if no diversion had offered from the circle in which she had come to argue about her conduct on her wedding day. Sometimes, in desperation, she would go into Maverick with Beatrice—the Vertners lived not quite in the town—and wait about while Beatrice did her marketing. She still hesitated before the thought of returning the calls which had been made upon her, in her capacity of stranger, during the month preceding her wedding day. When she said she did not care what people said she exaggerated as little as anyone who has made that hardy statement can ever have done ; but she owned to herself that, just at first, she could not like to court the questions, and the polite and in-direct, but not the less rasping comment that she must meet if she made these calls.

It was different with Dorothy, who had reached Maverick after that fatal day, and might be supposed not to be privy to her shame. Of course Margaret knew that she must

know ; but it was quite possible between them to sustain
the convention that she did n't. Dorothy would sometimes
come to the house, as they became better friends, and sit
for an hour or more accepting Beatrice's advice about arranging the house they had taken, while she was really
listening to Margaret's silence. Sometimes she would find
Margaret alone, and would make certain modest and doubtful advances. She liked her without being sure she understood her. They exchanged many confidences short of
the real ones. They never spoke of Deed, of course.

Maurice had preached a trial sermon, and was staying on
at Maverick in the hope of receiving a call to the pulpit of
St. John's.

Ernfield did not cease to be a question between Beatrice
and Margaret. But it was not until Margaret accepted an
invitation from him to ride up Ute Pass with him, that
Beatrice definitively washed her hands of her.

Ernfield and Margaret skirted the town, and directed their
horses toward the gulch that opened beyond the railway
round-house between the small, bare red hills that lay just
without the limits of Maverick to the North. These hills,
which rose from the plain abruptly, cut off the view of the
great mountains behind them unless one climbed to their
summits, when the horizon was seen to be populous with
snow-peaks.

The town, after they had passed out of the narrow belt,
which was really "city," and which was densely populated
by as many as five families to the acre, strayed lack-
adaisically along their road, until it reached the edge of the
hills, where it paused at an Irishman's cabin so suddenly
that after turning the first curve leading into the ravine,
Ernfield and Margaret seemed to themselves as much alone
as if Maverick were not engaged in rustling for the
mighty dollar just around the bend.

The bridle path, followed by their ponies at a canter, turned with the windings of the ravine, at whose bottom a stream might once have run. The rocks, rising in vari-coloured masses to the high brown hills above their heads, would sometimes fall back, and leave a space a hundred yards wide or more, in which the grass grew rankly, but not greenly, in the manner of the herbage of the West. In the early morning it had seemed cold enough for snow; but that was no hindrance to weather which habitually takes the Indian Summer bit between its teeth just after breakfast every morning and makes a break for the sparkle, the keenness, the unfailing sunniness of the typical Colorado day. It was December; but in the sun at this hour it seemed like a day in June.

Half an hour after they had entered the ravine their horses stood upon a height. The path wound up to this point out of the gulch on its way to the Pass. Indeed this was the beginning of what was known as the Pass— a road between the hills, which if one followed it far enough and high enough would bring one to Colorado Springs. They were on the summit of the first considerable rise of the foot-hills toward the mountains; and their station commanded the beautiful valley, in the centre of which Maverick spread its shabby architecture, and sprawling design. Behind, at their feet, lay a small park, into which the hills dipped from all sides, and through the midst of which a thready brook ran. Margaret, who had seen nothing so vast as this bewildering prospect, running on all sides to the horizon, caught her breath at the expanse.

The sunshine, bathing the tops of the white peaks far on the thither side of the valley with an enchanting radiance, danced above the plain on which Maverick sat. The kindling air that breathed about them on their height seemed, as always in Colorado, to be drinking the sunshine and making it part of its substance, as one is sure the nobler wines must have done, in their grape days.

In this atmosphere everything was seen afresh, and Margaret found all her thoughts of the time since she had parted with Deed discovering themselves in new aspects, as she and Ernfield looked out on this great world—this world thrilled with its own silence. In the face of the boundless light and air and earth, and the limitless sweetness of the sunlight her world, too, seemed large and serene again.

"We talk of dying when we are sorry," she said to him. "Suppose we should be taken at our word, and remember too late that *this* is life. Whoa, pony!" She leaned over and patted the restive animal's neck. She circled the hills with her eyes as she looked up again. "I believe I am accustomed to think that all the hard things are the real life; and I've been sure of it lately." The tacit reference to her trouble escaped her unconsciously. "But when one sees things like this, one is not sure."

"I don't know," said Ernfield. "I should think one might be sure they are not. The other things are nearer —the miseries and pains and disappointments; and I suppose they keep tugging at every one's skirts, and crying that *they* are life. But it's an awful whopper, you may be sure. If they are, the moon is our day, and the sun is the dead body."

He alighted to tighten the cinch of his saddle; the pony went through a series of obstructive manœuvres that gave pause to the conversation for a few moments.

"I wish I could be as confident," said Margaret when the animal was still. "But the things you speak of, Dr. Ernfield —don't you see that in one fashion or another they are so many ways of disabusing us of our cosy conceit that personal happiness is the main affair? And that, at least, we must be sure is not true. Can the wretchedness through which we learn that the world is not a contrivance for ministering to our self-love, but has other business in hand, such as crushing it, for example, be anything but very right ?"

"Oh, I suppose not," returned Ernfield, smiling; "but how about the pink light on Ouray over there ? Is n't that right too ?" He shook his head. "I shall never believe, Miss Derwenter, that the sun in eclipse is the normal thing. I have an endless faith—since you speak of contrivances—that the sun was mainly invented for shining purposes ; and I'm sure we were n't meant to grudge ourselves its shining."

"Perhaps !" murmured Margaret. "Perhaps !" Then, after a moment, she added, "You have a cheerful view of life, Dr. Ernfield."

Ernfield laughed. "Rather necessary, don't you think ? I've not enough left to waste in quibbles." It was the first time that he had referred to his condition.

"Don't say that," she begged. "You are going to get well. Since you talk of not grudging ourselves the sun's shining, you must n't grudge yourself that certainty. It has to be. Surely we have not all the responsibilities. And would it not be a shameful thing to believe that all your— your helpfulness and strength, Dr. Ernfield (I must speak plainly if I speak at all, you see), should be taken from the world while there are so many thousand drones and incapables left to go instead ; and so many thousand tired bodies and minds left behind to weary for the help that you might give them. I can't believe that, Dr. Ernfield, any more than you can believe what—what you were just saying," she concluded, with a sense of having said too much ; yet with a pleasure in having let him know her feeling.

"Why, what an abandoned moralist you are, Miss Derwenter !"

He caught his rein upon his arm, and made his pony stand

where he could tighten the cinch on her saddle, as he said,
" Who was it who was saying a moment ago that the teaching of life seemed to be that it did not exist for us ?   And
here you would have me flatter myself with the old fiction
that I—that any man—can count—that fate ought to clap
its eye on me and save me forthwith to be a comfort to the
world's declining years.   The world will decline nicely, thank
you, without me—are n't you sure of that ? "

His head was down against the pony's side, as he gave the
cinch the final twist.   Pulling up a cinch takes the breath.
But she fancied the long inspiration he drew, as he exclaimed " There ! " and put the strap at the end of the
cinch through the last ring, was more like a sigh.

" And besides," he went on, after a moment, " there's a
thing or so to be said in favour of death.   I wonder the poets
don't try to say it more, instead of gasping before it in the
craven rhymes that seem to please them so awfully.   It's
a pity, I grant you, that other people have to die ; but I
never could see why it should be so intolerable a thought
to one's self.   I mean, of course, if you have a certain
thought about death," he added, gravely—" the Christian's
thought, I suppose we should call it."

" But——" she began, and stopped impotently.

" Ah, yes," he owned, " I admit the ' but.'   The slow
ignominy of this stupid trouble of mine you were going to
say—the creeping weakness.   It's true.   I should have
chosen a great deal better if I'd arranged my own way of
going : anyone who knows what a luxurious dog I am down
at the bottom of my shirking heart would believe that of
me, I hope.   But I was n't asked."   He glanced at her
with a smile.   " No, no ! " exclaimed he, as she opened her
lips to reply.   " Don't try to deny it for me.   It's very
good of you ; but it's no use, you know.   I am a physician.
I don't deceive myself.   If I could only believe in

your denial, you know, I should be glad enough to let
you deny it for me by the hour. Or rather I should be
glad to have you affirm the other thing for me. To affirm,"
he said dreamily; "it's the only thing in the least worth
while." He paused a moment and Margaret wanted to say
to him that he must not go on ; but the processes of his
thought always excited her vaguely.

His instinct for relating the common, daily movement of
life to the confident morality which he seemed to keep with
an engaging ease at the centre of all his thinking charmed
her : since her talk with Beatrice she had never enjoyed the
certainty of innocence that this perceived and acknowledged
charm had not had as much to do with her persistence in
maintaining their relation on the same footing as her
consideration for him. She felt guilty about it now, as she
often did about anything which gave her happiness. In a
way he substantiated her dreams for herself. She could
arrive at the same ends by difficult and conscious means :
she could keep her impulses, thoughts, feelings at a certain
temperature by keeping them under glass ; she could water
and tend them and cut them back and get the blooms set
down in the Botany, in the end. But things blossomed for
him in the open, as if that were their natural atmosphere ;
and their flowering was not ruled—his plants, she was sure,
knew no rules—but abundantly spontaneous, like the Nature
of which they were part.

"When Agnosticism is the world's religion," he went on,
" I suppose affirmation and denial will be alike indifferent,
and alike uninteresting—as uninteresting as the world itself
will be then. But just now it seems as if all the work that
counted at all was being done by men with an awful lot of
' Yes ' in them. And even when a fourth of it is pure
doubt, and the other three-fourths shout to keep that
miserable fourth's spirits up, one has to believe, I think,

that a brave three-quarter affirmative is better than all the whole negatives between Maverick and—well, and Lieutenant Greely's ' Farthest North.' " He laughed painfully.

Margaret hesitated a moment. Then she said, shyly, " Do you know, Dr. Ernfield, I believe that is what has worn *you* out—affirming for other people. Nervous prostration—it's a kind of physical Agnosticism, don't you think ? It seems as if we did n't even believe in our own bodies any more."

" You are at least twice too acute for comfort, Miss Derwenter," he said, smiling. " My breakdown was n't due to anything so amiable. It was really because I had n't the temperance to stop there. The habit of absolute power is an irresistible one, I suppose. It made a despot of me, I know ; and whatever my subjects might tell you of *their* awful case—for I assure you I showed no pity—it is an exhausting thing to be a despot."

" What nonsense ! " She smiled.

" No, no," he disclaimed, " it's only right that my beastly satisfaction with myself should be taken down a peg or two. I accept this as my punishment." Margaret's lips framed a sound ; but he stopped her. " No, it's not gammon,—what I tell you. It's fact. I was outrageous about the whole business. I was young when I began, and I had a little success quite soon. It made me sure—infernally, intolerably sure. I led my patients a devil of a life. Don't think I'm inventing. That would be too shameful. Any of them would tell you as much—even those I have done something for : those more than the others, perhaps. Oh, I was a brute, Miss Derwenter, whatever you think ! But I've got my pay. It's wearing — being a brute." He smiled at her ; but she saw that he was in deadly earnest.

" I don't know what you were, of course, Dr. Ernfield,"

she said simply, " though I don't believe you were anything like that. Only one thing is clear to me: you must live to be more of the same sort."

He bit his lip and turned his head that she might not see his face. " I assure you," he said, huskily, " you must stop wishing me so well, Miss Derwenter. I'm not worthy of it. If I were I should be able to bear it better."

The too ready tears started to Margaret's eyes. " What shall I wish for you, then?" she asked. " I will wish anything you like."

" Wish the impossible, please. That is the only thing that can do me the slightest good. Wish me the man I was six months ago: wish me the love of the only person who matters. Come, don't be close, Miss Derwenter! Wish the Never Will Be for me! I might get well on the mere hope of it!"

" Do you mean—— ? "

" Oh, mean——!" he cried. " I *don't* mean to be rude for one thing."

" No, no!" exclaimed Margaret, her face full of earnestness, " I only meant to say——" She had not an idea what she had meant to say.

" The kindest and sweetest thing you could invent. Great heaven, don't I know that! And don't I loathe myself for letting you even think it for me!"

He glanced suddenly at her face, and saw the tears in her eyes. He bit his lips; an inrush of emotion mastered him. The uncommon mood in which the expression of feelings habitually restrained had left him, was defenceless before the impulse of love which sprang up in him at sight of the sweet tumult of compassion for him in her eyes. He was standing at her saddle pommel. Her arm hung by her side. He caught her hand to his lips in a long, blind reckless kiss. Margaret gave him a swift, scared look as he

L

relinquished it. Then, gathering her reins hastily, she turned the pony back down the road they had come up.

"Pride, ignorance, sufficiency, folly !" she said to herself with smarting eyes, thinking of her rejection of Beatrice's warning. Must she always be so grossly wise? She said to herself that Ernfield was not to blame, and shrank from the thought of him with terror, in a breath. It was her position— her intolerable no-position, that made such things possible.

As Ernfield followed her, she gave him a fleeting glance in which he read a reproach that cut him to the heart. He felt like spurring his horse over the edge of the precipice along which they were riding. But he decided to see her safely home, first. There were always precipices if one needed them.

He kept her in sight with difficulty. She pushed her horse down the steeps at a pace which made him fear for her. A single thought was in her mind : Deed. Her heart went out to him in a passionate appeal for shelter and defence. The silent loyalty which she had kept for him, in the midst of all resentment of his act, had leaped to flame at the touch of Ernfield's lips ; and she could not think how she could live until she could stand at his side again where he could protect her from the world and from herself. Pride and bitterness fell away from her like the properties of a dream. Her eyes were wet with joyous tears.

Ernfield wondered at the radiant look of resolve upon her face as he helped her to alight at her own door. She did not care what he did for her now.

CHAPTER IX.

DEED was pitching his effects into his trunk with nervous haste. If he paused for a moment to gaze at the confused heap, the ache at his heart reasserted itself, and he turned from his work, and went to stare miserably out of the hotel window. In these moments he tasted despair.

He had paid Philip. That was done with. He had made short work of his protestations; he knew on which side to place him now. He had gone Jasper's way. Deed told himself that he ought to be glad. He might have gone on trusting him as he had trusted Jasper, until he had confided enough to his honour to make the trust worth abusing; and a sickening breach of faith, like Jasper's, must have followed in due course. It was better to know the worst now. As he remembered what the worst was, he turned from the window dizzily, and sank into a chair, groaning aloud.

He no longer had a son. The misery of the words filled up the world's space. But a more hateful pain lay within the loss : that they had lost themselves to him. He could have borne that they should die—even if their deaths had trodden on each other's heels, as their falsities had done. But that they should live as ingrates and traitors to his love was a pain beyond the worst that death can bring.

What was it, he asked himself, as he sat crouched miser-

ably in his chair, with his head in his hands, that made
ingratitude so intolerable, so damnable, so unforgivable a
thing? Was it that it cut into the best of a man? Was it
because the loving acts on which gratitude follows proceed
from the richest, the tenderest, the secretest corners of a
man's nature that the agony of an answering baseness, where
one has a right to look for the answering love, is so un-
endurable? Of course it was a pain to receive a blow in the
face, and doubly a pain where one must rather expect a
kiss; but did that explain all the degrading, the soul-
nauseating horror of ingratitude? The pang of it was part
of the stock of familiar allusion; it must have been felt
since men first loved and served one another; shredded
echoes of quotation floated into his head and out again, as
he sat writhing under the torture of it.

> "For when the noble Cæsar saw *him* stab,
> Ingratitude, more strong than traitors' arms,
> Quite vanquished him: then burst his mighty heart . . ."

And Lear's cry—he had never felt its awful force before—

> ". . . that she may feel,
> How sharper than a serpent's tooth it is,
> To have a thankless child ! ' "

Common! Why it was in the School Speakers! Every-
one had felt the wound! And yet none of all the millions
who had suffered from it could say what it was—what
peculiar, stinging, maddening touch lay in it to make the
hurt of it beyond all other hurts. Ah, well! What
difference could it make to them or him? They knew the
pain, and he knew it. The pain was enough.

He got up and went restlessly about his packing again.
Where were the good hours of seven days ago? he asked
himself, as he folded his dress-coat. He smiled sadly for
the thought, and for the idea of taking a dress-coat on such
a journey. It was useless to take it; but it was equally

foolish to leave it : he did not expect to return immediately, and he did not wish to give it to the hotel people. He thought he should go on a long journey, to Florida, to Cannes, to Egypt—anywhere away from memory—when he had found the men at Burro Peak City who had once wanted to buy the " Lady Bountiful " and had made his sale. The hotel people might prove ungrateful, he said to himself, with a sorry laugh. " Ungrateful ! " he repeated, in the aimless need we feel to keep up a conversation with ourselves when we are miserable. The word flooded his heart with the recurrent ache ; and he dropped the coat listlessly into the tray, and returned to the window. Ah, where was the man of those good hours of a week ago ? He remembered vaguely that he had once been happy, as souls in hell may recall their days of earth : it was an unreal memory, as if it had been another's happiness. Who was the man who had ridden up to a certain door in Maverick a week before with life at his feet, and all the sweet airs of earth blowing for him? Not he. That man had two sons who loved him, and whom he loved.

Deed looked sadly on the spectacle of the street, crowded with men to whom life still meant something—men who had not lost their sons, perhaps, or had never known what it was to have sons, and to love them as one's soul. Why did they go up and down ? It fatigued his sight, this restless motion of which he had once been part—before his quarrel with Margaret, before Jasper had turned traitor, before Philip had cut the last tie that bound him to life, and set him adrift among the unfriended men to whom nothing matters. What was it all about? What was it for?

He remembered that they lived in a different world—his world of a week ago—and that they understood what it was all for, no doubt, as he would have understood, then. They understood ; but his present feeling would be as incomprehensible to them as theirs was to him. Would he have understood it himself a week ago? All happiness and unhappiness suddenly seemed to him to be shut up to themselves in chambers desolately aloof from each other, and from every other state of feeling. One sensation must for ever be as solitary, as incommunicable as the other. The unbearable sense of loneliness which the thought gave him made him shut his eyes against the sight of the going and coming in the street. The best sympathy, he knew, would be powerless to guess deeper than the outer envelope of his feeling; and these men, if they would imagine his misery ever so vaguely, must not merely be unhappy themselves, but must be like enough him to understand him; and he did not understand himself.

Could any of all the strange chances that brought men to a mining camp from the earth's dust-bins and coal-holes, leaving every colour of human experience behind them, have drawn here one man like enough himself to understand how, a week ago, in the crazy satisfaction of an impulse of passion, he could have forsaken a happiness filling and overflowing in the moment of his folly all his hopes? Was there one who could do an incurable wrong in such besotted confidence in one hour, and know it for what it was in the next? With others did the remorse follow instant upon the fatuity? With so much wisdom after the event, did others find none before?

But he knew very well that no one in his place could have done Margaret the unforgivable wrong he had done her. It was left for him to make a loving woman, guilty only in endeavouring to save him from himself, the victim of an infernal suspicion; and upon the head of it to abandon her on their wedding day. It was an insensate cruelty; and now it was his punishment to long hopelessly for a forgiveness which he should never insult her to ask. A moment later, thinking how Margaret would judge the expedient he had been driven to that morning in order to raise money to pay Philip, a sharp doubt of its innocence insinuated itself, and he would have been glad to undo it. But that was past praying for; and, on the whole, it was as safe and fair as it seemed, probably. The $25,000 which he had borrowed at his bank in the morning on the security of some Iron Silver stock—part of the Brackett estate of which he was one of two trustees—was a temporary accommodation from an estate which owed thrice that sum to his care, and one which could cost it nothing. If he could have sold his Burro Peak mine, the "Lady Bountiful," in Leadville, he need not have called on it ; but they did n't know the "Lady Bountiful," in Leadville, and the men at Burro Peak who did, and who had offered him $60,000 for it a year ago (when he had refused it) were a four days' journey from Leadville, beyond the telegraph and the railway, beyond even the stage coach. As it was he had simply borrowed $25,000 until he could lay his hands on his own money—a matter of ten days, as he reckoned it. He could n't wait ten days to pay Philip. He had found it irksome enough to wait for the opening of banking hours on the morrow of their quarrel; he had itched to have the money in his fingers when he had given him his bitter promise, and he had risen the next morning with his pride engaged to its last crazy and obstinate fibre in the resolve to keep the letter of that promise. He had kept it.

He turned to his packing once more, with a curse for Jasper on his lips. In the little space of a week he had lost all that made life worth while, and of all this devilish fatality of loss Jasper was the origin. The ruinous righting of himself which, in its endless ramifications, had now pursued him to the last covert of his happiness—whom else had he to thank for it but Jasper? Through him he had been brought to the madness which separated him from Margaret; through him he had just parted with Philip as a stranger; through him, worst of all, he had laid himself open to the unbearable reproach, from which he had just freed himself with Philip at a cost of which he preferred not to think. He saw all that had happened since the moment he had opened Jasper's letter as one piece of wretchedness, wrong-doing and shame, and of every inch of it he saw Jasper as the author. He longed, in the fury that seized him at the thought, to lay his hand on his throat, and crush out the life he had given him.

But his helpless rage against Jasper and Philip ended always in a remorseful thought. In the bitterest pain he suffered through their falsity it was a negative mitigation of his grief to know that he had not himself to blame. But as to Margaret it was his shame and torment to know that his own act had lost her to him. In this blackest hour of his life he knew that, but for himself, she might have been by. The single happiness which might have remained to help him to turn his eyes patiently towards the future had been done to death by his own folly. He cursed himself.

She would never look at him again. He knew that. He should be ashamed if she did. He would not have ventured to lift his eyes to her face if they had met in the street; yet he longed for her presence at this moment as never before. He would have gone half round the world for a touch of her hand; and he had cast away the right to take it as any stranger might.

"Fool! fool!" he roared to the unanswering air, as he paced the room. He flung his arms aloft in the last abasement of his misery.

His arms relaxed. He sank into the chair. Tears smarted in his eyes.

Margaret, when she stole into the room five minutes later, found him so.

CHAPTER X.

"YES," said Beatrice to her husband, a week after this—she repeated it because, after all, perhaps she was not quite sure of it—"it was the very best thing she could have done!"

This thought about Margaret's impulsive flight to Deed and her marriage had been reached by a circuitous route; but she clung to it now. When Margaret had come down stairs with her bag packed, after her ride with Ernfield, and had asked to have her trunk sent after her to the station, Beatrice had not discredited herself by a question. She divined, in the moment of pause which she suffered to elapse before she spoke, just what had happened, and all the feeling that was making a tumult in Margaret's breast at the moment, and casting her into Deed's arms; and after an awful moment of reflection, in which she reconciled herself to the odious surrender which Margaret was making, and taught herself to like it, and then to delight in it—particularly to delight in it as the act of Margaret—she fell upon her neck. She said it was the best, the wisest, the most womanly, uncharacteristic, human, every-day thing that Margaret had ever done, and that she deserved a triple kiss of farewell and approval.

She had her qualms when she had gone. Her jealousy for the integrity of the unassailable, the righteous position which Margaret had maintained since the event which would have crushed another woman returned upon her with a rush; and it suddenly seemed wholly wrong—what she had done.

It had all been a burning matter with Beatrice since it had happened.   She had felt more than she could ever say about it.   If she had said everything she thought she would have said that a man who could do what Deed had done deserved forgiveness at no woman's hands.   Of course any woman would forgive him, if she loved him; but that was another matter.   If he was to be forgiven, however, surely he should come suing for pardon on his knees.   In this light it became something perilously like a point of honour, involving the whole sex, that Margaret should not be the first to seek a reconciliation.

Beatrice simply could not bear to think that, without any merit or motion on his part, he should win back a happiness which he had not deserved.   But she saw that, after all, this did not count.   If women went into the question of men's deserts, where would they bring up?   It was the wrong way of approaching the question altogether.   The right way was one which she explained to her husband, who smiled at her over his lifted coffee cup—they were at breakfast—when she made known to him the conclusion at which she had finally arrived about Margaret.

"How is it the best thing she could have done?" he demanded.   "She did n't do it on your advice, Trix," he said with a twinkling eye.

"I don't care," returned Beatrice valiantly.   "She did right, if there was any right left to do in such a case. It was the womanly thing to have done."

"Yes," owned Vertner, "it was the weak thing."

"To be sure," assented Beatrice, accepting this version of her meaning courageously, "and that's its strong point." Vertner laughed.   "No, but I mean it," persisted his wife.

" In the dreadful situations women are always getting into, since they took to masterfulness and self-sufficiency, there's just one way out that's sure to be right ; and that's the weak way."

" When in doubt throw away all your trumps."

" When in doubt be a woman. Of course she abandoned her position. She threw away all her advantage. But her advantage was really too great—don't you see? She had to get rid of it. It was a bother. I suppose there is such a thing as being more in the right than you know what to do with. It did n't make her happy, and it must always have kept him from making the advance. I see that now. I used to want him to grovel. But I don't see that it would have done her any real good. It would have been a poor victory at best; and what she has done, if she has done it in the way I suppose she has, would be a triumph."

" Oh, you need n't trouble yourself to mention that when a woman does do the magnanimous, a man is wincing for it somewhere. I believe you."

" Hush, Ned ! You know she acted from the purest motives."

" Nonsense, my dear ! You would n't go and accuse any woman of pure motives, I hope—pure and simple motives. Let us admit that she acted from the purest adulterated motives possible. It's a handsome admission."

Beatrice was silent. She was thinking of something else. " I don't know," she said, after a moment doubtfully, " whether I quite like the mere act of her return to Mr. Deed. But that was inevitable ; and I've always thought it's a mistake that we ought to leave to men to be deterred by the look of an act. Don't you know, Ned? Nothing seems very right, let alone very heroic, when you are doing it. Taking the train, getting to the hotel, finding the number of his room—I'm afraid she found it all hard because it must all have seemed so small. She was doing a fine thing; and there ought to have been some very good music by a concealed orchestra, scenery by the best artists and electric lights. Don't you think so? But when they were in each other's arms and forgiving each other every-thing, and agreeing to forget that they had ever tried to forget each other, or do without each other, are n't you sure that she saw that it was the right thing to have done even if it was the weak thing and the absurd thing, and the—"

"Crawfish thing?" suggested Vertner. "I don't know. You would n't be up to any such game, Trix."

"I should n't have got into the situation originally. But if I had——"

"You would have done me up with a weakness to which Mrs. Deed's was hearty."

"Well, it would have been a different kind. I should have tried to select something that you would understand."

"Thanks. And do you suppose Deed understands?"

"I'm sure he does. No woman would do such a thing for a man who she was not sure would understand. He would understand and would be humbled into the dust by it."

"And you picture her spending the years to come con-soling him for the humiliation her brilliant weakness has caused—dusting him off?"

"I picture them both as very happy," returned Beatrice with dignity. Her husband laughed.

When Vertner came home to their one o'clock dinner, she perceived by the look on his face that he had heard something which he did not mean to tell her.

"What makes you like this business, Trix?" he asked her abruptly, as if they had not discussed the question.

"Don't you?" she asked, with quick suspicion. Like

a good wife, she kept a rational scorn for her husband's ideas about certain things—the sort of things which only women understood ; but she had a respect for his perceptions about character—as Vertner said, he lived "by sizing people up," and could n't afford to make mistakes—and, at the moment, she had a still greater respect for his news.

"I like my bread and butter better," said Vertner noncommittally, biting delicately at a mushroom.

It was one of the peculiarities of the Vertner household that their table, in the face of every sort of obstacle, maintained an almost Eastern decency and good cheer. As Vertner told Beatrice, they "would have fresh artichokes if they had to buy up all the canned goods in Maverick to find 'em." In a country where every one lived by grace of the tin can, the Vertners did not manage their good table without the use of an energy, ardour and inventive skill which would have gone a long way in felling the forests of a hardier sort of pioneering. Vertner did not leave it all to his wife ; he had studied household providing since his marriage, as he studied a number of other unrelated and unexpected things. In most of the other things he, more or less remotely, "saw a dollar ; " but in this he satisfied an instinct for propriety, for excellence, for "having things right," as he called it, which did not follow him always into other departments.

"Oh, Ned, do let us have *something* free from your wretched mighty dollar." There was the weariness in her tone which implies an old and hopeless subject between man and wife. "What can there be in Margaret's marriage to affect the price of corner lots ? "

She would not have been the loyal wife to him she was if, in accepting him, she had not accepted, without premeditation, the larger half of his theories. But even when she talked unconsciously in the too alluring, too natural slang, which was so native to the life he led, and either so shockingly or so admirably expressive of it (she was not always sure which), she was sorrowfully conscious of her reserves. She might easily have nagged him with them, but not merely her good sense, but a feeling of obligation to his honesty in having told her as much of his way of life as a man can convey to the woman who has not yet married him, withheld her. She could not say that she had not been warned. Yet, in her young girl's ideals there had never been any arrangement made for trimming her life by the market for her husband's new scheme. There was always a new scheme in the Vertner household, and they had it for breakfast, dinner, and supper.

"Corner-lots are all right," said Vertner. "The trouble is deeper down. Deed has left me with a flooded mine on my hands. If he had stayed where he was, I could have talked him into that pumping machinery."

"Then I'm glad he did n't. You have enough mines, Ned," said she. It was the kind of inapposite wisdom which does not torment a man less for being based upon a feeling to which he partly assents, and not at all on the facts which he knows contradict it.

"Have I? I sha'n't have enough mines, my dear, until one of them is a money-maker. I've got too many holes in the ground; but I'm mighty short of mines. This one I'm working with Deed—or should be if I was—has a vein in sight that—." He went on to tell her the seductive story of the assay, and of the wealth at their feet to which she had listened in the case of a dozen other mines. She knew how each of these other mines had turned out, and he knew; but there is a tameless sublimity of faith known to the man who has once owned a mine and to the man's family, which acknowledges no past and is as gaily independent of experience as the clouds that forage the air for the other clouds in which they lose themselves.

" But where has Mr. Deed gone ? " asked Beatrice at the end of his recital, as enthusiastic now as her husband.

" How should I know ? A man does n't give away the itinerary of his wedding journey from the steps of the County Court House. Besides in this case there was n't time. I don't see but they were married by a dynamo. Philip and I were both in the hotel office. He had just had his final row with his father. They had given each other that full material for the understanding of each other's character so valuable in family rows the night before ; and this was rather quiet—not actually, but by comparison. Deed paid Philip some money that he did n't want, that he hated and abhorred, and which he straightway took to the First National and deposited to his father's credit. Those being the facts, Deed naturally supposed Philip was hankering for it, that he was basely longing for it at any cost to him, and that he was suspecting him of having tried to do him out of it : a thoroughly good misunderstanding like that (without a fact in sight) is just the basis for a gorgeous family row. You know Deed's temper. It's like Barnum's rarities, the hottest, the most ungovernable, the most totally unreasonable temper ever seen in captivity. It's to his credit that he does keep it in captivity most of the time, so that you might think his disposition a good sort. But when it blazes——look out ! That's all. It was on the blaze this time ; and when you remember that Philip himself has n't the most—well, not the most angelic. . . . you can believe it was a rumpus. Philip refused the money, of course, and obliged his father to insult him to get him to take it. Then they parted for ever ; and an hour afterward, when Philip was just starting up stairs for the reconciliation that follows such fool rows, he stood aside to let his father pass, with a lady on his arm. Deed did n't look at him. The porters put some luggage on a carriage in

waiting, the hotel clerk threw an old shoe after them, and I
went back and inquired at the desk, and found out that
Philip had a new mother. They had been out to St.
George's between the time when Philip came out of the
hotel hot against his father and came to hunt me, and
the time when Phil, like the sensible fellow he is, went
back to make it all up."

"Well, I'm glad they were married in church, anyway,"
said Beatrice, "and the haste would n't make any difference
to Margaret. She would n't care any more what she was
married in than—than a cassowary."

"Yes," said Vertner, wickedly, "that indifference of the
cassowary to an appropriate wedding dress, and that vile
carelessness about orange blossoms is just one of those
facts of natural history that lend a charm to—"

But his wife had finished her dinner, and she came over
and shook him.

He grew serious when she asked him for his news. "It's
not my news, Trix," he said. "You must n't ask me."
He fell into one of the moods of sober thoughtfulness in
which his new schemes were usually imagined, and in which
Beatrice was always careful not to disturb him. It was
not a scheme to-day, she saw, however. His face was
almost sad ; and his musing was apparently often balked by
some thought, at recollection of which he would make a
wry face, and clench his fist.

Vertner's trouble was the practical disappearance of
Deed—or, rather, certain circumstances accompanying his
disappearance known only to Philip and himself. In the
midst of his wretchedness about this miserable business (it
tormented him more than anything that had ever happened
to himself—not only because if he had raised the money in
time it would n't have happened, but because he really liked
Deed, to whom he owed his present position in Colorado)

only one thing consoled him : that they had not yet got hold of it in the town, and so could not be discussing it. What Vertner feared was that it would get into the papers. It had not represented itself as a disappearance to the town, thus far. It merely seemed to the gossip of Maverick that Deed was taking an unusually long wedding journey.

There were, besides, other things still to talk of connected with Deed, and especially other things connected with Margaret and her marriage, from which it is doubtful it the town chatter would really have liked to be called while so much remained unsaid. Margaret's action, as being the most sensational occurrence in what began to be known as "this Deed business" — over-topping even Deed's desertion of her on their wedding day—needed most of the discussion, and it had held the attention of the ladies steadily since her sudden departure for Leadville, and the announcement of the marriage in the Leadville papers of the following day. In that matter they felt that they had been trifled with. If Miss Derwenter had the high strain of forgiveness somewhere about her enabling her to pardon a man who had publicly deserted her on her wedding day, why in the name of nameless things, had n't she found it out earlier? Was it for this that she had flaunted her pre-ference for Doctor Ernfield in the face of the town? And what, pray, did she mean by her actions with that gentleman? If she had really cared for Deed all along, her encourage-ment of Ernfield was simply shameless. The probability was that she had set herself to captivate Ernfield in the hope of breaking her fall; and that, when she found Ernfield obdurate, she had turned to her first lover.

At all events, when the ladies had been put to the trouble of arriving,—after a fortnight's fluttering among other opinions—at the belief that the affair between her and Deed was to be regarded as definitively "off," the necessity of

M

revising this belief was irksome.   The sense of the hard-ship of the situation of public opinion was liberally voiced wherever women met; and occasionally where men met. The ladies usually began with the admission that, so far as Margaret's "carrying-on" with Dr. Ernfield went—it was by this phrase that they alluded to the relation which Margaret had imagined so innocent; it was merciful that she was not in Maverick at this time to hear what was said of it—she could not be blamed.   What the 'ladies objected to was her playing fast and loose, and off and on, as they said.   "She did n't really seem to know *which* she wanted, so far as I can see," said Mrs. McDermott, whose husband dealt in hats on Mesa Street.

"She got to know at the last," suggested one of the ladies grimly, as Dr. Ernfield, on horseback, passed the church in which the ladies were gathered.

"Yes," laughed Mrs. McDermott.   "All of a sudden, as you might say.   No doubt Dr. Ernfield gave her cause."

"Well," exclaimed Mrs. B. Frank Butler, "I'm sure you can't say the poor thing was to blame for turning most any way for refuge just at first, when Mr. Deed deserted her on her wedding day—going off as casual as you please. And I'm not so sure, either, that I blame her for turning the other way for refuge, just at the last.   There was n't really anything left for her but that, if she wanted to marry at all ; and as to her flirting with Dr. Ernfield,—if you call it that, I don't   know what I *would* call it m'self—who can say anything against a woman that ain't past marriageable age, for allowing the attentions of a pleasant and agreeable young man that any one can see is dead in love with her ? "

She lifted her coarsely pretty little head out of the collar of her sealskin sacque at this, bridling ; and it was evi-dent that Mrs. Butler would not have been guilty of a wasteful discretion in such a case.

CHAPTER XI.

"SEE here," said Vertner to Philip, when he met him in Mesa Street in the afternoon, after his talk with Beatrice, (Philip had come down with him from Leadville on the day that the evidence of Deed's marriage had been offered them), "I've been thinking this thing out."

"You have n't thought it out in any shape that's going to wipe out my assininity, Vertner," returned Philip. "I'm at the bottom of this thing, I tell you. You can't get me out from under it. I maddened my father, and if I had had a grain of sense—or had had the sense to use the sixteenth part of a grain that I sometimes have when there's nothing to use it on—I should have seen that I must madden him. Taking Jasper's part at that! Well, the thing *was n't* square. I suppose I had to protest. But think of it's being Jasper! As if I did n't owe him enough!"

"*Now* you 're shouting!" assented Vertner cordially. "With a fellow like Jasper in sight, it's rank extravagance to waste your curses on yourself. And I would n't go messing with this question of responsibility, either. *I* don't believe we were meant to settle that," he asserted with his emphatic nod. Vertner had a turn for philosophy in his odd hours, and a sense of his responsibility to religion, to which, when his wife asked him, he gave proper financial expression. He secretly regarded the clergy as a kind of lame ducks whom it was the duty of men blessed with the capacity for turning a penny to help along. It was only vaguely conceivable, under his theory, that they would be in the business if they had known how to rustle for themselves. " The moment you get to portioning out blame, and saying where this would n't have happened if so and so, and how that would have been all right if what's his name," he went on, "you wind yourself into one of those snarls where the more you wind the more you snarl. The simplest way is the woman's way : scrape all the mud in the affair into one ball and fling it at the person concerned in the business that you like least. And the worst possible way is to be a pig about the sackcloth, and snatch it all for your own wear. Better turn over most of the sackcloth in this little matter to Jasper, I guess. He deserves it, and it won't trouble him. He'll keep it on the shelf in the original package. There's something about that brother of yours, you know, Deed, that simply takes your admiration by the collar. You can't resist his talent ; and it would be a shame to try."

"Oh, I don't try," said Philip, with a lack-lustre face.

He drew Vertner into a doorway out of the confusion of the street, crowded at this hour with the ranchmen and miners who had come into town for the day for supplies, for their mail, or for mining or cattle dickers, or for mere liquid sociability, and had not yet set out on their return. Their freighted burros and saddled ponies pawed the roadway in a long range on either side the street. Sometimes one of the ponies would lift a hoof to the board sidewalk which ran at the level of his knees above the road, and hammer about on the boards until a man would come from a neighbouring saloon and order him to " Whoa there, you——! "

" Well, that's right," said Vertner heartily in response to Philip's negative as they sheltered themselves in the doorway. " If you are a miserable man, and your father an utterly wretched one——if he has seen Jasper play him the lowest trick ingratitude could invent, if he has seen you apparently do the same, and has come within *that* of losing a wife, and now has had to make his wedding journey a flight from justice——"

" Oh, shut up, Vertner ! "

"——An opportunity for parley with the law, then. I don't care what you call it (it's what he thinks it that makes the difference, is n't it ?), if, I say, one of the first families in Lone Creek County has come to this in a week, it's a glorious satisfaction to know that the hand that pulled the strings belongs to a Jim-dandy of a talent. There's something nothing less than bang-up about.——Oh, I say, Phil ! " he exclaimed remorsefully, as his companion turned away. He clapped his hand upon his shoulder. " I don't mean that guff. I thought——" He caught his eye with a look like pleading in his own. " I thought the other view might comfort you a bit. The tragic we have always with us. Expressive of the feelings, but wearing, you know ! "

He blundered on, until Philip stopped him with, " Oh I know, Vertner. Don't think I don't understand that you've been my best friend in all this, and are sticking by me like the brick you are. Whatever rot I may talk, don't forget that. And when we find my father——"

" Which will be the day after to-morrow," interrupted Vertner cheerfully.

" What ? Have you heard ? "

Vertner rolled his lips over the cigar in his mouth ambiguously. " Well, there is a sort of clue. But I suppose I have to own that I 'm cribbing the date from the general stock of hopefulness. We'll find him, though, wherever he is gone."

" Find him ? Well, if I thought we should n't !——"

Philip set his teeth in a manner peculiar to him, which Vertner had learned to respect. When it had been a question in Chili of throwing a bridge across a mountain gorge and there had been a call for a volunteer to take the first line across, he remembered that Philip had said quietly, " I'll do it," with that tightening of the muscles of the jaw.

" I suppose he *is* suffering," said Vertner meditatively. " And it's so utterly useless."

" Suffering ?   A man who never stained his name with so much as the shadow of wrong; a man whom all the State trusts.   Think what he will be supposing that he has done. When I think of that, and think that I am responsible for the thing——! "

" Oh, confound your responsibility ! " exclaimed Vertner. " Did n't I say I'd get that money for you ?   Did n't I lead you to rely on me for it ? "

" Stuff ! "

" And did I get it ? "

" Yes."

" Did I get it in time to do any good ? "

" No, but—— "

" Well, then ! " said Vertner conclusively.

This money, which had come too late was one of the collateral misfortunes for which Philip blamed himself most severely in the trouble with his father.   He knew that Vertner, in the failure of all other chances, had humiliated himself before a man who he had been sure from the beginning would lend him the amount if he would consent to ask him ; and so had obtained it at a price he would not have paid willingly for any personal good.   The act, useless as it proved in the event, bound him to Vertner, Philip felt, by a peculiar tie.   He had always known him for a good fellow ; he had not supposed him quite as good a fellow as all that.   He knew what it was himself to borrow money where it was lent grudgingly. Some people were great duffers about money, he thought.

Of course neither Philip nor Vertner was in a position to know of the intention with which Deed had pledged the stock at the bank in Leadville; but they had been rightly sure (at first) that he must have gone away with the expectation of finding money elsewhere, and returning to redeem the securities before a question could arise. They had guessed so much as this, but as the weeks passed and he did not return, they were forced to believe that other resources (if he had really gone to seek them,) had failed him; and that, recognizing that he could not come back, he had at least not taken pains to make his whereabouts known.

"I should n't care that we could n't come at him," said Philip, "if we could only let him know."

" Yes, after the pains you took to explain to that receiving teller that your father had asked you to step around and redeem that stock for him, and the pretty way you manœuvred the return of the actual stock itself to Deed's tin box in the bank, where the co-trustee can find it any day he has an unnatural longing for the sight, and after the way you deposited the other $25,000 to your father's private account, it's a pity to have him glooming around in some Canadian watering-place, taking himself for an absconding trustee."

"See here, Vertner——" began Philip hotly.

" Oh well!" cried off Vertner.   " That is n't the only pity. What gives me a pain is to have to think that we went and wasted a good joke on that bank teller."

" What joke?" asked Philip impatiently.

" The joke of paying back into his old bank the same money your father had just borrowed from it."   He quizzed Philip's serious face with his audacious smile.

CHAPTER XII.

It had been Vertner's thought—mixed, like many of his thoughts, of kindly intention and an eye to business—to ask Philip and Cutter to take charge of the "Snow Find." As Vertner said, it would "bear a little more finding, and they were the men to do it." Beatrice had expressed herself freely about the double meaning which this last clause wore in her husband's mind without shaking him from his pur-pose. He said it was really one of the best mines in the State : that it would be another "Iron Silver" if you gave it time—and money. The money he hoped Cutter would get from his father, after a while. Cutter's father was not always rich, he knew ; but he often was. It was the inter-mittent stockbroker way. And Cutter, as he worked the mine for himself, would soon have the best of all possible evidence of its magnificent promise. Vertner had visions of fetching the father out in a special car to see the "Snow Find" for himself, if it came to that. The thing was a bonanza. Vertner even began, in the rosy dreams which he allowed to curl up out of the accomplished fact of the installation of the two young men in charge of the mine, to see the making of a man of business in Cutter. Even Cutter laughed at this, and Philip roared ; but Vertner said he knew what he was about—which was strictly true ; and he proved himself in earnest about working the mine by ad-vancing Philip a month's salary, when he asked for it.

The creditors at Piñon, whom Philip had been unable to silence, as he had hoped, with his father's aid, were growing impudent about the debts they had urged him to contract with servility; and money was a necessity. He sent all that he could spare out of the salary to his creditors, after lending Sandy Dikes $5, losing $25 on a horse-race at Pueblo, for which Cutter had given him a tip, and paying his share in a little monthly pension which he had got half a dozen others at Piñon to join him in arranging for Doulton. (Doulton's claim had caved in on him, and there was to be an amputation : they were paying the pension until Mrs. Doulton could get along on the profits of the saloon she had opened since the accident.) There was also a book for which he had heard Miss Maurice express a wish; and when the bill for it came from Denver, it was higher than he had expected. He told Vertner after the first week that he would have to raise his salary; and Vertner, who was generous and understood, and who was shrewd and remembered Cutter, yielded readily enough.

He offered to raise Cutter's salary also, but Cutter said he should want to get out of the country just as badly, if he had $25 more a month as he should without it ; he added that he was n't worth what he was getting, which he did not believe. He thought himself a good sort of mining engineer, now ; and if his present wisdom on the subject of mining were matched against the ignorance he had brought to Colorado in a Pullman, there was something in this estimate of himself.

The "Snow Find" was the mine which Deed had left on Vertner's hands, full of water ; and until he could find the money to purchase machinery to pump the water out, he had determined to bend his energies—or rather to let Philip and Cutter bend their energies—to working a new lead, away from the water. The new lead was actually a productive one when Philip and Cutter began upon it ; and they were now taking out ore which paid fairly.

When Beatrice questioned his motives, now, Vertner unscrupulously silenced her with the magnanimous half of them. She could not deny, when it was put to her with Vertner's cogency of statement, that Philip had been miserable, restless and tormented ; running off on every fresh clue to the end of the State, (at ten cents a mile—a subject for legislation, if there was one, Vertner said), and coming back weary, disheartened and discouraged. She admitted that an occupation which would give him an interest, and prevent him from brooding upon this business of his father's disappearance was a praiseworthy idea; and she praised Vertner for it, when she was not condemning him for including Cutter in the matter.

" And do you suppose Philip would have gone up there into the hills without him ? " Vertner asked securely. " A cabin in the hills, strictly by yourself, would cure anyone of the blues. You ought to prescribe for *all* the misery, Trix. Confining yourself to Philip is a limitation of talent."

" I suppose he does feel that he is doing the best thing he could do, until his father is found, in working at this mine for him," she admitted irrelevantly, in the need of admitting something. " And if it *should* happen that it turns out as rich as you expect, Ned, why what a splendid thing it will be for him to be able to turn it over to his father on his return, and say——"

" I don't think he'll have to say much. Deed will be glad enough of anything he can raise in the shape of money, by the time he gets back, unless I'm a particularly bad guesser."

" Yes; but he wouldn't take it from Philip—not after what has passed between them ; not after his casting him off like that, and vowing that he would never see him again. You said that yourself, Ned."

"Yes," assented Vertner, yawning,—it was the end of the evening, and he had finished his Denver newspaper, and was stretched cosily in his deep chair before the fire—" I said that he said it. But Deed's vows are n't always ' good until used,' you know. The very passion he expends in making them seems to have a tendency to wear them out early."

" I don't think this one will wear out. What he thought Philip had done was too bad. It had the touch of ingratitude about it that no one can forgive in any wrong. I know I could n't. And I think Philip is doing just the right thing. It will show his father——"

" That he underrated that mine ? " quizzed Vertner with a laugh, as he rose lazily, in preparation for bed. " It will, it will, my dear ! That is, it will if Cutter senior is the man I take him for."

" Ned ! "

Vertner smiled the smile of satisfied sophistication at her through his half-closed eyes, as he stretched his arms in a final yawn. " Come ! " he said. " Are you ever going to bed ? "

PHILIP was glad of the work Vertner offered him at the "Snow Find" because he needed money—he always needed money, and the search for his father was an added channel of expenditure now, and a further hindrance to the payment of his debts at Piñon—but he liked, besides, to feel that his work was doing something more for him than earning the salary Vertner was giving him. It was pleasant to feel that each bucketful of ore that he saw lifted out of the "Snow Find" was of direct advantage to his father. Until he could find him the next best thing was to be doing something for him. And meanwhile he spent a large part of his salary in following up clues of Deed. They all turned out alike ; after an absence of a day or two he would return with downcast face, and resume work at the mine silently ; and Cutter could not find heart to question him. Even Vertner's light spirit would sometimes droop before their repeated failures ; though he always waked the following morning with a fresh idea, which Philip followed out or pooh-poohed, as it happened, but which no longer excited any buoyancy in him. It was maddening to think that his father was making himself unhappy somewhere for the absurdly simple reason that they did not know his address.

The habit of seeing a great deal of Dorothy, and thinking much of her when he was not with her, went along curiously with his unhappiness about his father. He could not talk to her of his father's disappearance, of course, but to see her was to forget his trouble, and he and Cutter both found time from their duties at the "Snow Find," though they could not go together, to ride with her. It sometimes happened that Philip and Dorothy rode alone ; but it usually fell out that Dick Messiter and Beatrice were of the party. Beatrice was very fond of riding ; and Vertner had been buying her a horse lately with the profits of a little "flyer" in a Leadville mining stock.

Dorothy and Beatrice became fast friends in the intimacy of these rides ; and Philip, though he imagined, alternately, furtherances and failures in Dorothy's kindness for him day by day, was really in the unvarying enjoyment of the type of good-will a woman sometimes gives to a man whom she trusts. All their relation took its colour from those days in the cave, during which they had learned to know each other ; and this should have satisfied Philip, for the moment. Perhaps it might have ; but he was obliged to remember that Messiter had shared those days as well ;

and that, with him, they had succeeded many earlier days, the quality of which it was easy to imagine. It seemed impossible that there had been a time, before the snow had brought them acquainted, when he had not known Dorothy, whose existence now was of the fibre of his own life. But such a time had been, and Messiter had plainly been master of its opportunities. He saw him too clearly for the good fellow he was to believe anything else; indeed he liked him too well to believe anything else.

Messiter, who still remained, stimulating an echo of his early usefulness in settling the Maurices' house by inventing things to do for Dorothy, would have smiled sadly at this account of his favour with her. He would have said that for those who liked the unafraid, untroubled liking she showed him, it would probably be the sort of thing they liked. Some persons might enjoy the privilege of gazing into those gay, candid, tender, thoughtful eyes,—the eyes which were all these by turns to him, but, in his presence, never shy, nor downcast, nor in any kind of happy difficulties. But, for his part, he must have professed that the absence of all hesitations, all embarrassments, had its gloomy side. It was the kind of relation, he knew, which young men and young women were always pretending to themselves and to each other was their ideal of all that was blessed and comfortable. Had he not gammoned young girls with just such talk on the rocks at Mount Desert, at nineteen? But he found nothing in the situation, as it presented itself, either blessed or comfortable, though he stayed on.

In spite of these lover's doubts, it would be a mistake to suppose that this was not a happy time for all of them. It was clouded for Philip by the continued fruitlessness of all efforts to find his father, as well as by the fluctuations of Dorothy's feeling toward him, which he was partly conscious of spinning out of his fancy, but constantly ready to credit afresh. Yet he was happy enough to fear a change—to look forward to Jasper's return with a fierce repression of his imagination. How would he and Dorothy meet? What was their present relation? Where would they take up the thread? Was there a tolerable relation toward Dorothy for him, if Jasper still existed for her? These were the questions which he refused to ask himself. They were hints at the threshold of a whole torturing region of speculation, which to enter was to invite useless misery and the need for an immediate decision. Philip hated unpleasant thoughts, and detested immediate decisions; if the banks a mile ahead concealed the enemy, why there was still the mile! It might never be completed for one thing. If it were, one would find something to do when the time came. It was partly a reasonable confidence in himself, but chiefly a constitutional unwillingness to face disagreeable facts, which caused him meanwhile to lounge at the stern of the boat, finding the river water smooth and lulling under his hand.

Messiter's sunny temper, not being for clouds of any kind, he found what happiness he could in the immediate and agreeable fact that he was permitted to be constantly by Dorothy's side; while Beatrice, having settled Margaret's trouble to her satisfaction, had crossed her off her list, so to say, and, for the moment, concerned herself only intermittently about her (of course she knew nothing of her husband's concern)—awaiting calmly her return to Maverick, flushed with her bridal happiness, and filled with new ideas about things. She fancied her greatly changed; it would only show how marriage was the one thing for all women—even for those who did not seem at all to have been intended for its blessings. She fancied Margaret's severity, her primness, her "niceness" about certain matters, as smoothed and softened into the real niceness, against which not even Ned could say anything.

Dorothy had begun to plan for the future of her father
and herself in Maverick. The people of the church had
been charmed by his first sermon, and, as a matter of fact,
it was a capital sermon. Their liking for it suggested to a
number of minds at once that Maurice should be called to
the vacant pulpit of St. John's in the Wilderness. As
Beatrice said, it was a long time since they had had a
regular service, but the lapse had not been due to the unwillingness of the congregation to support a clergyman. It
was rather that there were varying ideals in the congregation.
But Maurice fitted, in a degree, into all these expectations and
wishes. He was a widower, he was not young, his graceful,
good-humoured, flattering manner commended him to every-
one, and especially to those who sought a successful parish
visitor; he was a High Churchman, holding with dignity to
his ritual, but careful to avoid grounds of offence, and he
preached undeniably good sermons. He was, besides, a
trained and enthusiastic musician : on his first trial-Sunday
the lady who played the organ fell ill at the last moment,
and until a substitute discovered herself, after the second
lesson, he himself accompanied the choir he had rehearsed
during the week.

It had ended, after some negotiation, in his being sum-
moned. Maurice had told them frankly that he could not
refer them to his last parish, giving them his own version of
the occurrence which had caused him to leave Laughing
Valley City ; but when the vestry had heard favourably
about him from the Dakota parish to which he referred
them, and had definitely offered him the post, he told
them, with some inward trembling—for his resources were
of the slightest, and if this opportunity should fail him he
did not know where he should turn—that if he was to
remain with them they must grant him a higher salary.
The vestry was reluctant ; he firm. It ended in their ad-

vancing the salary $100. It was more than they had ever
paid before, they said ; but perhaps they had never had so
good a clergyman. Maurice smiled, and did not attempt
to deny it. He did not believe there were many men of
his sort to be had for $800 a year.

He was now making ready to preach certain sermons
selected by Dorothy from a considerable collection sent over
the mountains on a burro by the ladies at Laughing Valley
City ; and was occupied in going about making the acquaintance of his new flock.

His portly, yet shapely and well-carried figure, his round,
rubicund, smiling, clean-shaven clerical face, his fortunate
voice, his admirable manner soon began to be familiar in
Maverick. It pleased Dorothy to see how popular her
father had already become. She looked forward with pleasure
to remaining a long time in Maverick. Perhaps he would set
about raising funds to build a more permanent church. She
remembered that the parish in which her father had remained
longest was one in which he had built a new church. But
there seemed no elements of discord here, none of the
foolish, tiresome people who had made trouble in other
parishes. Perhaps they should remain for ever. Perhaps
—it was a new country, a largeish town, there was an opportunity—perhaps he might one day be Bishop of the diocese.

Dorothy's plans were made with a pencil and a little
memorandum pad, from which she tore a number of sheets
without finding a comfortable relation between her father's
salary, (after adding their trifling income to it), and the
prices prevailing in Maverick for rent, food and clothing.
She avoided troubling her father about practical questions
when she could ; but, before they left the hotel, where they
had been staying since their arrival, she felt that she must
set the result of her calculations before him. When she
attacked him on the subject at breakfast one morning, he
smiled cheerfully.

"Oh, we shall get along, I think! We shall get along!" He rubbed his large, carefully kept hands together, after spreading his napkin over his ample form. "Have you included your mother's legacy in your calculations, Dorothy?"

"Oh yes! But with your salary it only makes a little over a thousand dollars. I'm afraid we ought not to have taken so expensive a house."

His smile revealed the even glitter of perfect teeth beneath a moustache which had been criticised as jaunty for a clergyman. "Why, my dear, we could n't live in an unplastered house, could we?"

His smile and tone made it seem preposterous, but Dorothy said, doubtfully, "I don't know. Perhaps when we found that we could get nothing plastered under $400 we ought to have felt that we must take one of the others."

"Oh, no! Why even at Laughing Valley we had a plastered house. Surely it does n't seem an unreasonable ambition,—a plastered house. And even if it were, depend upon it, the clergy get what they insist on. A man's needs are measured by the account he gives of them; and, in turn, he is measured by his needs. If a clergyman shows himself content with a hovel he not only won't get a decent dwelling; but when it comes to a question of some other need, he will be thought as capable of doing without whatever it may be that he wants as he showed himself capable of doing without the house. I have always found that I got what I wanted by taking the proper stand. I have found that people of a certain class respect the inability of a gentleman to do without things which they have never felt the need of."

"But, father—" protested Dorothy, and paused. She had been about to ask if the price of having all that one wanted might not be that some one else should have less

than he wanted—less than his own, perhaps. She was glad
not to have said it : an observation which seems true in
the largest bearing may be quite false to the little fact which
suggests it, and which one is tempted to try by it. Her
father was right of course. He was always right.

Philip and Cutter, in their cabin at the "Snow Find"
often discussed Maurice. They agreed that it was a pity
that Dorothy should have such a man for a father, or that
he should happen to have such a daughter ; but they avoided
the discussion of Dorothy herself by tacit agreement. As
Philip drew on his town-going boots for the fifth time during
a single week, however, and began to rummage in his chest for
a white shirt, Cutter made no further effort to contain himself.

"You 're not going in for a boiled shirt !" he exclaimed
as Philip exchanged the loose flannel of the West for the
Eastern affectation. Cutter—in pursuit of his loyalty to
the civilization which had produced him—had never disused it ; though the washerwoman at Piñon had forced him
to go to a Chinaman by returning the first white shirts he
sent her, contemptuously rough-dried. "Oh, I say ! This
is too much ! Do you know, I've had an idea once or twice
lately, Deed, that you are rather hard hit. Tremendously
nice girl !" he murmured to the cigarette he was lighting.

"Oh, yes, she's nice enough, if that's all," owned Philip,
rummaging in his army chest for some collars, which he
fished out at last, limp and yellow from their confinement of
a year. "Do you suppose there are any memories in New
York long enough to recall the time when this was the
pre-eminently pre-eminent shape in collars?" he asked,
holding up a bundle of them.

"Stocks may have come in again, for all I know," answered
Cutter. "Ask somebody more in the way of that sort of
information, Crusoe, my boy, than Man Friday. But, I
say, Deed : she *is* nice !"

"I think I remember agreeing with you in that observation," said Philip. "But I'll sign a treaty with you to regard her as nice, if that does n't satisfy you : I'll give bonds, I'll mortgage myself as security for her niceness, if you like. Come !" The eagerness of his manner was a trifle out of key with this sort of easiness ; but Cutter forbore his jibes.

"I say : I'm awfully glad for you, old man !" He had got himself on his feet ; and wrung Philip's hand in silence.

"Are you? What a romantic dog you are, Cutter ! It's uncommonly good of you." He turned to the reconsideration of the collars. "I wish I saw any cause to be glad."

"Don't you? Then it's because you are infernally ungrateful. I'm bound to say that I do."

"Yes," said Philip with a weary smile ; "it is you, I believe, who looks for big things from the ' Little Cipher.' You 've got such a lot of faith, Cutter. It makes a cheerful companion of you. But you are hideously unreliable, you know. You'll be wanting to convince me that it is the honourable obligation of a beggar to go and propose marriage to somebody or other, next. Jasper has furnished me with just the sort of situation for you to try your abominable cheerfulness on. Turn it on, Cutter. Rub up your lamp and get to work. I'm ready for any lie, if there's hope in it."

" Pshaw ! There are paying properties in the world besides the ranch your brother has swindled you out of your share in. You forget the ' Pay Ore.' "

"Oh, no I don't—not when I'm in high spirits, and don't need what hope there is in it. But a man can't live on a hope like that, Cutter ; and if he could, a woman could n't and no man could ask her to. And if he could ask her, he could n't ask her father to let her." Cutter smiled at this

N 2

reference to Maurice, who was a kind of joke between them ; and Philip smiled with him, ruefully.   The idea of Maurice allowing his daughter to marry any one but a rich man struck them both as humorous ; yet Cutter had to say, to console Philip, rather than because he believed it—

"I don't know.   There's some good in the old fraud, after all."

"Oh, don't go turning your cheerfulness on Maurice ! You have n't got the candle power."

" You might let me illuminate a little, and try," laughed Cutter.   " But it *is* a sombre subject, that's a fact.   You 'll have to elope."

"Shut up, Cutter ! "

" Well, then you'll have to wait for his consent.   Put it either way.   I'm only trying to please you ; and a dash of grey in the groom's hair is n't so bad, if you come to that."

" Oh, drop it ! Your despair is worse than your cheer- fulness."

" Well, it does seem to fit the facts of the case a little closer."

" Oh, you 're right !   You 're right.   It does ; and I know it when I'm not with her ; but when I am—— Damn it, man, I love her ! I *can't* lose her ! "

" Now you 're talking sense."

" Am I ?   It strikes me as a good deal more like the other thing.   No ; I always come around to a clear sight of the situation—— Jasper has fixed me out.   It's as if he knew I must meet and care for the girl he once —— Bah ! " Philip turned on his heel.

"See here !   Have you given up your faith in the 'Pay Ore'? "

" No ;" growled Philip, "and I have n't given up my faith in the coming Brotherhood of Man, but I would n't ask a girl to go to housekeeping on it."

This was no reason why they should not thresh out together again, for the hundredth time, the actual grounds for faith in the future of the "Pay Ore": they said together again, and managed to say it without smiling, that the ore-bearing vein was there; that they were taking out good mineral all around the "Pay Ore" on the Hill; that it was a question of finding out which way the vein dipped, and a question of the capital and patience necessary to reach it; and they agreed that Ryan had the capital and the patience. Philip ridiculed Cutter's faith, as he always did when they spoke of this subject together; but it was a way of playing his own hope, and they both knew it. Philip hoped rather easily; and most easily as a refuge from despair. He liked to be comfortable; and despair was uncomfortable. If he chose skepticism for an outward seeming, sometimes, it was by way of hedging: one's hopes did not always come off, and a sophisticated doubt looked better on the record, afterward.

"You'll live to see Ryan with his pick in that vein, yet," Cutter concluded. He had got to the end of his mining engineer's argument, and was indulging his gift of amiable prophesy.

"Shall I?" retorted Philip. "It will be a pretty tableau. But I don't know why we trouble ourselves about it, unless it is to avoid the point."

"What *is* the point?" He looked steadily at Philip who smiled without amusement. "Oh!" he exclaimed with intelligence. "Well, yes——" Cutter smiled. "But don't you think——?"

"No sir: I don't."

Cutter bent forward. "Why, what's the trouble?"

"Usual trouble. Another fellow."

"What? You think she cares for that——?"

"That gentleman, as you were about to call him, Mr.

Cutter, is a great sight too good for any shoe-string tying of mine."

"Oh, look here——Well, Messiter is a good fellow. I admit it. But what of it? Abstract considerations of that sort don't hold in a case of this kind."

"Oh, I beg your pardon, Cutter," exclaimed Philip, as he buttoned one of the collars about his neck. "I forgot that you were an expert in these things. Well, what does hold? Out with it! Let's have the latest! Don't put me off with any of your mouldy, out-of-date decisions. Give me the brand-newest opinion there is—something that can't be reversed before I can get her assent to it—Court of Appeals, preferably."

Cutter pulled at his moustache, thoughtfully; and blew some smoke in Philip's direction. "Well, *you* might hold, for one thing. I have a notion she likes you."

"Thanks," returned Philip drily. "I believe the worst of us have a kindness for our coolies, our dragomen, our slaves. *Would n't* a woman like a man who made a profession, a calling, a vocation of her; who revered her boots; whose idea of happiness was being stepped on by them; who spent his nights in dreaming new ways to be an ass for her sake, and his days in carrying out his dreams? *Would n't* she? I should hope so."

"You *have* been going it a little strong with her, this last fortnight. I suppose she has been rather enjoying the spectacle."

"See here, Cutter," said Philip hotly, "if you think Miss Maurice capable of torturing a man for her amusement merely, you never were more mistaken in your life. She's not that sort. The fineness, the dignity, the genuineness and truth of that girl, Cutter——Oh, the devil!"

Cutter was laughing.

THE servant at the Maurices' cottage said that Miss Maurice was in the parlour. The house on which Dorothy and her father had finally fixed was the usual frame shell of the newer towns of the West. There were better houses in Maverick—the Vertners lived, by comparison, in a mansion —but there were cruder buildings too : log cabins chinked with mortar, and houses constructed out of disused packing boxes, and roofed with canvas. On the ground floor, besides the kitchen and the dining-room, there was only the pleasant little room at the front of the house ; and it was this that the maid-servant called a "parlour." It was, in fact, Dorothy's sitting-room and sewing-room ; though Maurice spoke of it as their drawing-room. As Philip turned the knob on the door of this room, he felt a hand upon it on the other side, and releasing his own grasp, the door opened. Jasper stood before him in the act of farewell to Dorothy. He lifted his head, and seeing Philip in the doorway, stretched out his hand to him with his courtly smile. Philip, drawing back to let him pass, kept his gaze fixed on his face, looking him in the eye motionlessly, with a black glance of scorn. He would not see the hand. Flushing to his temples, Jasper gave a contemptuous little laugh and walked by him, turning once more to bow to Miss Maurice.

When Philip had got himself through the door and into the room, he went up to Dorothy in a dazed way, and offered her his hand. He thought he perceived a kind of reluctance which she conquered in the imperceptible moment that passed before she took his hand in the frank and hearty clasp, which had been from the beginning one of the little things that he had liked best in her. Then she asked him quickly if he had seen her typewriter.

CHAPTER XIII.

In his first groping, and bitter explanations of it to himself, Philip saw how natural it was that he should find Jasper with her. He had not known of his return; and he must have come this morning, as he was certain that he had not been in Maverick the day before; but being returned, and hearing of her presence in Maverick, what could be more in the course of things than a meeting of old lovers, long separated, in the first hours of Jasper's home-coming? Oh, it was natural enough!

"A typewriter!" he said, in the easy and flowing tones of one who tries to be easy. "I congratulate you. It's a great thing. You will write your father's sermons, now, I suppose."

"I don't know," she said. "Yes, perhaps, if I can learn."

It was, in fact, a longing desire with her,—to write her father's sermons for him at his dictation; he detested the manual labour of writing. But nothing seemed quite so possible and worth while as it had seemed a moment ago.

"Do you know anything about it? Perhaps you can show me," she said to make conversation. She chafed under this difficult exchange: it had never been like this between them, hitherto. They had always talked freely, and naturally; it was one of the things which made this Mr. Deed a pleasant man to get along with she had thought.

He was so straightforward, so simple and direct : he had no
attitude, he never got himself up, he had not even that
man's pose in talking to a woman, which she disliked.
He talked to her, she felt sure, as he might have talked to
a man. He understood things without being told. Men
to whom one had to explain irritated her. And now he
was not going to understand ; and he was defending himself from the natural course of their usual talk with an
artifice.

Was it in fact true, then, that such a thing as a frank
and cordial relation between young men and young women
was an impossibility? She heard Philip saying that he had
once spent a month or two in studying the typewriter, as
she asked this question of herself. It was going to fall in
with one of his young plans for being successful in some
other way than the way his father wished, and had been
dropped when the plan had followed the other plans. She
heard this distantly while she passed in hasty review all
possible and impossible occasions for the scene at the door
and for his constraint. Was the blame hers, in any way,
she asked herself? Or, whosesoever the blame, might it be
her opportunity to reconcile them ? Dorothy's goodness was
always impulsive : the people who did not like the consequences of some of her rash bursts of kind-heartedness,
said that it was absurd. It was true that she was good in
haste, and often repented at leisure ; but she liked better to
stumble and wound herself, as she must, in her rush to help
some one who had fallen, than to suck wise maxims about
prudence in contented inaction. She kept a generous scorn
for the mincing caution of the proverbs. All proverbs were
stingy and selfish, she thought, and taught one to live for
one's self in the handsomest security.

She went to the typewriter and began to finger it with the
gingerly deliberateness of the novice, while he stood above

her looking on, and they exchanged question and answer without much notion on either side of what they were talking about. She was feeling, with a woman's sense of social obligation, that she must do something to keep the affair moving ; while her kindly puzzlement about the little drama at the door went on steadily in her thoughts.

Philip was capable of listening at any time to the taking modulations of her sweet, rich Southern voice, without troubling his head about what she was saying; and it was in this dreamy way that he was listening to her now, thinking also, as if it were a novel thought, how utterly pretty she was. She was dressed in a house gown of black, with the daintiest suggestion of a dark green velvet at the throat, and shoulders, and sleeves ; and the quietness of this effect seemed to exalt the beauty of her fresh colouring, her good, honest, sincere, admirable eyes, her shapely face. How she stared at her typewriting ! He wished she would look about at him. It was two minutes since he had seen her eyes ; the whimsical brown, floating intermittently in their grey depths, would have had time to change or go.

There suddenly seemed nothing further to say, and leaning back from the typewriter she patted her hand upon her dress, and called, "Here, Jack ! " A great Newfoundland dog, which had been lying on the floor by the side of the typewriter leaped up, placing his forepaws in her lap, and wagging his tail. Jack had been given her by Messiter while they were at Laughing Valley City, and it had been one of the pains of her hurried departure that she must leave him behind ; but Messiter had arranged to have him brought over the Pass by careful hands, and it was a week since he had been restored to her. She was extremely fond of him. He plunged his paws in a moment into the keyboard of the typewriter, and Philip dragged him off.

The diversion seemed to restore them to themselves,

for Philip said, more in the tone of their usual talk than anything that had been said since he entered the room, " I did n't know you had a typewriter."

And, glad of the change, Dorothy answered, "I have n't. To really *have* a typewriter I suppose one should know how to use it, if only a very little ; and besides, it does n't belong to me, but to a clergyman, a friend of my father, who left it for me to try. He has gone East on his vacation, and spent a night with us on his way down from Leadville."

" You will like it immensely. You will hate him when he comes to take it back."

She shook her beautiful head, laughing. " I don't know. It makes me—wriggle ! " she said. " I can't bear to pick out the letters. I don't like the noise. And it's all so mechanical, so barbarous ! It's a great convenience, I suppose, and I shall go on with it on papa's account, if I find I can. But I can't see how any one could *like* it ! What is there to like ? "

" Everything ! Let me show you ! "

"Oh, if you do it like that ! " she exclaimed, as he rattled off a number of sentences, in the seat she gave up to him.

" You *must* do it like that ! " he rejoined, without looking up from the key-board over which his fingers twinkled bewilderingly. " You didn't think that you were to go hesitatingly from letter to letter, with a little fearsome pause between each jump, like Eliza in *Uncle Tom's Cabin* escaping across the floating ice, did you ? "

He was feeling much happier now. After all, it had only been a school-girl and boy engagement. He knew that it no longer existed——that it had not existed this four years. Was it likely that——? Pshaw ! Had not Jasper called on the day of his arrival in the place? He had not forgotten. Did he ever forget any purpose ? He brought

himself back to the consideration of the typewriter lesson
with an effort.

She was interested. "You won't mind if I ask questions?" she said, as she consented to try again for herself.
She let her fingers idle over the letters without pressing
their white circles. "Why is n't the alphabet set in order?"

"'The better to puzzle you, my dear,'" quoted Philip,
absently, but enjoying the use of the epithet.

"There is a better reason than that," returned Dorothy.
She laughed, flushing a little at his phrase.

"Yes," he admitted, "you will find it a very good thing,
after you have gone a little farther, to have the most-used
letters nearest your hand. Suppose, now, you put in a fresh
sheet of paper, and try a sentence or two on your own
account."

He inserted the paper, showed her the use of the little
device for separating words, taught her to pull back the
running gear at the top at the warning of the bell, made
plain the means of governing the space between lines; and
then gave her a little lecture on the position of the small
and capital letters, the punctuation marks and numerals.
She listened with serious attention, and, as he bent over to
illustrate his meaning, withdrew herself to leave space for
the play of his arms, while he pressed the letters, or caught
back the sliding rack.

In this close and amiable proximity the constraint between them, of a few moments back, seemed already to
have aged itself into an unhistoried past. She was wondering how this could be the man who had given Jasper
the look at the door which she could not forget; and he
was saying to himself that in all the world there were not
eyes like those he looked down into when she would glance
up suddenly from time to time to ask him a question, or
to give one of her flashing turns to his replies, with that

charming manner of reserved freedom which was constantly a new grace in her.

She became proficient enough at last to write out coherent sentences for herself, and together they found the things she wrote very amusing.

"Suppose you see if you can read what I write from the movement of my fingers, Mr. Deed," she said. "You are not to turn the cylinder up to look; but only to read, if you can, as I go along." She began in a kind of embarrassment, and did not get on as well with the first words as she had in her earlier experiments. But she tried again, in a moment, and completed the sentence with a little air of bravado.

She kept her eyes on the key-board, but as he did not speak she glanced up at him hastily.

"Oh!" exclaimed Philip recalled to himself. "I was to read from your fingers. Well, shall we begin?"

Dorothy laughed nervously. "We have begun," she said. "Did n't you see?"

"Oh, yes, yes!" assented he. "Or no—I was—." It was impossible to say that he had been watching the movement of her fingers and speculating upon the question whether all women had such hands, and why he had never noticed how adorably they were contrived for type-writing. He had got to the point of remembering that he had seen a number of young girls hammering away at type-writers in offices without being moved by the spectacle, when her glance called him back.

"Will you write it again?" he asked. "I will really watch this time."

"Oh, I don't think I could write it again," returned Dorothy quickly.

"Why not? As a punishment for inattention? I suppose I've deserved it," he said.

"No. I don't think I ought."

"It was a real sentence, then. I claim it as a right, in that case. You have made a communication to me, Miss Maurice. You've no right to withhold it. It has passed out of your hands."

"Yes," owned she, with amusement, "that's true, but it did n't pass into your eyes. I offered it to you, and you would n't look. You were engaged."

"Then you *are* punishing me, and that's equally unfair."

"No—no I'm not," she denied doubtfully, "but—" with a whimsical smile that enchanted him——"why it was not discreet, what I wrote." She smiled up at him.

"No?" he asked in pure enjoyment.

"No." And then, in a moment, "You would n't urge me to be *in*-discreet?"

"No, I should n't urge it. I should insist upon it. I do. Come!" he said, and she wondered why she liked his air of domination better than Jasper's, though she did not altogether dislike Jasper's.

"And the demon said unto me, 'Write!'" paraphrased she.

"It was an angel," said Philip.

"Was it?" She bent her hands hesitantly above the key-board. "But you must promise to stay, angel," she said, suddenly arresting herself. She glanced up doubtfully at his face. "No, I won't write it again. It was n't wise; it was n't—nice."

"That settles it, then: I *must* see it!"

"No," repeated Dorothy. "You would n't like it. It was a quite wrong thing to ask." Her fingers hovered above the key-board, meditatively. She suddenly began to pick out the letters.

Philip followed her fingers closely. He read, letter by

letter: "*Why would n't you speak to your brother at the door?*"

He rose abruptly from his stooping position above the machine, colouring painfully.

She looked up, at his impulsive movement, and rose herself. "Oh, what have I done?" she exclaimed at sight of his face. After a miserable pause, "You need n't tell me. It was very wrong of me. I knew it. But it was n't I who asked, Mr. Deed? I would never have asked,—not myself. I thought," she said, gathering her explanations painfully—"or the typewriter thought—it was n't I—it escaped me—that perhaps I could reconcile, bring you togeth—" The words died upon her lips. "It was a foolish thought, I see, and yet," she added, with recovered dignity, "perhaps I had a kind of right to it. Your brother is an old friend"—Philip looked up at this—"and you—you have been very good. We have always felt that we partly owe our lives to you—father and I—since the day of the storm, and—" Philip lifted his hand with an appealing gesture. "Well, there's nothing else to say, except that I'm very sorry. But, oh, Mr. Deed," she cried suddenly, "why won't you make it up with him, whatever it is—and be—be friends? I'm sure he can't have done anything very bad—nothing that could make it right that you should turn from him. He is good,—sometimes he is hard, and he is always masterful: yes—but he is good. You must feel that."

"Oh, yes," said Philip, "I feel that."

She glanced at him doubtfully, as if in question of his tone.

"I'm sure I've every reason to know of his goodness," she said, after a pause, with feeling. "If it hadn't been for that—"

"You would n't have been here to appreciate it with me,

perhaps.   No, I remember that.   It's another of the quiet
things, done without talk or fuss, by which Jasper has put
me in his debt.   I owe him a great deal, Miss Maurice—
more than you know."

Again she hesitated at an indefinable note in his voice;
but she said immediately with her usual openness,

"I suppose an elder brother has always that great advantage,—the advantage of being able to do a great deal
for a younger brother.   It must be very pleasant to him,
and he must always wish, if he is a man like your brother,
to do always a little more, that he may be able to make
you forget his friendly advantage over you by the mere
quantity of his friendliness."

In the midst of his pain and bitterness, Philip could not
help smiling faintly at this, but he said, with less care
about his tone, "Oh, yes! I've never had to complain of
short weight with Jasper.   He does n't do things by halves.
When he does a really friendly thing he heaps the measure
up and runs it over.   I don't always know what to do
with so much magnanimity.   You can't put a landslide in
your pocket, you know, Miss Maurice, and sometimes you
can't even find your manners in time to make your bow."

She could not avoid feeling the sardonic undertone this
time, and she thought she saw, at once, that the cause of
offence between them, whatever it was, was largely due to
Mr. Philip Deed's sensitive, almost nervous pride; and she
thought, too, that she could guess, pretty clearly, from her
knowledge of the two men, something about what would be
the usual situation between them.   She could see how
Philip might detest his brother at times for his very power
of doing him favours.   She knew how that was herself.
She was painfully aware in herself of the strain of meanness, or self-will, or conceit,—she did not know what it
was—that made the kind of generosity which is open-

handed enough to allow another to be generous among the
most difficult kinds of unselfishness and she could understand—yes, she could understand entirely,—how Philip
(whose pride would be less manageable than her own by
the degree in which it was a man's and commanding) would
feel this peculiarly. The very delicacy with which Jasper
would try to conceal a kindness would be an added offence :
the need for delicacy was itself humiliating. She could
imagine how Philip would become angered on provocation
of this sort, and how Jasper would helplessly make the
matter worse—not that there would be any way of making
it better—by his forbearance. It would be the kind of
case in which neither was to blame, and in which each must
blame the other.

Filled with this idea, she said, with a note of sympathy
in her voice that at first bewildered, and then angered
Philip, and finally caused him to laugh a little to himself
at the completeness of her error, "I'm sure we must all
have felt that. It's strange, isn't it, that it should be so hard
to *accept* a kindness as we all find it ? One would think
that the effort connected with a kindness would be all over
when it had been done. It isn't so very easy even to do
it ; but to receive it needs heroism. At least I find it does,
And I can understand how you would feel that way about
your brother, even when you were most grateful to him ;
and you would all the time be divided between a wish to
make him feel how much you appreciated his kindness,
and a wish to box his ears."

"Oh, it's not a *divided* wish !" said Philip, falling in with
her mistake, as the easiest defence that offered ; and at
this they both laughed.

"His ears must be smarting most of the time," said she
as her laugh ended in a smile.

"Why, no ; not all the time," returned Philip unwarily.

o

"You mean—?" she began, still smiling.

"Nothing that I'd better tell you," he said, quickly withdrawing.

"Oh, Mr. Deed," she exclaimed, with an electrical return to soberness, "I see that there is something really serious between you—something that I must n't intrude on. Forgive me! I have been thinking it one of those little disagreements that a word would set right—one of those wretched mistakes where two persons need only to be explained to each other. I see I can't do it; but you can, Mr. Deed."

"What? Explain myself to Jasper?"

"I don't know—Make it right with him, or whatever men call it. Some one has always to play the generous part, don't you think, where there has been—has been a disagreement?"

"No, Miss Maurice, I can't do that." He turned away from her and strode toward the window.

"Oh, that is not like you, Mr. Deed! He would not hesitate, I am sure, in your place."

"In my place?" returned he. She began to stammer a reply; but he said, "Oh, I beg your pardon—my place, in the wrong? No, my brother would not hesitate in my place."

"I did not say that," she put in sorrowfully. She saw that she had implied it.

"It does n't need saying, Miss Maurice. You only recognize a universal fact. There are laws of character, you know, and a planetary orbit is wobbly to them. Everybody who knows us at all would know, without telling, that in any question between us I must be in the wrong."

"And are you in the wrong in this?" she asked, earnestly. "Tell me frankly. I will believe whatever you say. You bewilder me. I don't know what to think. Tell me!" she repeated.

Philip laughed harshly. "You must ask Jasper that."

"I will," she said.

"No, don't, Miss Maurice. Don't on any account! Don't think of such a thing!"

"Ah, he would be more fair!"

"Promise me that you will not say a word of this to Jasper!"

"Tell me yourself, then, Mr. Deed."

Philip took a turn up and down the room. "I can't," he said at last.

"You see what you leave me to think," she said, sadly.

"Nothing good of me," he answered bitterly.

She glanced up at his face. The frankness and genuineness which she had always liked in his look shone through the hurt which possessed him, and gave her confidence to say, looking up to the tall, strong-limbed figure, standing above her, "Do you think it just to your brother to leave him under the imputation of such a silence?"

Philip started. "Jasper?" he said.

"Surely. Your silence implies—it seems to say that your brother is somehow much in the wrong; or else—"

"Or else?" asked Philip steadily.

"I will not say what else. But if that is so it is fair,—it is right that you should tell me." She sat down abruptly, as if not quite certain of herself.

Philip felt, girdingly, the extreme inconvenience attaching to all endeavours to do the fair-minded thing; the impossibility, namely, of explaining with decency.

"In order that you may not be thinking *me* much in the wrong?" he said. "No, Miss Maurice, I couldn't do that." He turned away.

"You are not fair," she said after a moment, with dignity. "I do not know that there is any right or wrong in the matter. I am ignorant of everything but that you would not bow to your brother in my presence. I have put my plea on the score of peacemaking, and if you feel that I have meddled I am rightly served ; but I have a right to ask why you should put a slight on a gentleman whom you meet here as——as "——her voice broke——"as my guest, Mr. Deed."

He came back and stood before her. "You *have* a right to ask that, Miss Maurice, and perhaps I have no right not to answer you. But I can not answer you."

"Then I must think——?"

"That I have done a wrong to Jasper which I am unwilling to repair or own. Yes, Miss Maurice."

"I do not mean that," she said wistfully, and he saw that she was on the verge of tears, yet had to blunder savagely on.

"What else can you mean? There is but the choice. You must believe in Jasper or in me."

"Oh, I knew it!" she cried, as if to herself. "I foresaw it! It was for that that I had to try to make it right between you. I could not bear——" She broke down suddenly.

"You mean that you wished to keep us both for friends. You know now that that is impossible. We are enemies. We cannot have or keep a common friend. Which will you choose?"

The passionate tone of demand roused her. She straightened herself imperceptibly in her seat on the couch, and raised her head, looking up and confronting his flushed face.

"I will answer your question when you have answered mine," she said.

She rose and held out her hand listlessly. Philip took it as formally, and suddenly left the room. His head was down. He felt sick—spiritually sick to his inmost fibre.

CHAPTER XIV.

PHILIP went out and got on his horse, and rode furiously toward the "Snow Find." This was the end, he supposed. And for this, again, he had to thank Jasper. He gnashed his teeth as he set his spur in the pony's flank and swept over the long level stretch by the river, outside the town. He had made a fool of himself again, and, as usual, not in a way in which Jasper would have made a fool of himself. His sense of the unhandsomeness, of the impossibility of telling her of the actual state of the case between them seemed in this open light of the prairie, with the wind blowing in his face, an incredible piece of folly. Why should he consider Jasper? Would he have spared him in the same situation?

He saw at once that this had nothing to do with the matter, and that it was not for Jasper's sake that he had held his tongue. It was for his own : he could n't have gone on living in the body of a man who had told her that. If he had told it he knew very well with what object he would have spoken. He would have done it to malign his rival to her ; (it had come to that between him and Jasper ; he might as well face it), he would have done it to take a sneaking advantage with a woman of an opportunity to spike another man's guns. That would be bad enough with any man for his rival ; but with Jasper it would be a thing which he would never be able to hold up his head after doing. It became too dirty a piece of reprisal to think of. The perception of the im-

possibility of doing anything to Jasper's injury, which he had
urged upon his father, had laid a firm and withholding grip
upon him in the midst of the temptation to tell her everything; and now it reasserted itself as a final motive—as a
thing not to be questioned, or dodged; as a principle to which
he must be faithful, wholly without regard to what it might
cost him. It had cost him indirectly his father's friendship,
already, and had driven his father to the wretched refuge of
flight from an imagined evil; and now it had probably
cost him his own happiness. He cursed Jasper, as he
thought of it, between his teeth.

He was glad to be going to Durango on the morrow to
seek his father; he thought he should remain a week. But
in the event he was back the second day. It had become
a necessity to him to see her if only at a hopeless distance.

Dorothy often bit her lip in the days immediately following Philip's call, when she thought of the part she had
played. She had been wrong in meddling, of course, and
she accused herself bitterly; but she also accused him.
What right had he to drag her into the question between
himself and his brother—whatever it was? Why should
she take sides? She said to herself that, whatever he might
do, he should not change her neutrality. She was the friend
of both. What effect could any quarrel between them have
upon that fact? She was most their friend when she refused
to allow their difference to invade her relation to them. She
was grateful to Jasper for refraining from making on his part
so difficult a demand upon her friendship; she felt his silence
about the whole matter to be a fine generosity. It delicately
implied the real character of the difference between the
brothers as she had guessed it from the first: it was part of
that forbearance which he would have used to avoid the
quarrel itself, and which he would now be the first to tender
to his brother if he would accept it.   The other kind of

generosity—the freedom with which Philip gave himself and all that he had in the smaller daily matters, she saw was, after all, a less deep and genuine unselfishness than this patient restraint and self-effacement of Jasper's.   In smaller things his attitude had not the charm of Philip's gay and thoughtless open-handedness ; but when a serious opportunity arose —an opportunity for a brave and self-denying magnanimity, it was easy to see which was the stronger.   She said to herself that it was true, what she had often thought: that Philip was light.

When a woman makes reflections like these it would be a mistake to seek their basis wholly in the psychological facts with which she believes herself to be reasoning.   It was at all events true that, before Dorothy had matured all of these thoughts about the character of the brothers, Philip had remained away from the house several days ; and that a certain chivalric reserve in Jasper's bearing toward an old question between them, had renewed in her a vague remorse.

She had supposed herself to have settled all that ; to have put it away in the lumber-room of her memory, where she need only visit it in those moments of sentiment when a dreamy willingness to pain herself possessed her.   But a discarded lover is both a more material and a more importunate fact when he happens to be in the same town than when he lives before the mental vision only in the letter of dignified complaint which must be answered with the statement of an unhappy truth.   Jasper, in the flesh, patient, unreproachful and obdurately faithful to a love which she had fancied as dead in him as it was in her, was a different man from the one she had pictured as suffering for as long a time as her action had remained a vivid theme of remorse to her ; and as getting over it by the same gradual process through which she had emerged from her remorse.   He had not got over it, and he was by her side.

Their engagement, if one could call it that—if it was the
kind of engagement on which marriage is supposed to follow,
Dorothy believed that she had never called it that to herself—had been one of the school boy and girl follies at
which one smiles with wonder at twenty-five, and tells to
one's grandchildren at sixty with a fond laugh, and a passing
inward question touching the colour of those curls now.   It
had been a pleasant diversion between them—the kind of
thing which is a little more intense and a little more entertaining than the tennis that one would be playing at that age
if one were not engaged in being engaged; but to think of
it as the sort of stuff of which one would make a life, was
to speak from the disordered outlook upon things in which
all measures and values melt into a mess of triviality.

It had lasted between them until Dorothy began to go
out into society, and to see the world and other men.   She
did not begin to compare, then, but she perceived a betrothal to be a different matter from the agreeable plaything it
had seemed at school : she began to question with her
conscience whether she had a right to go on with so serious
a thing unseriously.   Was it dealing fairly by him?   She
saw that it was not : yet she tried, with a woman's devotion
to an impossible unselfishness, to keep it up.   Jasper had
gone West to the ranch by this time, and in degree as the
affair seemed wrong and mistaken to her, she found herself
endeavouring to make up to him for the wrong (which, if it
was really any of hers, was hers unconsciously), by writing
him more faithfully.   This, too, seemed dishonest, after a
time, and, in despair, she let the correspondence flag,
believing, or hoping that he would divine what had happened,
and that he would save her the pain of explaining.   Surely
it was natural enough ; he was a man by this time, as she
was a woman, and he must know how inevitable it was.

He perceived as quickly as she could have desired that

there was a change ; but he showed no inclination to spare her in defining it. Brought face to face with the necessity for action, she passed a bitter time, in which she struggled with her conscience and the proprieties. To a young girl it still seems doubtful whether, after all, she may not better wreck her life and a man's than be talked about. In her highest moments of self-sacrifice she thought she could gc on with it : then it would come time to write him a letter and she would see that she could not even do so much as that. How was she to live with him for fifty years ?

Jasper's complaint took at last that tone of demand which lay under the surface of his most pliant moods ; and in the end she saw that she must write him all that was in her heart. It was a very right-spirited letter, telling him the bare truth : that she did not love him as she had supposed, that to marry with no better feeling than she could bring to him would be a permanent wrong to both him and her, and would merely procure their common unhappiness; and begging him to release her from their engagement. Jasper came on to the Pennsylvania city where her father was just then settled over a church ; and an interview followed of the sort which men and women remember on their death beds. But she did not yield. And Jasper went back to the ranch a changed man. He was hard about women, now : he felt himself cruelly misused. He was very bitter. He said to himself that he did not care what he did now. She was responsible for it. He had said as much to her in his anger. Dorothy, in fact, stood for and symbolized every good thought that he had ever had : she was the goddess of his dreams of being some time a little cleaner and straight-forwarder man than he had yet contrived to be. He was accustomed to say that she could do anything with him, and he had kept her in a species of bondage to this, while they had been together during their engagement.

This was one of the facts which had wrought upon Dorothy
while it was still a question whether she should do right to
break the engagement; it was part of the perilous power
that there is for every woman in the passionate need for her
of a man who does not on other accounts create an answering need in her. It is perhaps a phase of the mother instinct,
into which all forms of woman's love tend to dissolve; but
it is certainly always an argument with a woman strong out
of all proportion to its actual validity; and it had not only
been a part of the reluctant push toward the self sacrifice
she had once contemplated, but, in meeting Jasper, the
sense of it was found to have still a power for pain.

She was surprised and chagrined that it should be so, but
so it was; and in the solitude of her chamber at night,
after Jasper had taken away his melancholy eyes, with the
look of a settled sorrow in them, and she freed herself from
the influence of his patient reserve about all that had been
between them, she wept miserable tears. She dried them
when she remembered to be indignant at his attitude. She
would rather a thousand times be upbraided for what she
had done—if she had done anything—than to be arraigned
by that deferential silence which forbearingly would not
bring its charge. It was a studied insult she said to herself.
But the next day it seemed a chivalry beyond praise. It
seemed this most when she recognized, as she found herself
doing, in occasional flashes, her girlish ideal in his handsome face and figure, his daring and commanding manner,
his air of power, his effect of having his hand on the wheel
of the earth, his brilliant and indomitable will.

Jasper came often during this period of Philip's withdrawal; but she never proposed to him the question she had
told Philip she should ask him. Something in his manner
when she mentioned Philip forbade it; and it would be
unfair, she saw, to make him own up to the gallant gentle-

ness and magnanimity he would have used in all this affair with his sensitive and high-strung brother. The use of the adjectives that both condemned and praised him brought Philip sharply before her mind, and she felt again, as if it had been at the moment, the pain that the scene between them had given her. She liked him too well to wish to hurt him, and she had felt that she was hurting him with every word she said. Perhaps he was too easily wounded; but that seemed, now, a fault that one might forgive—nay, certainly ought to forgive to such an occasion. How hot-headed he was! She found herself saying this with a kind of laughing fondness to herself. It seemed suddenly almost a likeable trait in him. It was his fineness—the wrong side of it, to be sure—but still his fineness. And if he was swift to anger, he was swift to feel: it was because of that. It was easy for other men to be calm: they did not care so much—perhaps did not care at all. This made her think of Jasper; and to think of Jasper made her lift her eyes from her typewriter, and allow her glance to rove out of doors, with an impulsive wish that it might be Philip instead of Jasper with whom she was to ride at two o'clock.

The Maurices' house stood, not far from the Vertners', on the outskirts of the town, and the sun swept an unbroken stretch of plain to look on Dorothy at her window. The glowing light and the brisk air without, gave her a longing to be galloping away into the shining day. Her eyes rested with liking on the broad, sunlit level, reaching to the mountains. If she looked straight before her she could keep the prospect untouched by the sight of a single habitation. She heaved a little sigh. She should probably never meet Philip again, let alone ride with him. The outlook from her window gave all her thoughts a pleasant turn, however; and she saw herself forgiving something to any one who should ride up into the foreground of this prospect, leading a saddle-horse.

CHAPTER XV.

JASPER took up the interrupted thread of his life at the ranch with zest, in ignorance of what had happened in his absence. It gave him an agreeable thrill to resume 'his place ; to vault into the seat of authority, once more, in putting his leg over Vixen's back. He wondered, as he went about on his horse, hearing reports and giving orders, why he ever abandoned even temporarily this little kingdom, where his word was law, and where he could see from day to day his personal foresight, shrewdness, and force, taking visible shape in the increase of his herd, in the extension of his domain, and in the growth of his influence among the cattle-men of the district. Yes, it was a mistake to spend his time in running across the Continent, while this position was his at home—a position which he would not barter for that of any one he knew, which he would not sell,—knowing what he did of the future it promised—for any sum he was likely to be offered; and which he would not share with any one on earth.

Ah, yes! To be sure he had done right to go to New York. The intention he foresaw in his father to force the question of Philip's share in the range on him, before his marriage, threatened the position itself. It was not a thing he could wish to face out personally; and if he had ever had the slightest inclination to divide his power at the ranch this would have been the last time he would have selected. Just now, when the fruits of the hard work, the sagacity, the devotion of his five years on the range began to show, was he to share results—and much worse, control over future results—with Philip ? He had borne the burden and heat of the day, he had watered and tended his little tree, had suffered and groaned and sweated to bring it to bearing ; and here came Philip loafing, in his usual way, into a soft thing that some one else had paid for, and wanting to help pick the fruit and reorganize gardening methods. Jasper had looked on with a scornful eye while Philip spread his series of idle and fatuous experiments over a wide geography. If his father was willing to pay for such cleverness in devising schemes for dodging the main point, he was n't. The main point, as he saw it, was work—hard work, guided by stiff common-sense. He was a worker himself; and he was n't taking into partnership fellows who liked fishing better than fence-building, and who, in place of his capacity for making one dollar two, knew only how to spend one and borrow two.

In Maverick, Jasper was welcomed back heartily for the most part. There were men who had been over-reached in a cattle trade by him who marred the pleasure he found in the general acclamation by avoiding him, or greeting him surlily ; there was a widow whom he had been obliged to press in a little foreclosure matter, connected with a house he had bought on speculation in Maverick ; and she had her circle of sympathizers. But these were trifling notes in the chorus of good-will. Just before leaving for New York, Jasper had succeeded in organizing the cattle men of the valley into a Mutual Protective Association, designed to check cattle thieving, (by which many owners had suffered heavily of late); to apply a stricter system to the round-ups ; to put a stop to the loose practice of branding Mavericks wherever found, between round-ups ; to join other associations in petitioning Congress for a better law to prevent the spread of the foot and mouth disease among cattle ; and especially to keep all newcomers out of the valley—the Association officially declaring the range to be over-stocked.

There had been certain difficulties in forming the com-bination ; half a dozen forces, from different causes, were against it ; and the fact that Jasper, against all opposition, had pushed his plan to a successful conclusion had given him, in his absence, a new and stronger position in Maverick. He had always been popular ; but the town now began to feel that it owed him something. There was even talk of nominating him in the Spring for the office his father had once held ; and it was said that, if he played his cards well, he need n't stop at the Mayoralty.

At least one eye watched interestedly the subdued and decent air of triumph with which Jasper received these signs of the predominance which he might presently claim in the town. Mr. Snell's sagacious glance pursued him furtively from behind the windows of his Miners' Supply Store, as he rode by on horseback, when he came into Maverick from the ranch,—following his disappearance down the street with a sardonic smile, and a slow, humorous working of his tongue within his cheek, which seemed to do him good. .

They were all at Ira's one night when some one said that he supposed the next thing they would hear would be that Jasper had bought out his father's half interest in the ranch. He said that he had heard—he did n't know whether there was anything in it or not, of course ; but he *had* heard— that Jasper had made an almighty good thing in stocks while he was on in New York. Trust him for knowing a good thing ! He seemed to have his father's long business head with something else besides—something like clutch. Nobody ever heard of his letting go of anything that he once laid his fist over, and his father, spite of his dog-goned will, (it was a dose for an adult—that will : the speaker had tried it), had let things slip, and lost a fortune. It would be queer if Jasper *should* pull up and pass his father in the race ; now would n't it ? It would be like Deed to be glad. He was gone on those sons of his. He did n't seem to have his natural sense where they were concerned. But it would be interesting if, after his father had given him a half share in the partnership, Jasper should be able to buy the other half for himself.

"Queer partnership, that, anyway," grunted Mr. Snell from the other side of the cloud of smoke that filled the bar-room. Snell was reputed to have made a fortune in fitting out mining parties in the early days of the Leadville boom, with a very bad grade of goods at prices not without a touch of *naïveté* for the impartial spectator, not obliged to pay them. And he had made a good thing by "grub staking" two or three young men who had been lucky in prospecting the hills about Aspen. With the coming of fortune he had put on a precise habit of speech (it was a carefully made garment, but the old would sometimes play him the low trick of showing through, in patches), and had waked up one morning with a respect for himself which required the use of the third person in referring to Mr. Snell.

"What Mr. Snell says is like this," continued Mr. Snell: "A man's all off as soon as he begins bringing family considerations into business. Mr. Snell has nothin' against them: he's a family man himself. But he says to his sons, he says, Look here now, Fred, if you want anything out of your old father, you have got to earn it ; and if you want to do business with him you have got to do business on business principles, every time, sir. And he does it too, gentlemen. The rate of interest is just as high under Mr. Snell's roof and fig-tree, as it is down at his store. The multiplication-table was always good

enough for me ; and I guess it'll have to do for my boys,"
he added grimly, with an unwary lapse into the first person.

"Two per cent. a month, unquestionable security, notes
protested right along. That's what does it, gentlemen. Ask
no favours and take none ; and more especially have a cast-
iron, copper-riveted, water-tight contract with your relatives,
if you're foolish enough to have *any*, and bale the machine
dry of family feeling before you start. Now Mr. Deed has
got a notion in his head, near as I can make out, that there's
two answers to 'twice two.' Down in town here it makes
four; but out at the ranch, when he's dealing with that son of
his, Jasper, it makes five, or three, or some other fool figger."

A loyal murmur rose from the crowd at this, and Snell
concluded doggedly—"Well, anyway, what Mr. Snell says is
like this: 'There's a place for everything,' he says, 'and the
place for family feeling is at the family fireside.'"

"Family furnace up Mr. Snell's way, ain't it, Snell ? " asked
one of the group. He was joked on his peculiarity, of course,
but the town did not venture far in this direction. He owned
a good share of the houses of Maverick, was a hard landlord,
and employed a number of people in his business, and at
his mines. Times were not always—perhaps never—of
the best in Maverick ; and no one felt that he could quite
afford the luxury of making an enemy of Snell.

"I've put in a furnace lately, sir, I admit. Yes, sir," said
he truculently. "And I may be out of my count," he went
on, with a remote implication which was not lost on men
who liked their humour oblique, "but I think—I say I
think, young man—I've got a receipt for the coal bill."

"Come back to make things hum again out at your ranch,
I judge," Mr. Snell said to Jasper, when, about a week after
the talk between Dorothy and Philip, Jasper stopped his
horse in the street to speak to him. Jasper made a point
of speaking all men fair, and humouring the willingness of

everybody to believe his existence a constant matter for joyous surprise to all good fellows.

"Yes, Mr. Snell, yes—things get to loose ends in the master's absence, don't they? Personal supervision is the only plan, I find. I know it's your plan. Not many things escape your eye."

Mr. Snell drew his lips to a point, and, stroking them deprecatingly, pretended to weigh the question. "Well, not a great," he consented. "I suppose, now, you rather enjoy seeing the wheels start up again," he went on in a moment, in another tone—"like to crack your whip and see things moving—eh?"

Jasper glanced at him. "Why, it's pleasant to be back," he said. "When a man really likes his business there's nothing like business after all, is there, Mr. Snell?"

"Nothing!" agreed Mr. Snell. "Nothing! Not if it *is* your business at least," he qualified, "not if you run the machine, not if you're on top."

"Well, *we* should n't care to be anywhere else, should we, Mr. Snell?" laughed Jasper easily.

Mr. Snell flashed his furtive look on him, and dropped his eyes immediately. "No," he assented, with his dry smile. It was a wrinkled smile, like the skin of last year's apple: withered and pensive and loose. It seemed to become in a moment a little large for his face, and he hastily smoothed it out. "No," he repeated, "I don't believe we should. You would n't anyway, I judge. You would n't never be caught hankering, Mr. Snell guesses, for the place of that fellow in the theatre orchestras that hits them brasses once in a while, and dandles them sleigh-bells, and whacks his drum in between. I guess if any one *was* to do much figgerin' about your place, they'd see you belonged a leetle nigher the middle of the orchestra—somethin' not too all-fired far from the conductor's chair; and I should n't

P

wonder if they come around to the idee that the centre of his chair was not far off the right thing. You'd want a baton in your hand, and then matters would begin to rumble around there. Eh?" he shouted in enjoyment, rubbing his hands.

Jasper laughed. He could enjoy even Mr. Snell's attribution of the naturalness of the place of command to him.

Snell went away, rubbing his hands with a glee out of proportion to the superficial dimensions of the joke; and when he was alone in his private office at the store, drew a paper endorsed " Bill of Sale of ' Triangle Outfit,' " from a bundle of documents in his safe, and seating himself in his capacious leather chair, read it over in smiling silence.

When Jasper, while still at breakfast next morning, saw Snell's leathery face come suddenly into the sunny prospect from his window, appearing and disappearing with the motions of his horse, he was unable to imagine why he should be taking the long ride from Maverick at such an hour to see him. He had no dealings with him for nearly a year; what should he want of him? He accounted for his presence for a moment by the fantastic supposition that Snell was running out to see him for a little early morning exercise, and for the pleasure of a chat with him ; and he allowed himself a smile at this idea : Snell no more took aimless exercise on horseback than the other residents of Maverick did, and if it was a question of riding five miles for the sake of a chat with him, (Jasper), he thought he saw Snell wasting good business time in that fashion. The talk of yesterday came back to him : he had thought at the time that old Snell probably wanted something with all that palavering (he called him old, though he was scarcely fifty, because, in the absence of the absolutely old in the West, middle age has to typify senility), and here he

was to make what profit he could out of it. Jasper determined that it should be small. It was a bore, his coming
at breakfast time. Could n't he let a man eat his meals in
peace, he growled to himself.

Jasper combined with his habit of hard work certain
luxurious tastes, which he did not allow to interfere with
business. He rose early for work (it was one of his counts
against Philip that he was never up to breakfast); but he
liked a dash of Florida Water in his bath, and spent rather
more than an hour in grooming himself for the day. He
listened to reports about the condition of things within the
immediate precinct of the ranch-house from his cowboy
cook at breakfast, and gave him his orders then; but he
required a dainty table from him, and did not spare the
daily energy necessary to secure a luxury so foreign to every
condition of the life he was leading. He dressed like his
men because they would not have tolerated anything else,
and because it was part of his pose of good fellow to make
himself one of them; but it was one of the marvels of the
Valley that he should be allowed to go so neat without losing
acceptance with his cow-punchers. It was certainly not
because he was obviously a man who must be neat and dainty
to live, that this unworthy niceness was pardoned in him—
though the most casual glance must have shown any one
that—but through the respect he commanded among his
men on other accounts. For a range of fifty miles about
the ranch it was understood that Jasper Deed was not the
man one would choose to monkey with.

The loose hang of his dressing-gown about his stalwart
figure as he sat at breakfast, concealed the physical sufficiency
which was one of the sources of this feeling; as he rose and
stretched himself and went to the window to bow to Snell,
with his hands thrust deep in the low pockets of the robe,
it might have been guessed perhaps. He had, in fact, no

such strength as Philip's; but his closely knit frame gave
him the credit to the eye of every ounce of force in him,
while Philip's sturdy figure,—carried without Jasper's distinction,—had only the effect of its rude power. Jasper was one of
the perfectly moulded physical products which Nature turns
out in her most careful and workmanlike—perhaps not.her
most inspired—moods.   He was built like a firmly-rooted,
straight, strong young tree; and his grace, his refinement,
his physical adequacy were like that: they took the beholder
with their absolute adaptability to their function, with the
propriety of their place in Nature.   It was this effect in him
which made it seem natural that he should keep himself
trim: it was by way of being a tribute of respect to so right
a figure in the pageant of things.

His face had the symmetry that goes with such perfect
forms.   It was not very unlike certain other correct and
manly faces, of course: that is the penalty one pays for
having the standard face—that in degree as other faces
approach the standard they must be like one's own; but even
this fault was mitigated, when he spoke, by a hard line of
determination which formed itself on either side his mouth,
and by the glance of resolve shining from his eyes.   The
little frown habitually lowering his strongly marked eyebrows,
and a habit of twisting the end of his heavy golden moustache,
when he spoke, as if quelling things stronger than it would
be useful to say, contributed to his effect of force.

Jasper turned from the window, through which Snell was
visible, and threw two or three sticks of wood on the and-
irons.   The ranch house, which was a Queen Anne cottage,
built by an Eastern architect under the supervision of Deed,
but much influenced in its construction by Jasper's wishes,
was set directly under the range of mountains that one saw
from Maverick; and the rear windows looked out upon the
pine-clad lower slopes of Mount Blanco.

"Ah, Mr. Snell," he said, as he turned to greet him. "You're an early bird this morning. Take a seat. Nothing like an early morning ride to put life into a man, is there?"

"No! No!" assented Mr. Snell absently, as he took the seat, laid his hat carefully on the floor, and fumbled in his breast-pocket for a paper.

"Well, I'm glad to see you letting up a bit on the daily grind. We all work too hard out here. A little too hasty about chasing up the almighty cartwheel; yes, a little trifle too hurried—but it rolls, doesn't it, if you don't scramble after it with the rest?" Jasper put his hand to the back of his head and smoothed his carefully brushed hair. "It rolls. That's my experience.

> "'It is not wealth, nor rank, nor state,
> But git up and git that makes men great.'

Our Colorado maxim says it for us; and it's about so, I suppose. Eh, Mr. Snell?" Jasper gathered his dressing-gown about him, and seated himself luxuriously in his favourite chair before the fire, watching Snell warily from beneath his drooping lids, with every trading instinct in him alert under this rambling fire of amiability and worldly wisdom. Snell was there to get an advantage over him in some shape: he knew that as well as if he had carried a placard about his neck to advertise him of the fact. He gathered himself together with the secure consciousness that he knew whose the advantage would be when he bowed Snell out of his door.

"Well, it tain't quite a holiday that Mr. Snell's taking this morning," admitted Mr. Snell, smacking his dry lips, as a preliminary to business and observing Jasper, whose eyes were on his watch chain, with a curious look—a look instantly broadened to a smile at some subtle joke which at the lifting of Jasper's head, he apparently saw in this. "I guess Mr. Snell has n't taken a vacation from chasing up his own little mighty dollar, yet—not a very long one, anyhow—and he don't seem extra likely to, while the present scarcity rules."

"Are they scarce, Mr. Snell?" asked Jasper.

"Well, don't you find 'em so?"

Jasper hesitated a moment. "Why, to tell the truth, no, I don't. It takes all my time and some lively rustling to keep them plenty, of course. But I don't mind telling you, Mr. Snell, that I have a pretty good thing here—or my father and I have. With two or three open winters, like the last two we've had, we sha'n't be poor men. The increase is enormous, you know, if you don't lose all your cattle in the winter storms: and prices have been fairly good lately. I don't believe in the policy of running down your business, and playing poor all the time. I'm not poor, myself, and I don't know that I care who knows it."

"Why, that's good! That's good!" nodded Snell, and he let the gloating smile, which had been working about the corners of his mouth, go now, in sheer incapacity to contain his triumph longer. He longed to play his victim further, but he had to say it. "That's the kind of news that warms the cockles of an owner's heart, ain't it? Mr. Snell don't mind owning up, if you press him, that it warms his. He's been buying some cattle himself lately."

"Indeed, Mr. Snell!" said Jasper politely. "Whose?"

"Yours," returned Snell. He locked his withered hands within each other and leaned forward, resting his arms on his knees, and fixing his eyes on Jasper.

Jasper straightened out of his lounging attitude involuntarily. His face paled. He found his smile and cigarette instantly, and rose to pick out an alumette on the mantel, with a low laugh of self-contempt, which Snell took for derision of his statement.

" You don't believe it," said Snell to his back, with a
gurgling note of contentment in his voice. " Well, I don't
know as I expected you to," he drawled. " Mr. Snell said
to himself when he started out to pay this little morning call
that some of his remarks might require substantiation—not
necessarily for publication, but as a guarantee of good faith,
as the *Lone Creek Rustler* says in its ' Notices to Correspon-
dents.' Well, Mr. Deed, I dare say I can substantiate.
Might cast your eye over that," he said, coiling his tongue
into his cheek to keep himself in subjection, " and that," he
added, laying a second paper on the mantel, and still con-
triving to subdue an importunate smile.

Jasper stooped to the fire on the hearth and kindled his
alumette deliberately before rejoining. He was flushed, as
he rose—perhaps with stooping—but he turned and faced
Snell without haste or heat.

" Who's your employer in this game, Snell ? " He rounded
his lips and shaped a ring with the smoke, watching it climb
to the ceiling with affectionate solicitude. " Who are you
acting for, who's your principal—which of my well-wishers
put you up to this scheme ? " he repeated as Snell did not
answer. He looked down into Snell's bemused face, as he
thrust his hands into the pockets of his dressing-gown, and
puffed at his cigarette. " I swear, Snell, I gave you credit for
more penetration than to waste your time for *any one* on a
scheme that takes me for an unfledged tenderfoot. Do you
think I 'm here for my health ? "

Snell had recovered himself, and said, with patient good
humour, " No, Mr. Deed. I never thought that : your worst
enemy would n't accuse you of that. There's good reading
in them papers," he added with the effect of an after-
thought.

" Entertain yourself with it, then," said Jasper, taking
them from where they lay on the mantel, and tossing them

to him. Snell caught them dexterously, without relaxing
the smile which he no longer took pains to conceal, and
which spread beamingly now to all his features, affecting
even his sandy forelock, which had twisted itself into a curl
of sympathy. "I'm not in want of reading matter, here,"
continued Jasper; "and if you've nothing more to say,
Mr. Snell——"

"Oh, I've got plenty more to *say*, if that's all," responded
Snell, imperturbably, "and you'd like this reading. Hm-hm
—'This indenture—hm—this day—hm—party of the first
part, and Abraham Snell, party of the second part, witnesseth:' would you like to know what it witnesseth?" he
inquired, opening wide the document he had been pretending
to take stealthy peeps at, while he read. He looked up at
Jasper cunningly.

Jasper scowled back thunderously at him. "Oh, drop
that leer, Snell. What are you driving at?"

"Why, I've got a deed here of the 'Triangle Outfit,'—
whole concern, you know," he said, looking up into Jasper's
paling face blandly, "house, land, fences, water privileges,
run of the range, and one of the largest and finest bunches
of cattle in the State; increasing enormously, I believe you
said."

"A deed of *my* range—of *my* cattle?" repeated Jasper.

"Well," drawled Snell, with his habitual deprecating pull
at his puckered lips, "not too all-firedly, tee-totally yours.
Some of it your father's, ain't it?—say about two-thirds. *I*
guess it's a good deed. Ought to be—deed from a Deed,
you know." He leered up into Jasper's miserable face, with
a smile of enjoyment.

"From my father! Stuff!"

"Do you know his writing?" Snell began to open out
the paper. Jasper snatched it from him. At sight of the
signature he burst out in a great imprecation. He turned

livid, and Snell got hastily on his feet, fearing that he would fall. But he left the fireplace quickly, and going over to the window read the whole document slowly through.

" What devil's cunning did you use with my father to get him to sign this?" he asked, turning on Snell, as he finished.

" Not any," responded Snell cheerily. " I guess you used that for me, Mr. Deed, if all your father said was true. I'd have worked tooth and nail for a year to 'a got that deed signed, just as it is there, I don't mind telling *you*, Mr. Deed, and been glad of the chance. But your father saved me the trouble. He came and offered me the bargain, he urged it on me, he crammed it down my throat ; and after beating him down a trifle, just for self-respect, you know, I yielded politely. He was rather in a hurry, and I didn't want to bother him with a refusal—not at that price," he qualified, stroking his chin. " Ranges like this ain't going at $25,000—well, not every day." He glanced at Jasper, and his eye dropped irresistibly, in a wink. " It tain't no bad bargain," he went on, with a lapse into the cruder forms of his speech. " I don't mind ownin' up to that, now it's signed and sealed, and the outfit's mine." Snell did not miss the wince and the clench of the teeth with which Jasper received this. " But it was n't the *bargain* I was after—not entirely." Jasper stared at him. " I suppose you've forgotten that little transaction of ours a year ago come next Spring, Mr. Deed? Yes : I thought you would have. Well, you see I *ain't*. That's the difference. Oh, Mr. Snell's got a memory for kind deeds. ' Kind deeds can never, never die,' the old song says. We used to sing it in our Sunday School back in the New Hampshire days. Don't know that sacred toon, perhaps? But it's a good toon, all the same—a good, old-fashioned truth-telling toon. They can't die—kind deeds—and if they could, I would n't let 'em. But I ain't had no trouble keepin' this one alive ; it's got up with me every morning, and made my breakfast happy for me, and it's gone to bed with me every night and helped me to put in a good night's rest. I ain't forgot, Mr. J. Deed, if you have," he said, rising, and nodding his head bitterly toward him, " and I 've paid out a tidy sum for this here little dokkyment,"—snatching it from Jasper's loose clasp, and shaking it in his bony claws,—" just to get it to help say so for me. I hope the language is plain, Mr. Deed."

Jasper kept his hands from Snell's collar with difficulty. " Quite, Mr. Snell," he said, with his usual coolness. " You 've paid $25,000 for a piece of paper that is worth, at the outside, twenty-five cents. That makes the expense of registering your disapproval of something I 've done, or left undone—I really don't recall the particular villainy you allude to—twenty-four thousand, nine hundred and ninety-nine dollars, and seventy-five cents. It 's not a bad bargain as Mr. Snell's bargains go."

" What ! " screamed Snell.

" I say your deed, as you call it, is n't worth the paper it's written on."

" Oh, it tain't, ain't it ? " sneered Snell comfortably.

" No. My father had no more right to make that sale than you would have had."

Snell laughed cheerfully. " Think you 're the only man who ain't here as a sanitary measure, do you ? I took a lawyer's advice before I closed with that poor father of yours that ain't got no rights. *I'm* not here for my health —not altogether. When will you be ready to gim'me possession ? "

" Never," returned Jasper, closing his lips.

" Oh, come ! I'm willing to accommodate ; but the date's too late. Make it a day or two earlier—say to-morrow ! " He flirted the deed carelessly about in his hand.

" I'll tell you something I *won't* postpone," said Jasper, his fingers working by his side.

" Yes ? " inquired Snell with the irritating rising inflection.

" And that's putting *you* out of the house." He began to roll up his sleeve.

" Inhospitable, ain't you ? " said Snell, taking up his hat nonchalantly. " That ain't the way I'll treat you when I'm master here. Judge I'd better bring the sheriff with me when I come to take possession to-morrow," he said tentatively at the door.

Jasper glared at him. He shut the door hastily. When he had gone Jasper ran to his room, cast off his dressing gown, and drew on his riding boots. Vixen was ready for him when he came down the stairs, and flung himself upon her. He dug his spurs into her. Snell was making his way back to Maverick by another road.

CHAPTER XVI.

JASPER pushed Vixen across the five miles of level plain lying between the ranch and the mountains on the other side of the valley, with quirt and spur. It was an incomparable morning; but nothing in his mood answered to it. The stirring, potent, heady morning air swam richly through his blood, awakening him to a hotter anger, and a deeper resolve. He drank its strength as he rode on. It made him strong for what he had to do. He set his teeth and spurred forward, hammering his horse's flanks. The noises of the day's work were only beginning in the ranch houses he passed on the road. The spacious, deep-lunged, awful quiet that settles at night over the big hills and the stupendous prairie reaches of the West had not lifted, and the mountains, black and still in the motionless pines at their feet, and white and still about their snowy heads, looked down on the silence gravely.

Jasper was not thinking of mountains. His imagination, active enough within its own range of themes, was busy with a man who, up in the hills before him, would be just rising. The hills were not near enough. He cried upon the horse with an oath, as if Vixen could reduce the distance visibly at the leap she gave under a cut from his quirt.

At the "Snow Find" shaft a workman was busy lowering the bucket. Jasper tethered his horse at the cabin door and strode over to him. "Pull up that bucket, will you? I want to see my brother."

Mike Dougherty stared at him, and went on lowering. "Pull it up, do you hear?" said Jasper, laying his hand roughly on the man's shoulder

"Yis. I hear," returned the man. With his arm he followed the revolving crank stolidly. The rope unwound.

"You'll mind, if you know what's good for yourself."

"Yis, I'll moind me owners. I takes me orders from Misther Cutter and Misther Dade, d'yez moind?"

"I *am* Mr. Deed—Mr. Deed's brother."

Mike shot a look at him as he stooped to his work. He may have found warrant for the statement in the resemblance Jasper bore to Philip: "An' how would I know that?" he said, reversing the crank, and fetching up the bucket, hand over hand, with the same deliberation. Jasper cursed him silently. "There yez are. Yez'll find Misther Dade in the big drift to yer right at the bottom." Jasper got into the cage, and Dougherty lowered away. "The second to the right, d'yez moind?"

Jasper had thought out his meeting with Philip as he rode. He had decided, if he did not find him at his cabin, to go down into the mine without asking for him. He preferred not to give him the opportunity of refusing to see him.

He dropped past a stretch of pale green earth out of the light. After the mellow stratum of brown he was in the dark, and all colours were alike. The firmament shrank above his head to a narrowing circle, the size of a man's palm. When he looked over the sides of his swinging, sinking bucket, the darkness deepened thickly into the abyss. He told himself that he was a fool to so put himself in Philip's power. But he could not stop now, and at the moment a pin head of yellow flame danced in the depths, and he shouted at it.

The man behind it caught the bucket as it settled on the floor of the mine, lifting his candle to peer into the visitor's face. All the morning shift was in the mine; and both the Superintendents. Any one who came now was a stranger, and, in a productive mine, a stranger is likely to be held an enemy until he proves himself a friend.

"Well?" interrogated the figure in shadow behind the candle.

"Is Mr. Deed here?" asked Jasper, stepping out.

"Yes; but he don't allow no one in this here mine," returned Henry Wilson, formerly of Missouri.

"He'll allow me. I'm his brother. I settled that at the top." As the man still scrutinized him, without offering to move, he said, "You don't think I lowered *myself* down in the bucket, do you?"

"*I* don't know what you did," growled the figure, which now showed a face, as the candle was lowered to the level of the head.

"Well, I do, then. I satisfied the man on duty at the top before getting down. You can lay odds on that."

"Yes," assented the man. The candle showed a smile in the recesses of his tawny beard. "I guess you would n't be let by Mike very slick without you halted and gave the countersign. Who did you say?"

"I sha'n't say it again. Come! Get a move on!"

The man surveyed him again surlily, and turning suddenly away with his candle, left him in darkness. Jasper lighted a cigar and sat down on the edge of the bucket. The man's stumping step died away in the lateral gallery into which he had turned.

Two minutes passed without a sound. The air of the mine laid a clammy hand on him. He puffed vigorously at his cigar. The silence in the black space not lighted by the fitful glow of his cigar was like a thing in the darkness.

Then he heard a quick step coming along the same gallery, a candle wavered into sight down the long passage into which he sat looking, and Philip stood above him. They gazed into each other's eyes.

" *You!* " cried Philip.

Jasper lifted his eyes lazily to the candle Philip held aloft, and merely smiled. "Yes." He bit at the end of his cigar. " I want father's address."

" I can't give it to you."

" You mean you won't."

" I said ' *can't,* '" returned Philip, thrusting the steel point of his candle-holder into a soft space in the wall, and advancing on his brother with bent brows. "I don't know where my father is ; and let me tell you that you will do well to measure your words." He looked steadily into his eyes, across the candle glare. " This interview is not of my seeking."

" Hum," uttered Jasper meditatively. " Your manners have rather gone off since I met you last. The life of a mining camp seems to have been—relaxing."

Philip bit his lip. " You should not be the first to say so," he said.

Jasper laughed. " You have n't looked me up with your report of my mine," he said, with impudent perception of Philip's meaning. " No, I understand ; it was n't ready," he continued, lifting his hand deprecatingly at Philip's motion to reply. " I quite understand the delay : there was something else that was n't ready. *You* were n't ready." A dangerous light kindled in Philip's eyes. " A man who has done a sneaking thing behind another man's back usually *is n't* ready, I've noticed, to face the man he's injured."

Philip's hands twitched at his sides. " Ingrate ! " he cried. " Keep those words to ticket yourself with ! "

Jasper looked at him quietly from between his half-closed lids. "I'm talking of *you!*" he said. "Bluff is a good dog—for tricks; but I'm dealing with facts; and I say that to rig a game on me with father in my absence was a dirty act. You can turn it back or front, or upside down," he went on with mounting anger, "but you can't get around that. It was a dirty act, and calling me names won't whitewash it." He came close to Philip, casting the words in his teeth.

The creak of an ore car on a distant track cut upon the silence that fell for the instant, while Philip searched for words. The preposterous reversal of their positions dizzied him. For a second everything went round in a whirl, in the midst of which Jasper's adroit shifting of the question between them seemed to take on a demoniac physical body, and to go capering through the candle flame, jibing at him. The right which he felt at the centre of Jasper's accusation quelled him, and beat back one after another the answering words thronging to his lips. He clenched his fist and dropped it at his side. Everything in him called upon him to choke back the falsehood in his throat as it touched *him;* but as his words touched his father, he owned sickly to himself their truth. The thought dashed him, and Jasper took the word before he could choose between one of the half-hearted answers that lay upon his tongue.

"You thought I would n't see through this thing—you and father—did you? You must have taken me for a bat. Why, you'd see through it yourself—yes, even you, my helpless, pottering brother, who don't know as much of business in a year as I could guess before breakfast any morning! Yes, you who never turned an honest dollar in all your life, and who have managed to lose a pretty number; even you would see through it! The thing's childish, I tell you—

hiring Snell to make a show of buying the range, and fixing things to take it over on your own account and father's as soon as you've quieted me. There were just two leaks in that chivalric scheme, let me tell you: First, the idea that I would n't see the point of all this roundabout trick for doing me out of my range; and second, that I *would* be quieted. I do see the point, and I won't be quieted. There's going to be a row about this thing before we're done with it, let me tell you! I should n't wonder if you heard the echo of it as far as the ' Snow Find,' " he sneered. " I'm just the sort of man to sit down and whistle at my fate, I am! Huh! " he grunted, for lack of all other expressions of his scorn, and turned away.

" Do you find yourself safe in *always* judging other men by yourself? " asked Philip, after a pause.

Jasper stumbled, and Philip caught up his halting words. " You think you know me. You have said how I am this and that. Answer me! Am I the man to meet your vile blow with a viler? Have I ever played the black-guard with you since you've known me? You must wish to have an accusation on your side. The circumstances make it desirable. It should be a big one too, since it has to shelter you, and stand for answer to an act you know of. But it should be credible. Come! Spin a yarn you can believe yourself! Make yourself believe that I could stoop to your low-lived notions of what a man may do, and trim my actions by yours. Bah! Was I ever a sneak? "

Jasper clenched his hands. " Yes! " he cried hoarsely. " Yes! When were you ever anything else? Your life has been one long slinking out of every sort of duty, re-sponsibility and hard work. Your father has fed you since you were a man: he has kept you in amusement, and helped you in every fool scheme for dodging disagreeable things

Q

that your ingenuity could invent. You've gone on horseback, from the first, young man ! Do you think I have n't
seen it ? Do you suppose I have n't watched you, while I
was putting my back into my own work, and sweating to
pull up this ranch you talk about ?" Philip had not mentioned it. "*Sneak*, do you say ? Why, if you were mous-
ing about for a type of all the sneakingest things a man
can do, you would n't have to go far. Fancy your demand
that I should give up a share in this range to *you*, after what
I've done for it ? You always had an eye for a soft snap;
but I swear you never had the courage before to put in a
claim for such a soft snap as that."

"Oh," cried Philip, "you should add that. You do
well ! Your hellish ingratitude would lack its final touch if
you left me to go free of your crime ! It is I who have
dealt my father this coward's blow. It is *my* act that tortured
and maddened him and sent him to fling away his fortune
distractedly, that he might stab me back with the loss of my
share in it ! It is like you to be the innocent one, and
mighty like me, is it not, to be in the wrong ? Was I ever
anything else ? And it's I, too,—it must be I, for if it's not
I, it must be you, and that's not possible—who begged his
brother to stake out a claim for him in the mountains, and
then got him without much bother (for you were always an
easy-going fool about taking trouble for others, were n't you,
Jasper ?) to work the claim for him, alongside his own.
Ah, yes !" he cried, with a derisive shout that went echoing
under the hewn roof above his head, and ran stormily among
the galleries, "it would be I, would it not, who took such a
service from my brother, who left him to slave for a year
for me in an ungodly hole among the hills, and paid him at
the end with a coward's trick of fence that has its name
among gentlemen. Yes, it would be I ! And it is you,
basely wounded and heaped over with injury,—it is you who

come out of this thing with white hands ! It's a fine saying—a monstrous fine saying . . . . *brother !* "

Jasper slashed away with his cow-puncher's knife at a strip of iron pyrites in the rock at his side, as Philip went on. At the last word he twisted the knife violently and brought away the glistening little stratum at which he had been quarrying. It dropped to the floor of the mine with a tiny note that was like a crash in the silence which fell as Philip ceased. Jasper paled to the eyes.

"Words ! " he said, in his throat. " Words ! Better stick to them. Keep away from facts ! They hurt. Where is my father ? "

"I have told you that I do not know," returned Philip in the tone of enforced patience which one uses toward a guest who has outstayed his welcome. He folded his arms.

"And I think I've said I don't believe you," answered Jasper. "If you hope to force me to a quarrel with *you*, by keeping me from the bigger game, let me tell you that you are badly off your base. I've got a juicy bone to pick with you, later; you've given me matter enough this morning for all the quarrel you'll ever have any real need for, I fancy. But I choose my time for quarrels. This is n't my time for a quarrel with you. I'm not gunning for assistant sneaks to-day. I'm looking for the brains of this deviltry. Tell me where my father is, and when I've made him disgorge, I'll be ready to give you all the attention you can want."

Philip fixed his eyes steadily on him, above the candle. It began to gutter, and flared between the brothers.

"Damn you ! " he said deliberately, from within his teeth. " Keep your foul tongue from your father, or by heaven, I'll teach you courtesy ! '

" T-s-s-s ! " uttered Jasper. " An interesting person to

teach courtesy ! Tell me," he cried, taking a stride forward (and in the baleful light that suddenly entered his eyes, Philip guessed, as by a fatal inspiration, what he must say) ; "tell me," he repeated, "what did you say of me to Miss Maurice when I left you alone with her not many days ago ? What pleasant tales about me did you entertain her with ? Ah, my knightly brother ! You were asking if you were ever a sneak since I've known you. To abuse me to a woman in my absence with the mean hope of undermining my favour with her, and slinking into my place ! There's chivalry for you ! The chivalry of a confidence-man ! The courtesy of a back alley ! "

With a single movement Philip whipped past the candle, and took him by the throat. "You hound !" he cried. " Breathe Miss Maurice's name again, and I'll. . . . . You never had a decent thought ! You are as incapable of under-standing the movements of a gentleman's mind as if you had sprung from the gutter ! Who taught you such thoughts ? Not your father, damn you ! "

"Take off your hands ! Take your hands off, I say," shouted Jasper.

" Must I be a cad because we are sons of one father— more shame ? Must I use my position to slander you to a woman because you would have done as much in my place ? How *should* you guess that your father could wipe out your share in that cursed ranch in the pure generosity of his anger ? It needs a *man* to understand certain things !" Philip's voice was a sob. " You think it like him to turn a penny from his revenge, do you ? You can't understand his un-reckoning love turned to unreckoning hate ; you can't understand his ruining himself to even things with you, eh ? Cur ! Do you suppose he knows *how* to do a thing you could understand ? "

Jasper cast himself free, and fell upon his brother in blind rage. They clenched in silence and swayed in each other's arms.

"Curse you!" muttered Jasper, as Philip forced him to his knees. He caught fiercely at him, and, rising suddenly, by sheer strength, ground Philip back inch by inch, and, with an adroit twist, had all but thrown him. But Philip, winning a fresh grip, cast him back against the wall, where the candle leaped in a dying flame. Jasper's head struck upon a point of rock. He fell heavily to the floor. They had gone crashing into the candle together. It lay upon the floor, extinguished.

In the darkness Philip stooped in horror, and thrust his hand under his brother's clothing, feeling for the beating of his heart.

CHAPTER XVII

THE minutes lengthened as he crouched there in the still-ness, dazed and shuddering. In the silence he heard the dull, regular stroke of a sledge upon a drill in the recesses of the mine. His eyes seemed bursting in the darkness as he strained them upon the still figure beneath his hands. The blackness began to pale. The daylight, streaming through the shaft, reasserted itself vaguely, and, with his eyes, Philip devoured the motionless form. Its outlines slowly discovered themselves in the sick uncertainty of the yellowing light.

Steps drew near in one of the lateral galleries, and the gleam of a candle suddenly floated over the white face. Cutter laid a hand upon Philip's shoulder, and he looked up, turning a drawn visage on him.

Cutter raised his candle, peering upon the prostrate figure ; and as Philip gave way to him, bent above it, and, after a moment's study, gave Philip his candle to hold and put his ear to Jasper's heart.

"Pshaw ! He's all right !" cried Cutter, in a cheerful tone which shook Philip out of his labouring nightmare. "Come ! let's have him in the bucket."

Philip stooped without a word, and they carried him to the bucket, and stepping in, gave the signal. As they rose, with their freight between them, Cutter caught out his handkerchief at sight of the wound on the head from which the blood still flowed, and bound it up.

They laid him on the grass in the wide sunshine, at the top. Philip fetched water and they dashed it in his face. They loosened his collar, and plied him with brandy. He stirred.

Philip, who had been bending over him, sprang up. "Here, take this!" he muttered hurriedly, pressing the flask into Cutter's hands. Mike came up with a telegram which had come from Gasher's—the small railway station, a mile from the "Snow Find." Philip tore it open, and with a glance at it handed it over to Cutter.

"PIÑON, *Dec.* 22.

"The Ryan outfit have made a strike in the 'Little Cipher.' Assays $1,200 to the ton. You are a rich man. Come at once to protect your interests.

"HAFFERTON."

"By *Jove!*" shouted Cutter as he read. "Did n't I tell you!" He rose in excitement. Jasper moaned uneasily.

"No," said Philip.

"Well, I told you the other thing. It's all the same."

"You told me that the 'Pay Ore' was a great mine, and that the 'Little Cipher' was no good," returned Philip. His voice had a hollow sound.

Cutter looked at him. "Well?" exclaimed he impatiently. And after a pause, "See here! Will you take my advice?" he asked, laying a compelling hand on Philip's listless arm.

"I don't know," returned Philip, out of the mazy seizure into which the despatch seemed to have plunged him.

"You don't want to see this fellow when he comes to. And you ought to be at Piñon by the first train that will take you there. Take his horse over by the cabin, and catch the 11.12. It's only twenty-five minutes past ten now, and you can make it on that horse of his with hard riding. I'll send Mike after you to fetch back the horse, so that it will be at the ranch when we get there."

"When you get there?" repeated Philip.

"Yes; yes! Don't make objections, but start. The Ryans will have time to play the deuce with you if you don't start at once. I'll get Wilson to help me make up a bed for him in the Studebaker wagon, and I'll drive him over to the Triangle myself. I'll see him through. Don't bother! And get on that horse!"

"Cutter!" said Philip, in a tone of conviction, "you are a brick!"

He gave him his hand in a silent pressure, strode over to Vixen, flung himself on her back, and with a wave of his hand to Cutter, disappeared below the brow of the hill on which the "Snow Find" buildings stood.

Jasper opened his eyes.

PHILIP saw the meeting hills, within which Maverick lay, part before the climbing progress of his train, and then close in behind it again, as they issued from the valley. The train writhed upon itself, crossing and recrossing its track, snatching an advantage where it could, and winning its way from height to height by breathless climbs, by level tugs, in which the engine seemed to fill its lungs, by stealthy curves, by assaults. They stood at last, where a mountain side dropped sheer away, below the rails, and, looking out from the dizzily clambering train, Philip saw beneath a white world, out of which the melancholy firs lifted their wailing arms in scattered companies. Ouray impended spectrally above the opposite window for a moment ; and then the train was at rest upon the summit, within the black hole which snow closes at all seasons. The scene was the same to Philip's heated sight within the tunnel and without : the monstrous bulks of the interfolded hills, the vision of a white, tumultuous wilderness, desolately broken by rocks and pines, ran upon his distracted sense like frost tracery, dissolving unintelligibly as it shaped itself.

He was facing a new fact, with a thousand consequences, and watched the marching panorama as one watches a play in an unfamiliar tongue. He had only known his fact an hour ; but a year's pain had gone into it, and a year's idle wrestling.

The mine in which the Ryan outfit had struck a fortune was Jasper's.

As the train pulled out of the tunnel, and slipped down the first stretch of the descent on the other side of the mountains, Philip dreamed in rage of the day in which Jasper should take over with a silent smile the fortune he had won for him. It was the twist too much in this devilish business, he cried to himself, in speechless bitterness, as he stared from the window again. The train swept into a snowshed or burst out of one momently, and he took the white and glistening sweep of the wilderness upon his unseeing eyes in abrupt flashes. In the snowsheds where the other passengers could not see, he beat the arm of his seat in wrath.

He could bear that Jasper should give him no thanks for the year he had divided between the two mines ; he could bear that he should cheat him of his inheritance, and, in the helpless tangle of fate in which that act had involved his father and himself, and even Margaret, he could bear to owe to Jasper the loss of his father's trust. He could suffer this and not attempt reprisal ; he could even feel how deeply, fatally wrong all reprisal must be. But he could not heap a fortune on the man from whom he had borne all this.

He frowned on McCormick, as he threw his leg over the pony he hired from him at Bayles' Park, for the ride over the Pass.

"Been gittin' bad news?" asked the hotel proprietor. He had got the best of him in the bargain for the pony, and could afford to be sympathetic.

"Heard of the strike up at Piñon?" asked Philip with an idle willingness to amuse his misery by what the man should say.

"Don't mean the 'Little Cipher?'" You ain't got nah-thin' to do 'th that, have you?"

"I leased it to the Ryan outfit a couple of months ago."

"Why, shake!" cried the hotel man with honest pleasure. "You don't tell me! They tell *me* it's a Josephus dandy. Moshier come down the other day on his way to Leadville —you know Moshier—and he said it was the biggest strike they've made at Piñon: the hull town's wild about it." Philip conquered the envious pang for which he began to despise himself.

"How long ago did Moshier say they made the strike?" he asked, to stifle his thoughts.

"'Bout a week? Have you jist heard about it?" asked the man interestedly.

"Yes. They were n't in a hurry to let me know."

"No—nachully," mused his interlocutor. "Did they tell you what it assayed? *I* heard $1,500."

Philip found a smile. "The assayists get a little rattled when somebody really strikes something, I've noticed. Trying to find pay ore in iron pyrites three hundred and sixty-four days in the year dulls a man."

"Well, you take it easy," said McCormick admiringly. He had spent a good part of his life on an Illinois farm where things do not happen so often as they do in Colorado. "If any one was to have asked me before you spoke up about the 'Little Cipher' bein' yours"—Philip winced—"I should have said you had been losin' a near relation 'stid of strikin' it rich in a mine—somethin' a little nearer 'n an uncle, and a little further than a father—'bout a brother, say." McCormick laughed for enjoyment of his humour, but he changed the subject at Philip's scowl. "Say, what become of the pretty young lady and her father that you come through with a while ago, after the big storm?" And at Philip's answer, "That's good," he said. "Glad to hear it. She was lookin' shaky. I was a little mite afraid she would n't pull through. It was a close call you had up 'round the Fifth Cascade, there. We ain't had such a storm since. Well, better luck this time! We can't afford to lose you, you know. You'll be one of our millionaires, now. Come in and have something before you start!" he urged, in the overflow of his hospitality.

Philip said it was too cold to get off his horse again, and offered him a nip from his flask, if he must pledge him. They drank together, McCormick praising the quality of Philip's whisky. "One more? Well I don't mind! Here's to the success of the 'Little Cipher' and its owner."

"No," said Philip. He laid a hand on McCormick's up-lifted arm. "There are better toasts than that, McCormick. Drink to the poor devils who have n't struck it rich!"

"Oh, all right," returned McCormick, surprised. "To the poor devils who have n't struck it rich, then! That takes in me," he added, as he smacked his lips.

Philip rode away and over the Pass with set teeth. Jasper would be even richer than he had fancied—brutally, damnably rich! It was the chance of mining: Jasper had won, and he had lost, and it was the kind of chance for which he could see himself being almost glad, under certain conditions; he

could not imagine himself grudging a brother a fortune, if
that were all.   Very likely he could do more with a fortune
than he could: he had never learned how to use money, or
even how to keep it; and at least there would be something
to say for the wisdom of the Fate which should pick out
Jasper rather than him for her money favours.   But after all
that had passed, to choose him as the instrument of her
bounty, was an odious freak.   Contrived in this way, he did
grudge the fortune to his brother—and grudged it to him
savagely.   He felt like howling in his rage to the cañon walls,
as he thought that it was for this he had spent that cursed
year at Piñon.   He thought of their fight in the mine.   He
thought of what he had said to him, and now took none of
it back, as he had begun to take it back when he stooped
over him in the awful fear of what he had done.   On the
whole he was glad that he had not known then what he knew
now: no one could say to what he might have been tempted.
The thing was too intolerable: to suffer the ignominy of
Jasper's swindle, to lose his future, to lose his father through
him, and to answer it all with a gift!   So did fools!   So did
the whining cowards who saw their account in it!   So did
the sort of men whom every fibre in Philip's nature went out in
contempt for.   He pulled himself up with the irrelevant
thought that so did Christians.   "And if any man smite thee
upon thy right cheek, turn to him the other also."   One
knew what to think of that in these days.   But of course it
was not meant for these days.   The habit of intellectual
pity for those who took injunctions of this kind literally and
sought to make the impossible application of them to the
conditions of every-day life, rose to wash the whimsical
thought from its momentary lodgement.   And yet, why not?
There was a thought there.

There was no snow in front of the cave near the Fifth
Cascade when he reached it, though a heavy fall lay upon

the hills toward which his face was set. The thought of
Dorothy and of the days they had spent in the cave—days
in which the friendly meeting of a common danger, and the
natural, candid, almost happy conditions of their situation
had drawn them together—taught him a new pang. His
heart laboured thickly with the sudden pain of the thought
that she was lost to him. If he could still hope to restore
himself to his place in her thought—when he recalled how
he had lost it through a sentiment of delicacy about Jasper,
he loathed himself—what sort of man was he now to propose
marriage to any woman?

He said to himself, with a smile of irony, that he was in
just the condition to tempt a woman to marriage whom
he had given reason to distrust and dislike him; and,
especially, he was in a state which commends itself, everywhere, to the careful fathers of lovely girls, and would be
certain to commend itself to her money-loving father.

Not to put too fine a point upon it, he was a beggar; and
a beggar, now, without hope. He saw, now, how he had
built upon the expectation that the Ryan outfit would strike
it rich in the " Pay Ore "; he went back and told himself
that he should never have gone on seeing so much of Miss
Maurice if he had not made sure of this in his own
musings upon his future. His visible resources during the
time when he was seeing Miss Maurice every day, and for a
good part of every day, were contained in a leather trunk,
the worse for mountain travel on pack animals. But he
had been rich in confidence. He smiled wearily as he
remembered that he was always rich in that; if at any
moment of his life he could have realized the wealth that he
saw in " futures " he would seldom have needed to wonder
where he could borrow money to lend good fellows, or to
buy a useless third pony. It was an instinct with Philip to
want the third pony; and an irresistible instinct to buy it

when he lacked money for a new hat.   In moments like those he was enduring as he rode forward over the Pass toward Piñon, he recognized these instincts for follies at least as cordially as his wisest friend could have wished ; he even said to himself that it was cold-blooded to have borrowed that last money from Vertner for the purchase of Dan ; but he excused himself by recalling that he had ex-pected the " Pay Ore " to do something for him then : it only needed to be sunk deep enough, he remembered having repeated to himself, when he was turning over in his mind the idea of asking Vertner for the loan.   But Dan was a good horse and worth the money ; and, anyway, he felt himself absolved by Vertner's own shrewdness.   Even with his talent for friendliness, Vertner would hardly have lent him that amount just then if he had n't believed in the " Pay Ore."   Surely it was n't in the " Little Cipher " that he was putting his trust ?

And at this he said to himself for the hundredth time, that if any one liked that kind of humour, it was a pretty stroke on the part of fortune, to have wheedled him and every one who knew the situation existing at Piñon, into the belief that she would one day give him a rich mine for his portion ; and to keep her word in the fashion she had chosen.   She had struck it rich for him as she had engaged, but she had struck it rich in Jasper's mine.

> " ' That keep the word of promise to our ear,
>   And break it to our hope,' "

he muttered to himself.   Was it not even in his mine, that she had uncovered the ore-bearing vein, if you would, ac-cording to the letter of her agreement—his mine in trust : his mine for Jasper !

The thought was too bitter.   He turned from it to wonder sarcastically if Jasper's luck would hold in the search he knew he would be making for his father, as soon as he was able to be about again. It would be like the way things had been going since his father had struck back at Jasper, if he should find him, and revenge himself as Jasper would know how to revenge himself. Ah, that was the mistake! It was useless to regret it now; the thing was done. But what, of all that had happened since, was not the fruit of it? It would have been a wise or a very hardy man who had ventured to foretell what shape the sure train of evil must take, when his father answered Jasper's blow with another; but a child could have foreseen the inevitableness of the pursuing chastisement—of all this horrid, fertile coil of wrong begotten of wrong. Subtle, ingenious, pitiless—by what sureness of indirection, by what deadly certainty of straight-forward vengeance, the Law which his father had outraged was taking its satisfaction! Was it only nightmare? Did it not truly seem that the wrong which his father had dared try to cure with wrong must go on helplessly begetting other wrong, after its kind, and in its own image? Philip felt as if he were getting his Bible mixed; but Nature seemed to have her own idea of the eye for an eye doctrine: that was what he was thinking. She did n't spare.

His thought ricochetted, in the aimless manner of thoughts, toward the ever-recurring theme of his debts. With his horse's head turned toward Piñon they became a subject of immediate, of even pressing importance. What was he to say to those fellows? He had staved off men to whom he owed money before; but he had never made so many promises about any other set of debts, nor broken so many. The letters he had received lately from Piñon had made him writhe; for it is a curious truth that reminders of debts contracted in carelessness about the means of meeting them, are often felt to be more insulting than reminders of the same nature conveyed to conscious inno-

cence, whose cheque-book is in its pocket. Philip hated
the men to whom he owed money. They represented the
difficulty of life. Worse—they stood for his weakness:
they *were* his weakness in material form. From this point
of view their mere existence was insulting.

He chose to hold in his pony after passing Laughing
Valley City. There was snow at this height, and he did
not wish to press the animal. Besides, a plan of getting
into Piñon after dark and up to his old cabin on Mineral
Hill,—a plan of investigating the find at the "Little Cipher,"
leaving Hafferton in charge, if he was still there, and getting
away again before the shopkeepers in the town below should
have the opportunity of representing disagreeable facts to
him, had been forming itself in his mind.

In the event Hafferton hailed him from the sidewalk as
he rode into the town, and Philip had to alight and walk
along with him, while he heard Hafferton's story. It was
an interesting story; and they were at Hafferton's cabin,
and Philip had consented to stay the night with him, and
allowed his horse to be stabled in the burro shed, behind
the hut, before he knew. A party of four were playing cards
in the cabin which Hafferton had shared with the editor of
his old paper since he had returned to Piñon (his leased
mine at Leadville had ceased to pay lately): and in the
doubtful light cast by two candles, set in a couple of whisky
bottles, Philip saw at once that one of the party was Charlie
White—red-haired Charlie White, the newsdealer, whose
bill he knew by heart.

"How are you, Mordaunt?" he said, giving a listless
hand to the editor, who rose with his cards, and wrung his
hand.

"Lucky dog!" said Mordaunt, in a hearty half-whisper,
which Philip felt was intended for congratulation. He half
withdrew the hand which Mordaunt was crushing; and then

let it lie. They all rose from the table and crowded about him, eager to snatch his hand. "Oh, come!" cried Philip, as his bones crunched upon each other in the grasp of a hairy paw, "I can't interrupt the game."

"Game be blowed!" replied the owner of the paw cheerily. "What's the latest from the 'Little Cipher'? That's a daisy strike of yours, Deed!"

They liked the coolness with which Philip took his good-fortune. When they heard that he had n't seen his mine yet, they formed themselves into a committee on the spot, to escort him to it in the morning.

"Better hire the 'Silas R. Phinney' brass band," said Philip, sickly laying hold of the humorous view of the situation; and staying himself upon it, as the only perma-nent object in this lurching welter, while he went on to chaff them.

None of them knew. But, of course! Had he not known that no one knew? Yes, yes! Oh, no doubt! But he had not fancied them ignorant in this way. He had expected. . . Heaven knew what he had expected! Or, yes—he remem-bered what he must have expected. He had understood vaguely that at Piñon they could not know the mine to be Jasper's—how should they? They had never heard of Jasper. It was all in his own name : both mines had been known in Piñon as equally his : "Deed's mines;"—Philip Deed's mines. Yes; he had said this to himself; but never the other thing : that they must think the "Little Cipher" *his*. Was it too obvious, he wondered, now? Had he been crazed by Jasper's damnable good fortune? Well, what matter! They thought the mine his.

A black suggestion—the devil's—plucked at him as he stood among these fellows, giving back their congratulations with dazed looks and half-hearted raillery. It came upon him suddenly, fatally, as if this, too, were a fresh thought.

R

The thought was that Jasper knew no more than they. He
knew that he owned a mine at Piñon. But which?

Philip turned pale, and tried to cry the truth at them. It
would not utter itself. Then some one proposed a toast to
the owner of the "Little Cipher," and when at last he lifted
his voice to explain their mistake at any cost, it was drowned
in the uproarious shout of congratulation.

But Philip was determined, now. He waited until he
could catch Charlie White away from the crowd; and
drawing him into a corner said, "That bill I owe you——"

"Oh, that's all right, man! You did n't think I was
anyways worried about that, did you?" asked White
jovially.

"Yes. You have n't left me at a loss to understand that
you were worried."

"Oh, my letters!" cried Charlie, waving them off magnificently. "You surely have n't been taking them seriously!
What? My little joking way! Why, I thought you were
too much of a joker yourself not to understand a bit of
fun, like that, Mr. Deed!"

"It is n't my idea of fun, Mr. White," retorted Philip,
reckless of consequences with a man whom he might have
to sue for indulgence the next minute. "I can't meet
your bill in cash at the moment," he went on haughtily.
"But if you will allow me to return the set of Thackeray,
and some of the other books in good bindings—it's coming
Christmas, and you'll have a sale for them—I can make a
small payment, on account, on the magazines and other
things I owe you for."

They spoke in an undertone; but Philip felt that they
were watched by the others, who went on drinking, leaving
the new-made Mining King to his royal whim.

"Why, what the——?" began White; and Philip saw
that he had humiliated himself for nothing. Then, as if

taken with discretion, White went on—" Why, pshaw, man !
What's the use of talking ! Charlie White ain't the last
man to understand how a fellow can be hard up with a
leased mine where they've only just struck the dust. I
don't want neither books, nor payment. Not I ! Why,
you must come down in the morning, after you've been up
to your mine, and see what you want in our line. We won't
stand on the question of credit. Five years and no
questions asked is my motto with Mr. Deed."

If he could have drawn a cheque for $69.17 then and
there and handed it over to him, Philip would have answered this as he was aware that it ought to be answered.
The consciousness that he had less than $15 in cash in the
world ; and less than $10 in his trousers' pockets, taught
him to parley with the situation, as it had often taught him to
parley with situations less vital. A wandering recollection
came to him of something he had been hoping to be able
to send Dorothy for Christmas—something which he could
get at Charlie White's, on credit, as he faced, for a moment,
the opposite prospect of a suit. White would n't want his
books, nor the small sum on account, if he knew the truth :
he didn't need to glance at the hard lines under the smile
he was wearing at the moment, to understand this quite
clearly. What he would do would be to sue him, now that
he was within reach again ; and bring down the whole
howling pack of his creditors on him. It would be an
infernal row, and he should be spattered with a lot of mud.
Why not postpone the question until he could look into
the mine quietly, and take himself out of Piñon? Then,
they were welcome to bay at his heels, if they liked : it
might amuse them and would n't hurt him. But to bring
it on himself while he was here. . . . The horror of the
temptation came over him again, and to shut out the vision
of the man that it sought to make him, he plunged into,

" Don't rely on the mine, White, if you know what's good for yourself."

"Why not?" asked White sharply. "You have n't assigned your interest in it, have you?"

Philip saw what was in his mind; he was imagining that he might have assigned his interest to avoid his creditors. He might better risk the truth than that; if that idea got abroad to-night he might as well drop everything in the morning and give himself up to his creditors. But he knew that the moment when he was likely to risk the truth was past, and in despair he said—

"No. I have n't assigned it."

It occurred to him that he should have to send his gift to Dorothy anonymously.

CHAPTER XVIII.

BEATRICE in these days was busy with her boy, who had begun at the age of four to develop a profane habit of speech which Vertner by turns laughed at and promised to punish him for. He never did punish him, for he said the child could n't help it; he was bound to hear it all about him from boys of his own age, in this rambunctious country; it was part of the country's routine of getting its growth; Edward the Second would forget all that if he was given time. When Beatrice, in doubt of time's chastisement, would punish the child with a grieving heart, herself, Vertner would bring him consolatory candy, or promise him a ride on mamma's pony, next time she came back from a ride; and this sort of promise he always carried out. He was very fond of Edward the Second as he called him, though Edward was sometimes very "bad," in the phraseology of his mother — especially when she was about to set forth on her rides. The desertion pained his young spirit, and though he was to be left with his nurse, he would occasionally lie on the floor and kick, howling out that he "hoped the pony would buck her off." This pleased Vertner, too; he would snatch him from the floor, kicking, and having set him on his shoulder would inquire vainly through the noise and dampness if he "wizshum papa's boy?" He would stay half an hour after Beatrice

had gone to hold a romp with "son bun, Ned," as he called
him on these occasions, in a contempt of English which
seemed to soothe the boy; he would stay in the face of
schemes ripening to their fall, and to the loss of plain
opportunities of rustle.　Beatrice　said　he　spoiled　her
son.

"Spoil　him?"　retorted Vertner.　"I don't know about
that; but I'm spoiling his future.　There won't be anything
left of his estate if I keep on this way.　He lost me a couple
of hundred dollars yesterday!　Too late.　Man could n't
wait.　*I* don't know what we can tell him when he asks
what we've done with his patrimonial acres.　He would n't
believe　me, I suppose, if I said I 'd had to cut off the
entail."

"Well, if you *will* stay at home with him, Ned, I wish
you 'd keep him out of the irrigating ditch!" exclaimed his
wife irrelevantly.　"That cold mountain water will give the
child his death, some day."

"Oh no!" said Vertner cheerfully.　"Not unless he
bathes in it!　You have n't lived in the West as long as I
have, Trix, or you'd know that paddling around in an
irrigating ditch can't hurt a Western born child.　Some
hygienic star watches over the nativity of a young voter who
adds himself to the population of Colorado from the start.
It's when　the　child comes West as a tenderfoot at
eighteen months, or so, that he dies of croup after his
first stolen wade under the cool shadows of the cotton-
woods."

Vertner won the last word by the usual unfairness of making her laugh.　The idea of an umbrageous shade cast by
the sickly and spindling trees, which, in this dry climate, were
kept alive only by the ceaseless flow of the irrigating ditch
about their roots, was irresistible.　But his wife followed her
own ideas of the training of Edward in a soberness which

had nothing to do with her toleration of her husband's fooling.

Ernfield had been very ill after Margaret's departure, and none of them had looked to see him again ; but he was out now, once more, and, when patients did not press, would sometimes join them in their rides. Dorothy was silently kind to him ; and Beatrice and he talked together as they always talked. Ernfield had not been able to bring himself to renew his old habit of calling on Beatrice—the habit established before Margaret came—but he went to a poker party which Vertner gave, that Beatrice might understand he was not staying away for any reason but the one she must guess. He was sure she knew about his feeling for Margaret, though he was equally sure that no one else knew through her. He lost all his original purchase of chips at the poker party, and bought a second supply of Vertner, who was banking and, by a quiet system of play of his own, winning the better part of the small stakes for which they were playing. Poker parties were the fashion in Maverick this year : they often took place on Saturday nights ; it was entirely good form for the ladies to play, it being only understood, (the casuistry was their own,) that their winnings belonged to the plate at church the next morning.

Kiteva Snell did not approve of poker parties ; but perceiving that the fashion was setting against her in this, she let Cutter teach her one night—he would sometimes amuse himself with the ghost of a flirtation to assure himself how wholly he still belonged to Elsa ; his only rule being never to flirt with a girl he respected—and a few days later she gave a poker party herself. Every one went everywhere in Maverick. There was a rigid theory of caste, of course, but it existed chiefly in the confidences exchanged between the ladies who held themselves to be not as other ladies. There was, in fact, as everywhere in the West, too little amusement of any sort to permit one to allow one's self the luxury of rejection, or differentiation.

When Mrs. B. Frank Butler sent out invitations to a "pink tea," however, some of the ladies debated as to whether the line might not perhaps exist somewhere between the railway track, and Mrs. Butler. This lady, who was the wife of one of the railway conductors, lived across the bridge spanning the mountain river flowing between the track and the town—much worse, beyond the track itself; and was reputed to have married her submissive but clever husband three years earlier in Indiana, because she thought she saw the making of a division superintendent, or general passenger agent under his freight conductor's jacket. As a matter of fact, her own ambition and resolution had urged him so far on the way to one of these offices as the position of passenger conductor may be— she having insisted that he could find such a place in the West until he had left his position on the Indiana road out of sheer weariness of her insistence. He often said that he did not see what he had gained, as he had forfeited a place worth $60 a month for a place worth $90, and had at the same time doubled, by his movement West, the cost of living. Mrs. Butler's answer to this was the purchase of a sealskin sacque (short, and possibly not quite new, but indubitably seal) with which to sustain the dignity of her new position as the wife of a passenger conductor.

"You never know who may see you," she said (it was not clear whether she had the president of the road in her mind, or the receiver, who was just then the more important functionary), "and I'm sure the impression a man's wife makes is often half the battle."

It was out of this feeling, of which she made no secret, that she gave her pink tea; and the two or three ladies who had doubted came at last, to humour it, as they said. Philip was away upon one of his searches for his father, but Dorothy, as the daughter of Mrs. Butler's clergyman was there, and Beatrice, in her capacity of social representative of Vertner's universal good humour, was there also. The men came in after the tea, and were allowed oysters.

CHAPTER XIX.

I PLEASE myself by thinking of Dorothy just at this time as the centre of all the young sentiment gathered about her. In the East, where we know that things are not what they were, a young girl is no longer likely to be called upon to choose among three lovers, a privilege which ought probably to be the inalienable right of every nice girl on both sides of the Continental Divide. But the eager army of adventurous spirits who populate the West, crossing the Mississippi at an age at which a nice girl seems much the nicest thing there is, are apt to find her the rarest product of the country; and to hold her in proportionate esteem. That one man should alone be in the secret of her niceness would, under Western conditions, be a painful extravagance; and though the instinct of the West is not for economy, it is never, in this regard, other than frugal. By a fortunate provision of Nature the pretty contest between the members of a group of young ranchmen, or mining engineers, or the galliard lieutenants stationed at a frontier fort, cannot go on for ever, else the nicest girl might finally lack niceness enough to go around. She usually mobilizes her straggling lines of amiability, and throws them upon a single knight, after a time, and if they hardily resolve to undertake the Western experiment together she commonly finds, during the first year or two, that she needs all her niceness to keep the experiment going. Sometimes she returns to the East, and marries, in the end, some

humdrum New Yorker or Bostonian. In cases like this she
leaves a reproachful sentiment of regard behind her, which
half a dozen agreeable young fellows may share without enmity
until the next young girl comes from the East to divide their
good-will ; and she often takes with her a romantic regret :
she sees how the West,—or, at least, these young Westerners
—need her, or some one not too unlike her ; she pities their unfriended, unfeminized lot; she thinks how, if she were braver,
she should have courage to share it with them ; and after
her humdrum marriage she has moments of despising the
weak-heartedness which withheld her from sharing it with
them. Fifth Avenue is a long way from the Rocky Mountains: through the mist of distance in miles and in years she
finds it easy to imagine herself suffering the West for love
of one Jack or Harry—if she had only loved him enough
—and she keeps a perfumed corner of her memory for the
real romance that clings about the whole great, rude, un-
spoiled country beyond the Mississippi : the romance which
seized her young girl's fancy, even more than the battalion
of young men, and which makes the unceasing and inexhaustible interest of the West.

Dorothy's heart and her conscience were sadly occupied,
as, with Jack by her side, she went her parish-visiting way
some days following the encounter of the brothers at the
" Snow Find." She had heard nothing of this as yet.
Her trouble was an ill-starred instance of the imperfection
of the frank and abundant Western love-making. Dick,
whom she liked so much, Dick who had been so generous
and tireless a friend to her, in ways unknown to any
friendliness but the very kindest, Dick who had come
to her rescue in one of the most difficult hours of her
life, and had ever since been beyond all saying good to
her and to her father—Dick wanted to marry her ! The
fact, when it was fully explained to her, almost caused

her to revolt from the whole institution of marriage. *Why* should Dick want to marry her? Why could he not remain her dear, her very excellent, her never-to-be-enough praised or liked friend? Why must the tiresome question of love perpetually rise to haunt the fine and cheering and noble friendship which might bind men to women, if men were different?

She saw this to be childish, or even pettish, but it was a deep feeling in her. If it was wrong, she felt that she was wrong—deeply, painfully, wrong. If every social motion between young men and young women must be conceived as charged with meaning—as trembling toward love, or away from it, the whole affair of a young girl's relation to a young man became intolerable—a game of hide-and-seek, or puss-in-a-corner, unworthy of rational beings. If she must measure her glances, or qualify her hand-clasps, or weary herself with the question of relative cordiality to this man or that, it would be a happiness to be delivered from the whole problem of marriage, or no-marriage. All Dorothy's free, gay, generous nature recoiled from this conception of her relation to anybody whatever. The heartiness, the instinct of good comradeship which differentiated her from other women, affected her with a contempt for this hair-splitting code, which forbade, and made a shameful thing of the major part of the natural, candid, human instincts of her heart toward men. She could not help grieving for Dick—poor Dick!—but she would not allow herself to be sorry for the pleasant days which had led to this. It had been very pleasant to her—his friendship; and if it was at an end (at least on the old, kindly, unconscious ground), it was not her fault, but her great misfortune. She could not see, as girls often see remorsefully, in such cases, with no better reason, how she had been to blame. Was she to have imagined, then, that Dick was in love with her? She said to herself indignantly that no such discreditable and vexatious thought about Dick could ever have entered her head. But as the full meaning of Dick's passion for her made its way into her consciousness, her heart bled for him, in perceiving how just this frame of mind, on her part, must lend poignancy to his regret. That she found him impossible and incredible as a lover, was not a thing to console his lonely sorrow at Laughing Valley City. It was to Laughing Valley that he had returned the day before with a gentle air of asking forgiveness for having spoiled their relation, which went to her heart.

"Ah, well !" she said to herself, as she caught sight of Vertner coming toward her down a side street. "He will find some good girl after a while who will see how splendid he is, as I do, and will love him besides. The worst is, we never can be friends again !"

Vertner, as he joined her at the corner, asked if he might walk along with her; and then inquired where she was going. Dorothy said she was going on a round of duty calls, but that she was glad to see him : she wanted to ask him about his plan for enlisting her father in the publication of a Church paper. She spoke anxiously, and Vertner had his unfailing cheerfulness ready for her.

"Oh, that's all right," he said. "It's a wonderful field. Its' curious some clever chap has n't worked it before." He was distributing his happy, indomitable little smile, as they walked, to every one they met. Dorothy, who had come to know a great many people in Maverick herself, by this time, was surprised and amused by the extent of his bowing acquaintance. She said he seemed very neighbourly ; and Vertner laughed. Oh, yes, he owned, a man had to know everybody. There was no telling what business he would be wanting to go into, one of these beautiful

Colorado days; and perhaps from a willingness to avoid plumbing the depths of his Church paper scheme with her, he called upon her to admire the unwearying and systematic goodness of the Colorado weather, and insisted upon the admission that there was no place in the world for a man to settle in like Maverick. "I used to think Leadville was about right," he said, with a smile which admitted her into his professional insincerity, "but that was when I owned more corner lots in Leadville than I do now."

"No, but about the paper—" began Dorothy, again.

And, as if it had slipped his mind, "Oh, yes, about the paper!" he exclaimed; and changed the subject.

Dorothy had intended to make her first call on Miss Kiteva Snell; but, perceiving that Vertner hoped that she would be obliged to leave him before they had definitely arrived at the subject of the paper, she changed her course, determining to begin with Mrs. Felton, who lived much further out, not far from the river road.

"Why, you see it's this way," said Vertner, when he found that he must make a virtue of necessity. "There's no diocesan paper; and your father and I thought it would be a good thing to start one." Dorothy laughed boldly at Vertner's use of the word "diocesan"; if she had not been much concerned about her father's share in the paper, she would have taken time to be amused by the idea of Vertner as the publisher of a Church journal—a function which he presently explained that he was to assume, if her father decided to go into the enterprise, and would accept the post of editor.

It appeared that this was to be a weekly—"a little weekly for a cent," Vertner called it; it was really to be very small, but was to be sold at rather less than a cent, in quantities, to the various congregations of the diocese. "We'll take in New Mexico and Wyoming after a while; but we thought of beginning with Colorado," said Vertner, modestly. " In these missionary dioceses, you know,"—Dorothy could not help admiring the glibness with which he used his second-hand knowledge procured, she felt sure, from her father,— "they have n't got around to the little diocesan papers that are so common in the East. But all dioceses need them. They are popular with the Bishops because it gives them a channel for direct communication with all the people of their dioceses—appointments, pastoral letters, and all that, you know ; they are popular with the priests," (Dorothy wished not to be irreverent, but she was forced to smile at Vertner's confident use of her father's high-church word,) " because we print a special edition for each church, with local announcements, and the people like them because they get them for nothing."

" For nothing ?" inquired Dorothy, not understanding how her father was to profit by such an arrangement.

"Well, the same thing. They feel as if they got them for nothing. Of course each church will subscribe as a body, but the papers will be distributed every Sunday in the pews, free. Every church will subscribe. We sha'n't stick them very much for the paper by the hundred."

" But how do you expect to make your fortune, Mr. Vertner, by that plan—and papa's ? I suppose you intend to make your fortune ?" she asked, with twinkling eyes.

Vertner smote his hands together with delight. He was wearing a pair of sealskin gloves, and the concussion made a resounding noise. " Yes, yes ! " he cried, generously enjoying his foible with her. "Of course ! What are we here for ? "

" For your health, Mr. Vertner ?" suggested Dorothy roguishly, under her breath.

Vertner smiled with her. " I 'm afraid it would n't do to trust you with our scheme for making a go of this thing," he said, looking at her with admiration. "You might understand it."

"Thanks."

"It's a good scheme," he said, fondly. "Do you think I could trust you?"

"To misunderstand it?"

"No—not to go and give it away to the big advertisers." They laughed together at this, and Vertner said he thought he could rely on her friendliness to her father to keep her from indiscreet revelations, and explained how they—he always implicated her father, Dorothy observed, with interest —were only going to charge for advertising in proportion to the circulation, and were only going to charge a cent a line per thousand of circulation, at that.

"But that is worse and worse," cried Dorothy. "I don't see but you are sure to lose money. You are taking every precaution."

"Um," meditated Vertner, with a cheerful smile. "Strikes you that way, does it? Well, it does most every one, to tell the truth. I've mentioned the idea to half-a-dozen men in Denver who do a good deal of advertising, and that's what they said. They asked me if I could n't corner enough annual ruin in mines without monkeying with Church newspapers, at a cent a line, and prove your circulation by monthly affidavits? I had to do a little fright at that, of course, as if that view of the case had n't occurred to me. Your intuition, Miss Maurice," he said, making her a flattering bow, "taken in connection with their business judgment, makes me feel happy about the scheme. So you think your father and I would drop our molasses jug if we went into the *Church Kalendar* on that basis?"

"No, Mr. Vertner," returned Dorothy, with an unperturbed face, which Vertner resisted an inclination to applaud, "if you say there is a fortune in it, I shall get myself a new pair of gloves to-day. I'm sure you always know when you are going to make a fortune."

"Ah, that makes two persons who believe in me!" exclaimed Vertner. "The other is a man in Denver who dropped to my scheme. He fell off a ten-story building on it. It was glorious. I chummed with him for an hour like a brother, and swore him to secrecy."

"Oh, please chum with me like a sister, Mr. Vertner!"

"Shall I? Well, the man said it was too pretty a scheme to give away. I believe you'll have the same feeling," he said with a reverence which he failed in burlesquing. "You see—"

He hesitated.

"Well?"

"Well, we don't make any guarantees about the circulation. It may be small or it may be—large." He paused for the effect.

"But—" began Dorothy, not finding herself more illuminated.

"Well! We make them take out a yearly contract in consideration of the lowness of the price."

"But still I don't see," cried Dorothy.

"Don't you? How many subscribers do you think we shall have at the end of six months?"

"I don't know," returned Dorothy, laughing. "Five thousand?"

"What! Five cents a line! Do you want to starve us? The circulation at the end of the first half year will be a quarter of a million. How many churches do you suppose there are in Colorado, Wyoming, New Mexico, Arizona, Montana, Dakota, Washington, Oregon, California and Nevada?" He rolled off the portentous list with enjoyment. Dorothy again replied that she did not know. "Well, neither do I," owned Vertner frankly; "but there must be a quarter of a million regular attendants at those churches at a low calculation. Now do you see?"

Dorothy laughed aloud. "And are you going to make every one of those people subscribe to the *Church Kalendar?*" she asked.

"I'm going to *give* it to them!" replied Vertner. And at Dorothy's look of bewilderment,—"On a *bonâ-fide* subscription plan, of course. We'll arrange that with the rectors. But you see the point, perhaps?"

"With the advertisers?" faltered Dorothy.

Vertner nodded, happily. "But will they—will they like it?" asked Dorothy.

"Well, I don't believe they will renew their contracts for the second year," admitted Vertner sententiously.

Dorothy did not instantly see her way through the sinuosities of this ingenious plan; but she thought she was sure that there was a lurking wrong to somebody involved in it. She reserved this for her father, however. She meant to ask him all about it, and to beg him, whatever the honesty, and whatever the promise of the enterprise, not to share in it. She doubted all projects for making money, *primâ facie.* She had not merely a woman's conservatism about finance; she had the timidity of all who live on a stated income; and to this she added a rooted distrust of her father's financial capacity. It was the only distrust she allowed herself regarding him; and even this was affectionate : how should such a man be skilled in the ways of trade?

She formed a project of asking Jasper to advise him not to engage in the plan. She knew that her father respected Jasper's judgment; and perhaps he would suffer himself to be persuaded by him on the business side, when her own remonstrances would not avail. Jasper and her father had been even more intimate since the renewal of their acquaintance in Maverick than she remembered them in the old

days ; Jasper had once come and sat out the evening with
her father in his study, smoking a pipe, only looking
in on her to say "Good night." Possibly Jasper would
go into it with him ; that would make it safe, for she
was sure that any business project of which Jasper approved
and to which he gave his mind must prosper. But she was
in a moment not sure that she wished this. She would
not say to herself all that this thought implied to her
own consciousness. She shrank from putting it before
herself, as she had begun to shrink lately from her pre-
visions of the final outcome of her present singular relation
to Jasper. She had said to herself that she must bring
the matter to an end, but she had not yet found the
hardihood for that, and meanwhile she felt herself being
surrounded, she had the sense of being softened and
drawn to him by a slow, certain process, like the fatal
eating of the sea into a rock. Jasper's will was in itself a
reason for anything that he strongly wished : through all the
strength of her own will, she felt this. Sometimes she felt
it insupportably, and it was at such times that she said to
herself that she must end it. Alas ! it is really only the
man who can put an end to such a situation. A woman
can only make her way out of it by a violence, an un-
womanliness. From all that could be held unwomanly
Dorothy shrank with much more reluctance than from
anything that the situation into which Jasper had contrived
to bring her with himself could have to offer ; and she
helplessly let the affair lapse and drift.

Thinking of Jasper led her to speak of him ; and
Vertner's extraordinary interest in the subject was causing
her a vague wonder, when they met Dr. Ernfield, driving
back to Maverick from a professional visit which he had
been paying at Loredano. He drew up to the sidewalk and
they paused to speak to him. Dorothy thought, sadly, that

he was looking very weak and ill again. Dorothy had last seen him at Beatrice's card party, where he was looking much stronger than now; and she was grieved by his appearance of illness. She begged him to come and see her; she said she was in shockingly good health, but she would come down with any new and unstudied disease that he liked, if he would not come without that. But she hoped he would.

Ernfield said he should be glad to come without excuse, if she would let him. He had often seen Dorothy at Mrs. Vertner's while Margaret was in Maverick; and twice since Margaret had gone, he had been to the Maurices' cottage: once to see Maurice himself, when he had been suffering from a bad cold, and once again to call on them, with no business reason. Dorothy's cordial freedom, her sweetness, and the candid openness with which she lavished herself on him when he came, were not things which any one could fail to like and certainly were not things which a man in his position could be other than grateful for. When he had last seen her he had scorned himself for the stealthy pain which ventured to show its head at the thought that it was only to a man out of the running that a woman could venture to be as good as that; and he was willing to go again to punish himself for the thought, by enjoying her kindness as whole-heartedly as it was offered. Surely, in so far as any one could imply by words said, and left unsaid, that he was a robust marcher in the ranks with the rest, with a brave, rich, life before him, she implied it, with her woman's tact. It was himself he must accuse; and he did it handsomely, as Dorothy, with the yearning painted on her face, in spite of herself, to do something for him, to somehow give him a lift, to cheer and comfort him, begged him to come and see her.

Vertner asked the news at Loredano. How was the strike Pope had made in the "Nugget" coming on? And had Metuchen driven his bunch of cattle over into Bayles

Park for the winter? It was part of the kindliness and inbred courtesy, which oddly mingled themselves with other qualities in Vertner, that he forebore to follow Dorothy's suggestion with one of his hearty invitations to Look in on a fellow, once in a while, won't you? He did not care anything about Pope's mine, or Metuchen's cattle; but he felt the obligation to bridge the gap. Ernfield did not want to be asked to that house of painful reminders, *he* knew; and he didn't even want to be reminded that anybody was taking care not to remind him.

Ernfield, after a word of inquiry about Dorothy's church work, which had always seemed to interest him, drove on, turning back to say that he had met Mrs. Vertner coming out of Mrs. McDermott's house, on the river road: they would meet her if they went on. Fred Kelfner, who occupied his usual seat beside the doctor, lifted his hat to Dorothy as Ernfield whipped up his horse.

They were out of the town now, and walking toward the mountains against the brisk wind which often blows at these altitudes. Ouray was behind them, but on their right the long serrated rib of the Sangre de Christo range cut the fiery welter of the western sky. The range hung a curtain before the setting sun, which went on shining behind it. Over the white flanks of the sweep of hills walling the other side of the valley there began presently to spread a tender, subtle, infinitely delicate glow, like a maiden's blush, which is and is not.

Vertner talked gaily on, in the wind; but the still peace and beauty in which the hills lay about her, and a flying rack of thoughts within her mind, kept Dorothy quiet. She began to wish that she had not set out to make a round of visits: she had come out to escape, if she could, from her miserable thoughts about Dick, but she had not lost them, and this new trouble about her father, about Jasper, seemed

to connect itself with the other, and to agglutinate the
whole into that single mass of vexation which will sometimes cloud over a day or an hour for the lightest-hearted.

She would have turned back, but she bethought herself
of Mrs. Felton, for whom she had set out, and who, she
knew, was battling with a misery of her own, which her
visit might lighten momently, perhaps. She did not say to
herself that to solace Mrs. Felton's homesickness might be
a roundabout way of helping herself to climb a little out of
her own depths ; though she knew, well enough, that the
only real happiness lay, and must always lie, in some one
else's happiness.

Mrs. Felton had lately come to Maverick from Philadelphia
as a bride—having married a capital young fellow, originally
from the same city. He had founded a prosperous Real
Estate and Insurance business in Maverick within the year,
and had lately been encouraged by his success to return to
the East long enough to marry the faithful and charming girl
who had waited four years for him. She was just passing
through the first homesick time in which young wives, fresh
from certain traditions of the East, sit in puzzled and miserable helplessness before the conditions of Western life. Mrs.
Felton felt that the desolation, the strangeness, the hideous-
ness of her first month in Maverick—the month which she
had looked forward to as the happiest of her life—had left a
permanent mark on her. She wondered whether they would
see it in her eyes at home when she went back. But she
was determined that they never should. They had told her
that it would be something like this,—not guessing, in their
ignorance, a thousandth part of the fact, but prophesying in
the cheerful manner of kinsfolk, before one's marriage. They
should never know how she had realized their prophecies.

She planned to confide the truth to Jessie Kidder, who
was betrothed to a young man who had just left Harvard,

and had gone to Dakota to start a horse ranch ; she planned
to warn her under the seal of confidence. It was wrong to
let a young girl venture upon such a future blindly. Jessie
would be dazed and troubled by what she should say to her ;
but she heard her answering that she did n't care ; that she
was not marrying to live in this place or that, but for love
of her husband, who would be sufficient for her anywhere.
And then Mollie Felton saw how she must tell her that that,
too, was a mistake : that what she said was true enough, in
a way, and more than true enough. She herself had never
been so happy. No. But then, she had never been so unhappy. She perceived that it would be useless ; but if she
ever got home again—she no longer really believed that
they should ever be free to retraverse all those dreary miles
of rail—she should tell her. It was a duty.

Mrs. Felton was of course not very well seen in Maverick.
She was thought too Eastern ; too exclusive. She had an
honest hatred of gossip, and, in other ways, had not proved
as " adaptable " as some of the ladies could desire. It was
reported that she had once said that she did not think herself better than her butcher ; but different. And opinions
like this separated her from such society as there was in
Maverick, and had helped to make her first month difficult.
Dorothy understood her trouble exactly : when she had first
come to the West she had passed through a time not very
unlike Mrs. Felton's, herself. Even in the midst of her
week or two of homesickness, however, she had been able to
see it, partly, as the joke it was ; and when she was better of
it, the humour of the whole Western situation had soon so
penetrated her that she remembered her first feeling about
the West, now, only as a sentiment which she could call up,
at need, to assist her sympathy for another in like case. She
did not pretend to delight in the West, now, as Kiteva Snell
did ; but she was busy, she was absorbed in making the

West bearable to her father (who hated it), she was up to her eyes in the business of tempering the situation to him, in the enterprise of making him happy, and for herself she had ceased to care very definitely. One was happy anywhere where one had an absorbing occupation; and it was this wisdom that she was presently preaching to Mrs. Felton, when she had left Vertner with Beatrice, whom they met near Mrs. Felton's house.

Mrs. Felton had often accompanied them on their rides lately, and Dorothy pretended that it was to invite her to join Beatrice and Ernfield and herself in a ride on the morrow that she had called.

Mrs. Felton was not like the pretty little Jewess, upon whom Dorothy called next, unhappy because she "did so miss the *matinées*." Mrs. Felton's homesickness, if passionate, was not fantastic. Dorothy did not ask Mrs. Stern (who for an occult reason, of the sort that no one thought of questioning in Maverick, chose to go to Maurice's church) why she did not complain of the indigestibility of the clay in Lone Creek Valley; but a number of impossible questions were on her lips.

At Kiteva Snell's the atmosphere was amusingly different. The Snells, of whom Kiteva was most in evidence, socially, were very happy about themselves and the West. Miss Kitty, in particular, would hear nothing against any State West of the Mississippi, and she kept alive a fine enthusiasm about Maverick and its future which had the fire and the taking largeness of a sentiment of patriotism. She had not seen New York, and did not care to; but she knew and loved the Omaha of her birth, though she could seldom be persuaded to go so far East, when her father would go on his pass. She was glad to remember that even her name was Western, for she had been christened Kiteva in honour of a summer resort for the people of Chicago, which her father had been engaged in booming, at the time of her birth. It was a regretable fact that the books she wanted to read were, for the most part, published in New York or Boston, and she could only balance this misfortune by ordering them through the local newsdealer (there was not a bookseller in Maverick), in order that "the money," as the Western phrase is, "might not go out of the town." It happened also that the centre of her present intellectual life had its physical habitation on the shores of a New York lake ; but she tried not. to remember that the advantages of the "Chautauqua Literary Association" were derived from Jamestown.

Kiteva had acquired her fondness for reading at a Toledo boarding school, where one could acquire a glossy coat of Culture in three years, with diligence. Kiteva had used the diligence, and when Dorothy first knew her, she was in the earlier maturity of that habit of exactitude and impeccability, which are the very things for general conversation. Her *a* in "squalor" was quite, quite long, and she pronounced her "Asia" between her teeth, with the alluring sibilant effect : *Acia*. She accented her "le-gis-lative" on the second syllable, and could pronounce a great many words just as they are in the Dictionary, without smiling. Nothing, though, was so nice in her conversation as her elegant habit of bridling the shambling looseness of our common speech in colloquial phrases, like "could n't you," which she prettily replaced with "could not you," and the sloven "a-tall," to which she restored its printed aspect—so that "at all," with a proper fence between, lived again. Her favourite books of reference were *The Orthœpist, A Thousand Words often Mispronounced,* and *The Verbalist.* Her *vade mecum,* however, was *Don't,* and it is fair to say that Miss Snell did n't.

Kiteva did not talk of the things of the mind, as she

called them, with Dorothy; she talked of Jasper—a little
persistently, Dorothy thought. She had heard that he had
returned, and had seen him ride by from her window, but
had not yet met him face to face since his return. How
was he looking? Had he enjoyed his visit to New York?
He seemed very fond of the ranch, and of his work there.
He had done wonders with it. She quoted sayings of
Jasper; she rehearsed incidents of the time before Dorothy
came to Maverick. She gave the impression of having
known Jasper very well. Dorothy wondered if this was
the kind of young lady with whom he occupied his leisure
when she was not near.

She left Kiteva a little abruptly at last; and took her
way back to her own end of the town with a vague feeling
of weariness tightening about her heart. Too many things
had happened to-day; there was too much to think of.
Her head went round in a whirl.

She entered her own home with Jack, at last, on the verge
of tears. The day and the world seemed to have gone hopelessly wrong. Her father, who had learned to interpret the
signs of suppressed emotion in her, patted her hand quietly
as, with her hat and jacket still on, she took her accustomed
seat in his study, on the arm of his big leather chair.

"Well, little girl, what is it?" he asked, laying down the
volume of Guy de Maupassant he had been reading.

"Oh, I don't know, father! I don't know. I wish you
would n't go into this paper of Mr. Vertner's," she said
abruptly.

"But my dear young woman——!" He smiled vaguely
at her.

"He told me all about it this afternoon. I don't
believe," she told him, stroking his beard, as she bent over
him, "that you know as much about the *Church Kalendar*
as I do, papa. Ask Mr. Vertner about his advertising; and

his—his ' scheme,' as he calls it. It is n't nice. It is just
like you, papa, not to have looked into the details of it, at
all ; and to have accepted the idea because Mr. Vertner
says it is a good one."

" Pshaw ! pshaw ! There's nothing wrong with the idea,
child. What do you know of papers, Dorothy ? " He got
up and went over to the upright piano which filled a corner
of the study.

This room, in which Maurice wrote his sermons, and
played on his piano, was the largest in the house, and occupied
the whole front of the second story. Dorothy never interrupted him here in the mornings, when the superstition was
that he was hammering out his sermons ; but she often
spent the evenings with him in its smoke-laden atmosphere.
Sermon writing, with Maurice, required the consumption of
a number of Havanna cigars, and was accompanied by a
good deal of Sullivan and Offenbach on the piano. Dorothy
would hear him playing and singing snatches of comic opera
in the mornings for half an hour ; then the piano would
suddenly go silent ; and, from below, she would hear him
pacing the floor. Then this sound, too, would cease, and
she would know that he was at work, until the piano burst
out again. In the moments of silence he was as often
reading as writing ; but this would have counted as work,
too, with Dorothy, if she had known it. She had a little
pride of her own in his learning. Maurice's smattering of a
number of subjects was far from that, but he was by nature
a bookish man ; he read the poets, whom he was fond of
quoting in his sermons ; he had once relinquished the
thought of a book on the Old Dramatists ; he had a pretty
taste for Barrow, whose sturdiness and solidity attracted him
by the law of the attraction of opposites, perhaps ; he rambled
through him from time to time, pencilling his winged
adjectives ; and regularly, once a year, he read Thackeray

from start to finish. His contemporary reading was, for the most part, French; of the older writers he liked Dumas, whose *Trois Mousquetaires* he read at all seasons; he was a subscriber to the *Revue des Deux Mondes* and the *Saturday Review*; and he loathed the present school of American fiction; he said it lacked—but we know what it lacks.

"Come and sing ''The Bailiff's Daughter,'" he said, as he took his seat on the piano stool.

Dorothy, who had taken up her knitting, shook her head. She seated herself in the chair he had left, and, lost to his sight in its depths, she stared into the fire through the tears of overwrought emotion which stole out upon her eyelids, and coursed silently down her cheeks. Her father, after a dreamy prelude, had rattled into the "Entrance March" from the *Mikado*.

"Did Vertner say how he was getting along?" he asked, pausing in the middle of the march.

"No," Dorothy managed to reply in a muffled voice.

"I should like to get out the first number in January," he said meditatively. He whistled a bar or two of another air from the same opera thoughtfully over to himself; and turned to the piano to finish it.

"Papa!" she said, loud enough to be heard above the music. He rose and came over to her.

"What! crying?" he exclaimed. "But this won't do at' all." He drew up a chair beside her, and took her hand. "Why, girlie, there's nothing in this. Nothing!" He regarded her tenderly, as he stroked her hand. He let her sacrifice herself to him from habit, he postponed her to many things; but he loved her. One saw it in his glance even when it rested on her casually; no one could have seen him at the moment without feeling sure of it. "I won't enter into it at all if you take it so hard. But you've been accepting some of Vertner's joking literally. You must allow for his way of looking at things. Why, I don't believe he would care for this paper idea at all if he did n't see a joke in it."

"Yes, papa," rejoined Dorothy, starting up in her chair, "that's it. It's a joke—a practical joke; but it is n't—it is n't quite what you would call a fair one, I think, papa, if you understood it. Do look into it before you give your word to Mr. Vertner to be his editor."

"Of course I will, little girl! Vertner must n't be allowed to compromise me. Perhaps I 've let him have it too much his own way. But he knows about the business side of it; and, after my experience with the Church School of Music, I 'm willing to let some one else take all that responsibility. You can understand that, Dorothy."

"Oh, father, I'll be so glad if you will! And let some one else find the money, too!"

Maurice pensively stroked his long, golden moustache, with its young-mannish upward turn at the ends, without speaking. "I suppose you see the necessity of my making more money, my dear. The last monthly bills look bad. Maverick seems to be dearer than Laughing Valley. This editorship is more like a necessity than a choice. It is n't time to be too nice," he said, with the doubtful accent of waiting her opinion on this.

This man, who could satisfy his own conscience about one and another matter of daily dealing with his fellow-men, and forget it lightly; who could shuffle and balance before doubtful questions, and choose the easy issue with a sigh for the man he might have been if things had turned out differently with him, was afraid before his daughter's moral judgments. Their certainty, their bare, blind justice were more than he could bear at times. He avoided all such questions with her when he could; but he had committed himself to this paper with Vertner; and, since he must go

on with it, and she had learned of his connection with the
plan, he would go on with her support rather than without
it. They lived too much alone, he was too dependent upon
her for sympathy, to make it pleasant for him to carry on
constantly, by her side, a work which she disapproved of.
He was sensitive; he always reckoned with that. If he had
not been it would have been easy to use his authority, as he
sometimes did in cases like that of the money he procured
from time to time to meet their bills. No one knew better
than Maurice how to put aside discussion of painful subjects
with dignity; but no one liked less to accept what such
uses of power involved.

He did not think for a moment of abandoning the
scheme of the paper; he believed that he and Vertner
should make a very good thing of it together; and it was
five years since he had drunk just the wine he liked. The
moral question, which had never occurred to him until
Dorothy suggested it, he had dismissed without a thought.
He understood Vertner's advertising plan at least as well as
Dorothy; but he saw nothing wrong in it, as he had told her.

He explained to her, now, that it was not original with
Vertner; that it had been tried in the East, where a man
had made a small fortune out of it. There was no harm in
it, except as there was harm in all business. She did not
hope to bring in a new sort of business transaction, which
would leave the money in the same pocket, after it as before
it, he hoped. They did not dispute—he and Vertner—that
they were going to take money for the advertising; but they
were going to give *quid pro quo*, strictly. They did not
even leave the degree of circulation given to the advertisement in doubt as was usual. The advertisers were to pay
for what they got; and for no more than they got. She
heard Vertner in all these phrases, yet it was her father who
spoke, and she did not know how to put her doubts together

and bring them to bear on him. She found herself shaken by his confidence; but she said, "I see you think you understand, papa. But you don't; you can't, or you would n't have anything to do with it. These advertisers you speak of—they are not to know what Mr. Vertner means to do. They will suppose that they are giving their advertisement to a little paper which will have a circulation of a few hundred copies. When the bills come to them, if Mr. Vertner succeeds in what he hopes to do, they will be for a circulation of a great many thousands; it will go on increasing every month; and they will have no redress because Mr. Vertner is going to make them sign a contract for a year."

Maurice laughed lightly. "Don't you think you may safely leave Vertner's scheme to the business men of the Great West, Dorothy? Do you think it likely that they will not understand all the bearings of a proposition that a girl like you can understand?"

Dorothy stared at him. "Oh, I suppose so," she said after a moment, daunted. "But promise to insist on Mr. Vertner making it plain to them what they are doing." She laughed herself at the futility of this. "I mean," she amended, "that the contract should imply what Mr. Vertner is about—what he hopes to do."

"They would laugh at what he hopes to do. You do, yourself, Dorothy. Every one who knows Vertner understands his disposition to add ciphers to his schemes. You may be sure he has given them all the ciphers that he thinks they will credit. After all, you know, Vertner is honest. You must n't be losing yourself in any theories depending on the opposite supposition, you know, Dorothy."

"Oh, of course he's honest!" sighed she, parting with her position, in fragments, as she felt, but with a deep reluctance. She saw that it was one of those obscure cases where the ethics have a tendency to liquefy, to escape from the instinct which is their only witness, and to melt into the medium of the business-like, the practical, the customary. She could not detain them; perhaps she was wrong to try. Her father must know; and "Yes, I'm sure Mr. Vertner is good," she found herself saying, "in spite of his ways— perhaps because of them. There is something very charming about him. He is so sure, so gay! And I don't believe that he would deliberately do anything that he thought wrong" she argued aloud with herself.

"Certainly not!"

She balanced it all in her mind a moment, and then with the recurrence of her loyal trust in her father, which at the end of everything had always to be the permanent fact in her relation to him and to his doings, she said, with a brightening face, "Oh well, if you have really looked into it, papa, and think it right, why——"

"Yes?"

"Why, of course it *is* right! But you will look carefully after Mr. Vertner, won't you, papa? You will see that he makes an agreement that will be fair to everybody?" He gave the promise readily, though he had no intention of interfering with Vertner. She leaned over, and kissed him. "Dear papa! And shall we be shockingly rich?"

"Appallingly!" laughed Maurice, easily, as he returned to the piano. "Come and sing that for me."

She came over to his side, adjusting the light so that it should not fall into the eyes he tired by late reading at night.

"Then you can have a horse and phaeton," she said, stroking his hair, as he spread out the music for her.

"I am not so ambitious, my dear. What I'm hoping for is an income which won't force me to look three times at a dollar. Twice, I can bear. Well, are you ready?"

He struck a chord on the piano, and she raised her voice to the first notes of the quaint old air.

CHAPTER XX.

PHILIP remained a fortnight at Piñon; and it was a week before Jasper was seen in Maverick again. Dorothy heard from Dr. Ernfield on the day following her parish visits and her meeting with Vertner that Jasper was suffering from the effects of an accident; but Ernfield either knew no more, or thought it well to say no more, for she got no particulars from him. Vertner had heard all about the affair in the mine from Cutter; but he had left town the day after their meeting to look after a contract for the electric lighting of Empire, a mining camp lying to the northward, and was not expected to return for some days, so that Dorothy learned nothing from him.

Jasper's first clear thought on returning to consciousness was of her. What would she think of the fight, if it should come to her ears? Her swift, pitiless moral judgments were as terrible to him as they were to her father. Suppose she thought him in the wrong?

But he believed she had not the material for such a thought. Philip's freak of reserve had spared her some facts that might affect her judgment; and he believed that, in any event, the initial faith in him which Dorothy retained from the habit of an earlier day, would carry him through a good deal with her. He accepted, now, in good faith, Philip's assertion of his forbearance from his obvious opportunity, and he saw that she would never hear Philip's story until

T

he should force Philip to defend himself by telling her his own. What a frightful ass Philip was to play the chivalric at that rate, he mused. But that was his affair.

His thoughts melted dizzily into each other, as he lay half awake on the morning after the accident, trying his eyes in a blinking way every little while on the view from his bedroom window. The cowboy who had been nursing him assured him that the hill he saw was Mount Blanco, fast enough. To Jasper it was a green blur. Some sort of film seemed to be crackling and sparkling before his eyes, like a kaleidoscope, eternally breaking up and renewing itself. He saw objects as the natural eye sees the page of a book held within an inch of the pupil. He felt vaguely for the bandage on his forehead, and then remembered again how it came there, and all that had led up to it. At recollection of the blow, the suffocating sense of hatred and rage he remembered as he fell, was fresh in his mind again. He clenched his hands under the bedclothes. When he was well again, he should not spare.

The thought that Philip might be making favour with Dorothy, or that she might have learnt what he had refused to tell her, and that the knowledge might, nay, certainly would have effected a promotion of him in her kindness, caused him to thresh restlessly about in the bed. He told Ernfield, when he came, that he must get up to-day. Ernfield smiled quietly, and asked him to try sitting up in bed. He straightened himself and sat up painfully, his eyes wild and unseeing, his carefully-kept hair in disarray. The air dissolved about him; he clutched at his fading consciousness and fell back among the pillows with a moaning curse on his lips.

It was the fourth day before Ernfield would allow him to sit about in his dressing-gown, and write a letter, and the sixth before he pronounced him well enough to try the voyage down stairs, staying himself upon the balustrade.

He made Ernfield remain to dinner with him the first day. " I say, I've been taking a simple cut pretty hard, seems to me. What's been the matter? What have I had?"

" Why, you have n't had it,' said Ernfield.

" How's that? You mean I've escaped it. Well, what have I escaped?"

" Congestion of the brain."

" Humph!" exclaimed Jasper, without troubling himself to explain the connection. "That brother of mine is a brute!" He asked Ernfield if he would take another bit of venison; and Ernfield did not pursue the subject. He had his own notions of the way his patient had come by his cut.

" I say, Ernfield," Jasper went on, after a moment, "you knew something of my new mother, when she was here in Maverick. What was she like?"

" Like?"

" Yes. You know I never saw much of her. Was she the kind of woman to make my father happy, for instance?"

Ernfield busied himself with his fresh slice of venison, pursuing a bit of currant jelly with his fork. "I did n't know your father well; I could n't say," he answered. "One ought to know more than one party to a marriage to answer a question like that."

Jasper had heard fragments of the talk which still went on in Maverick about Ernfield and Margaret, of course. He was revolving the gossip of the town in his mind, as he bent his shrewd, penetrating eyes on his companion's face.

"Yes, to be sure. But you would form some idea of her temperament. Would she be the sort of woman, for example, to support my father in—well, in what you might call the extravagances of his temperament? I suppose you know him well enough to understand what I mean."

Ernfield looked at him for what seemed a long time without speaking. "Yes," said he, at last, with intention, "I know what you mean."

"It *was* rather rough, was n't it?" agreed Jasper to the unspoken comment.

"It was cowardly," said Ernfield briefly.

"It certainly left Miss Derwenter with a nasty position on her hands. It was a test of character—abandoning her on her wedding day," he said tentatively. But Ernfield did not offer to discuss this. "She came out of it curiously—on a plan of her own," he mused. "But it's given me a kind of respect for her! Not every woman would have done it, you know, Ernfield."

"I know," nodded Ernfield to the canned peaches, which had been set before him.

"She answered my question for me, there : she supported him with a vengeance. But would she in a case where she was n't concerned in just that helpless way?"

"I can't answer that," said Ernfield, after a moment. "She would do what seemed right to her."

"Yes," rejoined Jasper, "I gather that. She seems to have a conscience. But she seems fond of father, too. What I was wondering was whether in a case where he was on one side and her conscience on the other, she might n't— well, negotiate with her conscience."

Ernfield glanced at him without speaking.

"Well, I'm glad you think so," said Jasper, after a moment, in response to Ernfield's contemptuous glance. "Father needs a check." He turned the subject then; but as he lighted Ernfield's cigarette for him. "Where did the wedding party go? Did you hear?" he asked, carelessly.

Ernfield perceived that he meant to imply that he might have heard from Margaret since her departure from Maverick. But he chose not to resent this. Jasper was not worth the powder.

"No," he replied. He puffed his cigarette in silence.

The following day, seeing how Jasper chafed under his confinement, and thinking, on the whole, it might be less harmful for him to venture out than to remain within doors lashing himself into a state of morbid irritation, Ernfield consented to allow him to drive to town. Riding he forbade; and Jasper found that the jolting of his buckboard was all he cared to bear, for the present.

He had not seen Snell since the day he had called to make his preposterous announcement; but this had not surprised him. His father and brother were too wise to attempt to push the matter to a conclusion while he lay ill; but they should see that he was not seeking a prolongation of the truce. He meant they should hear from him at once.

When he had been to his lawyer, and arranged with him to secure a temporary injunction against Snell and to begin suit against his father he drove to the Maurices' cottage, smiling for the first time since his discomfiture at the "Snow Find."

He had made up his mind to a definite move which would at least relieve him of the fear of what Philip might be accomplishing with Miss Maurice, behind his back.

She came in to him with her face alive with sympathy; and Jasper was agreeably sure that he had not been wrong in thinking she had warmed to him with a new kindness in the week before his accident, while he added to himself that his illness and the wound on his forehead were not things to diminish her mood of good will. He lacked material for guessing that part of her mood of sympathy was due to the fact that she had just parted with Dick Messiter, who had stopped over a train to call on her father in regard to some business on his return from a visit to Denver. (She had found him much changed in the week which had passed since his return to his work at Laughing Valley City.) Much

more he lacked facts to understand that her recent disposition
toward him was the outcome of the talk between her and
Philip which had followed his encounter with Philip in the
doorway of the room in which he was now sitting. He was
occupied, so far as his mind turned toward Philip's refusal,
for motives of his own, to give him away, with the negative
good fortune that she had no information about their quarrel.
It did not occur to him to imagine that if she knew of a
quarrel between them, she must believe one of them in the
wrong; and that Philip might be suffering for his Quixotic
silence.

"You have been ill," she said. "You have been suffering."

"Oh, so, so!" returned Jasper. "I got a rather nasty cut."

"Tell me how it happened. No one has been able to
say—or perhaps no one would." Jasper slipped down in
the sleepy hollow chair she had forced him to take, and
toasted the foot he stretched towards the fire, enjoying her
interest in his illness. His pallor, she thought, became
him; and the firelight, playing on his handsome face, and
twinkling whimsically upon the court-plastered wound, lent
his solid, prosy good looks a remote effect of distinction,
and of glamour. "Don't let me ask if it's a secret. But
if it is n't a secret," she went on, with a laugh, "you can
make it as romantic as you like, for I've heard nothing.
You can make out that you have been rescuing a lovely
maiden from the Utes, if you wish. That would be as
pretty as anything. Or you can have been dragged by
Vixen, with your foot caught in the stirrup: that would be
exciting. Or a fight with the Eveleighs about your
water rights, or fences, would make a good story. I like
mining stories, too, Mr. Deed." She smiled at him from
her seat at the other corner of the fire. She often chaffed
him to avoid the serious talk with him which she had begun
to see must one day come; and which she feared.

"This *is* a mining story," returned Jasper, staring musingly into the fire, with a disengaged look.

"How nice ! Well ? "

" Well—I think I must n't tell it," he said, still seeming to muse. He glanced at her speculatively ; and Dorothy thought she saw that she should not be overstepping in urging him.

" No," he said, shaking his head slightly, in response to her mock humble entreaty. " It is n't altogether my story."

"How tiresome ! Could n't we buy out the other man's rights in the story? Is he the same man who owns a part of the mine—was that it?"

The guess was wide, and yet so near that Jasper smiled. "Something like that."

He glanced at her with intelligence, and she suddenly paled, and cried, in a kind of fright, "Surely it is n't your brother ! Surely you have n't been—been— ? " She breathed quickly, and stopped.

" Yes," owned Jasper, with the air of a man who yields to a revelation past remedy, " Yes—since you have guessed it, there is no reason why you should n't know. But don't ask me any more about it, please. I could n't tell you."

" Oh, no, no ! " cried Dorothy. " Of course not. And it was he who— ! Oh ! " she exclaimed. Her tone expressed reproach and repulsion, and withdrawal. She shuddered away from the thought of Philip's act. " And you have been very ill ! I can see it ! Dr. Ernfield would not own it, but I could see that he was anxious. He was afraid of its affecting the brain."

" Yes," said Jasper lightly—"congestion and all that. But there was never any actual danger of that, I fancy. Ernfield did n't really know what had happened to me, you know—one would n't feel inclined to tell even a physician a thing like that, of course—and he thought my little scratch more serious than it was. You see I have scored on him. Here I am."

"Yes! oh, yes!" breathed Dorothy in an absorption of which she was unaware, and which was far from being as wholly related to the man beside her as he was believing with a joy which he could not have concealed if she had been more attentive. "But you might not have escaped. A little more one way or the other, and—! Oh, how could he!"

Jasper had not expected such success. He thought of Philip's chances with her, now, almost with compassion. It was a pretty outcome of the fight that it should make for him in her favour, and lead her to so desirable a thought of Philip. In the luxury of success, he felt that he could afford to be generous—generous enough, at least, to let her see that he was.

"Oh, I don't know!" he deprecated.

"Oh, but I do!" exclaimed Dorothy quickly. All her old thoughts about the relations of the brothers returned to her; and she now caused Philip to suffer for all the excuses she had found for him.

"No, no! It was fair enough—as fair as such things can be."

"Would it have been fair if he had killed you?" she asked conclusively.

Jasper bent quickly toward her, fixing her with a passionate glance. "Would you have cared?" he asked.

All his love for her was in his eyes. She lowered her own.

"Of course," she stammered. "Why, yes! But of *course!*"

"Would you have cared in the way I mean?"

She controlled her eyes now and swept his pale, eager face with a furtive look.

" I don't know," she said hastily. " I·—I think not."

"Oh, but Dorothy, girl, surely this time you know? I have loved you ever since! I love you even more, I think, than then. It has gone on. It has grown. You won't say that you have n't seen this—that you have n't been answering it a little bit in your heart. I can't live without your love. I've tried it a long time. I can't," he cried, " I *can't.*"

It was the thrilling, irresistible note of passion. It seemed to enfold and seize her; to benumb her will; to make a reason of itself for a return. She remembered thinking, in a prevision of this scene, how his will must always make a reason for anything he strongly wished. The old fascination of his feeling for her returned upon her. Re-created, and palpitating before her as if it had never ceased to be an active part of her experience, the remembered charm went through her veins exaltingly.

For a moment she felt herself slipping, slipping.

Jasper read the half-consent in her eyes. He rose and drew near her, but at the touch of his arm she started away.

" No, no," she cried, rising in her turn. " I don't know! I must have time to think! Don't press me for an answer, now! Don't!"

There was a moment in which Jasper stared hungrily into her eyes, balancing in the remote second consciousness the wisdom of pressing his advantage, or of complying with the frightened longing for escape from this moment's decision which he saw in her face. Her look at once promised his bliss and confounded him.

It was at last his willingness to use the subtle rather than the direct means of arriving at any object which decided him.

" Well," said he, " let it be so, then. But you will let me have my answer soon, Dorothy ? "

" Yes,—soon," she murmured breathlessly.

" You have seen that I still cared. You have let me go on. I really don't believe you could have the heart, you know, to cast me off, now. I don't ask you to say anything to that. I only tell you to let you know that I trust you completely."

He snatched her hand to his lips and was gone. Dorothy trembled to a seat, torn and pulled by a mob of emotions—excited, intoxicated, exhausted.

How could Philip have done a thing like that! She wondered languidly where he was.

CHAPTER XXI.

On the next day Dorothy received the following note :—

Dear Miss Maurice,

I am leaving town to-morrow for a week. Will you give me, to take with me, the hope of an answer on my return? I won't bother you to say good-bye.

Yours—whatever your answer, always yours,

Jasper Deed.

And to this temperate note she wrote " In a week, then." It was like his invariable consideration to deny himself a word of farewell. Indeed she could not help imagining in this intended absence a more intimate chivalry. It was a fine withholding of himself from so much as the colour of seeming to influence her decision.

The truth was that Jasper had found a clue to his father's whereabouts through the Leadville lawyer to whom he had written the first day he had been allowed to sit up; and after a visit to Leadville he was going in pursuit of him.

The impulse of another man would have been to try to make sure of his future with Dorothy before leaving Maverick; but Jasper saw clearly that this course, to which everything, save his discretion, urged him, would only make sure of a failure which no after patience could retrieve. It was better to use a little patience now; and to go away.

But he thought it worth while to have a little talk with Maurice, whom he found at the station, as he was boarding his train.

He took the sleeping car for his destination with a cosy prophecy of success warming his heart. His reverence for Dorothy's instinctive purity and rightness of feeling, which was at the root of his love for her, consorted with his half-conscious habit of trading on these qualities in her, and he was estimating, as he stepped into the train, the construction of his departure which he could rely upon from her recti-tude. He fancied her construing it almost precisely as she did; and, as he settled himself in the smoking compartment of the sleeper with his cigar, he experienced an inexpensive thrill of virtue at the thought of the nobility she would be imagining in him.

THE sun shone at Mineral Springs as it did at Maverick, though there was no snow at Maverick, and at Mineral Springs the snow lay hugely heaped as far as Deed and Margaret could see from the hotel portico. The snow, in fact, covered all the one-storied houses in the place to their roofs, and lay in the Pass at a depth which for over three weeks had cut off all communication with the outside world and kept them prisoners. The stage had ceased running on the day of the snowfall, being caught in the Pass, and snowed up there out of sight. It was likely to lie there until the succeeding spring. The driver and his one passenger had ridden into Mineral Springs on the backs of the horses.

Mineral Springs was usually cut off for three or four months in the year from the outside world. At its altitude, and in its situation, approachable only by a narrow defile between close-lying hills, this was expected, and as the inhabitants would have said, discounted. But the snow did not usually come so early.

Margaret had smiled with the wistful smile of happiness which had made a home for itself about her mouth since the day of her marriage, at the intelligence which Deed brought her on the morning after their arrival, that they were "snowed in"! And Deed had found an ambiguous laugh. Margaret said it was delightful. Now they could be sure of quiet. Now they should know that the disagreeable visitors to the Springs whom she had feared when he first suggested the place, would stay away. Of course it was n't the season for them, anyway. She knew that. But those half dozen stray people who sometimes came to such places, late, were worse than a mob. One could decently withhold one's self from a mob; but the half dozen, if they were in the same hotel, demanded sociability, sat at the same table, wanted to organize excursions, to get up amusements, to talk at unpropitious times, to discuss—the women were the worst—the new stitch, and the children left at home, and the altitude.

When she found that there were no visitors whatever at the hotel besides themselves, she had a moment of bewilder·ment; but she said she liked that, too. The hotel, which was a large frame structure of three stories, built for the summer season, when it was crowded by invalids and tourists, was a building designed to shelter forty guests; and even Margaret found the great dining-room a little daunting for two. She went to the wife of the landlord—a hospitable creature, largely planned like the hotel—and begged that they might be allowed to dine in modified state. The landlady was glad to close up the big dining-room, she said, and after that she gave up her usual winter sitting-room to them, and Deed often wrote or read there while Margaret sewed. The hotel was itself set on a high hill above the town, and the windows of this room commanded an extraordinary prospect of the snow-covered mountains rising on the other side of the narrow valley. They called it a valley in the town, but it was, in fact, more like a slit in the hills, which plunged precipitously down on either side, fronting each other at a distance of less than half a mile.

They had stopped at Mineral Springs for the night on the way to Burro Peak City, where Deed hoped to sell the "Lady Bountiful." Deed had not meant to take Margaret on, but to leave her at the hotel for the necessary day or two until his return. Then, he had said, they could remain at Mineral Springs, or go on to another place to spend the remainder of their honeymoon, as she liked. Ah, yes; with that money once restored to the bank, with that stock placed to the credit of his trustee account again, he did not care where they went. He had proposed Mexico to Margaret in the anticipatory relief of having made all that business straight, in the relief of feeling himself again in anticipation not only an honest man by brevet.

And then the snow had come. The way to Burro Peak was blocked absolutely; and he could not even get back to Leadville to make a struggle for his good name, or to face the consequences, if necessary. To Burro Peak not even a post had ventured since the storm. The drifting snow had buried the narrow trail along the mountain sides, which men took in midsummer with caution, to a depth where only the May sun would find it; and the people at Burro Peak City, who had once wanted to buy the "Lady Bountiful" when Deed had refused to sell, might as well not have existed.

But it was probably too late to do any good, now, if he could reach them; he believed Barney Graves would have made the quarterly examination of the affairs of the estate at his usual time, and he knew what must happen then. His fellow trustee lived at Red Cliff, and as Graves knew Deed to have been chosen by Brackett to be one of his trustees as a lawyer, while he knew that he himself had only been chosen as a friend it had been his custom to leave the actual work connected with their common trust to Deed. In atonement for this seeming neglect of his dead friend's interest, it was his habit to come to Leadville quarterly to go over the accounts of the estate with Deed, note his investments, and, as a matter of form, to make a memorandum of the securities in his hands. Deed, who had rather relished the trust, on the whole, had been able to add largely to the value of the estate by judicious management of the mining properties partly making it up; and he recalled the satisfaction with which Graves had glanced over his last quarterly statement, with a miserable wonder as to his present thoughts. He made sure that Graves would have postponed the examination when he did not find him at Leadville, but his continued and unexplained absence could have had but one effect: it must long since have come to be believed in Leadville that he was dead, or that he had intentionally disappeared. In the latter case the course was obvious, notorious; the very children knew it from the newspapers. In a simpler state of society he said to himself, scornfully, when a man disappeared his friends might imaginably organise a search for him; in his own world he knew very well that they examined his accounts.

The intolerable simplicity of the barrier which withheld him from even so much as the chance of making a fight for his reputation, goaded him at times beyond endurance. Each morning he waked to scan the sky for signs of a thaw; and each night cursed the royal setting of the sun which had shone through all the day without diminishing the snow. Sometimes in his walks with Margaret through the town, or out to the springs on the hill near their hotel, he would gather up a handful of the sparkling, fluffy, almost ethereal flakes which held him prisoner, staring at them in contempt, and flinging them away at last with a helpless shrug.

What he had done had seemed innocent to him, and at worst it was a potential wrong; the remorseless snow, and the unwilling sun were making it a crime, day by day.

Margaret saw that he was troubled, and was grieved for him, but it was because of the chagrin of which she knew— the chagrin which was cause enough, it seemed to her, for any sickness of heart. She comforted him as she could about Jasper and Philip (she had of course Deed's version of the difference between Philip and himself), but she knew that trouble to be beyond any one's consolation. The double faithlessness and ingratitude, the sudden and absolute loss of both his sons, represented a pain to Margaret which she dared scarcely approach; she felt that she could not under-stand it. It was all that she thought it; and even in the face of the haunting fear which now lived in him, it had its way with his heart. He was sometimes almost grateful for that other trouble, which was at least superior in its immediacy and claimed a part of the thoughts which must otherwise, it seemed to him, have destroyed him. With the black misery of his real trouble—the thought of Jasper and Philip—he got along for the most part, as strong men do with the grief of death; he said nothing and ground his teeth; and did not suffer the less.

If it had not been for Margaret's presence and for the happiness of their new relation, he must have been utterly overthrown. She helped him not only by her love, her kindness, her unfailing watchfulness and care and sympathy, but in unconscious ways which she did not suspect. When she perceived that his sadness and abstraction persisted, she began to charge herself partly with it, in her own way— accusing herself of not knowing what to do for him—be-

lieving that another woman would have known how to comfort him. She tried not to let him see that she was searching her conscience for grounds of offence, but Deed surprised
her in it; and blamed himself. After that he joked her
steadily, as of old, and maintained before her always a
gaiety of demeanour which finally almost helped him to
forget the gulf at the edge of which he was living, even
if he could not put away from him the corroding thought
of his faithless boys.

When the fatality which lurked at his side like a shadow
would take form before him, in spite of all the resources by
which he denied its existence, he usually saw himself in the
newspapers. He saw in shuddering fancy his "case"—it
would become his case at once—treated in the usual newspaper fashion, picturesquely, lamentingly, speculatively,
mock-sympathetically, high-virtuously, and all the rest of it.
Then the State would have its wonder at this latest stainless
name in the dust, and would have its talk, in which it would
recognize the entire and cheering fallibility of every one else
in a world where one could n't one's self be as straight as
one would like. His enemies would enjoy the realization
of their prophecies, while his friends.—Ah, his friends! He
could not bear that thought. When it occurred to him he
would fall to teasing Margaret about something. They had
discovered together an infinite number of points at which
she was teasable—Margaret even learning to enjoy the
exploration of her seriousness with him.

She felt that she owed him this; and she encouraged him
to joke the seriousness which had come so near to wrecking
their happiness, as a kind of expiation. It had also the
advantage of being a refuge from the chivalrous gentleness
and humbleness in which he now sued silently for her forgiveness. She could not bear that he should humiliate himself before her as she had once said coldly to herself that he

U

must; if there was any forgiving to be done, he must do it. She felt blessed in being forgiven, even if he had been at fault; she found it an odious attitude, as a wife, to be brought to book, and forced to forgive him.

For the most part they did not even impliedly discuss the question which had separated them, and gone so near to part them permanently. In the happiness of possessing each other they could not wish to go back and live that nightmare time over again, even in imagination; and it only recurred as an actual question between them when Deed, in their happiest moments, would question his right to such bliss—— to the bliss which he had once thrown away, and trampled under foot.

He made her many promises in moods like this that she should never know him again in the convulsions of passion which snatched him away from himself, and left him to do any evil—the nearest, the readiest—in the devil's mind which then replaced his own. Margaret would not let him talk of such things for long; and she would not suffer him to reproach himself since the hour at the hotel at Leadville when he had done penance before her in an abasement which would have satisfied even Beatrice.

In the long evenings they played at cribbage or bezique, or, less often, at chess. Chess was Margaret's favourite game; but seeing that Deed lacked patience for it and only pretended a pleasure in it for her sake, she would not let him suffer at it, but won him back to the lighter diversions in which his lighter spirit expanded. Sometimes they would set the cards and the board before them for cribbage, and fall to talking, and forget, until the evening was over, that they had meant to play. Deed made her tell him, at these times, of her travels.

In the absolute confidence of their new relation it was a curious pleasure to her to tell many things which she had hidden away in her soul as things impossible to tell any one. The budget of her adventures in the roaming life she had led before she met him, and even after, seemed exhaustless, and Deed was constantly calling for more. He roared with delight at the follies she confessed, the *gaucheries* she owned up to. He said it was a new revelation of her—this history of her independence. He urged her to admit that she had lost by the exchange ; he said that she had sold herself into slavery ; he did n't see how she contented herself.

"Don't you?" she asked, letting her eyes rest on him a moment.

"No," he said, promptly. He leaned toward her and took her hand.

"Why, James, that's just it ! Neither do I ! But you see I do content myself. I'm not planning an escape, I'm not thinking of running away."

"Oh, that's the snow !" he said. "You could n't."

"No ; that's true. But you'll see when it thaws. It will be the same." She said this earnestly. Even when she let herself go, Margaret held on a little.

"Ah, you say so ! That's like the bird that never shows a wish for the old freedom until you open his cage. Then, —whisk ! And away he goes ! Margaret," he said seriously, "don't you sometimes—just a little bit—catch yourself longing for the old, free life? You remember your hesitation about marriage—and how you came and held back, and consented and refused, and ran away and took refuge in your wretched idea of independence, and sometimes would n't so much as look out to take a peep. Occasionally I used to think you actually feared a future in which you would n't be allowed to take care of yourself."

"Yes, yes !" she said. "I know. It was so. And now I like to be taken care of !" She nestled up against him. " I *like* not to be free. I enjoy being *de*-pendent ! Oh, I was

U 2

foolish !" she whispered. "It seemed right—that life I was leading. It seemed good and natural. But it wasn't. *This* is right !" She looked up at him.

Their love was good to them ; and not the less good because they won from it the sane and tempered bliss of a man and woman past the dithyrambic joys of first youth. They had been parted by such a difference as might have risen between the hottest blooded pair of young lovers who ever cried off with each other over a ribbon or a photograph ; and they had come together no less eagerly and gladly, in the young lover manner, as if nothing had ever been between them. But now that they had each other, their happiness was the quiet, full-bodied content of the long-married. To have surprised the glance of serene trust that would pass between them, when their eyes met, to see the unafraid tenderness which had come to Margaret since her marriage, to see her lay her hand on his, or stoop to press a fleet kiss on his forehead, as she passed him during the day upon her errands from place to place, would have been to be taught a great kindness for the marriage state.

If he could have escaped the pain about his boys which was always by him, and could have banished the threat hanging over him, Deed might have been continuously happy. As it was he was very happy when he could forget ; and Margaret (who had nothing to forget, save her permanent trouble about his act against Jasper, of which she forbade herself to speak), was exaltedly happy.

They went upon walks within the valley over the beaten snow, where paths had been cut, amusing themselves in the town by the sight of the entombed houses sending up a pathetic slip of chimney into the air, out of which the smoke curled steadily. They liked, too, to see the nimble house-holder come out of his home through the roof, using the aperture prepared for such emergencies in building mountain houses. Once they went down at night and watched from the snow, ten feet above the sidewalk, the crowd which gathered nightly at "Mulvaney's" to hazard their earnings at faro and stud horse poker. Margaret disapproved of it, even as a spectacle, but she listened when her husband told her how, the night Philip had maddened him, he had gone to Pop Wyman's and lost a thousand dollars in an hour. He did not tell her how he had settled with Philip, of course; that might have involved the other.

The path to the springs, which gave the town its name and part of its prosperity, was one of their favourite walks. It ran along the mountain side on which the hotel itself hung; but the spot at which the water bubbled warm out of the earth, and spread itself steamingly about, commanded an even opener prospect of the hills than they got from their window; and they were fond of coming here at sunset, to watch the great disc go palpably down behind the summit of White Face, scorching the snowy ridge with colour.

The sun had set and left the air chill, and the evening was suddenly grey as they turned one day from this spectacle, conferring pensively on their happiness, as people will who can keep their happiness at this hour. They saw the figure of a man coming toward them along the path, and began to abuse him to each other for poaching on the solitude. Then they saw it was Jasper.

CHAPTER XXII

As Philip's train felt its way cautiously down out of the mountains into Lone Creek valley, on his return from Piñon some days after this, he was hoping that he should find Jasper well enough to see him. He meant to seek him at once on his arrival at Maverick; and give up the "Little Cipher" to him. He had borrowed the mine from him, when he found it served his purpose, with the thought that Jasper had left it with him for a year, and could probably spare it to him for another week or two; and to himself had added that, if he couldn't, he didn't care. It was the first good the mine had ever done him, and it was certain to be the last. He took what advantage there was in the attribution of proprietorship during the ten days he remained at Piñon, reminding himself smilingly that he might considerably lengthen his tenure of the "Little Cipher," and still leave a good balance on the credit side of his account with Jasper.

But, as he drew near Maverick, he was seized with the desire to have the thing immediately off his hands. He did not like the suggestions that were bred of this seeming ownership; and, since the bitterness of giving up his find to Jasper must come, he wished to have the business of the surrender over.

Philip's habitual choice of the comfortable issue from a difficulty sometimes led him (out of mere need for an untroubled mind) to march up to troubles which he loathed and feared, with an unintentioned effect of heroism. The idea of turning over to Jasper the mine he had discovered, staked out and worked, was galling enough to be more comfortable as an accomplished fact than he could hope to make it as a prospect.

Now, too, that he knew what the surrender meant—since he had seen for himself the possibilities of this mine which he and Cutter and Vertner had made a jest of, the splendour of the prospect would sometimes thrust itself luminously before his eyes, in empty moments when he would let his gaze wander from the plain fact of Jasper's right to the "Little Cipher."

The ease with which he had, for the moment, reaped, without his will, the advantages of ownership at Piñon, polluted, every little while, the wholesome current of his thoughts. He put the fantasy from him, when it would recur, with the sense that he could not be well; it was in this way that murderous aberrations and the lunacy of suicide assailed men. And yet there would return upon him that air-born phantom of a thought : That the fiction of his ownership, which had lasted a week, needed no motion 'on his part to make it permanent : that he had only to keep silence.

The arrangement by which he had carried on the two mines in his own name lost its old naturalness, as he found himself wishing heartily that Jasper had always known which mine was his, or, at all events, that some one person—only one—knew at this moment which was his, besides himself. He could easily have told Cutter in the Piñon days ; but he was n't protecting himself against himself in those days ; and he should n't tell him now—he could fancy even Cutter, with all his right-mindedness, palliating the obvious facts of the situation, or diminishing his clear obligation. The person he wished to tell, now, was Jasper. He could be depended on not to diminish the obligation. He would

demand an account of every penny he had expended on the
"Little Cipher" since the first pick was driven into the
claim ; and would ask for any stray bits of silver he might
have brought away in his pockets. Jasper knew his rights.
That he (Philip) had staked out both claims in the
beginning as his own, was nothing. That he had mentally
turned over the "Little Cipher" to his brother when Jasper
had written, asking him to see what a "flyer" of $500 would
do for him on Mineral Hill, was all that would interest Jasper.
Bless you! he would n't care for the registry at the Land Office.
If it had been the other way about there might be some
sense in showing by the Land Office books, the advertise-
ments, and all that, that only one name had appeared in all
the transaction, and that, legally, the two mines belonged to
but one person. But, in the present situation, Philip's
mental cession of the "Little Cipher" to him plainly settled
the question. Jasper could n't care to "go behind the
returns," Philip said to himself, with a curl of his lip, as the
spire of St. John's in the Wilderness came in sight, and he
began to get his hand-luggage together.

The sight of the church recalled Dorothy to his mind—
from which, in fact, she had never been absent since the
memorable day of their last interview; and he said to
himself that it was because he was unhappy, not because
he was unwell, that the vile thought of the simple—the
fluidly simple—course open to him, dared dance about him
beckoningly. If he had not wrecked himself with her, if he
could think she could ever care for him, his normal state of
cheerful spiritual health would come back to him ; and
such thoughts must find their proper place as nightmares.

"Oh, Dorothy! Dorothy!" he caught himself crying inwardly. "Can't you see that I must have you! Can't you
see that I can't live without you!"

As he left the train at the Maverick station, and went

into the hotel, which stood on a level with the station platform, overlooking the arriving and departing trains, he met Maurice at the door coming out.

Maurice's round, handsome face, which we know found a smile readily when the occasion seemed worthy of it, wrinkled into a beaming smile of welcome for Philip. He offered him his large, fair, fat hand.

"Why, my dear boy!" he exclaimed in his mellifluous accents. "Just returned, are you?" with a glance at the traps Philip was carrying in his hand. "It's good to see you again. It's a long time since you've let us have a glimpse of you. Oh, I know, I know!" he exclaimed at Philip's deprecatory beginning. "We've been hearing of your doings." Maurice spoke with a benevolent smile. Philip wondered what he meant. He made a motion to walk by Maurice, whose considerable bulk blocked the narrow hotel-entrance, with the purpose of depositing his luggage with the clerk of the hotel, whom he knew. But Maurice laid a fatherly hand upon his shoulder. "Don't do that! You are going on to the 'Snow Find' in the course of the afternoon, I suppose?"

"No," returned Philip abruptly, "I'm not. I am going on to 'The Triangle' to see my brother."

"Oh, indeed! He left town a few days ago to be gone a week; so that what I was about to ask you to do holds good," he went on, without pausing to observe Philip's agitation. "You will be going on to your mine later in the day, as you can't see your brother, and you must come on to the house, and lunch with us, and take on your things from there."

"Why——" began Philip, confused and baffled by the news of Jasper's departure, and at a loss to understand Maurice's sudden warmth. This had hardly been his tone at their last meeting. Philip was about to say something which

would have implied that Maurice was presuming on a relation between them which did not exist, when his companion
broke in with,

"Ah! That's good! I hoped you would! Well, that's
settled then. You will want to get rid of the railway grime.
We will go right on to the house, if you like. I was just
returning home from some parish calls at the hotel. You
know Mrs. Montgomery Bolton?"

Philip said he had seen her, as he walked on by Maurice's
side, dazed and irresolute. He wished to see Dorothy, of
course; would he not be a fool to quarrel with his luck;
would he not be twice a fool to demand of Destiny, in
Maurice's shape, the cause of this temporary amiability.
He could have laughed, if he had been in a mood to laugh
at anything, at the recollection of Maurice's cold and formal
greeting at their last encounter. What intention toward
him, what hope of service from him, was in the clergyman's
mind?

CHAPTER XXIII

MAURICE did not leave him long in doubt. He congratu
lated him on his "strike" in the "Little Cipher," using the
slang. He had heard of it from Cutter, he said. Was the
assay as large as Cutter said?

Philip had begun to hate the word "strike"; and in his
loathing for the congratulations which had pursued him
since the first day, he was much further gone. The very
conductor of his train from Bayles' Park had wanted to
smoke a cigar with him on the strength of his strike. He
had ceased to start at these felicitations, but they were irritating. If anything could have increased his grudge against
Jasper for being the man to whom he must surrender the
"Little Cipher" it would have been that the circumstances
of the case were things that one could n't explain to a man
who wanted to smoke a cigar with you. It was a fact, if any
one liked to put it in that way, that he was turning over to
his brother a mine to which Jasper had no claim save such
as existed in one conscience; but it was n't the sort of fact
that one could mention as one observes that it rains.

It was impossible—he said this to himself when he found
that he was not denying Maurice's congratulations in the first
instant of hearing them—that he should expose his motives
to the comment of every mind he met on his way to Jasper.
It was n't decent; and, at all events, would be intolerable.
Yet, in the next moment, he saw that though Maurice was

the last man to whose eye he should care to submit the spectacle of his moral processes, he must tell him. The moment lengthened, however, and he did not tell him.

As the gate slammed behind them and they stood in Maurice's front yard, Philip felt again that he must speak. It came upon him with renewed force that Maurice had a right to know ; and that he should be wronging him in keeping silence. Maurice stood in an entirely different relation to the fact from any one else he had met since he knew it himself. To keep silence in Piñon, or before his conductor, might be a matter of taste : but not to tell Maurice was a kind of fraud, perhaps.

He had opened his lips on the doorstep, with no notion of the way in which he should begin, when Dorothy appeared at the bay window which jutted out into her flower-bed in the yard. Philip had a vision of a black skirt and an electric blue blouse on amiable terms with the fair face above it. She waved her hand gaily to her father with a gesture in which Philip might include himself or not, as he liked. It seemed a very long time since they had spoken together ; it was a fortnight since he had seen her. The apparition at the window filled all his senses. He did not go on with what he was saying.

The stainless white brow of Ouray, visible from the doorstep, fantastically seemed to be wrinkling itself in reproach as he went in with Maurice.

Maurice opened the door into the parlour far enough to say to Dorothy that Mr. Deed would stay to luncheon with them, and to ask when it would be ready ; and then led the way upstairs to his own bed-chamber, where Philip got rid of the railway dust, and did what he could by way of freshening the effect of the miner's dress in which he had hastily set out for Piñon, a fortnight before, lacking one day. He wondered how she would receive him. He braced himself for the reception which he feared, and which he felt he had probably earned.

She received him, however, as he might have guessed, as a hostess, not as a woman. Her expressionless cordiality, her meaningless courtesy daunted him. He would rather have been snubbed outright. Her father, who had taken up his stand with his back to the wood fire in the grate, smiled on the meeting. A moment later he was called from the room by information from the servant that his sexton, Sandy Dikes, was waiting to speak with him.

"Miss Maurice—— !" began Philip, entreatingly, as the door closed behind her father.

She stopped him to ask if the room was not too hot for him. Philip was going hot and cold by turns; but the temperature was not at fault. He said it was not too hot for him, unless— "Oh no," she shook her head.

Her smooth tones, her conventional smile of good society began to madden Philip. He felt like an unpractised skater slipping impotently about on new ice.

The passive *rôle* assigned to women, which laid them under so many disadvantages, certainly had its moments of triumph; Philip wondered if women must always use them as cruelly as Dorothy was using them, out of a willingness to avenge themselves on the other moments of helplessness to which the *rôle* condemned them.

At last he looked into her eyes, and asked, without preface, "Is there boiling oil in *all* your punishments, Miss Maurice?"

"I don't know," she returned politely, with the same glittering and correct effect of having said nothing.

"Because if I might choose the quality of my mercy I should like it strained. I suppose I am not worthy of the unstrained. At all events the steady drip, drip of it, does n't soothe me as it ought to. Please strain your mercy, Miss Maurice. What I need, I see, is open cruelty."

She stared at him a moment, in doubt how she should answer this. "I am glad you think that," she said seriously, at last. "But you must look to some one else for it."

"You mean that it is enough to have deserved such a punishment from a person without asking her to be at the pains of administering it?"

"I think you are much in the wrong."

This time there was no mistaking her earnestness. "Good heavens, Miss Maurice. Have I been guilty of other crimes besides those I know?" He paused nervously, observing to himself how beautiful she was in the sudden pallor for which he blamed himself. The fair hair curling spontaneously about her high, white brow, those melting grey eyes, dashed with the whimsical thread of brown, the delicate little mouth, which he had set vaguely quivering now, the poise of her exquisite head, seized him with an irrelevant, and fruitless yearning.

"You know best about that," she said, and he saw she was answering a question he had forgotten the purport of. In an instant, however, he remembered.

"Oh, Miss Maurice," he cried, "are you fair? I give you my word I don't know what you are talking of, unless you are still thinking of the wickedness I know of; and I can't believe that it's only that."

"No, it is n't that," she told him, a little wearily.

"Is it *anything* to do with that—with my brother?" he asked, desperately.

"Yes."

"I might have known it! Well, what, Miss Maurice?" he demanded, in unconscious rudeness. "I have borne pretty much all I am up to from Jasper Has he been telling you how I have wronged him?"

" Do you think that would be like your brother ? " asked
Dorothy with an implication in her voice which nettled
Philip beyond control.

" No, I don't, Miss Maurice. He probably told you how
finely I have been behaving toward him, and you guessed
the other thing from a combination of your knowledge of
me, and your certainty that Jasper would always have a
chivalrous word for his enemy."

" Now it is you who are not fair," she rejoined.

" I don't mean to be unfair," he said, and there he
stopped. " Did he tell you of his visit to the ' Snow Find ' ? "
he asked suddenly. " Is that it ? "

" No," she returned tremulously. " I guessed it ; I forced
it from him ; I surprised his confidence. And after all he
would tell me nothing ; I would not let him tell me anything.
But I understood."

" Ah ! " exclaimed Philip bitterly, " You understood ! "

She rose haughtily. He saw that he had gone too far.

" Oh, I am abominably rude ! Pardon me ! Or don't
pardon me ! Tell me to go. But if you knew, Miss
Maurice—— "

" Tell me," she begged. She put forth her hand. Philip
seized it, and dropped it instantly. He turned away.

" No, no ! I can't," he cried. " Somebody ought to tell
you perhaps. But I can't. It is n't—it is n't decent. He
clasped his arms despairingly behind his shaggy head as he
walked from her toward the window and stared out at the
long backbone of the Sangre de Christo range.

She guessed this for the pride it was ; but she had no
information which could have enabled her to justly estimate
the obscure and multitudinous motives which made it up ;
and she was far from guessing the rightness of feeling which
actually lay at the root of it.

" But there *is* something I can tell you, Miss Maurice,"

he said, turning suddenly, with a new light in his eyes which awed her. She shrank from him, and sat down hastily. "Perhaps it will explain for me—not this precisely, but everything, and if it explains nothing, why I shall be content that you should not understand my relation to Jasper, either, because nothing will matter, then. I have no right to tell it to you ; though you have a right to know it. But I can't tell you unless you promise me to understand that it asks nothing of you, that it has no relation to you except as your knowledge of it may help you to—to understand——. I love you. That is all. I love you."

She dropped her eyes.

"I wanted you to know," he said, in the silence that fell.

"Yes," she whispered, in assent to this.

"But I did n't want—I don't want the fact to exist for you, except as it may help you to think more kindly of me ; to—to understand." Philip believed that he meant this. "I have no right to speak of it—and absolutely no right to found anything further on it." He did not say it in the hope that she would contradict him ; but a pang shot through him when she did not. He should not have told her any more, he said proudly to himself, whatever she might have urged against this statement ; but her silence whetted the pain at his heart. He rubbed the two half dollars left over from his journey to Piñon against each other in his pocket, and thought how the actual occasion of his forbearance lacked dignity; it really was n't as noble as it seemed, perhaps, for a beggar to refrain from a proposal of marriage. When the beggar happened to be as much in love as he, however, it was hard.

"Well," he went on, as she still kept silence, "there's nothing more to say." He came over to her, and offered his hand in farewell. "Good-bye, Miss Maurice. If you ever give me a thought after this, remember, please, that whatever you have to think of me, it was in this way that I thought of you—that I shall always think of you."

She said nothing, still ; and he turned to go.

"But," she called after him, raising her head now, with a smile in which many emotions played, "you are going to stay to luncheon, Mr. Deed ? "

He turned at the fancy of a note between roguish and caressing in the sound of her unsteady voice, and started toward her—withholding himself instantly. Then he remembered what she had asked him and could have smiled for the absurdity of his unhappy lover exit arrested by the banality of a luncheon engagement.

"No—no, I must n't," he found himself saying; but he heard the door knob turn in Maurice's firm clutch, and knew that he must.

Maurice came in upon them rubbing his large hands in smiling hospitality ; and abandoned the amiable commonplace he had ready for Philip, to glance sharply at the two. He concealed adroitly his sense of having interrupted an intimate collision ; but he followed them into the dining-room, after having asked Philip to give his arm to Dorothy, with a look of grave satisfaction on his face.

x

THE luncheon lagged, though it began with salmon, and went on to escalloped oysters, to quail on toast, and finally to a California fruit, which none of them knew. Dorothy said she had forgotten its name; it grew in a tin can—like the oysters and the salmon. They ate, save Maurice, as if the quality of the luncheon alone concerned them. Maurice talked beamingly about a host of subjects, in the full, orotund voice which sounded so well from the pulpit. He made all the talk. Philip was silent and ill at ease; Dorothy answered her father, and kept him going. She flushed when Philip once looked her way. After that they avoided each other's glances.

When they were alone with their wine and cigarettes— Maurice kept up the customs of a higher civilization jealously—the clergyman told Philip the history of his purchase of the claret he was drinking, with the deliberation which characterized his talk. Philip writhed inwardly. He longed to get away.

Maurice seemed to have plenty of leisure, however, and made no move to rise. He left inviting gaps in the conversation when he had done his story of the wine, as if he expected Philip to take it up, and Philip had begun dimly to divine an intention in this, when Maurice finally said nimself,

"I think, Mr. Deed, we may deal with each other quite

frankly." He cleared his throat, caressing his wine-glass meditatively.

Philip bowed politely across the table, not knowing what was coming; but feeling the assumption to be a safe one. He had always been on his guard in his few conversations with Maurice. He did not trust him. He found himself constantly wondering what he was up to; what purpose underlay the obvious meaning of the things he said.

"Yes, so I thought," continued Maurice in response to his nod. He offered him cigarettes. Philip took one and struck a match. As Maurice lighted his own, he glanced at his companion through the smoke and asked, as if it were a casual question, "May I ask if I rightly infer that you have a more than common regard for my daughter?"

Philip flushed. He was wholly at a loss for an answer.

"I need not say that it is not to challenge such a regard if it exists, nor to question your action in any way, that I speak," continued Maurice in a conciliatory tone, anticipating the resentment of his inquiry which he began to see rising in Philip's face. "I should not ask if I had not good reason—the best of reasons. You will quite agree with me, I am confident, when you understand what they are. But first, as to the main question. I need not repeat it?"

"No," said Philip, and was going on angrily, but stopped himself. "Yes, you are right. I love Miss Maurice."

He remembered that he was talking to her father, who after all, had an excellent right to question him.

"Ah!" said Maurice, "I have long believed as much. May I ask—it is my last question—if I am right in supposing that you have made Dorothy aware of this?"

Philip remembered the scene on which the clergyman had just come in. He had hoped that it might never be known to any soul; least of all did he like to talk it over with Maurice. But he said helplessly and a little savagely,

"It is true. Yes. But —— "

"She has refused you, then?"

Philip frowned. "I don't know why you assume——"
he began.

"Mr. Deed, we shall get on in this delicate matter only
if we understand quite clearly that I speak as your friend,"
interrupted Maurice. He sipped slowly at his claret. "I
know that I may not always have seemed so. But I have
learned—some things have come to my knowledge."

Vaguely and doubtfully at first, and then surely, Philip
had seen for himself that Maurice's inclination toward him
was friendly.

From whatever cause, out of the coldness he had kept
for him hitherto; out of the warm and friendly association
with Jasper of which every one in Maverick knew; out of
the old liking for the match broken off by Dorothy, which
Philip suspected in him; and at all events, out of the open
favour he had lent the new relation between Jasper and
Dorothy, this was the issue. It was strange, but he did not
doubt it, and if he had doubted it, Maurice's next words
must have been convincing.

"I have heard the truth about you and your brother;
and I have reason to believe that Dorothy is still in ignorance of it. You are aware of the feeling I have had
towards Jasper. I have liked him—we have liked him;
and Dorothy still does. It is because I believed that
Dorothy's proper understanding of some things, just at this
moment, may deeply affect her future and yours, and—
mine, that I wish to offer you a friendly word."

"You are very good," murmured Philip, plunging about
in his imagination for a final meaning beneath this.

"No. If I am good, it is to Dorothy—to myself. You
may believe that I should hardly be speaking to you in this
way if it were not of vital concern to me that I should,"

He judged it unnecessary to enter with Philip into the facts he had lately learned regarding Jasper's present tenure of the ranch. The injunction against Snell had become town talk within two days of Jasper's departure; and had set all Maverick agog for the painful but interesting story which must be lurking behind this action of Jasper's. Maurice had heard the entire story from Cutter, who saw no reason to withhold the truth when Maurice questioned him at the post-office on the day he heard the rumour of the injunction.

"I shall speak plainly, Mr. Deed, for both our sakes," the clergyman pursued. "I think it right you should know that your brother has proposed to Dorothy."

"Jasper!" cried Philip. He fronted Maurice abruptly, perusing his face with an estranged regard.

"Have you not known?" exclaimed the clergyman.

"Known!" repeated Philip, with a haggard face. "Yes. Oh yes!" And, after a moment, "He has offered himself. He has been accepted. Why do you bring me here to tell me this?"

"He has offered himself," assented Maurice, passing over Philip's tone with dignity, "but he has not been accepted. Dorothy has promised him his answer within a week. The week will be at an end to-morrow." Philip opened his lips with a passionate impulse, but swallowed back his words, grinding his teeth. "What his answer shall be depends, as I believe, upon the way in which you may receive what I have to say."

"For God's sake, man, go on! I'm listening."

Philip bit his lip, and waited for what might follow, with his eyes fixed on the line of low-lying hills, opposite Ouray, which were visible from the dining-room window.

"Quietly, if you please, my dear young sir. This matter, let me remind you, concerns me at least as much as it can

concern you. Dorothy is my only daughter. My life goes
with her happiness. But we can gain nothing by haste."
Philip made an impatient gesture of apology.

He stared at him restlessly, across the table, with his chin
in his hand as he went on.

"What I am about to say," continued the clergyman, "is
most intimate. It touches a subject which I had hoped
never to be obliged to re-open to any person living. Circumstances have ruled otherwise, and I have now only to add,
in disclosing certain facts, that I shall look to you to regard
them as communicated under the most sacred seal of confidence."

These cautious guards and defences, these precautions
against one knew not what, by turns tortured and sickened
his companion. He found his perception reeling giddily
every little while, before the clergyman's abominable flow of
language, which seemed one sheen to him, like the glaze on
paper.

"I don't know whether you know precisely the circumstances attending my departure from Laughing Valley City?"
said Maurice interrogatively. He tried for a parody of the
importance of the name in his voice; but his anxiety came
uppermost.

Philip turned toward him quickly and said, "I am glad
to have the opportunity of letting you know, Mr. Maurice,
that I *do* know rather more than it seemed a kindness to
Miss Maurice to mention in the cave that day. I have never
felt quite right about that. But it seemed to Cutter and me
that she would not care to know that we had seen what
passed on the hillside above the cañon, the day of the storm.
If I had imagined that it could make a difference to you I
should have spoken long ago. It was Miss Maurice who
was in my thoughts," he confessed.

"Ah, I am glad of that—yes," mused the clergyman;

"glad, because it will help you to understand a feeling of mine about that—that circumstance. I have never told Dorothy the actual—the exact occasion of that scene on the hillside." Maurice leaned over toward Philip, and questioned his face closely. "Do *you* know it?" he asked.

"No," said Philip.

"Ah, well, perhaps that is as well, too. You will believe, when I tell you this, that I am concealing nothing from you. The Vigilance Committee," he gave them the title with a curl of his large, handsome lip, from which he stroked away his jaunty moustache, "thought me in the wrong in refusing to go and read the funeral service over two men who had died at Laughing Valley of small-pox." Maurice's face worked, and for a moment he did not attempt to go on. "The right or wrong of that we must leave to a higher tribunal," continued he, dismissing the ethical question with a gesture. Philip shuddered. "What immediately concerns us is that Dorothy has never known why I was forced to depart from the place."

"She must never know," said Philip huskily. A vicarious sense of shame for the clergyman would not let him lift his eyes to look in his face.

"Exactly. She must never know. But there is another matter of which she must not know."

He turned a doubtful eye on his companion as he paused. Philip turned cold, wondering what worse thing this man could have done to shame his daughter.

"It is, in a way all the same matter," Maurice was saying while his companion dumbly waited and wondered. Philip drew a breath of relief. "Information reached me a week since through a good friend of ours—of hers, of yours; in point of fact, through Mr. Messiter, that—"

"I beg your pardon. Is Mr. Messiter back in Maverick? I heard that he had returned to his mine at Laughing Valley."

"So he has," responded the clergyman, with the ghost of
an indulgent smile for Philip's transparent impulse of
jealousy. "He came here a week ago for the day only, to
see me—in point of fact to warn me. He had heard rumours
at Laughing Valley that some of my enemies there had been
inciting the Bishop when he visited the place a fortnight or
so back, to take some action founded on this—this accusation
against me ; and like the dear, good fellow he is—knowing
what that must mean for Dorothy—he had posted down to
Denver without stopping to consult me, in the hope of
inducing the Bishop not to move in the matter." Maurice
sighed. "It was good of him, but it was useless. Once
brought to the ears of the Bishop I have always known what
must happen." Philip saw the green hills outside the window
swim before his eyes. "And—well, the end of it is that I
have this morning a letter from the Bishop—generous and
temperate,—even fatherly, but quite plain—suggesting that
it would be convenient if I should let him have my resignation of my charge here."

Philip took the letter he handed him, as he started up
with an inarticulate groan on his lips. He carried it to the
window, and stared at it for a moment helplessly ; the
words refused to relate themselves to one another and he
finally turned and gave it back to Maurice, in silence. The
clergyman shrank from the look on Philip's face as he put
forth his hand to take the letter.

"Yes," owned he ; "it's bad. It is a blow. I won't deny
it. And yet not an unbearable blow to me. I have
expected it, for one thing ; and I see, now that it has
come, that I have long been half willing." He looked
at Philip sharply. "I was not made for a clergyman,
Mr. Deed."

"Oh, don't say that, man !" The cry was torn from
him. "For Heaven's sake, don't say that !" The igno

minious, the disastrous fact seemed to connect itself intolerably with the thought of Dorothy; it seemed to leave two lives in ruins. If it had been the clergyman alone, one would have seen only the tragic waste of a career. But as the fact involved Dorothy, Philip could not face it.

Turning toward Maurice he saw that a ghastly pallor had stolen over his face, which was sunk upon his breast. He went over to him and clapped him on the shoulder.

"Come!" he said gently, with an indescribable mingling of contempt and pity pulling at his heart. "Take this! You will feel better." He poured a glass of the wine Maurice had been discussing in that moment of after-luncheon talk which seemed now so far removed. The clergyman snatched it, and drank it off.

Philip was ashamed to be witness to his recovery of himself. He turned his back, and went to the window, within sight from which a rider was endeavouring to break the spirit of a bucking pony. There was a large open space behind the house, not yet built upon, and untamed bronchos were often brought here from the neighbouring livery stable for this purpose. The tiresome iteration of the see-saw motion by which the brute was viciously endeavouring to throw his rider renewed Philip's restlessness.

"You must go away from here," he heard himself saying to Maurice, as he turned in the need of action, or the suggestion of action. "You must go at once!"

Maurice shook his head with the sadness of a superior knowledge.

"No! No! It is ended. I shall never preach again."

Philip was appalled.

"Oh, my dear sir! Shake this off. For your daughter's sake—for Dorothy's sake! Shake it off!"

Maurice looked up at him with a mournful smile. "Shake it off! My dear young man, I have been dismissed.

I have been disgraced! Oh, my God!" he cried, breaking down suddenly, and burying his face in his hands.

Philip bit his lip. For a moment there was silence in the room. Then there came a ring at the outer door, and a knock at the door of the room in which they were. Philip darted to it, with the fear in his throat that it might be Dorothy. It was the servant, come to say that Mr. Vertner was in the parlour. "Say that Mr. Maurice will see him presently," he said.

" Do you mean to say that you could not secure another parish?" he demanded, as he returned.

Maurice, who had risen at the knock, and was himself restlessly pacing the room with his hands in his pockets, stopped before the table, littered with the remains of the meal, and absently took a *bon-bon* from a plate.

"Secure it? Perhaps. Keep it? No. This story would rise. Oh, I'm not degraded from my office; I'm not unfrocked, as they used to call it!" He laughed scornfully. " It's simply a story—the most powerful, the most subtle, the deadliest, the most pitiless enemy a man can know. If I were younger,—or, let me say it all; if I cared for my calling as I once did, if I could be back at twenty-five again, fresh from the seminary, a young divinity student, with the old fire, with the old feeling that the priesthood was the holiest, the noblest, almost the only possible vocation in the world: ah, then I might go on and fight it out! I might try to live it down. But I don't care! I have learned to live another life. I have always wanted to do other things, and even when I cared most for my work, I have done them. I have done them, at last, so much that they own me. I don't *care*," he repeated in a kind of cry of pain and stopped short in his march from end to end of the room, to add, looking Philip in the eyes—"except—*except* for one thing."

Philip framed her name with his lips. Maurice nodded.

"For Dorothy I would give all that remains to me of life; for Dorothy I would go on in this work of mine, if they would let me, always. *She* cares for it. To see me give it up will be a shock to her. To see me forced to leave it in disgrace would kill her."

"She must not know it," said Philip, setting his teeth.

"*Must* not," repeated Maurice. He stopped again, and faced Philip. "Ah, I hoped you would say that! I knew it .... You understand, then, my purpose in telling you. You can see, now, how it is that the man who is to marry Dorothy should share this purpose with me?"

"To keep the knowledge from her?" asked Philip quietly. He divined with contempt how Maurice must be doomed to long with all his cowering soul that Dorothy should never come to know him as he was; but he forced himself to do justice to the impulse of love which had the same need. Maurice loved his daughter; he forgave him much for that.

"To keep the knowledge from her," repeated Maurice. "Perhaps you can also understand how it is necessary that he should be *able* to keep it from her."

"Able?"

"If I give up my calling, Mr. Deed, I give up the only means I know of earning a living. I can stay in it, and fight, and she must know; or, (the question of livelihood being done away with,) I can leave it, apparently, of my own will, and she need not know. I must stay in it, if I must go on earning my living; I must leave it if she is not to know."

Philip regarded him in amazement. The words sang through his head backwards and forwards. He made nothing of them.

"Yes," he assented, without knowing to what he assented.

"A week ago I should have been saying this to your

brother. I know him now. It is impossible that I should any longer wish his marriage with Dorothy. And yet it may still have to be. You know Dorothy's relation to Jasper. Why not say it frankly? You know that she once cared enough for him to engage herself to him." Philip bit his lip. "You can judge whether it is unlikely that she will accept Jasper to-morrow when he comes, if nothing happens."

Philip clenched his hands. "Likely? It is certain! You don't know!"

"I do know," rejoined the clergyman quietly. "I have gathered my own impressions—from Dorothy, from the discontinuance of your visits to us, from other things. I know what Dorothy thinks; and I know, now, that she is wrong. It is because of that I speak." Maurice looked at him keenly. "I *wish* something to happen," he said.

Philip felt himself choking. "Do you mean—? Speak out, man! Do you mean that—that you think I have a chance with her?"

"Ah, I must not say! I recommend you not to be discouraged."

"Oh, if I thought it!" cried Philip.

"I only ask you to remember my situation, hers—what we have said."

"Tell me!" exclaimed Philip fiercely, with a sudden thought: "Have you told all this to Jasper, and has he refused to listen?"

"No," returned the clergyman, without offence, and with the sad calm that remains to the purposes of a broken man, "I have spoken first to you. I shall state the necessities of the case to him, only if you force me to."

A wild joy played through Philip's veins. He turned away to hide his unhoped-for happiness, with its perfect mingling of a satisfied—a richly satisfied debt. He drank deep of the pleasure of holding Jasper's fate in his hands before he would turn and face Maurice again. It was worth while to have borne what he had borne from Jasper for this moment.

"You will see now—I may say it frankly, since you understand, now, that it implies no reflection on you—how, in my present situation, in Dorothy's situation, I could not let her think of a poor man, even if she were inclined to."

Philip started. He remembered his old, his rooted distrust of Maurice. Was it possible that all this story was devised —cooked up? But, if it was, what was its object? He had nothing to give Maurice; he could do nothing for him. Surely he was the type of poverty!

And then, in an instant, he saw. He perceived that he stood on the brink of a precipice, and realized that he had brought himself to it. It was not Maurice. Beside him the clergyman was a man of truth and justice and honour.

"That is so," he heard the clergyman going on, "because the man who marries Dorothy must be able to make it practicable for me to leave the ministry, now, at once; and naturally, and without the scandal which would kill her." He paused. Then, after a moment, "But if Dorothy should listen to you," he added, "it must be so for another reason. If Dorothy should engage herself to any one but your brother, it is right to tell you that I must be prepared to find a considerable sum at once."

Philip's eyes fell. The clergyman studied his face attentively.

The younger man raised his eyes at last, and gave back Maurice's look.

"Why?" he asked, coldly.

"Because I owe your brother rather more than five thousand dollars."

"Jasper? Why? How?"

" The larger part of it was a loan from him to enable me to take a share in Vertner's paper, *The Kalendar.* The rest is made up of smaller sums, borrowed before and since. It began with a trifling loan to assist me in escaping from certain difficulties rising out of my Church School of Music in Michigan. You may have heard of my failure there. I have always been grateful to him for that. And from time to time I have wanted money. I have never been able to make my tastes harmonize with my income. I think you know how that is, Mr. Deed ? "

Philip winced at this home-thrust, and winced even more at the association of himself with the pitiable man before him. "Things which to a certain order of mind seem luxuries, to us—to me, are necessities. Jasper has found his account in this. When I have wanted money he has always pressed it on me. He has had his purpose. But he has not let me feel it. A week ago, after he had spoken to Dorothy, he sought me out at the station. He reminded me then."

" Cad ! " exclaimed Philip under his breath ; but his mind was already far away. A thousand thoughts went racing through his head, grouping themselves odiously, and dissolving again in strange and alluring shapes.

His companion did not respond, and the conversation fell.

Philip sat staring moodily at the stove which, in this room, replaced the usual open fire. A kettle hummed on it, purfling into the air its leisurely cloud of steam. The cat lying before the stove purring regularly, and the ticking of the clock on the mantel made the silence hideous. Philip knew that his hope of Dorothy, his future and his honour lay on the other side of this silence.

In the swift, final moment of temptation, if a man may be said to think it is at least not his present thought which decides. The thoughts already allowed himself; the trivial consents; the reasoned compliances gone before, determine for him. He may even find himself bound by his silences. And for Philip, casting about in the blind fever of his hope to save himself, the right and wholesome thoughts which he could still conjure to his aid were answered, not by another and an evil thought, but by a feeling—a sweet, strong ecstasy, that gripped and held him, and seemed to have its own sacredness.

Maurice's secret—was it likely that Jasper would keep it from Dorothy beyond the moment in which it served his interest to guard it? Had not he, Philip, the pre-eminent right of reverence, of tenderness over a future that must always be threatened by the knowledge of what Maurice had told him? And he loved her. Did Jasper love her as he loved her? A passionate belief in the supreme right of his love filled him.

Yet all the rectitude of a life unspotted by an act of wrong rose in protest. Little impulses mingled with the big. A certain pride which he had always kept about his final integrity in money affairs, in the midst of the looseness about them, of which every one knew, caused him to smart in imagination. He seemed to see that he could not do this thing; not for any happiness the earth could hold; not for Dorothy.

He opened his lips to tell Maurice that the "Little Cipher" was Jasper's; and that, if he sought a man strong in the strength that wealth gives, it was to him that he must turn. But the silent shaping of the sentence in which he should tell him, gave the whole story of his real relation to Jasper back to his memory.

Was it more, or other than a fair exchange—the ranch for the mine? It was ever Jasper's taunt that he did not pay his debts. There was a debt he would pay. The accumulations, the additions, the compound interest of insult and

offence, gathered themselves, now, in his mind into a single
bulk, in the face of which all scruples grew absurd.

He would pay the debt; and if he overpaid it, there was
always the obligation his father owed Jasper. The balance
could be credited to that account. As he thought of his
father, the savage impulse of hate which had caused him to
gloat a few moments earlier in the knowledge that Jasper's
future lay in his hands, sent a sweep of exultant yearning for
vengeance through him.

He saw that in all his forbearance toward Jasper, in his
softening of his father's wrath, in the just course he had
tried to walk with his brother since Jasper had wronged him,
the black hate which now rose in his heart, had its part. It
must always since have lain crouched there. It seemed now
to spring out from him into an awful aloofness where, with a
beast's instinct, it had the will, if he would let it, to rend
and tear.

Was he to give this man a fortune? Was he to beggar
himself for him? He was ready to do that. He had meant
to do it. But how if to impoverish himself and to enrich
Jasper was to lose the new hope of Dorothy, thrilling along
his pulses like wine? Could he bear it? Perhaps. But to
lose her that Jasper might win her? . . . He shook his
head with a gentle smile of scorn.

" Well ? " inquired Maurice.

Philip rose suddenly. A light shone in his eyes.

" May I speak to Miss Maurice ? "

The clergyman glanced at him in surprise. But he rose
and went to the door with him.

" Yes."

Philip passed out into the hallway with the flicker of a
smile on his set lips.

CHAPTER XXV

THE sun was dyeing the paper stained-glass in the hall
windows to a similitude of the costly beauty they imitated
as Dorothy went to the front door at sound of the bell.
Through one of the palest lozenges of glass she discerned
a figure which she knew for Vertner's. His hand was on
the bell when she opened the door to him.

" Oh, are you back, Mr. Vertner ? " she said, offering him
her hand.

" Yes. You just saved yourself. In another moment I
should have started that slam-bang gong on its errand of
destruction." It was one of the gongs, set in the door
itself, which explode a clangour through the house, sending
a shiver to the remotest nerve of the structure. " There
would be bells in your landlord's house if we had the building of it, would n't there ? We'd have them in the window-
sashes, they'd go off when Cozzens opened his bureau
drawers ; they'd be concealed in chairs ; we'd pave the
house with them ; he'd go to sleep to a weird whirr from the
cellar, and wake to the unmerciful buzz of one of the things
by his bedside. I think we could fix him out. How's your
father ? "

Dorothy smiled and changed the subject with his own
facility. " Papa is very well. Would you like to see him ?
He is at luncheon with Mr. Deed, but he will be in, in a

Y

moment." She opened the door into the little parlour at the front of the house.

"Don't disturb him," said Vertner as he walked briskly over to the plant stand on which Dorothy kept her winter flowers, and put his face down into a geranium. "You made out with the cactus, did n't you? You must show Beatrice. No, it was only a little matter."

"About the paper?"

"Well, partly. I've got a new idea about the *Kalendar.* But I think I must have wanted to see you as much as anything. We have n't talked 'schemes' for a long time, have we?"

It had been a joke between them since the day of their conference about the paper that Vertner must always discuss his new scheme with Dorothy before finally committing himself to it. He pretended to defer to her advice; and Dorothy pretended she believed that he did.

"Oh, no !" assented Dorothy. "What is the new one, Mr. Vertner? Is it a 'bonanza' or 'a gold mine'? I'm sure 'some one is bound to go into it if you don't,' and that it will 'give you the cinch on the whole business,'" she said, parodying his phrases fearlessly; "but do you think we ought to go into it? Should we 'come in on the ground floor'? That's the important point for us to consider, is n't it?"

She made these suggestions absently. She was thinking of something else.

"Well, I don't know," rejoined Vertner, gazing at the blooming cactus, while he swung his hat between his legs. "Don't you think we ought to make sure first whether Schlesinger will sell?"

Dorothy brought herself back to give this question the advantage of her judgment, and they laughed together, as Vertner explained his plan of forming a syndicate to buy up the entire municipality of Spesiana, a deserted city in the mountains, which had enjoyed its boom but had not lived through it. Vertner meant to organize another boom. Schlesinger had bought most of the city lots on speculation, but he would sell, now, if he was approached right. The boom would begin after the sale. He said he could work the newspapers.

Vertner noticed that Dorothy's attention wandered. She usually listened to his schemes intently; and guessing that something interested her more at the moment, he changed the subject with, "So Jasper is back?"

"Mr. Deed? No. It is Mr. Philip Deed who is with papa."

"No? Is it? I want to see him. I want to congratulate him. You heard, of course?"

"About his mine? Oh, yes. Mr. Cutter told us."

"You don't seem very glad," he said, glancing at her.

"Glad? Oh, yes."

"Well then, not enthusiastic."

Dorothy regarded him studiously a moment without speaking. Many thoughts were going through her mind—many considerations; and at last a resolution seemed to enter it, for she said suddenly, and with an effect of bracing herself,

"Mr. Vertner, do you know Mr. Philip Deed very well?"

Vertner was instantly serious. "Yes, Miss Maurice. Very well. Why?" he asked kindly.

"Because—— You will know of a difference he has had with his brother—a quarrel: I—I don't know what. I have n't liked to ask. But I must ask some one, now. And you—you will know." .   .   . .

The uncharacteristic hesitations, the tremulous advances and retreats seemed to Vertner to call on his chivalry.

"But surely you have heard——?" he began blunderingly.

"I have heard of the injunction which Mr. Jasper Deed has secured against his brother—something about his ranch. Yes. He has had to defend himself, at last."

"Who?"

"Why, Mr. Deed."

"I beg your pardon, Miss Maurice, but which?"

"Mr. Jasper Deed, of course."

"Jasper?" She nodded. "*Jasper?*" he repeated. "Jasper defend himself, and 'at last'? Oh, Miss Maurice! Why, would you mind telling me how much you *do* know of this?"

She shook her head in rueful bewilderment. "I don't know."

"Well, you know how things stood when he went away. Let's find a basis, Miss Maurice. This hurts my poor head."

"But you don't suppose he would tell me, surely? You know him, Mr. Vertner. Does it seem likely that he could condemn his brother to me if—if he had suffered from him. You don't know. Even if it were likely, it would have been impossible to him, to any one, as—as things have been."

"Would it?" asked Vertner, in a daze. "Oh, yes, of course it would!" And then, "To whom?"

"To whom?"

"Yes, whose impossibility—who could n't? Yes, that's what I mean?"

"Mr. Jasper Deed," she said quickly. "Who else could I mean?"

"Oh, I don't know! I don't know!" cried Vertner, beating back an imaginary army of conjectures with his out-stretched palm. And, falling sober again, "Philip, for one, I should say, Miss Maurice?"

" Before *he* went away, did you mean ? "

" Well, yes," drawled Vertner.

" But—— "

" And did he never tell you how things stood in this case of Deed *versus* Deed?"

" Ah, you expect him to have condemned himself? So did I. I thought him strong enough. I believed he would rather condemn himself than let me doubt his brother wrongly. Oh, if he had been strong enough for that, I should have believed in him always! I should have known. He did not believe that I would know. He would not believe that I should understand how his brother could be maddening, and he—he hot-headed."

" And do you mean to say——?" cried Vertner. "Oh, no, no! It can't be! I knew the boy was a wild and roaring unicorn on some subjects, but I never supposed he could go and be such an ass as——. And you have been thinking that *he* was the one to blame in all this row with Jasper! Oh, that's very pretty!" He paused a moment to contemplate the beauty of the idea! "And you never knew that Jasper had done his brother out of his share in the ranch by a foul trick, and broken his father's heart by the same operation: and sent him to——! You never knew all that!" he exclaimed, breaking off suddenly. "And you've been thinking—— Oh! Wow! Wow!" howled Vertner, inarticulately. "Why you must keep up with the news of the day, Miss Maurice," he told her, when he could speak. "You mustn't let these facts of contemporary human interest get by you, in this way—though, come to think of it, I don't know how you would have heard about it, unless Phil had told you. Except Deed and his wife, who have taken their knowledge off to heaven knows where, no one knows anything about it but Philip and myself. Jasper knows about it. But he did n't tell you? No, naturally.

There *has* been one other—the fellow who bought the ranch, Snell. But he's been keeping it dark. *I* don't know what's possessed *him!*"

"Bought the ranch?" gasped Dorothy. "Mr. Snell?"

"Yes. Oh, yes. That's just a little bit from this picturesque muss. You shall have the rest if you like the sample."

"Tell me the whole, please, Mr. Vertner. Tell me everything," cried Dorothy in a brave voice that died away in a quiver.

When Vertner found himself in the street a little later, after telling her the whole story, including Deed's and Margaret's share in it, he turned toward home, cursing himself roundly. He did not like to see a woman cry.

DOROTHY stood with her face pressed against the pane, looking out desperately toward the big, uncaring mountains. She felt Philip by her side, and could not turn her face. They stood together in the window, for a moment, in silence.

"Would it matter if I said——" began Philip, in a low tone. But at the sound of his voice she turned her streaming eyes upon him, and he stood gazing into them.

"Don't!" she begged, brokenly. "Don't!"

He shrank. It was like a ghostly voice crying out on him to stay his purpose.

"No, you must listen!" he had said incoherently, before he knew. He did not know what he meant to ask her to listen to.

He seized her hand involuntarily. She caught it away. "No," she cried. "No! You don't *know!*"

His conjecture darted instantly to her father. Had she heard? Was the little leaven of another's good to fail his act? Was she to suffer notwithstanding? The flux and influx of his will about the odious thing he was doing went on in him sub-consciously in the face of his resolve to take his right, to use the mine which was not his, to square accounts with Jasper, to deal with him as he had been dealt by.

The thought that he should not benefit her daunted him. He seemed now to himself to find his only warrant for his act in this little note of right, of kindness, or love which sang within it somewhere.

"I have wronged you, Mr. Deed," he heard her saying, as all his resolve seemed sucked away from him in the sudden outflow of his will. "Oh, I have wronged you bitterly!"

He looked up. "Wronged me?" he cried.

"Yes, yes! Oh, yes! We can't speak of it. There's nothing I can say or do that could make you know how—how I feel to have—to have——"

He saw the tears start in her eyes with a shock of shame. "I hope there is n't, Miss Maurice! Don't try to say anything like that! Pray don't! I could n't bear it."

"But I must. Your silence—I misconstrued it. I thought——"

"And you don't think so, now? I'm glad of that." He took her hand, and this time she let him keep it a moment.

"But—you don't know what I have thought of you!"

Philip frowned, but he said with a smile. "I don't care; or I sh'a'nt if you'll tell me what you think, *now*." He bent over her, looking into her eyes. She dropped her gaze to the carpet.

"Look up!" he said. She obeyed him slowly. They let their eyes rest on each other, and melt and mix in a glance that taught them one another. Then he stooped shyly and kissed her.

CHAPTER XXVI.

THE days that followed were very dear to Dorothy. She had given herself wholly to him in that first meeting of the lips which seemed to make all things straight, and straight for ever; she had her reserves with him, but she had no doubts. She knew, now, that she had been his and only his, from the beginning. She thought of Jasper, as she now saw him, with a shudder, and made up to Philip in her heart, if not in the outward expressions she allowed herself, for every kindly impulse toward Jasper she had known.

For the contumely which she seemed to herself to have heaped on Philip in believing him in the wrong in the question between him and Jasper, she could find no proper penance. But the purity, the instinctive morality, the pitiless, colourless sense of right which Jasper feared and admired in her, saw in this silence of Philip's, which had gone so near to cost them each other, a nobility beyond praise. Philip laughed at this when she told him of it in the long interchange of confidences which filled the afternoon, after he had spoken and had taken his answer from her. She liked to have him laugh; but she said that however wicked and wrong and dangerous it was to have kept that silence, it was fine, and she would not have had him speak (especially when he saw that she doubted him) even if——

"Even, if——?" queried Philip, with the rising inflection of impudence.

She looked at him for a moment in affectionate musing. He reached from the other end of the sofa, where they were sitting, and took her hand. "No," she said, as her eyes filled spontaneously with happy tears, "I should never have forgiven you if you had let it go so far as *that!*"

She began to abuse his foibles to win her way back to her reserves. She said it would n't do to spoil him too much. He had spoiled himself enough already. It was no wonder that she had been a long time making up her mind to accept such a reckless, careless, extravagant, haphazard lover.

"Oh, come!" cried Philip. "There was nothing haphazard about my love. I wished sometimes that there might be."

"There's something hap-hazard about a young man who buys three ponies when he can't possibly use more than one."

"Not when one of them is for a young lady, who chooses to take a view of things, after the purchase of ponies, which makes it impossible to ask her to ride one of them!"

Dorothy blushed. "Oh!"

He made her agree to use one of the ponies as her own; and when he had taken himself off to the "Snow Find"— having first given his orders about the pony at the stables, where he had left the animal after he had ceased to see Dorothy—she sent word to the livery people that she should want to ride in the morning, early. She caught sight of Ernfield's boy passing the house on his way to the stables, and despatched the message by him.

"Benn gittin' good news, Miss Maurice?" inquired Fred, as she laid a hand on the phaeton she had come from the house to stop.

She saw that he recognized the happiness in her face; and she liked Fred well enough, and felt safe enough with him to say, "Yes, Fred—very." But she admonished herself that this public impression of her happiness would n't do; and she asked Fred about Dr. Ernfield.

. "Oh, Doc's all broke up lately," said the boy. "*I* do' know what's the matter of him. He use n't to be like that. He don't seem to have his old git up an' git any more,— Doc don't ! Here I benn drivin' round to tell our patients that we can't come to-day. We're laid up, we are, and that's the way it goes ! "

Dorothy's heart went out to Ernfield in a pity which took a new edge from her own fortune. She asked Fred, while she smiled at his invariable air of proprietorship in Ernfield, to tell the doctor that she was coming to see him next day, if he would let her. She felt as if her love somehow consecrated her to all the suffering and failure and misfortune everywhere. She felt as if she must be worthy of her bliss ; it must teach her to look out, not in. There was a fresh force in the world ; it was created anew. It seemed to her that her whole life must be an outgiving of the great spiritual truth which had descended upon her. Her one word, of which she had learned the meaning for the first time to-day, seemed to explain so much, to make so much perplexity smooth, to melt so much doubt and trouble, to make foolish so much striving. The joy which knocked at her heart, and seemed to beat there sometimes as if it would burst its gates, was not a thing of which either she or Philip should take all the good. It was for everybody ; only, she thought, they should not know what blessed them. And, in the morning, as a beginning, she took her ride.

It was a good ride. She seemed to find herself in it, and these early, sunny morning hours, in which she fled along the *mesa* alone, in a sweet abandonment to the joy of the motion, of the morning, and of the inward tumult of her thoughts, remained always in her memory as moments a little better than speech could report. Even Philip she never told of this ride.

They took many rides together, however, in the valley, and among the mountains, and up the mountains; and the compensatory law of Nature by which the work of the world is continued in the face of an engagement, enabled the usual output of ore to be taken from the "Snow Find" daily, with little assistance from Philip. Cutter was one of Nature's assistants in this, and the lovers recognized together his unfailing goodness. Philip went back and told her about their life together at Piñon. He said affectionately that Cutter was an awful ass, and the best fellow in the world. He should be sorry when he grew less of an ass, because he might be less entirely the best fellow. He said that he was afraid that the West was teaching him something; he feared he was acquiring sense about some things; he could see his affectations dropping away from him, one by one.

And then he told her about Cutter's affair with Elsa Berrian, and Dorothy compassionated him tenderly. She wished every one they liked to be engaged, to be happy in their love. She said hard things of Elsa, but she professed to be sure that she and Cutter would understand each other, finally, as *they* had. Surely they had suffered enough from misunderstandings, but all had fallen out well with them. Philip ridiculed her optimism; and then he asked her if she was quite sure that even they were beyond the reach of the accidents of fate. They would sometimes feign themselves lost to each other for the pleasure of surprising their happiness afresh; but something in Philip's voice made her turn upon him quickly.

"Why? *Is* there something? Have you heard from your brother? What is it, Philip?" She laid a gentle hand on his arm.

They were riding on the pine-covered *mesa*.

Philip denied to himself the ache and the foreboding out of which he had spoken, as he held aside a bough to let her pass.

"Nothing," he said. "Why should there be anything?"

"I don't know. Everything makes me afraid. It was never so until—until I had this to lose. It seems to me every little while as if something must happen. Perhaps we are too happy!" She sighed, and Philip laughed down the wasteful use of a present happiness as an object for the threats of destiny.

"Do you suppose," he asked, "that no two people were ever happy enough before to excite the jealousy of the evil-minded fates?" And he added that the fates were still kept so busy on the Atlantic seaboard that they had n't had time yet to come West, and grow up with the country. "They may be wrecking the happiness of some loving pair in Connecticut, or Massachusetts, or New York at this moment. In fact, it's likely. But they have n't time for Colorado. Business is too brisk where they are."

She laughed, and Philip proposed a gallop. He was willing to be rid of his own thoughts.

Dorothy liked to make him see how she had come to be such a goose about the proportion of his guilt in his affair with Jasper. It involved accusations on both sides, and, on the whole, they liked the security with which they might now accuse each other as well as anything. She asserted that her idea about that affair was not merely the natural conclusion; but that she should think the same thing again

"Oh, come!" cried Philip. "Not quite!"

"I don't know," said Dorothy judicially. "You see what I went on. I was sure you were a hasty, hot-tempered, sensitive, high-strung, harum-scarum young man," she said smiling at him, "and I knew your brother for a gentleman of judgment. You must remember that he had never given me any reason to doubt his honesty or his—his virtues. They were n't romantic, like the vices of some other people I could name, but they were solid. At least they seemed so. I believed in them at any rate; I suppose I 'esteemed' them. Is n't that the word?"

"You took good care not to esteem *my* virtues, I observe."

"Did I?" quizzed Dorothy. "I had n't noticed. Were they about?"

"They were n't estimable."

"I'm sure I did n't esteem them."

"I believe you. You were busy."

"Yes," she said, with a little arch lift of her eyelid, "—loving them."

They had been climbing the hill which Margaret and Ernfield had once climbed. He caught her hand to his lips.

It was easy to answer such expressions—of which, however, she was very frugal—in the manner allotted to them; and to find the moment's happiness which they should produce in the normal lover; but it was impossible to keep this content. And when he was away from her, in the face of every reason for joy, he was blankly miserable. Cutter, who was the first to whom he told the news of his engagement, and who rejoiced in it as became a friend, noticed his moodiness, as Vertner and Ernfield did, also, after a time; and they twitted or jibed him after their several fashions, until Cutter saw it was serious, and set himself to help him, if he could. But Philip repulsed him, almost rudely.

In the long nights he thought he must tell her; but when he saw her radiant face again, it was seen to be impossible and absurd. No; he had bought his happiness with a price. If the price was high the more reason for not risking

it by suffering foolish qualms to tempt him to the revelation which hung always on his lips. He thought,
sometimes, she must read his secret in his eyes. How
could it be that a man should lose the power to face himself
in the defenceless moments of solitude, and fail to show it
in his countenance?

He could still make it seem right—what he had done—
as it touched Jasper. Nay, it sometimes seemed as finely,
as excellently right as it had seemed in the moment which
had persuaded him to the wrongful silence he was now
committed to. But as it lived in the same world with
Dorothy, it was a foul and unspeakable thing; it was to the
full the wrong, or more than the wrong it could have
seemed to his old rectitude, if it had approached him in its
naked guise, with no question of Jasper, of vengeance, of
wrong for wrong, or of the love for which he had done it.
This love was now good and sweet to him only as he could
find a purity of impulse in himself answerable to the purity
of hers; he felt soiled by what he had done, to his inmost core. Her very caresses were a shame to him. He
thought how she must start away from him if she
knew.

In these moods he framed a dozen passionate confessions
in which he told her that he was a scoundrel beneath the
least of her kindnesses; he said that he had her love on
false pretences; that she should know him—all of him—to
know how unworthy he was. He said in these confessions
which were never made that he would go away; that they
would not meet again; and that—at this point a crazy pang
of jealousy would intrude and he would remember that he
could not leave her to Jasper. He knew that she now
despised Jasper. Yet this seemed possible, or even
probable.

In the midst of this harassment of mind, small things

gave him pleasure. It was with a strange joy, for example, that he arranged the details of borrowing on the security of the "Little Cipher" the sum which Maurice owed Jasper. He transacted the business, giving him the money that was to deliver Maurice from Jasper's hands, and to place Dorothy for ever beyond his brother with a pleasure hardly diminished by the sense that he was at the same time giving the final sanction to his deed, and making retreat impossible.

He recognised, with a start, as he stood by the banker's counter, the feeling which he had accused in his father. His own perception of the unwisdom, the wrong of reprisal upon Jasper, he had played utterly false, and he found himself rejoicing in having done so. He knew, now, the exultation his father had felt in squaring himself with Jasper. Still more clearly, but sadly, he saw how his father had been led to cast back his own seeming ingratitude in his face.

Ah, if he could but get at his father, they might understand each other, now. His father was the one person to whom he could fancy himself telling his story unreservedly, if he could but find him and reconcile himself to him. He did not believe he would be the surer that his plea for Jasper had been the false one it would now more than ever seem; though he thought of this. What came to him was that his father was the one man who could wholly know the goaded mind in which it had come to him that he *could* not let Jasper win his love from him, too.

The thought made the discovery of his father's whereabouts even more than the immediate necessity it had been for the past two months. He enjoyed the reflection that Jasper would now be indirectly furnishing him with the money for lack of which he had hitherto failed to find him. He said to himself that he would start soon—at once; and then he recalled that he had promised himself to remain in Maverick until Jasper's return. If Jasper should ever come to know of what he had done he did not wish to give it to him to say that he had dodged away. He wished to face him. He was not ashamed of what he had done—not, at least, before Jasper.

He did not find his feeling about it, even as it touched Dorothy, continuous. There were odd lapses in it, followed by quick returns of remorse. It would die away from him, in good hours, when they talked together, and grow a callous lump, which he was conscious of carrying about in his bosom as a burden ; but he was not constantly sure of its meaning. At these times his willingness to enjoy the nearest pleasure, his liking for the comfortable, the agreeable arrangement, minded him to keep it out of his sight, if he could, and forget it. Surely he had a right to his hardly-won bliss ; and if he had not, no one was likely to be benefited by any foolish asceticism about it, unless, indeed, Jasper,—whose enjoyment of his brother's incapacity to taste the joy he had snatched from him, being imagined, helped Philip to forget manfully.

They talked of Jasper sometimes, to make sure of their possession of each other ; they even indulged a wonder why he did not return, though, in their hearts neither wished his return. They felt instinctively that his return would set a period to their present state ; their next state might be better or worse, but it would not be the same. The first days of betrothal came but once, and they hedged them jealously from the world. Dorothy would not let him make their engagement known beyond the little company of their friends, and made him pledge each of them to secrecy, for a time yet. She said she knew it must come ; she should have to be congratulated ; she should have to see her engagement take its place among the gossip of the town, in the news of the day, but she was not ready for that yet. It was only one degree from having to feel, as she knew she should be made to feel,

that a marriage was just a marriage—an interesting public
function, surrounded by the usual circumstance of ushers,
orange flowers, white silk, carriages, subdued whispers, rap-
turous comment, Lohengrin, and all the rest of it. She
might as well be a statistic, and done with it. She admitted
that their marriage would be in the census; but she was
willing to postpone her sense of its civic importance.

Sometimes in their rides long silences would fall, and
perhaps they communicated with each other most fully in
these. But they liked to speak of the time when a little
turn, one way or the other, might have lost them to each
other, as it seemed.

Dorothy would not admit that any chance could have
been strong enough to really keep them apart : on which
Philip asked her what she said to the chance which she had
given herself to accept Jasper.

"Suppose I had n't come along ! Suppose Vertner
had n't let on what an extra abused fellow I was ! It's
even betting what answer he would have got."

"Well, he has n't come back for it," suggested Dorothy

"No, but if he had ?"

"I gave myself a week," she said, demurely.

"Do you mean that you gave me a week ? Take care !
I sha'n't believe that you were spending *all* your time
disliking my part in the row with Jasper!"

"Oh, you may believe what you like !" she rejoined
flicking her horse with the quirt Philip had given her.

But, at another time, when they were sitting before the
fire in her own home, she told him that it was really he
who had gone nearest to make the impossibility of their not
coming together possible. What did he say to the extreme
folly of telling a young woman he loved her, and asking her
in the same moment to understand that the fact was n't to
count ? To be sure he had suddenly thought better of this

z

absurdity.   It was a great point that he *had* thought better
of it.   But why ?

 A sick feeling stole over Philip as he parried this question
—so obvious, so just—for the dozenth time, with a weary
joke.   It reappeared with the haunting effect of a threat.
Must this ghost always stand at his elbow ?   Might he not
better tell her the whole story of his temptation and his fall,
and throw himself on her mercy, and her belief in him.

But he remembered Maurice, who would be so far too
much involved in anything he should try to say.   He could
not wound the faith in her father, which he had given so
much to preserve.   He wished that Maurice would at least
take the action which was now a matter of days, and which
could not be much longer postponed.   And he wished
Jasper would return.   There came a point in all threatening
discomforts where all his thoughts and desires about them
resolved themselves into a single longing to have done with
them.

When he and Maurice met in Dorothy's presence, now,
they avoided each other's eye.   Philip felt degraded by
their common secret.   He saw that he must tell Dorothy
what he had done if the present situation did not come to
an end soon of itself.

CHAPTER XXVII.

Margaret clung upon her husband, as Jasper left them, and took the path back into the woods. She looked wistfully into his eyes. "Tell me it is n't true!" she whispered huskily. "Say that he is wrong! He would say his worst. I know that! Oh, James, tell me that it is n't true!"

Deed was silent. He watched Jasper's form slowly disappearing among the twilit pines, with blazing eyes. He took his breath shortly.

"True?" he asked from his absorption. He stroked her head absently. "What true, dear? Scoundrel!" he muttered.

"What he said—that you—you——?"

"That I pledged bonds left with me in trust to raise money to pay Philip? Yes. It's true," he said, clenching his hands, and staring over her head at the point where Jasper had vanished among the trees. He was less than half conscious of making the confession which he had considered so often and painfully; but at her shrinking from him he knew that he had told her, and that he was alone with her knowledge of him. "Do you object?" he asked abruptly.

The soreness of his spirit spoke. Every nerve in him ached from the interview which he had just cut short fiercely with a word.

She could have comforted him, without a backward look

on the story Jasper had told, and he would have blessed
her; and, later, would have humbled himself before her with
the truth.   At the moment the hand of pure kindness must
have been a pain; and the probe, even in the hands of love,
was torture.   "Do you object?" he repeated, as she did
not answer.

"Object?" she cried.   "Oh, my husband!"

She saw that he was in the mood when he must be hard
with the person nearest him.   She had just seen him
tormented beyond endurance.   She meant to be gentle, to
be tolerant.   But she could not be silent.

"I see!" exclaimed Deed.   "You need n't say it.
Well, the law objects, too.   You are in excellent company."

"Oh, James, how should I care for that!   You were in
the right.   I believe it.   I only ask you to say it, and I
will believe you.   Can't you see that I can't bear to think
you in the wrong?"

"Ah yes!" he exclaimed sadly.   "You care too much
for the right to bear to think that!"

"That is true!" she said simply.   "I don't think you
could want me to deny that, James, though you say it as if
it were an accusation.   You mean that I care for that first,
and then for you.   I care for you as you *are* right, *the* right!
Can't you see how it's all the same thing?   You have
become my right.   Oh, James, did n't I take you for that in
marrying you?"

"Reserving your own definitions," said Deed bitterly.

"I don't define," she murmured entreatingly.   "I only
ask you to say!"

"And I can't say!   Nothing that I could say could make
what I have done seem right to your ideas of Right.   You
would be forced to condemn just as I should be eternally
forced to do it, in the same situation.   It's temperament!
It's character!" he cried miserably.

The twilight had deepened during the brief minutes in which Jasper had told his father that he knew the secret of the hypothecation of Iron Silver stock at Leadville, and had given him his choice between retreat from the sale to Snell, and an immediate publication of the facts of the hypothecation in the newspapers. He had taken his scornful answer away with him into the dusk. The darkness was now falling about them, touched only by the last reluctances of the day, which the reflected glimmer from the white hills detained vaguely still.

"Yes, yes!" assented Margaret. "I know. But what can matter if we love each other—if we trust each other!"

"Trust, Margaret! Did you trust me when I sold the ranch away from this fellow! Would you trust me, now, if I were to tell you how I used this mining stock out of a need of the same kind? I am made that way, Margaret. I could n't have helped doing it any more than you can help loathing it, now," he repeated.

"I don't loathe it," she said patiently. "I am sorry—sorry. What you say about the other—yes, I see, now, that I was wrong, or unhappy, or—I don't know what—in my way of asking you not to do that. Perhaps I shall never be able to find words, or ways—whatever it is with which other women explain such things," she went on, with a little note of humility in her voice which touched Deed indescribably, and caused him to take her hand in his in a quick pressure as she stole it gently, almost timidly toward him. "But James," she continued quickly, "we were not married then. I am your wife, now. That has changed everything. I can't judge you. I am part of you. If you have done what—what he said, the error, the sin, if there is any, is mine, too. Let us help each other about it, James. Tell me—how was it?"

The moon stole an edge above the summit of Monk's

Head, etching the dusky outline of the mountain against its peeping disk. The light kindled along the snowy flanks of the opposite hills, and ran tremulously into the black depths of the cañon beyond. He told her of the means by which he had paid Philip, as they stood in the broadening glow.

"But you meant to do no wrong!" she said as he finished.

"Oh, meant!" he exclaimed. "Do you think they will care at Leadville what I meant to do?"

"Perhaps not," she said. "But I care. If it had not been for the chance of this snow, which might have happened to any one, you would have sold the 'Lady Bountiful' to those people at Burro Peak, and no one would have been the worse for what you did." She said this stoutly, as much by way of trying to believe it for herself as to comfort him. But her conscience forced her to add, immediately, "But it was an awful mistake—it was —it was not right, was it, James?" She looked up into his eyes, questioning him doubtfully, as if she had never known days in which problems like this were decided with instinctive confidence within her own breast.

"No, Margaret, no! It was like other things—a muddle of right and wrong, I suppose; but certainly not right. Perhaps I might say for what I did that it would n't be fair to judge it in the gross. But that's the best I could say. I did it because I had to, Margaret. I did n't *mean* one thing or the other, as you call it. The position in which Philip placed me was intolerable. I changed it—I righted it. God knows with what show of justice!" He turned away. They stood for a moment, silent. Then he said, "Does it not seem my destiny, Margaret dear, to hurt you, and always at the tenderest point? I seem to have to do the things which must wound you deepest, and then to have to hurt you deeper by wickedly trying to make you pay for

my error through your sensitiveness to it. From the hour
that I borrowed money at Leadville on those bonds which
did n't belong to me I have been ashamed to face myself;
what I did has seemed to debase me deeper and deeper
every day. I have hated myself. I have wished to tell you.
But when you question my act, ever so gently, I must make
you suffer for my pain about it. It is because I know the
things I do for what they are that I can't bear your sure
eyes on them. If I believed myself as much in the right
as I am always ready to say I am, I could not shrink from
your brave, judgments."

"Oh, James, it is n't for me to judge. But, don't you
see, dear—what you say gives me courage to ask—that—?"
she hesitated.

" What, Margaret ? " he asked gently.

"That—that all you have done—all that you have been
led to do since Jasper turned false, is all of one piece,
really ? "

" No," said Deed gravely, " I don't see that."

" But I do ! Oh, James," she cried, " what you did to
Jasper was wrong—wrong from the beginning ! "

Deed frowned heavily. " Margaret ! I thought you——"
He bit his lip.

" That I said I was mistaken in that ? In the way I
chose to make you feel what I felt—yes ! But in my feeling
about it—oh, no, no, I was right; and if in nothing else,
then right in my instinct that it was wrong for *you !* Poor
James ! It has been wrong, has it not ? " She slipped her
hand within his arm. He dropped the arm, and looked
away toward the gilded white hills. But she went on, un-
daunted. " We have tried to cover it up in our happiness,
these last few weeks. But it's true ; and I see now—I'm
sure that you see now—that we must face it. Do you think
I don't understand how, having done what you did with

Jasper, what you did with Philip had to follow? It was that I feared for you—all the endless consequences, all the suffering, all the remorse, all the snarl of wrong! I feared them for *you*, James, because I knew you—because—" her hand stole into his, and this time he held it fast—" I loved you ; and because I saw—oh, so clearly—how it would all be worse for you than for another man—how you would make it worse, because you would be trying always to burst your way through the misery ; and because you would suffer more than other men from your failure, and—and your wounds ! It was that that forced me to ask you not to do it. And it's that that makes me ask you now, James, to *undo* it ! Don't speak ! Don't say you won't or can't. You can, James, and you *must !* Can you wish to be subject for ever to such attacks? Jasper has to make them. They are in his nature ; and they are part of the sure result of what you did," she said bravely. She was launched now, and did not care what she said. " What you did to right yourself with Philip was wrong, of course ; but it was not the first, nor the chief wrong." She caressed his shoulder vaguely with the arm she ran about his neck. " Whatever you did, it all came from the other. It could n't have happened if the other had n't. And we must go back to that. I see now that we have been mistaken in pretending to each other that that question is dead and all its consequences buried. It can never die, James, until we face it together, and do what we still can." He turned and looked into her pleading face. " It lives between Jasper and you, and will always live until we have the courage to give up our wrongful right ; it lives between Philip and you, and perhaps that is past help—perhaps that is to be our punishment—but worse, much worse, it lives between *us*, James ; and we shall never be happy until it is dead and out of sight ! Oh, I have been thinking while we have been standing here ! I have been seeing, more than ever before, how different we are, how hard it will be, always, for us to understand each other, to make allowance, to remember that we love each other, and to keep that uppermost. But I have become sure that never, for either of us, is there to be peace until this is made right!"

Deed drew her to him, and folded her in his arms, "My wise, good Margaret!" he said. "My gentle, sweet, just girl! You said a little while ago that I was your right—that you had taken me for that. But you see, now, how I could never be that. My right is personal, whimsical, fantastic, brutal, selfish. I construct it myself. I take it habitually as if it were the one right in the world, and as if it might not be the wrong of a dozen others. It is you who must be my right for the future; and I will obey it humbly. Your Right is certain because it is *not* yours—because it is the Right of others. I will do what you say, Margaret."

He bent and kissed her. Margaret touched her eyes hastily with her handkerchief. "And will you—will you restore the ranch to Jasper? Will you give him back his share?"

Deed's brow knit darkly. "My girl, my girl," he exclaimed in sadness, "you don't know what you ask!"

"But you would do that, surely. You would not hesitate now, for any feeling of—of—"

Deed shook his head bitterly. "Is it a light feeling? Do you think I could do it? Oh, Margaret, you don't *think!*" An inflection of reproach stole into his voice.

Her ear did not fail to note it. But she said, "I do! I do! It is because I think—and for you—that I beg it of you."

Her husband bit his lip. "It's preposterous, Margaret! Ask something reasonable. Would you have me humble myself before Jasper, *now*—after all that has passed, after to-day? Would you have me go to him,—his father—

confess that I had been in the wrong from the beginning, and beg his permission to restore, to give back what I stole from him. I should be lying. I don't believe him in the right; I believe him hellishly in the wrong. But besides, see what he must think—that I do it in fear of his vile threat! Could you wish that humiliation for me, Margaret? I don't believe it."

"No. We must wait, I see. We must make the other right. Then this will come right of itself. You must go back," she said. "You must find your way to Leadville the moment this snow releases us, and restore what you have borrowed."

"Borrowed? Do you think it is by that word they will know what I did at Leadville? It will be a harsher word, Margaret—a word with a penalty."

"Well then," returned she with a simplicity which at once appalled and enchanted him, "you must go back and make it right on those terms."

He stared at her fascinated. "I will!" he said at last.

"I don't mean to urge you to anything your own judgment does n't approve," she said, temporizing, as even a strong woman must before consequences which are to be wrought out beyond her sight in the man's world.

"No, no! It has been in my own mind a long time. I would have done it gladly long ago if I could have got out of this prison, and could have believed that I had a right to commit you to what must follow. I must have my own respect back again, Margaret. You are right. I will go to Leadville, as soon as we can get away from this place, if Jasper does not contrive that I shall go earlier. And I will take the consequences."

"And then—?" She looked up into her eyes confidently, joyfully.

"Jasper?" he asked frowning.

She nodded. He shook his head.

CHAPTER XXVIII

BEATRICE folded Margaret in her arms and kissed her repeatedly and took off her cloak, and asked her where she had been, when Deed brought her to the house one evening a week later. She said that Ned was down town; and Mr. Deed was not to think of going on by the nine o'clock train to Leadville. She was charmed to keep Margaret while he went on; but he must stay, too, for the night at least. Ned would be back soon, and he was so anxious to see him.

As she spoke Beatrice glanced from one to the other. In Margaret's face she thought she saw some of what she had expected—a development, a softening, an effect like that which photographers get from the process they call "toning." It was not merely that usual, though indescribable difference which distinguishes the matron, however recent, from the maid; Margaret had changed almost in proportion to the area she had offered for change; almost in proportion to what Beatrice had always called to herself her "unmarriageableness." What she saw made her retract silently some things she had said to Vertner; but still left her wondering. Had Margaret contrived to attune herself to her husband; or had he, feeling the sacrifice she had made in coming to him, at last, after what had happened, made the history of his sex memorable by shaping himself to her? Did they get along? That was what she asked herself. She had decided that they did (Deed's face looked

strangely sad and worn ; but that was, no doubt, the other
matter) as she intercepted his answer to a glance from
Margaret in the pause which fell at her hospitable entreaty ;
and yet . . . . . She went back to her old feeling that the
difference between them was too irreconcilable ; and that
Margaret, of all persons, was the last to be able to reconcile
it (it was always the woman who had to play that part in a
marriage, and when the woman was wrong it was hopeless).
She said, as these thoughts passed through her mind, that
they had been greatly concerned lately when no one heard
from them.

Deed said Yes, they had been snowed up. They had
been unable to get out; they had feared their friends would
be anxious. He gave this explanation like a lesson learned
by rote. He was conscious that people would be curious ;
it was necessary to supply an explanation for current use,
and the simpler it was, and the sooner made, the better.
Margaret glanced quickly at him as he spoke.

He would not take off his overcoat in response to
Beatrice's entreaties : and in a few moments rose, and made
his farewell. Margaret followed him into the hallway. She
threw her arms about his neck.

" Oh James," she begged, through the lump that hung in
her throat, " are we doing right ? or no—of course we are
doing right—but do you think— ? "

" Margaret ! " exclaimed he reproachfully. He took
down her hands, and gazed into her eyes by the dim light
of the hall lamp, under which they stood. " It isn't you
who persuades me to falter, is it ? "

" No, no. But it is so easy to persuade ! It is you who
have to act—to suffer ! Perhaps I am wrong ! Oh, think ! "

" I have thought," he said soberly. " You are right.
We are both right. We cannot do otherwise. Tell me,
dearest," he whispered, stooping to her, " can we ? "

Their eyes confronted in a look in which each seemed to search the other's soul.

She turned away choking. "Go! go!" she cried in a stifled voice. She caught him to her and kissed him once, twice, and held him to her in a ravenous embrace, from which it seemed she would never let him go. Then suddenly she pushed him away, and, snatching her hands to her face, ran into the room where Beatrice awaited her.

It was finally because she was ashamed of her cowardice that she forced herself to look into the *Maverick Sentinel* the next morning. She glanced at the head-lines with a cowering heart; and when she found nothing in them beyond the usual budget of snow-slides, murder trials, Washington gossip, European war-clouds, local news, mining and cattle notes, booms and rumours of booms, she began to search again incredulously. Could it be that Jasper had held his hand? She asked Vertner, in as steady a voice as she could command—they were at breakfast—if Mr. Jasper Deed was in town.

"No," said Vertner. "Want to see him?" He smiled over at her, unscrupulously. She shook her head, without smiling. "No," he repeated, "he isn't in town, and it's even up when he will be. He was going to be back in a week when he started; that was the word he left; and there was plenty to call him back. But it's nearer ten days and no one's heard anything of him. I *did* think some of organizing a search expedition to go and find him one of these days when business was slack, but, come to talk to the fellows in town about it, there seemed to be a general agreement that *they* had n't lost Jasper Deed. I didn't know as I had myself, so I let it drop. But if you want to see him—" he offered, with twinkling eyes.

"No, no," she said. And then she told him—there could be no harm if she did not tell his errand—of the visit he had paid them at Mineral Springs. Vertner pricked up his ears at the first words, and, at the end of her recital, was leaning forward with his face supported between his hands, listening in unconscious absorption. As she finished, he emitted a little whistle.

"What a fellow!" he exclaimed, under his breath. "*What* a fellow! Snow so deep the drummers didn't try to get out, you say? Pass blocked! Everything battened down for the Winter! Drifts, probably, until you couldn't rest. And that *cuss* fought his way over into the Springs and saw Deed! My! My! But there was a rustler lost to the honest paths of speculation when that remarkable young man went into the business of being a confounded scoundrel! Like to have him in partnership with me for a year with his claws cut! Wouldn't we make this old Centennial State hum! But what's become of him? That's what I want to know. I believe I *shall* have to go after him, now. We can't leave a man with all that sand to die in a snowdrift. Come to think of it, there might be a chance to reform him if we could meet in a snowdrift—he underneath, and I on top—with a whisky-flask. It would be a pretty triumph—leading him home captive, warranted kind and gentle, and trained to go in harness. What a scoundrel! I'm afraid he made Deed unhappy," he said suddenly.

Vertner had executed a circumscribed war-dance in their bed-room when Beatrice had told him of Deed's safety, on his return the night before. He had said that Deed was a fraud not to wait; and then had said that he should start for Leadville in the morning to hunt him up. He had something to tell him. But, in the morning, when Beatrice asked him if she should pack his bag, he told her that he had decided not to go—not to-day, anyway. Deed would probably find out at Leadville for himself, what he had to tell him, and it would be all the better.

Margaret's eyes filled with tears alarmingly at his suggestion, and he shyed hastily away from it, and asked her if she would n't go with them on a little picnic they had arranged for that day. They were all going to the Iron Mine. Oh, yes, certainly she would go. But there was no question about it! Margaret protested. It seemed wicked to be enjoying herself, or even to permit herself the colour of enjoyment, while Deed was away from her on such an errand. But Beatrice's assurance to Vertner that she would go, and the "talking to," which Beatrice gave her when he had left them, silenced her.

She was full of her own thoughts as she prepared for the long ride to the Iron Mine; and they were not all of Deed in Leadville.

She must meet people since she had come back. Some of those she had known during her earlier stay were sure to be of the picnic party. She must bear to guess the comment that had gone on in her absence from the looks she should receive. Ah, well! She did not care. There were other things to think of. Yet she caught herself wondering if Dr. Ernfield would be riding with them to the Iron Mine. She had not dared to ask Beatrice who was going; she had not even asked how he was, though she wished much to know.

She recalled the occurrences of her former stay in Maverick, one by one. Some of them—the days of courtship for example, when Deed and she had seen each other daily, in perfect love and confidence, were sweet recollections. But others crowded these out. The morning when she had so nearly sacrificed his love for her to save him from himself, and had failed; the desolate days which

followed—Ernfield, her flight, her happy flight from this
house to which she had come again ; these were haunting
memories.

It was a beautiful day. The sun was shining with that
effect of never having shone before, mingled with the sober
purpose of going on shining just so for ever, which Colorado
knows, and which all December picnics should arrange for.
The fact that the entire sum of the grey or doubtful or
lowering days in the course of a Colorado year would not
make up a fortnight, mysteriously seems not to dull the
edge of one's pleasure in each new sun-soaked day.
Dorothy was saying something like this to Philip, as they
rode out together to meet the party. Vertner had brought
Philip the news of his father's arrival in town, and had had
hard work, as he told Beatrice afterwards, to restrain him
from following Deed to Leadville, forthwith. It was only
by representing the case to Dorothy that he had succeeded
in keeping him for the picnic, he told his wife. He did not
mean that he had told Dorothy anything she did not know ;
he had merely indicated to her the propriety of his remaining and he had remained.

Philip rode by Dorothy's side with a happy smile on his
lips. His heart stirred joyously in time to the hoof-beats
of their horses. To know that his father was found ; to know
that he must by this have learned that he had a loyal son,
was cause enough for throwing up one's hat, and to turn his
own trouble idle and foolish. As they rode, Dorothy would
occasionally look across the space between their horses and
smile with him ; and at these times a gleam of intelligence,
of sympathy, would light in her eyes, which seemed to
double his happiness. His head swam with it. He would
not talk, and Dorothy also kept silence ; but when their eyes
met Philip thought how, with every look, she endeared
herself more to him, and how she must make her way into

his father's heart. How his father would like her! She should make up for many things to him. She should be a daughter to him——not in the conventional sense, but truly. He fancied her replacing Jasper in his father's heart; he imagined her atoning for that loss, in so far as any one could. He knew that must always remain an unhealed sorrow, an incurable bitterness; but she should console it.

When he met Margaret, for the first time, a few moments later, he seemed to see something in her face which told him that his father must already be as happy as the love of woman could make him. He had had his one glimpse of her on the staircase of the hotel at Leadville, as she was leaving it, a bride; but her face had been veiled. He saw, instantly, that she was good. She was such a woman as he could fancy his father caring for. He saw why he had married her. These perceptions passed through his mind rapidly as he flung himself from his horse, and took her hand warmly.

Margaret had imagined this meeting. She supposed she must speak to him; but she had intended to make it a formal matter. She could not believe him as much at fault as her husband did; but his attitude bound her, she felt; and she must be the more careful since he was not by. Poor Margaret! Her judiciousness was always a failure. It was not less so in this case, for Philip's warmth disarmed her, and with the whole party halted and looking on she could not treat him with obvious coldness. She could only say to herself that, at least, it was not Jasper. Even her husband could not feel Philip to be as much to blame as his brother. And, before she knew it, a wave of tenderness for Philip came over her, like the tenderness she had felt toward him when Deed, for so different a reason, had left her before. He was at least his son. She had not yet found courage to glance at him. She wondered if he looked like *him*. She made herself glance down into his honest eyes ; and suddenly believed in him.   He *was* like his father ; his eyes were particularly like his.   She returned his hand-clasp.

" I have hoped we should meet," he said.

"Yes!" she murmured breathlessly.

" Will you tell me how my father is ?   You can't know how anxious we have been about him—about you."

"He's not well.   He has been—he has been troubled. You knew that he had gone on to Leadville ? "

"Yes, yes !   But he is coming back ? "

"Soon, I hope."   She lowered her eyes.

" Only soon.   Then I must run up   I had hoped he would be back to-morrow.   Vertner assured me that he would."

" Oh, don't do that ! " she exclaimed hastily.

" Don't ? " He hesitated.   "Ah, you mean . . . . No, I suppose father has n't forgiven me," he said gloomily.   Then, with recovered buoyancy, " But that's almost part of his fineness is n't it ?   If I had done what he supposes, he *ought* to hate me.   But does he still—or, no, I ought n't to ask that ; it is n't fair ; perhaps I ought not even to have spoken to you ; but I saw you.   I could n't help it.   You can't think what finding father again is to me—to all of us.   It's mixed up with so many things.   But it does n't need to be mixed up with anything to make me glad.   He's not like every father, quite, you know ; he's not been at all like other fathers in his goodness to me.   And he's such a *man !* "

The tone in which he said it sent a thrill leaping through her pulses, and it was hard for her not to shout what she answered a moment later, in an agitated whisper, struggling to control herself.

"I know your father," she said.   She took a hand from her rein, and offered it to him, in a torrent of feeling, for which she could find no words.   He caught the hand in a grasp that hurt her as he wrung it.

"I believe you do," he said, almost reverently.

The cavalcade had passed them as they paused together. She touched her horse and, with a single glance at him, started in pursuit of the party at a gallop. Philip joined Dorothy and they cantered on slowly after the company together, talking of what had happened.

They caught up with the others in the gorge making into the hills outside the town—the gorge through which Margaret, and Ernfield had once ridden on their way to the neighbouring summit. Cutter, Beatrice, Vertner, Ernfield and Mrs. Felton were among the group in advance. Margaret, who had rejoined the company before them, they perceived riding by Vertner's side. Every one, save Margaret and Ernfield, appeared in a festival mood; and their shouts and laughter echoed from wall to wall of the ·gulch, and floated up into the still, keen air, like a kind of offering to the perfection of the day. Ernfield was with Beatrice, far in advance, and they saw him stoop to her in quiet talk. Beatrice would sometimes turn in her saddle and laugh gaily at something Cutter and Mrs. Felton, who seemed to be having a pleasant time together, would call out from behind. But at these times Ernfield did not turn. Philip guessed that he was willing to avoid Margaret's eye; and Margaret for her part, kept in the rear with Vertner. Ernfield had joined the van of the cavalcade after it was in motion, and they had not encountered yet. Both were willing to postpone the meeting.

The gulch narrowed presently, and forced them out of its bottom to a narrow path along the ledge which hung above it. Opposite them a gash in the hill, the effusion of a mass of green earth upon the rocky slope, an abandoned cabin, told the familiar story of failure, the little daily tragedy of disappointment. The memory of another mine, which was always with Philip, now, but had seemed to leave him in the happy hours since he had known his father to be found, returned upon him with a fresh pain. It was a richer mine of which he was thinking. He had been about to say to himself, more fortunate. But was it fortunate? If he could choose would it not be his wish, now, that the ore-bearing vein in the "Little Cipher" might never have been opened? He could not wish that it should give out, now: his future had been wagered on it. But what would he not have given to know that he had dreamt the essay, the exploration of the mine, the fingering of the ore in his own hands? He wished heartily that he had never leased the mine to the Ryans, who must go blundering about and snatch a fortune out of the bowels of the earth, to show his conscience the way to the hell in which it now lived.

"Poor fellows!" said Dorothy, looking across at the deserted mine, as they rode along the path slowly, in single file. "What work, what hopes they must have put into that mine! It is hard, is n't it, to think that where one succeeds, a thousand must fail. It must be so, I suppose; but what a price for the success!"

"Do you mean that these men—the men who worked that mine—and others like them all over Colorado, and elsewhere, really pay for the lucky fellow's good fortune?" asked Philip, turning in his saddle (he was riding in advance) to look back at her. "That's a hard thought for the lucky fellow, is n't it?"

"Oh no, Philip, I did n't mean that!" She saw what he was thinking of; and hesitated a moment before trying to say just what she did mean. "It's Nature that pays. I suppose we must think that. The men will feel that they have played against Nature and lost; and that is right, too, no doubt. Some must lose; the chances are infinitely in favour of loss. Every one knows that who sinks a shaft, or digs a tunnel, I fancy. And then some must win. That is

natural. The men who fail don't grudge the successes. I
think they like to know of them. It is a comfort to them
to know that there *is* some success somewhere. But it lays
a great responsibility on the successful ones, does n't it ? "

" Yes," said Philip.

They rode on in silence. The hoofs of their horses seemed
to make a loud noise as they struck on the rocky path.
The others had been moving more rapidly while they talked,
and the hoof-beats of the animals in advance, as they died
away, seemed to leave them more solitary in this lonely
path between the hills than if a party had not been within
hail.

" Philip," she said softly, not guessing his thoughts.

" Yes."

" Was n't it fortunate—Mr. Cutter and I were talking of
it the other day—that it was the ' Little Cipher' which
turned out so rich ? "

" Why ? " asked Philip, turning to face her again suddenly.

" Why, only think if it had been the ' Pay Ore,' and you
had been obliged to give it up to your brother, after—after
all that has happened, and after your making it a success.
Fancy your having to think that all the work you had given
to your own mine had come to nothing; and the same
work in his had brought him a fortune. Fancy your having
to know that *you* had done it for *him!* Why, Philip, when
I think of your being forced to go to him in the face of all
the wrong and suffering and insult he has heaped on you,
and having to say——! B-r-r-r ! " She shuddered prettily.

It had come. He felt, now, as if he had paltered and
doubted and hesitated, to his shame. How could he have
believed that she would not find a forgiveness in that
heavenly sympathy for the means by which he had won her.
These gentle words,—the first in comment on that bitter
situation which had found their way to any lips—were like

dew in a thirsty land to him. She must know. He would not wrong her by another moment's shameful silence. His secret choked him. Their love seemed worthless while it remained between them.

"It *would* have been an odious position," he said with an effort at lightness. "Perhaps a man might be forgiven for shirking it."

"You mean he might send some one else to tell him?"

"No. I suppose I was thinking that he might do nothing at all."

"Wait; and let his brother find out, do you mean?"

"Well, yes; something like that!"

"But that would only be postponing it. His brother would be sure to learn of it, sooner or later. And then he would have his silence to accuse him of. If one had a brother like Jasper I don't think one would like to give him an accusation—even an accusation like that, where no real wrong would have been done him. Do you?"

"I think I should let him find out," said Philip. He was speaking with his head half turned toward her, and with one hand resting on his pony's flank behind the saddle. This kept his body swaying with the animal's forward stride. The others came into sight for a moment at a bend in the road, and vanished again. They probably thought to do the lovers a kindness in leaving them to themselves. "Even suppose he never found out?" he pursued after a moment, as he turned and leaned forward to adjust the pony's forelock, which had not been properly smoothed under the head strap.

"But I can't imagine that. His brother would hear. He would know that the strike had been made in his mine."

"He might n't know which was his. You can imagine that surely."

Something in his voice startled her. " Why, Philip——?
But what do you mean?"

They had emerged upon a vast open green upland, and
their horses by a common impulse changed their pace to a
canter. The others were visible, now, far in advance, upon
the road winding as far as the eye could reach between the
grassy acres of the park. They cantered along side by side
in the sunlight, taking the pure air of the table-land on their
faces.

The interval gave Philip time. But he could not think.
Her smiling face, as she glanced towards him in their
buoyant flight, daunted him. Would she smile so when he
had told her? He was suddenly afraid to speak.

But as the animals fell into a walk, " Suppose his brother
did n't know," he repeated ; and this time she was sure of
the strange inflection.

She stared at him. " It would be an awful temptation,"
she said under her breath. She gazed thoughtfully into his
eyes. He dropped them.

" Yes," he said.

He kept his eyes upon the moving roadway. He felt her
glance upon him. She was reading him. He knew it.
Would she never break the silence? Then, at his side, he
heard a low moan—not like Dorothy's voice—a moan of
perception and reproach and heart-breaking grief.

" Oh !" she murmured desolately. " Oh-h-h !" The
wail trembled from between her trembling lips ; it seemed
torn from her soul. She paled. He saw her sway in her
saddle, and stretched out a quick hand to stay her fall
She waved him off, brokenly. " No. No. Don't! Don't
please !"

" Dorothy—" he began.

She commanded herself and looked into his eyes again
with a look of love and longing and despair, with a face of

sorrow and indignation, and scorn and pity which shook his heart.

"How could you!" she cried in a stifled voice, through the tears that began to come. " How *could* you ! "

" It was for you," he said.

"For *me !* Oh, Philip, don't say it !"

" But for whom else, for what else ? You can't think that I would do it only for money, for revenge ! It was for you—only for you ! "

"And you think that makes it better ! Oh, what can you have imagined me ! How little—little you have understood me. Better ! Oh, Philip !" she choked.

" It was a question between losing you and doing it. I did it. It was wrong, it was wicked, it was base if you like. You may think what you will of it. I don't defend it. But I did it for you. And I would do it again."

"Don't !" she cried again, shrinking away from him " Oh, no one could accuse you as you accuse yourself. Knowing this—this thing that you have let yourself do to be all you say, how—oh, Philip, *how* could you stain our—our love with it ! I don't know what you mean. How could it have been ? Did I make you do this !" she cried suddenly. She stretched out her hand toward him. " Was it my folly, or vanity, in letting Jasper go on, that forced you to it—that seemed to give this a reason ? " Philip shook his head. " Oh no, no ! Of course it could n't have been that. But why—? " She stopped short. " What difference can it make ! It's done ! It's done ! And for me—for our love. Oh, how could you hope that any happiness could be bought with such wrong ! Can't you see how it soils and degrades and shames every moment that we have ever had with each other ? Can't you see how it must kill me to think that we have come by all that has seemed so sweet and precious and good through a fraud—through a trick."

"No," said Philip stoutly, "I don't see that. I won't
see it. If we really love each other, *that* counts ! But nothing else counts. I can make this right. I have taken.
I can restore." He said it, though he knew otherwise.
"Why, Dorothy, no one knows. And no one can ever
know. I see that you look on me as a common robber. But
it's not so. They were both my mines. Jasper sent me
money to work a claim for him. The money went into the
common fund. I don't know which of the two mines it
was used for. I shall never know. When I began to work
with his money I said to myself that I should look upon the
' Little Cipher' as his. But both still belonged to me. I
did all the work on them. They only existed through the
work I directed upon them. Jasper never thought anything
of his chances at Piñon. It was like giving a man $500 to
place on a horse for you ; or to buy a lottery ticket with.
And I thought so little of the chances, one way or the other,
after the first month, that I swear to you it was never in my
thoughts which claim was his, and which was mine. Legally
they were both mine. In fact they *were* both mine, not
only for all practical purposes, but actually. For Jasper
had never *bought* anything from me. He had given me
some money to expend in working a claim." Dorothy
opened her mouth, but he went on with a gesture, "Yes, I
know. It's true. Don't suppose I shirked the truth for
a moment. The difference is no difference. In my conscience Jasper was the owner of the 'Little Cipher,' and
all that might come from it. He is so yet. I don't dispute
it. It has never been present in my mind in any other
way since the temptation to keep silence and let him take
the other for his, came upon me. Since you must judge me,
it is fair that you should know how it has been with me. If
it is worse to have done what I did knowingly, I tell you
freely that I did it in the face of the knowledge that not all

the deeds and registrations and formal evidence of ownership in the world could make Jasper more the owner of the
'Little Cipher' than he was through my word to myself.
I know it; but I did it—I must n't tell you why or how—for
you." His voice dropped, and as their horses went slowly
along, he leaned over, and took the hand she had let fall by
her side. "Does that count for nothing with you, Dorothy?"

She had been listening to him wearily, wonderingly—
hoping against hope that he could excuse himself; that he
could make the obvious wrong seem right. But at this she
started as if waking herself from a sleep, and answered,
"Oh, for too much! Too much!" She released her hand
quietly. Philip felt a shock go through him. "Every
word you say makes it a more impossible thing for *you* to
have done, Philip. And to do it, above all, in the name of
our love! You had an opportunity such as comes to a man
in a thousand. You could have been strong; you could
have turned from that awful temptation, and I should have
loved you for it as women have loved heroes and martyrs.
I understand the temptation. It was cruel—even leaving
all this miserable thought of me out of it, it was horribly cruel.
I said how it would seem very hard to do right in such a
case. That was my first thought. But, oh, Philip, can you think
that it makes it easier for me to think you have failed—to
know that it was hard! Because the right is hard the wrong
is not good—is it? And surely the right is dearer for being
difficult! Any man might have resisted if it had not been
bitter to be strong. Only such a man as I have believed
you, could be great enough for the noble thing that was
open to you."

"Stop! Stop!" he cried, in pain.

"No, let me speak now, please. The truth is better.
Oh, Philip," she cried, "when I think of you with those two
mines in your possession, with the knowledge that one of

them held a fortune, and that the other was a mere opening in the ground; and when I think of you with the other knowledge that the one that held a fortune was your brother's, for your conscience, and the empty one, still only for your conscience, belonged to you, and that no one knew this—*no one!*"—she drew a deep breath—"when I think of that, and remember that that brother had wronged you to the death; that he had made it seem right to rob him by robbing you; that he had driven your father to desperation, and brought you to poverty—when I think of all those things, and see the splendid, generous, heroic right you might have done, and have to know that you chose to do *this*—oh, if I could have died before I knew it!"

A convulsive sob escaped her. She pressed her cheeks rapidly and repeatedly with her handkerchief. When she looked at him again it was with streaming eyes. "Say you were not in your right mind—that you did it in error! Say anything rather than leave me to believe what I must! It *was n't* you! Oh, Philip! Was not the man I have known you for too proud? Would he not have seen how the very security with which he might take, and keep silence, forced him to hold his hand? And would he not have felt, proudly, that every one's ignorance of his duty, and the infinite delicacy that ignorance forced upon him—yes, that the mere thread which bound him must be stronger for him than the strongest bond, because it bound him to himself? Oh, Philip, say you did n't do it!"

"I can't! I can't!" he cried. "It's true!"

She gazed at him with eyes of unspeakable reproach; and he dropped the eyes he had fixed upon hers while she spoke with the fascination of a criminal who hears his sentence. The party in advance had almost disappeared. The wide plain, hemmed in by hills, seemed a world in which he and she alone existed.

She checked her horse and held out her hand. "Good-bye, then."

"Good-bye?" he exclaimed, stupefied.

"Did you think we could go on?" she asked, sadly. "Did you think it could all be as it was? No. It is ended for us. Good-bye," she repeated. The tears fell from her eyes in a rain, but there was no relenting in her face. "Give me my ring," she said dully.

He stared. "Dorothy!" he burst out. "You can't! You won't."

"I must!"

"I have wronged Jasper. I confess it. Nothing that he has done excuses it. It makes it worse. I own it. But I can right that. I will. Dorothy! Surely—surely this need not touch us!"

"Oh, what do I care for Jasper?" she cried in misery. "It is for you I care, and you have lost yourself to me. It is n't the wrong to him! It is the wrong to yourself, to me, to all that we—to all that has been. . . . Oh, is it for me to show you such a thing? You have murdered our love! All the atonements in the world can't change that!"

She buried her face in her hands. Her horse stamped an impatient foot, and swung his head free of the rein.

"You despise me! You hate me! I see *that!*" exclaimed Philip. "But you sha'n't throw me off! You sha'n't raise me to such a happiness as you have let me know to cast me back! You should have thought of that before you stretched out your hand to lift me up. You should have known that I am not made of the stuff that bears. I can't bear this! I won't! Dorothy, girl,"—his voice fell to the note of tenderness—"I can't do without you. You have taught me not to be able to do without you. You won't do this thing. Oh, my God, could I live and know that you were lost to me—and lost through Jasper? Have you thought of that? Can you think that I could bear to know that, after all that has gone and passed, it is Jasper who parts us? You see how it can't be!"

"Give me my ring, please," she said, not coldly, or hardly, but resolutely.

He tore it from his finger. "As you wish!" he said with blazing eyes. And then, with cold courtesy, "You won't want me to go on with you. I will wait here until I see you with the rest."

"Oh, Philip," she trembled. She reached out her hand.

He would not see it. He leaned forward and gave her the reins she had allowed to slip from her. He lifted his sombrero.

"Good-bye," he said coldly.

She gave one glance at him. Her mouth twitched pitifully. Then she struck the pony a sharp blow with her quirt. The beast leaped forward.

Philip watched her steadfastly until she had melted into the dust cloud which indicated the position of the picnic party. He knit his brow upon his straining eyes and bit his lip fiercely as he gazed. When he had seen the last of her he whirled his horse, and dug his spurs into the animal's flanks with a wild sob of pain.

CHAPTER XXIX

VERTNER took the picnic party over the entire Iron Mine, inexorably, when they came to it. They watched the drilling, a blasting was set off for them, they rode in the ore-cars; they clambered down ladders into black pits, where only the candles lighted them, they clambered up again; they crouched and crawled and stumbled after their guide through galleries and passages which never ended; and four of the party were conscious of it all. Dorothy and Margaret and Ernfield and Cutter were thinking of other things.

Margaret sat down in her old room, when she was back again that evening, and wrote Deed a long letter, begging him to return; and tore it up.

Dorothy, on her return, found her father in his study chair. She curled her arms about him, and asked him without preface if he would not give up his charge at once, and leave Maverick—for ever. The blood tingled in his veins, and he drew a long breath. The relief of receiving the proposal at last from her silenced all speech for a moment. He had paltered with the need of breaking it to her, he had postponed the evil day through the forbearance of the Bishop, with the fear of what she must feel, of what she must say; and while he waited, the difficulty was solved for him. He was too happy in the fact for the instant to question occasions or causes.

" Why, I don't know, Dorothy," he said, endeavouring
to hide his pleasure, " if you don't like Maverick, I dare say
I should find reasons for not liking it, too. In fact, now I
think of it, I've been impatient and restless here for some
time. Yes, dear," he said, patting her hand, " since you
wish it, let us go."

" How good you are, Papa! I knew you would say so.
And where shall we go ? "

" Why, that's for you to say, partly, is n't it ? "

" But I can't call you to a new parish. I'm not a vestry
or a church committee. I wish I were. You would have
ten thousand a year for your salary, and have all the things
you have to go without now—poor Papa!—and never do
anything you did n't want to."

" What a picture! But I thought we were all to revel in
something of that sort, without the assistance of church
vestries, in that fine future of your own that you've planned.
I never consented to it, you know. I never agreed to play
the part you've assigned me in your drama of two happy
people and another."

" Oh, don't speak of that, Papa!" she cried, stooping
over him, and burying her face. " Don't speak of it ! "

" Why—why— " he exclaimed, in alarm, " what is the
matter, my girl! Have you and Philip been——? What
is it? Tell me, child ? " A stern and impatient note came
into his voice.

" Oh, I can't tell you ! It is n't anything that I can tell."

" Nonsense, Dorothy! Don't make all this trouble
about a lover's quarrel, child ! Do you suppose two lovers
never quarrelled before ? "

She lifted her tear-stained face from his breast, and
looked in her father's eyes, as she said : " This is not a
quarrel." A look passed over her face such as she might
have given Philip if he had been before her—grieving and

miserable, but proud, self-contained, resolute. Her father did not understand it.

"Oh," he said, relieved, "Well then, don't let him suppose it is ! " He rose and lit a cigar. Dorothy stared at him from the seat which she kept on the arm of his chair. "Don't play with a man, Dorothy. It is n't nice," —he blew out the first slender whiff of smoke contemplatively, as he brushed a speck of lint from the new clerical coat to which he had treated himself since he had been at ease about the future,—" and it is n't fair. It's even unwise when a girl is making a marriage so fortunate and desirable in every way as yours." He frowned slightly.

Dorothy raised her eyes and looked into his. "You don't understand, Papa," she said quietly. "I shall never marry Mr. Deed."

CUTTER went to Ira's, Ernfield's office, the Vertners, and finally to the Maurices on his return, without finding a trace of Philip. He thought the clergyman's replies to his inquiries short. He stabled his horse, and walked about the town, looking for him.

The shops were still open, and men and women paused before them to price the goods displayed outside, or went into the vividly lighted interiors, where the arc light glowed and glared. Trade was going on listlessly. It was near the end of the month, the pay-car was still to come up from Denver, and the railway *employés* of all grades awaited the monthly guest. The hands at the mines, and the cow-punchers were paid off at the same time, in order to keep the festival which followed pay-day, and which disorganized the town in the process of enriching it, within as narrow limits as possible. The lull that precedes a *fête* therefore lay over Maverick. Only two-thirds of the electric lamps were turned on; but there was nevertheless more light than noise. Suddenly a clatter of hoofs sounded above the vague and leisurely murmur of the quiet thoroughfare, and those on the sidewalk turned at sight of a horse ridden at a furious pace. No one save Cutter recognized the rider. The hoofs hammered across the bridge leading to the hotel; and Cutter followed hastily. The whistle of the night train sounded down in the valley at the moment, borne for miles through the clear air. Philip was standing at the bar of the hotel, draining a stiff glass. As Cutter laid his hand upon his arm he raised his eyes and regarded him strangely. He motioned to the bar-tender for another glass. Cutter shook his head; he looked anxiously into his friend's face.

" Where have you been? "

" To the devil—to Jasper." His voice was hoarse, and his black eyes stared from his haggard face with the effect of a man long ill. The train whistled again, nearer. Philip swallowed what remained of the spirits in his glass at a gulp. "Come, I'm off." He gathered his change from the counter, and made a rush for the door, as the train roared into the station. Cutter caught his arm at the door.

" Hold on, man! You're mad! "

Philip turned a weary face upon him. He smiled sadly. " Yes," he said.

" You're not well. It's crazy to be careering over the country in your state. Come back with me to the 'Snow Find' and go to bed and behave yourself."

" Oh, I'll behave myself. That's what I'm doing now. I've dropped the other thing. Come along." He made for the train, Cutter following him.

" See here. You're not going to take this train. You're a sick man, I tell you."

Philip gave him his weary smile again as he put his foot on the first step of the Pullman. "Yes, Cutter, I'm a sick man, fast enough, but not in the way you mean. I've got to go to Piñon. It won't hurt me. Come along if you don't believe me."

Cutter gazed up at him for a moment, where he stood on the platform above him, in helpless perplexity. Then he said, "You know what you are?"

Philip laughed, almost with pleasure. "Yes, I know."

"Just stay there, then, till I get a ticket."

The full moon was flooding the valley as the train ran out toward the mountains—beaming virginally, in this crystalline atmosphere, through a medium no grosser than its own. The purity of the air gave a new effect of luminosity, of splendour and abundance to the great lamp swinging aloft. It was light distilled; the air was not conscious of it. It fixed the valley under its cold, bare, hard gaze, etching the circling hills against the sky with a finger dipped in light, which seemed to bound, to outline, to select, and finally, as one looked, to detach it all from neighbouring sky and earth, and catch it away into that strange effect of being a picture which we know in all memorable scenes.

They began to climb into the recesses of the hills after the swift run through the valley. The opposite range of mountains was behind them, and as the young men looked out in silence from the windows of the compartment they had taken together in the Pullman, a liquid tract of radiance shone on their eyes from time to time far away; it was the snow, crusted in molten reaches along the mountain sides. Beside the silvery lakes of crust what one knew by day for the wooded hollows of the lower slopes were black mysteries under the light.

Philip turned from the scene with a heavy sigh.

"You can catch the 9.47 back from Barker's," he said

suddenly, catching the eye of Cutter, who faced him from the opposite seat. "You must n't think of coming along with me"

"I have an errand of my own, over the range. Don't bother about me."

"Come! No nonsense!"

"I have, I tell you!"

"Oh, well!" He dropped the question listlessly.

"I say, old man, what's the matter?" Cutter laid a hand on his knee.

"The devil's the matter," groaned Philip. "What do you suppose?"

"I don't know. Jasper?"

"No, sir. It is n't Jasper. I'm sick of that pretence. I cheated myself with the idea that it was Jasper when I let myself do the thing. But it was n't. It was I."

"I don't believe it."

"Well, anyway, it's I who suffer for it."

"I see that," returned Cutter, gently. "But how? Why?"

"Because I'm not the fine fellow I have liked to think myself—not even the fine fellow you think me. I'm not a fine fellow at all, Cutter; and I've done a low thing."

"Pshaw!"

"Is it lofty to abuse a woman's confidence, then? Is it admirable to rob a man who has trusted you?"

"What have you done?" asked his friend, quietly.

"I've taken a mine which does n't belong to me because I could, and because the man to whom it belongs had done me a wrong, and wanted to marry the girl I wanted to marry Is that plain?"

"The 'Little Cipher'?" stammered Cutter. "Jasper?" Philip nodded.

"But see here——" began Cutter.

"Oh, there's nothing to say!" cried Philip. "A man is

one thing or the other. I'm the other. She despises me. She hates me "

"Why?"

"Why!"

"Yes, why? Does she know what Jasper has done?"

"Yes. But she knows what I have done. Nothing else makes any difference. It can't to a woman, and probably that shows it should n't to any one." He told him of Maurice's situation; he explained his temptation, palliating nothing. "I thought the wrong Jasper had done me made my wrong right," he said. "It did n't. It only made a new one with separate consequences. I thought my love for her justified it; to her that seemed the damning touch. I believe she could have forgiven my villainy; but not that—not that! I fought it; I would n't see; I took my stand upon our love; I made her suffer as much as I knew how, and parted from her in anger. But all the time I felt her contempt scorching through me. When I got away from her it was more than I could bear. I hunted up Jasper, when I found he was back, and turned over the mine to him, as I ought to have done the first minute I heard of the strike."

"What?"

"You would n't have had me keep it, I hope?"

"I know, Deed. But owning up to Jasper——?"

"I did n't say I liked it. I was pursued by the thought of her scorn, I tell you. Do you think I could bear to know that she despised me, and that she was right? I had to do something. If she ever hears of it, she will know that I tried to do what I could."

"Yes, yes," cried Cutter impatiently. "But the humiliation!"

"Have I deserved to please my pride? Jasper was a blackguard, as usual; but there were two of us this time. It seemed to help the business along."

" And you've told him ? "

Philip nodded ; but at Cutter's look, " Oh don't ask me what he said ! " exclaimed he. " It was a damnable scene. The fellow is ill ; coming back from his journey he was caught in a blizzard ; for three days he was under a rock, in the snow ; he's in a bad way. He got up in bed ; he raved. Ernfield came in and I went. I looked back at him at the door ; and he nodded to me with a gloating smile. I know what he means. He has me, now. I've put myself in the wrong. All that has gone before—all that led up to this, is cancelled. He'll take his opportunity. It's all right."

He buried his face moodily in his hands. Cutter sat silent. He opened his lips to speak once or twice, and found nothing to say. The moon, which had been hidden since they had entered the gorge between the hills, and set out on their climb to the summit, gleamed suddenly upon a field of snow, lying high betwixt the mountains into which they were steaming up. It shone into their windows and filled the dusky compartment with radiance.

Cutter began to speak in a low voice. He said Jasper would do nothing ; he did n't doubt his will, but nothing was open to him ; and he went on to tell his friend that he exaggerated the enormity of what he had done. " You say that you've always looked on the ' Little Cipher ' as Jasper's," he said. " But we've only your word for it—and your word for a mental process so intangible that even you can't say when or how the ' Little Cipher ' became Jasper's mine, or by what process it ceased to be his and became yours." And he added that whatever might be true about this, surely the provocation made a difference ; surely it counted that it was done against one man rather than another. He did n't see why he should concern himself much about anything done against Jasper.

He believed some of this ; but not enough to enable him

to face Philip, as he stared at him with a miserable smile a moment before he muttered, "Rot! rot! rot! Very kind of you, Cutter, but no good! I can't deceive myself with such notions as that. It makes no difference, though. If you want to console me, don't talk about Jasper. I can get over that part of it myself. It's the other—Oh, Cutter, can't you see it's the *other* that matters? It's that I have done it against *her!* I thought if she cared for me she would pardon it because I had done it *for* her. Crazy fool! Not to see how it abused all her trust in me; how it must wound her at her tenderest; how it must profane all our relation. She will never forgive me. She hates me. She despises me."

He rose with a groan, and took a restless turn within the narrow space of the compartment, throwing his arms wide, and letting them fall again in despair. Suddenly he stood still and faced his friend. "My God, man! Do you know what that means?"

CHAPTER XXX.

MARGARET went to call on Dorothy the next morning. She had been thinking a great deal about her since the day before. All forms of misery seemed especially grievous to her just now; and useless forms of it seemed merely wicked. She had heard nothing from Deed, but there had not been time; he had telegraphed to let her know of his arrival, and had promised to telegraph again as soon as he had anything to communicate. The dread in which she awaited this message created in her, for the moment, a need to befriend some one's else sorrow. She felt a certain shyness. She had been conscious in their earlier meetings of the vague hesitation about her which Dorothy had tried to conceal. But she would not allow this to make a difference.

She found the house upturned when she arrived at the Maurices'. Dorothy came into the little parlour after a moment, apologizing for her appearance; she was in the disarray of the house-uniform in which she was accustomed to attack the heavier household problems. She kept on her apron. Margaret, glancing at her, saw the traces of tears on her cheeks.

"I have come——" she began, doubtfully. Her slow eye for such things showed her suddenly the pictures packed and standing in ranks against the wall, the upturned carpet, the dismantled walls, and swathed furniture. "But are you moving?"

"Yes; there is no reason why I should not tell you, Mrs. Deed. Papa has sent in his resignation." She met her interlocutor's eyes for the moment as if with the intention of putting some face upon the action. Margaret was the first to whom she had been obliged to make the announce ment'; put into words it sounded barren ; she saw that she had unconsciously relied on her father to front the inquiring world with an excuse. She found none for herself, and dropped her eyes before Margaret's clear, kind gaze.

Margaret's own thought leaped to its decision with its habitual certainty where Deed was not concerned. Dorothy was sitting on the sofa ; Margaret rose quickly and came and stood in front of her. " Won't you let me help you ? " she said.

"About moving ? " asked Dorothy, with troubled eyes. "Oh, there 's nothing ! Thank you very much, of course ! But we have so little."

" I did n't mean about moving, though I should be glad if you *would* let me do anything for you in that, if you must go. But you had better stay. I was thinking about——" She sat down on the sofa beside her, and stole her hand upon Dorothy's. "Listen," she said, in a low voice, "I am in deep trouble—I, too—the deepest. Won't you let me help you ? "

The sudden tears started to Dorothy's eyes. "But how ? " she stammered. " But why ? "

" He is near to me as well as to you, you know. It seems to give me a sort of right to speak. But perhaps you won't think that. Perhaps it hurts you to have it spoken of. I know—trouble is like that ; we wish to keep it to ourselves. But it's better shared, is n't it ? It might be needless ; it so often is. It's hard to be wise, but we may be quite sure of that—don't you think so—that needless additions to the misery of the world are wrong ? And even if it must remain all the trouble it seems to one's self, it is good to let another feel part of the ache with one. It somehow helps."

Dorothy listened with averted face ; she kept her glistening eyes on the opposite wall ; she pressed the kindly hand as Margaret went on. When she finished she seized it, turning to face her, and gazed into her eyes for a moment through a mist of tears.

"Oh, you are good," she murmured, chokingly. "I am very unhappy !"

She sobbed out her story in Margaret's lap. They remained a long time when she had done in each other's arms. "I see how you feel. It is hard," murmured Margaret, drying her eyes. "But you must forgive him !"

The fair head on her shoulder was shaken violently. "Yes, yes," said Margaret, gently, "you must, and you will." She felt herself very old in the presence of this violent young passion ; she felt rich in the abundance of her experience, and the richer because it was so recent. "You love him, don't you ?"

Dorothy raised her head and regarded her in a kind of amazement.

"Then you will forgive him," said Margaret, quickly. "Things don't matter so much as we think. I have learned that. One thing matters—only one ! And you may be sure he has his excuses if you could know them. My husband is suffering from a wrong he believes he did him ; we have been very confident about it ; but since I have seen him I have doubted. We must both wait. Why, you saw him ! You heard him ! His honest eyes, that true voice—I don't believe he's false ; not intentionally ; not wickedly ; not without excuse."

"Oh, don't ! Don't !"

"Yes, I know. If he is false, in spite of all that, it's the worse—infinitely the worse. But be sure he would have something to say if you would give him his opportunity."

"He has had it; it is he who has condemned himself. It was from his own lips. Don't think—please don't think that I would believe any one else about him!"

Margaret observed her irresolutely, a little dashed. Her will to help her was unaltered, but she had not the habit of quick resource.

"He said that he had taken his brother's mine?" she repeated.

"Yes, yes. He said—how little men understand!—that he did it for *me !* That was his excuse!"

"Yes," said Margaret, slowly, "I know what you mean. I can see how that would seem the worst pain of all; and yet, don't you see, too," she added, meditatively, "how perhaps it *is* an excuse, and if an excuse at all, the best?" She put this forward doubtfully.

Dorothy shook her head. "Oh, don't you think I have tried to believe that? Don't you think I tried to give him opportunities to excuse himself, to make it seem right? and that I have done my best to excuse him to myself since? Sometimes I have made myself believe that if I couldn't pardon his doing it for me, I ought to pardon him because it was done against his brother; it was a cruel position. But that makes it only worse—a thousand times worse— doesn't it?" She asked it as a question. Margaret was silent. "Doesn't it?" she repeated.

"Yes. No. Perhaps. Do you know what his brother had done to him? Do you know it all?"

"Oh, yes, yes! It was very hard. But that's what I mean—it was *so* hard that it was for him all the more to hold his hand. It was his privilege *not* to strike. It seems to me no one ever had such an opportunity. And to use it as he did—— ! Oh, there is no excuse—none. The excuses only make it more wrong ; they make it impossible to forgive."

Margaret bit her lip. She did not know what to say. But she reached out her hand suddenly, and said in a low voice, " If you have no excuse for him, think how much less he can have one for himself. Have you thought of that ? Doesn't it seem as if it almost *forced* you to forgive him ? Think how he must be suffering ! Remember, he loves you too ! Think how his love must be making it a torture for him that you should think of him as you do, and that you are right."

" Yes, I have thought of that. I have thought of every-thing. But nothing helps. It is done, done ! If he loved me "—a sob caught at her throat—"if he loved me, it ought to have been a reason for him against this,—this that he has done. It's not a reason to forgive him—I can't feel it. I have prayed to feel it. I have prayed——" Her voice died away. She avoided her companion's eye.

Margaret looked at her longingly, tenderly, helplessly ; and Dorothy gave back her gaze. In Margaret's plain, wholesome face, in her genuine eyes, in the wide, clear benignant brow, Dorothy read goodness and strength—nothing but goodness and strength. The primness and precision she had been used to fancy in her, seemed resolved into these ; the qualities which she had been used to wish that Margaret would let her like in her seemed somehow to have freed themselves from the old bondage ; she saw that she had in some way misconstrued or wrongly imagined her—or perhaps she was changed ; perhaps experience had taught her. Did one come to see things differently, then, in time—did one's way of looking at certain matters alter ? Should she ever think differently of Philip ?

Margaret, on her side, was looking into Dorothy's eyes, thinking how gentle and sweet, and true and right-minded she was; but thinking too, that in a way, a very remote way, she stood where she had once stood; where one saw the right so clearly, that one was in danger of not seeing all the pity of the wrong; where it was hard to forgive. The cases were not at all the same: it was the youth that spoke in Dorothy, of course—the intense, impulsive, passionately certain youth; and it was not youth, whatever else it was, that had worked in herself to the same ends. But, at all events, she felt drawn to her by a mysterious bond of sympathy; she felt that she knew enough of her state of mind to comprehend, to sympathize, and she yearned to say certain things to the young girl beside her; but she found no words for them. Even about Philip's offence itself (a simple and concrete subject) she could not trust herself to speak; she wished only to say what should be quite, quite true. She could not let herself comfort Dorothy against her own conscience about what Philip had seemingly done; if he had done it, it was hateful and wicked to her; yet there was another point of view. . . . . . Perhaps Margaret was less entirely illumined by her experience than she thought; perhaps none of us escape out of ourselves, through any experience, beyond recall.

She rose at last, and Dorothy rose with her. "I don't know what to say," she said. "I'm not sure what it would be right to say. I am not sure of anything, any more. But you will let me come to see you again, I hope, and we can talk."

"Oh, come! Pray come," begged Dorothy, taking her hand.

"And you won't move, yet. You will wait?"

Dorothy seemed to take an inventory of the dismantled room and of the situation in her swift glance. "I see what you mean," she said, in a moment. "But I dare n't say that. The thought of seeing him again, of meeting him— you don't know what it is to me. I know I'm not reasonable about it. But I feel as if I must go away. I feel as if we should only be happy again—father and I—and get back to our old good times together before—before he came, by going to some place a long way off, and very different from this. And father has sent in his resignation—he would n't like to recall it." She pressed her companion's hand. "It is so good of you to come—to care. You won't think me ungrateful if I can't see it quite as you see it—not yet, at all events."

"Oh, I don't know how I see it !" exclaimed Margaret hastily. "I am the last person you should trust to ; I make a great many mistakes ; I am not wise. I used to be very certain ; but things have happened to alter that lately. I am not sure of anything—but—but perhaps this is true,— that, if we have charge of men's ideals, as men say, we must n't be too hard in judging them by them. If we love them we must wish to help them back to them, I think, when they fall ; and, at all events, I don't think it can be wrong for us to remember always that they have to do their good and evil in a different world from ours—a world we don't understand, perhaps." She gazed over Dorothy's shoulder, with a far away look in her eyes, in which she seemed to herself to be questioning and resolving her own future.

"But right and wrong remain—surely they are the same in all worlds," said Dorothy, bewildered by this strain of reasoning from Margaret. "And our loving—that seems to me just it ! It does n't matter that some one for whom we care nothing does a thing beneath him. When—when another does it——" She did not finish.

"I don't know—I don't know," mused Margaret, with the same far-looking eyes. "It's true, of course ; but it's not all the truth—or, at least, there is a better truth, perhaps. Love is better." She bent over and kissed her. "Good-bye !" she said.

Dorothy watched her go away with many feelings.

CHAPTER XXXI

MARGARET'S way home took her by Dr. Ernfield's office, and, as she passed, she heard a rap on the window. Beatrice's face appeared at the pane, and she went in, at her silent gesture. They encountered in the outer office, where Beatrice whispered that Dr. Ernfield was ill. His long ride of the day before, followed by a night of watching at Jasper's bedside had brought on another hæmorrhage.

"Is Jasper back, then? Is he ill?" she asked quickly.

"Yes, he's back, and he's very ill," returned Beatrice; and in a hushed voice she told her of the blizzard in which he had been caught on his way back over the mountains from Mineral Springs; how he had spent three days without food or drink under an overhanging rock, dying slowly of exhaustion, cold, and hunger, and how he had at length been found by a lumber team going up Ohkay valley for a load. The men had taken him into the town of Ohkay, and he had been laid up at the hotel there until now.

"Poor fellow!" exclaimed Margaret. "Poor fellow! I wish I could go out and nurse him. Is he alone?"

"He has his cowboys."

"Cowboys!" cried she. "No; I must n't," she added after a moment's meditation. "But how like Dr. Ernfield to sit up with him. Tell me," she said, laying a hand on her companion's arm, "—— he is better?"

"Yes, he's better; but he has been very ill. Ned is going to take his place with Jasper, and I'm going to ask you to take my place with him for a moment. I left Edward in the irrigating ditch. He will be wet through."

Margaret was about to say that she could n't stay; that it was impossible; but this seemed foolish, on reflection. She put off her shawl on a chair in the outer office, and went in to him, while Beatrice silently gathered her wraps in the inner room. Beatrice hushed her entrance into the room where he lay, with her finger on her lip. He was asleep, she saw. So much the better!

Beatrice indicated the medicine he was to take next with her finger, whispered one or two further instructions and glided out, saying she would be back immediately. Margaret gave a quick glance about the untidy, mannish room. This, then, was where he lived. There was an unframed medical print or two, and some stuffed specimens. The walls were almost bare, save in the corners, where they were cobwebbed. Margaret could never have lived for a moment in a dishevelled room. The desolateness of this one gave her a pang of homesickness for him. She saw that the fire was dying down, and looked about for wood. He stirred uneasily as she softly put on a log, and opened his eyes on her. She rose quickly. His bewildered stare broke into a smile. "Have you taken Mrs. Vertner's place?" he asked. His voice was quite strong. Perhaps, she thought to herself—perhaps he would yet live to conquer his disease, and to take his place in life with the others. She knew that this could not be—that it was impossible; but the other seemed too dreadful. They faced each other alone for the first time since the day they had ridden up the Ute Trail together.

"It is good to see you again," he said, as he put forth his wasted hand. She took it and held it a moment silently, as she gazed out of the window, thinking of many things. The sunlight was pouring into the little space of Mesa Street, on which Ernfield's rooms looked.   From where she stood she could see the office of the *Maverick Sentinel,* which she recalled as the name of the paper she had cause to remember. The days following Deed's going returned to her, as she stood looking out at the sign and holding his hand, and it came to her that it was Ernfield, in a way, whom she had to thank for her husband and for her happiness.

The wind hid the office of the newspaper, and "St. Ann's Rest" and the Post Office next door, when it raised, as it did from time to time, a mighty cloud of dust.   Women who were walking would sometimes pause before one of these gusts, and turn their backs, burying their faces in their muffs.   The men often wore protecting goggles or glasses, and seemed to take the wind and dust as part of the circumstance of the universal Joke.

As she stole a glance at his face again and saw in his look the illusory brightness and vitality of the consumptive, grave and silent tears started in her eyes.

"I sha'n't be so sorry not to get well, after all," he said, suddenly, observing her from under his half-closed eyes. She looked, he thought, even more than she usually did, the benignant goddess of all right-doing. He was conscious of an absurd wonder whether she must dress her hair in that way because she was herself, or whether she had to be herself, having once brushed those silky brown strands back from her forehead in that severe fashion.   He was as much at a loss to say why he liked her way of parting her hair uncompromisingly from forehead to crown, without a decoration or extrusion of any sort, and smoothing it simply down to the ears, where it curled back in a way that made him long to tell her how utterly nice she was, as he was at a loss to say why he liked her—why he loved her, in fine, to his madness, his torment.   "I sha'n't be so sorry not to get well," he repeated, "because by the time I could get well,

Mrs. Vertner and you would have spoiled me past remedy. I should n't be able to resume my place in society, decently. No one would be able to tolerate me. If you really want me to have courage to get well, you'd better go before it's too late." She answered him with an indulgent smile only.

"Ah, well!" he went on. "It's little matter, either way. The game will soon be up." He put away the instinctive denial that leaped to her lips, with a gesture. "Don't say it," he asked her. "There's no need." A whimsical little groan escaped him as he shifted his position. He stared at her in far away thought. She moved uneasily. He caught her hand. "I thought I could die without asking it. But it can't hurt you—my question—not from a man who has his death-warrant. Tell me—are you happy?"

She gazed down into his eyes a moment doubtfully. She felt herself choking; she nodded painfully.

"Ah, that's good!" he exclaimed; "good! And it's true?"—he turned a keen glance on her—"everything is well with you?"

She shook her head.

He regarded her for a moment thoughtfully. "May I guess your trouble?" he asked, with a deepening of the kindly note in his voice. She said nothing. "Jasper told me a long story when I was called to him last night."

He told her what she already knew about the origin of Jasper's illness, and how, in the watches of the night, as he sat by his bedside, he had poured into his ears the whole narrative of his relation to his father and Philip. Margaret flushed ; how much did he know?

"It must have been very hard for you," she heard him saying.

"How? What?" she asked, startled.

"All of it. You can't think how it came over me, sitting there in the dark with him—what you must have suffered.

I have never known anything of it all. I have fancied things, now and then, of course, but I have always liked to believe you happy, and I did n't allow myself to fancy much. The truth is worse than my fancies. It must have been very hard for you," he repeated.

" It hasn't always been easy," she owned.

" Ah, if I could forget the time I tried to make it harder ! "

" Don't think that, please. It was you who made everything plain. It was you who helped me. Why,"—she hesitated—" I don't know why I should n't say it. I owe you my happiness."

" Do you ? " He reached up and took her hand again. " Do you ? " he repeated. " You don't. You must n't. But perhaps you may, too, if you like," he added with his smile. " Leave the idea with me for a while. I sha'n't need it long, and it will do me good." " Yes," he said happily to himself, " I could go away with that thought. You'd better not stay. You'll take it back."

" But it's true ! "

" Is it ? Well, no matter. I like it just as well false. Your seeing it that way—that's all that counts. And about the happiness—you manage to find it in spite of what we were talking of just now ? If I've given it to you, I want more than ever to know that I gave you the genuine article."

" Yes ; in spite of that and—some other things, I think l may say I'm happy. Or at least I should n't know how to choose any way to be happier."

" There *are* other things ? "

" Nothing that we shall not solve at once and have done with for ever. Whatever comes we have that comfort, now."

A shadow passed over his face at that tiny world-including, world-excluding " we "; but he repeated fervently " Good ! Good ! "

He saw her eyes light suddenly with a light that he had not brought into them. She went to the window and rapped briskly upon it. A figure on the other side of the street turned at the sound, and recognizing the face at the window came quickly across the road.

"Excuse me if I leave you a moment," she said, and turned at the door, with a beaming face, to add, as she nodded toward him, "We shall know now!"

When she had opened the office door to Deed she drew him in, and folded him in her arms, and then held him off and questioned his face, reading the good news in his smile with greedy eyes. Ernfield in the next room turned wearily to the wall. She found him so when she ran in for a moment to see that all was well with him. Then she returned and questioned Deed. She saw before he spoke that he was very happy; his face had taken on a radiant look. It was like the face of the man she had known in the year before their marriage. She was conscious for the first time how old and worn she had grown used to seeing him look; he was not looking old now; he was looking young and buoyant. Beatrice came in upon them before he could give her his news, and Deed must greet her, and Margaret must show her the last medicine that Ernfield had taken, and must linger a moment alone by his bedside to say, leaning over him as she buttoned her gloves, "I came to help you, and you have comforted me. It was always the way. Some day you must let me change it : you don't know how much I should like to feel that I had the advantage of you in that, even for a moment. I should like to help you."

He stretched up his hand to her; she noted with pain how frail and thin it seemed. "You *are* my help," he said with a sad, eager smile. "I think you know that. It is you who make things possible for me."

A sudden flood of compassion filled Margaret's heart as she looked down into his weary eyes. In the great relief which had come to her at sight of her husband's face; in the joy of having him back, which seemed to give him to her as if for the first time, the thought of this maimed and broken life, so poor in joy of any sort, went through her with an afflicting pain. Her own share in his fate enlarged itself, and seemed to press upon her stiflingly; myriads of memories went electrically through her brain. So poor—so poor he was! And she so rich! She stooped with an irresistible impulse, and pressed a fleet kiss on his forehead through her blinding tears.

She seized Deed's arm passionately when they were outside, and walked swiftly with him toward the main street, with her muff to her face. For a long time neither of them spoke. Then he began in a low voice and told her his news.

WHEN the servant brought Deed's name to her next morning Dorothy experienced a sinking of the heart; but she renewed her resolution with a stern word to herself and went down to him. As she took his hand a little shock went through her that was not all pain. " His father! His father! " she caught herself murmuring. To him she said in a scarcely audible voice, " I am very glad to see you." Her manner was at once eager and reluctant.

She suddenly looked up, encountered his kindly eye, and coloured. His eye was at the moment tenderly studious of her. He saw what Philip perceived in her outward aspect, at least, to like. As she stood before him, a little shyly, taking his hand in her cordial pressure, and lowering her eyes after the first full, frank, pleading meeting with his, she seemed to him very charming.

"You know why I have come?" he said, bending over her.

"About——?"

"Yes. I want you to save him."

She motioned her visitor to the couch, taking a chair herself. "Save him?" she repeated. She clasped her hands in her lap and drew herself slightly together in unconscious resistance. She had instinctively pushed her chair back a little as she sat down; she found the mere potency of his presence, his individuality, vaguely controlling.

"I want you to let him make it right with you, I want you to let me bring you together again; and I want you to do this not for his sake, but for mine. When I tell you, you will understand; and you won't think, I hope, that I ask as much as I must seem to. Last night, Miss Maurice, I came back from Leadville happier than men often are. I had heard great news of him—news that changed all I had been base and cruel enough to think of him. I wanted to hug him. Instead I found him gone, and *this* for news of him—first what he had done, and then that you had broken with him. You were right. You could do no less. I understand all your feeling. But, Miss Maurice, you must take him back. It was I who took Jasper's mine."

"You!" she cried. She smiled nervously.

"Yes, I. Not by the outward rules of things. That was Philip's part—to seem to do it. But the real doer of an act is the one behind it all who is responsible for it. I was responsible for this. You know what I did against Jasper. This is one of the fruits of it. If I had not done that this could not have happened. I made the situation. He had to act in it as he did. The blame's mine. Lift it from him! It's that I want to ask you."

She was bewildered; she did not know what to say. She stole a glance at him where he sat, and perceived the look like Philip's look; it was about the mouth, perhaps; it was his smile that was like Philip's. He was more handsome than his son; as she whipped another furtive glance at him, she found herself trusting him; his sturdy frame, the clear-cut, powerful face, the alert and genial eye, had all an effect of gentle force, on which she instinctively reposed. To her it seemed that he looked very *right.* He went on in a moment to tell her what he had learned at Leadville— beginning with his quarrel with Philip, and taking pleasure in condemning himself. He said that he had made an egregious and wicked mistake. And then he made her see (he told the story with glistening eyes) how this precious boy of his, whom he had dared to cast off for a fancied baseness, and against whom he had hardened his heart, had all the time been sheltering and righting and saving him behind his back, by the most shameless trick. . . . He broke down in the midst of it. Tears of pride filled his eyes.

"That was good, that was noble of him!" said Dorothy quickly.

"And you will forgive him? You will pardon him? You will take him back?"

"Oh, don't you think I want to? Don't you suppose I long to? I can't!"

She did not know how she said these things. It seemed easy to talk to him; but difficult—impossible not to do what he wished. The effect of his presence grew upon her rather than diminished; and a kind of diffidence lingered in all she said. She felt keenly how much he had put aside to come to her; that gave authority to all he said—that, and the sense that he was older than she, that he was his father, that he was in trouble; and she felt her own young girl's feelings, opinions, judgments, shrinking in the balance by the operation of an instinct almost like one of decorum.

But she called upon her resolution. In the time which

had passed since Margaret had left her she had gone over the question between herself and Philip with all the honesty she could find in herself. She had forced herself to face it with absolute pitilessness for her own pride, and for all that might be merely extraneous or selfish in her feeling. She had rehearsed it all, as well, with the tenderness for him which, alas, she did not need to force; and she believed that she had taken her resolve. It was taken in bitterness and tears; but it was fixed.

Deed leaned over from his place on the couch, and took her hand. "You won't punish him for what began with me," he said.

"I see what you mean," she said, in a dry voice, out of which she kept her feeling as she could, "but I fear that can't be true for me. I can perceive it; but I can't feel it. I have thought a great deal of what you speak of, though, since he—since Philip told me of it; I have thought of what the punishment you found for your son must have cost you, I mean, and of his ingratitude; and I've been very sorry for you. May I say that?"

"I am very glad to have you say it. I see that you're good, that you're kind."

"No, don't think that, please," murmured Dorothy, painfully. "I am hard; I must be hard."

He regarded her for a moment as he withdrew his hand. "Then we shall understand each other, Miss Maurice," he said. "I am hard. It is that which has brought me here. If I had n't been hard, I should never have got myself and Philip into this miserable mess with Jasper, which has led Philip to do, now, what you see."

"But what you did, and what he has done—they are very different. What you did—do you mind my saying that—may not have been right, perhaps, but it was splendid."

His face confessed his pleasure in her praise, but he said

quickly. "Are you quite sure, Miss Maurice, that if you knew all Philip's motives, you would n't find something heroic about them, too? What I did used to seem to me fine, too; it does n't now. But it makes no difference; I had to do it, and every one near to me has had to pay for it. It's taken its revenge," he said sadly. "I was right, perhaps, but I was not right to take my right. An injury began with that which has gone on ever since. There was no injury until I did it to Jasper, for his was what I made it. If I had not resisted it—I see that, now—it must have stopped there. I was not wise enough. I answered his villainy, and the penalty has been brought home to me since in every form through which I could be made to feel. It has not always been myself; it has been Margaret's fate to suffer for it, too, and now it's Philip's. Don't force him to suffer more for it than you must. That's what I've come to beg of you."

The dignity and reality of his trouble affected her deeply, as she listened. Her generous instinct to rush to the aid of any one in pain or difficulty came over her. But what seemed a final obstacle rose to withhold her. She did not know how to explain it. She lowered her eyes to her lap. "Mrs. Deed came to see me; she has been more than good. She will have told you how I—what I feel," she said huskily.

"I know. It's not only the wrong he has done Jasper—culpable, strange, and mistaken as that is. There is more to forgive."

"Oh, if it were only to forgive——! That would be easy; I suppose I have forgiven now. When one gets over the first pain and shock, one forgives if one loves, instinctively. But that is nothing—a form of words. He would not care for that; and I could n't offer it to him. What he wishes is something else. The only thing I could do that would do any good would be to bring it all back,—our old relation—

as if this had never been. I can wish it back, and I do. But I can't bring it back. Nothing, it seems to me, can do that! Nothing!"

"You mean that you can't bring it back for his own sake or for yours? I know that. Won't you try it, then, for the sake of some one outside of it all—some one who has no claim?"

"You mean——?" she began.

"Yes," he answered eagerly. "Will you do it for me?" A flush mounted to her face. "I have told you how I wronged and misunderstood him," he went on. "You know how he has rewarded me. You see—I'm sure it's natural to you to see such things—how I must long to do something for him : how I can't bear to think, however much he has deserved it, that he should be unhappy."

Dorothy looked over at him compassionately. "I see that!" she breathed.

He leaned forward and took her hand again. "He will pardon me ; he will run to do it. But I can't take his pardon on those terms. You understand. He has humiliated me : he has heaped burning coals of fire on my head. I can't face him in his trouble empty-handed."

"No," she murmured. She was much shaken.

"Listen, my dear girl," he went on. "Do you think that what he has done is less a pain and trouble to me than to you? Have you thought how he is repeating my experience? In attacking Jasper, after all his forbearance, he is beginning as I began, and must go on as I have gone on. You see that. It does n't make what he has done seem less wrong (though it must have excuses of which we know nothing) but, to me, it makes it more pitiful. You understand how I can't look on, and see that happening, and do nothing to stop it. I *must* stop it. Oh, Miss Maurice, I'm sure you can't have the heart to let him stumble on into the mire where I've been struggling these last months—you won't let him do that for lack of a word. I'm sure you will help me !"

He stopped, and a great pity for the man into whose eyes she was looking, for Philip, and for the situation Philip had made common to both of them, came over her. It was almost impossible to her not to try to help them. "Oh, if it were a question of pity, of tenderness, of love, of anything but what it is I" she burst out.

"But finally that *is* the question—how much you love him, is n't it. And is anything impossible to love ? " He leaned forward suddenly. " My dear girl, will you let me tell you of something which has come very close to me?" She was gazing at him in absorption ; she nodded tremulously. " You will understand, if I tell you this, that it is necessary—*necessary* to me that you should take him back ; you will see that I could n't speak of it for a light reason. You have heard how I abandoned Margaret on her wedding day?"

"Oh, don't speak of that ! Don't make me feel that I have forced you to speak of that," she exclaimed in a kind of panic. She was not sure of what she was saying.

He silenced her with a sad and gentle gesture, and sketched the occasion of his difference with Margaret quickly. "You see," he said, at the end, "I had no excuse. It was simply a monstrous humouring of my passion. I forced her to pretend, if she would unselfishly save me from myself, and then savagely punished her for it. I left her as if I had never had an obligation to her. It was an insult, and not a brave one. To desert a woman on her wedding day could never be a handsome thing to do ; in this case, where her only crime was caring for me too well, it was an abominable cruelty. And how did she reward me ? Ah, my dear girl, you know ! I could never come back to her ; she knew it. She knew that I had shut the gates of Paradisc behind me, and that, except for the chance of her mercy, I must remain at the decent distance I had chosen for myself, cursing my folly, and longing vainly for her. It was her right never to suffer me to so much as see her again—a thousand times her right. I had outraged her pride; I had wounded her at a woman's tenderest and dearest. And she forgave me! Don't ask me how. She found a way." He got up, abruptly, and looked down for a moment in silence at the stooping figure in the chair before him. Dorothy's head was in her hands. She was weeping bitterly. " My dear girl," he asked with grave tenderness, " won't you find a way?"

She rose, and put her hands in his.

" I will try," she said, lifting her tear-stained face to his, bravely.

" And I may tell him—? "

" Tell him I will see him."

He looked at her long and questioningly, while he held her hands.

CHAPTER XXXII

"But you did n't tell him that there was any difficulty between Miss Maurice and Philip, I hope. You were n't such a dunce as that, Ned?"

It was two days later, and they were seated at dinner. Margaret had secured rooms at the Centropolis House against Deed's return from Piñon (with Philip she hoped), and had taken up her own residence there, though she was much at the Vertners. She had said that she felt that they— she and Deed—must begin to think of settling down, like sensible people (she had begun to make plans from the hour in which she heard Deed's good news about the Leadville business); and though she did not pretend that apartments at a hotel were even by way of gratifying this ambition, she said that they at least did not constitute a step in the other direction, like staying with one's friends.

Vertner arrested the carving knife with which he had been inquiring his way to the joint of the fowl before him, and levelled a glance of scorn at his wife in response to her question.

"Well, I should hope not," she rejoined to this disclaimer, as he busied himself about the fowl again. And then after a pause, "I shall always say it was very good of you to go out to the Triangle to see what you could do for him, Ned."

"Shall you? Well, I should think more of it myself if Jasper interested me less. I did n't go to nurse him; I went

to take a look at him.   He has a special effect on me ; I'm
curious about him ; I'm always wondering what he will do
next."

"Well, you see what he has done next."

"Yes, but just before he did it, I thought he was going to
do something else."   Vertner asked Edward to hand him
the cranberries, as he finished cutting some of the fowl for
himself, and settled himself at the table, with the conscious
pleasure of the carver who has earned his contentment.   "I
had got his next move all planned out in my mind ; I thought
I saw that he had seen a point which dawned on me while
I was sitting with him ; perhaps he has seen it—indeed I'm
pretty sure he has—but he has n't acted on it.   He has done
something even more brilliant."

"Do you call it brilliant to go after Mr. Maurice and
Dorothy by the next train ? "

"From his point of view—certainly.   Do you suppose
Jasper could sit still under the thought that, after all that
has happened, it should be his brother who succeeds with
her. He will know how to reconcile himself to it if it happens ;
but he is n't going to let it happen if he can help himself.
The first news that reached him when he was brought back
to Maverick was that they were engaged ; and if I know
Jasper he wanted to break something in celebration of that
news.   But then along comes Philip and puts a weapon into
his hands, and he rages, but chirks up.   He sees the opportunity his brother has given him.   And then he hears
that the engagement is broken on account of the same affair,
and that pleases him down to the ground."

"But how did he hear that?   And how do you suppose he knew that Mr. Maurice and Dorothy were going
yesterday afternoon, when no one else knew it?"   ·

"Well, I think I could imagine.   Who has always been
his friend here? "

"Why, Mr. Maurice, but—"

"There is no 'but.' Maurice was angry when she broke the engagement, of course; he supposed Philip was the rich one then. But the transfer of the 'Little Cipher' to Jasper changed his mind, just as she was beginning to change her mind back again. I don't believe he was very sorry that, if the *Sentinel* had to copy that article from the Laughing Valley paper about his doings over there, it should choose this time for it. Perhaps she gave him more definite reason to believe that she would forgive Philip than she gave Deed. At all events, he would n't care to keep her where Philip would certainly find her within a day or two and make it up with her. He decided to take an early train, for various reasons; but first he let Jasper know where he was going."

"I wish we knew. I begged her to telegraph. I knew Margaret would never forgive me if I did n't. But I wanted to know for myself. I am very sorry for her."

"So am I. But I am still more sorry for Deed and Philip. Think of Deed bringing him back here to find her gone! He's set his heart on this thing. He is in such a position that his peace of mind depends on his success in it. I sha'n't forget for a while the after-dinner cigar I smoked with Deed the day before he called on Dorothy. I've seen men crushed before; but not like that. Well, of course it tore him up to have to feel that Phil had turned round and been his salvation after all! After quarrelling with him, and casting him off because he thought he was unfaithful to him, it *was* pretty rough. He could have stood it to know that he had been in the wrong, and that he had accused Philip without any too much excuse; but this was another matter. It's awful for a generous man to have to see that he has done a nasty thing. From the hour when he faced the fact that his son had really been fixing things up for him at

Leadville—doing his best to stop the boomerang Deed had
started on its cheerful career before he left Leadville; using
the $50,000 he had flung at him to save him, and generally
toeing the mark, and doing his duty like a little man—from
that hour he has been the happiest and the most miserable
man going. To know that Phil was all right tickled him to
death, but it shocked him to think how he had used him.
His going to Dorothy yesterday did n't surprise me. He
did n't say he was going; but it was the only thing left to
him. When Margaret told him about it, I guess he felt that
this little rumpus between Miss Maurice and Phil was a
kind of providence. It gave him a show. He could n't
take Philip's hand again, until he had made it right with
him, somehow. That was his chance. He took it and won
—or at least, if Maurice had let things alone, he stood a
first-rate chance to win. And now he will be bringing Phil
back with him to-morrow morning, both of them all ready to
be mighty happy, and I don't know which the gladdest to
be friends with the other again, and they will find her gone.
It makes me tired!" exclaimed Vertner, pressing his handkerchief nervously to his brow, and ejaculating the slang as
if it had the force of a phrase sacred to grief.

"I'm not sure whether Philip deserves much pity," said
Beatrice after a moment. "Of course I'm sorry for him;
but, as Margaret would say, I'm not sure that I ought to
be. She could n't do anything but give him up after he
had done such a thing."

"Perhaps *she* could n't. I'm not sure that another
woman (a little different, or a little older woman : say a
woman of thirty, instead of a girl of twenty-one) might
not have found that she could do something else in her
situation, though—dodge around a bit, and find her feelings
coming up in unexpected places to square things with her
conscience or her other feelings."

"It's easy for men to say such things; and perhaps you are right—about some women," responded his wife, after a moment. "But you can't judge, Ned. You can't feel as a woman must in such a case. The circumstances were peculiar."

"Peculiar mainly in his not being so all-firedly guilty as her treatment of him makes out. Of course it is n't proper to take your brother's mine; but that is n't the question. The actual question is surrounded by a thousand reasons for thinking that it *is* just right to take your brother's mine, and that it might be a hallowed duty. Besides, he did n't do that—he merely failed to let on that he had once thought the 'Little Cipher' would be a good mine to give to his brother."

"Pshaw, Ned! You exaggerate!"

"Well, I'm stating the case for the defence. You don't expect me to stick to absolutely undecorated facts, do you? Still, I stand by that. That's the gist of it. You get into a hair-splitting region when you try to say whose mine that actually was. My mind is too gross for it. And, at all events, you must admit that she has been pretty hard on him; she's too clear-headed. Women *are* that way when it comes to the wrong doings of the man nearest to them; and especially if it touches them, directly. I see it in you sometimes, Trix; but Dorothy is much worse."

"Oh, she sees things," owned Beatrice.

"Sees things! Well, I should remark—outside and inside, and underneath and all around. That's what makes me pity Phil. No man can stand that kind of soul-plumbing, straight in the eye, unforgiving, undiscounting, heavenly stare. We're not built that way—and Phil, poor fellow, less than most of us. Phil makes allowances for himself; he knows where he needs them, and he puts them where they will do the most good. It has got him into the habit of thinking that other people will be making the same for him; and some of us crude sinners, who know how it is ourselves, make them right along, and glad of the chance, with one of the best fellows in the world. But, bless my soul, is that the way she takes him! Is that the way any woman takes a man? Not much! She takes him on the ground of the fellow she's dreamed, and he has to live up not only to the man she thinks him, but to the kind of man she thinks all good men. It's the sort of thing to do a man good. I don't deny it. It puts stuff into him; it's a tonic and a stimulant and a bracer. But it's hard, constant, ticklish work. And the worst of it is, it don't count,—not for what it is. Women, dear things, fancy it as the every-day attitude of the sex; and when, some fine morning, you relax a bit, you're punished not on the basis of what you are, but on the basis of what she's all along been thinking you."

"Oh, you don't get any more than you deserve," laughed Beatrice.

"It's all right. I don't say it isn't. I only say that we're entitled to warning; it's like playing poker, without notice that you are playing 'straights.' I like to be familiar with the rules, myself, before I risk my money."

"The rules are perfectly simple. You've only got to be good."

"You call that simple! I fancy Phil wouldn't agree with you. Shut up, son," he said, in an aside to the young man who was strumming on his plate with his spoon.

CHAPTER XXXIII

In the late afternoon of the following day Dorothy was sitting on the piazza of one of the smaller hotels at Colorado Springs watching the sun go down behind Pike's Peak. The little city of invalids and tourists, which has easily one of the loveliest situations in the world, was at one of its best moments. The sun had not gone ; the. clear air seemed more clear for the tinge of rosiness, and the splendid bulk of the Peak, cut crisply against the dying light, looked down on a cluster of villas and hotels, in which each structure seemed to stencil its Queen Anne jaggedness, or Late Colorado vagaries of outline against a sky which invited stencilling.

She was alone on the piazza. Some of the other people staying at the hotel (there were not many) had made up a party and driven over to the Garden of the Gods and Manitou; two or three young men had gone on a walk to Cheyenne Cañon ; some ladies, left behind, were in their rooms. It was just before the supper hour, and the excursionists would soon be returning. Her father had left her half an hour before, saying that he wanted a walk ; he had not suggested that she should come with him, and she had made no movement to accompany him. She was glad to be quiet and think.

She sat thus, for a long time, meditating about many things, and working at some embroidery in her hands in·

termittently, until suddenly she felt rather than saw a shadow fall between her and the sun, and, looking up, she perceived Jasper. She rose instantly. A shock went through her. She felt herself gazing at him defiantly; and then she saw how very ill he looked. His face was almost spectral; its old firmness was gone. His hollow cheeks and cavernous eyes gave her a start. Her glance roved hastily over him; she saw that his clothes, which had been used to set so trimly on his figure, hung on him with an almost shambling looseness. In her surprise she remained motionless, arrested half-way in her intention to go in and leave him standing there. He perceived his advantage and said, in the thin and wasted voice which had replaced his former manly tones,

"You' are wondering at the change. Did n't you know that I had been ill?"

She made "Yes" with her lips.

"But you did n't think it was so bad? It was a close call."

"You ought not to be out. You ought not to be up," she said. She forgot that she had not meant to speak to him. A ball of worsted with which she had been working fell from her arms, and rolled out on the piazza. He stooped with his old precise courtesy, and restored it to her.

"I had a very good reason for getting up," he said. "I heard that you had gone away—that you were leaving Maverick for good. I had meant to wait until I could come to see you in the usual way; I should have managed it in a day or two. But your going made everything different."

"Excuse me," rejoined Dorothy hastily. "I can't allow you to include me in your plans."

He smiled tolerantly. "You remember our last meeting,

do you not? You remember your promise. I have been waiting for your answer."

In all the reflections which had contemned Jasper and put him for ever out of the case for her, she had not thought of this; that, in form, he was entitled to some word from her. She saw that it put her for the moment in the wrong with him. But she said with disdain,

"I did n't think it necessary to tell you that I had found you out. I supposed you would guess that."

Jasper bit his lip, and waited a moment before replying. He had determined, in seeking this interview, to keep his temper.

"I knew that you had resolved to break faith with me when I heard of your engagement to my brother. I don't see why I was bound to suppose that your reason was one discreditable to me."

"Break faith with you?" she repeated scornfully.

"You won't say that you had n't as good as promised me; you won't pretend that if you had never said a word, you had not still given me the right to believe that I was something more to you than another. You distinguished me, you encouraged me; it might not have meant great things in another case. But you have n't forgotten that we were once betrothed; a woman does n't single out for favour a man who has once occupied that relation to her unless she means something in particular."

The truth of this came over Dorothy helplessly. She gathered herself to confute it, but before she spoke she knew that he had, in a sense, the right of it. It was not in her to lessen a fault because it was hers; rather it pressed on her the more closely. But she saw that if she let Jasper make this point, it must be the end of everything.

"Does it really seem to you that you have a right to expect the same consideration as other men?" she asked, looking into his eyes.

" Why not ?   You give it to him."

Dorothy caught her breath, as he said this—not bitterly
or heatedly, but with the quiet manner of stating a consideration which she had omitted.   She saw all that he
meant ; it quelled and beat her down.   She glanced at him
where he stood with his back to the sun, supporting himself
lightly against a pillar, and fixing her with a glimmering
smile.   She opened her lips to speak and closed them again,
thinking better of what she had been going to say.   But
in a moment she raised her head, and said quickly :

" I can't discuss that with you ; " and made a motion to
pass him.

He put out a gentle hand to stay her.   " Please don't
go yet, Miss Maurice.   I've left a sick bed and come a long
way to see you.   I'm sure you won't refuse to hear me.
You have not been fair."   He did not strike this note at
hazard ; she stopped ; he had known she must stop.   " If
you don't think me worthy of ordinary usage because of my
treatment of him, what do you think of his treatment of me ?"

The question sent a chill through her: she knew what
she had thought of it.   Was that still her thought ?   Confronted with her own sense of Philip's act, balanced in this
sort against her sense of Jasper's, she had suddenly the
need to take refuge in any denial of her old feeling.   She
could not bear to think, even for that passing moment, that
a feeling of hers was sanctioning his comparison.   For a
moment no answer befriended her ; it was because from one
point of view there was no answer, she saw.   But the necessity to defend him, to cry out against this odious grouping,
brought her the certainty—the sudden, illuminating certainty
—that hers was the other point of view.   She saw surely, for
the first time, that the mood of her talk with Deed was a
finality ; that love had conquered in her.   It was her love
that spoke now.

" And have you the courage to think the two cases in any way alike ? " she said.

He had counted on her inward assent to the soundness of his position. He had it; but he was dealing with another force which he could not measure. He was shaken by the assurance with which she answered. Was he mistaken, then : had she not thrown Philip over because she hated the injury he had done him ? He had reckoned on this and on the revulsion of feeling toward the injured one which he had imagined in her generous nature. Taking his own act for a moment from what he supposed to be her standpoint, and putting it at its worst (he knew what to think of it himself, but he could fancy her ignorant objections to it readily enough), in what way could she in justice feel it to be more heinous than Philip's ? Jasper was, of course, better at almost anything than in estimating the moral value of his own actions; his sincerity in believing them "all right" from the standpoint of a man who did n't pretend to the priggishness of being better than his neighbours disabled his usual cleverness at this point. But he saw his mistake and manœuvred an inward retreat and brought himself into line at another place, before he answered.

"Suppose I say I have that courage ? " He stroked his moustache lightly. Its rich, bright abundance made the cheek behind it seem more pale.

She met his eye fearlessly. "I should ask you if you had given your brother back the share in the ranch you took from him if I believed you.

" Why should I ? "

" Why should you ? "

" Yes. It is mine for one thing, but that apart, he has n't done as much for me."

" But he has restored the mine to you—he has surrendered everything."

"The mine—yes; but not everything. There is a matter of $5,000."

"What do you mean?" She swept a thousand possibilities with her mental vision while she waited for his answer, and rejected them one after another.

"My precious brother negotiated the loan of that sum on the security of the mine, I find. That was one of the first things he did with his borrowed claim."

"It is not true," said Dorothy simply.

"You might ask your father!"

"My father?" exclaimed she.

"Philip borrowed it for him. It was at a time when your father found it inconvenient to owe me as much as that." He smiled with intention.

"Do you mean to say that—that——?" she gasped.

"That I had the presumption to lend your father as much money as that? Yes. I suppose I must n't expect you to like it, but I did it."

"And he—he, took it from *him* to pay you?"

Jasper nodded. She gave a little moan, and sank into one of the seats on the piazza.

The young men who had gone for a walk to Cheyenne Cañon were visible on the road before the hotel. Their woollen stockings and knee breeches were covered with dust; they came along at a swinging pace, laughing and talking. They passed into the house through the wide entrance, casting a glance of polite curiosity at the intent group at the further end of the piazza.

"Will you do me a kindness?" she asked in a husky voice, as he dropped into the seat beside her. He protested his eagerness. "Go away, please!" she entreated.

"I beg your pardon," exclaimed Jasper, as if he had not understood.

"Please go away. You have made me hear it. I could n't

help that. But you won't stay, now!" She paused, and clasped her hands before her. A wretched sigh escaped her. "Oh, how could he?" she cried to herself, in the words she had once used for Philip.

"You are not fair, Miss Maurice," he said, rising with dignity. "Am I to blame because my brother has chosen to borrow money on my mine and has failed to return it to me; am I to blame because your father chooses, for reasons of his own, to make such an arrangement with your affianced husband?"

"Oh, don't! Don't! Have you no manliness?" She felt her cheeks burning with the horror of the ideas that were coming to her; she turned away to hide their shameful confession. She was trying not to hate her father; she was searching for excuses for him. Was it to this, then, that Mr. Deed's allusion to Philip's motives pointed? Was it her father that she must blame for what Philip had done?

"Is the truth so hard, then?" Jasper was asking. "Would you rather believe what you wish to believe; would you rather think well of certain persons, even if you knew it was not the truth? But I need n't ask. You take the side toward which you are drawn for the moment—like a woman, and everything is indifferent to you but the illusions by which you make yourself think that the right side at all hazards. The truth does n't matter to you—nor justice, nor fairness. You need n't tell me that; I know it," he said.

She winced; the stroke was well aimed. "You know much better than that," she answered feebly.

"Say rather that I used to know better. But I knew it of another woman, I think. The woman I used to know, Miss Maurice, could n't be so resolved to think badly of a man who has openly taken his right, and so determined, at all costs to think well of a man who trades on his brother's ignorance to cheat him out of his property." She shrank

where she sat, and he pressed home his advantage. "Is it
the motive that makes the difference? Is it so wrong, then,
to take what belongs to one, without malice, or double
thoughts, or hope of any gain but the plain one; and is it
so right to take what does *not* belong to one with the admirable motive of revenge, and the other admirable motive
of winning a sneaking advantage with a woman? Ah,"
cried he bitterly, "it makes a difference who does such
things, and even more it makes a difference for whom they
are done!"

"Oh no, no!" she began vehemently. But she sank
back in her chair helplessly. She shook her head. "You
would not understand," she said.

His voice took a note of tenderness, as he dropped again
into the seat beside her, and said in low tones, "Are you
sure of that, Miss Maurice? I think I know what you have
been thinking of me these last few weeks, since we met.
You have heard things about me which could n't make you
think well of me. But I want you to do me the justice to
remember that they were not told you by my friends. There
are always two sides. It would be fair to hear mine, before
judging. But I don't ask you to do that. Suppose I admit
all that you are thinking, suppose I say that I see it, in a
degree, from your own point of view, suppose I agree to
make it right with my father, to restore what he thinks I
came by unfairly; suppose, in other words, I agree to take
your view—would you care, would it make a difference
to you?"

She glanced up at him in bewilderment. "I'm not sure
that I know what you mean," she said quickly. "I could n't
care that you should agree with me, merely to agree.
You must know that. But the other——" She paused a
moment. "You must be equally sure that I should be glad
of anything that made you think it right to do that," she

said gravely. It was difficult to think of anything but the near and personal trouble which was gnawing at her heart; but his suggestion opened vistas ; it stimulated and engaged her.

" Would you care so much then ? " he asked, regarding her curiously.

She hesitated a moment. " Yes, very much," she said heartily. " I have seen your father. Knowing him has given me a great wish to help him. If you could see how what you did has wounded and broken him you would wish to do what you say even more than I could wish to have you do it."

" He has n't treated me well," said Jasper laconically.

" No," rejoined Dorothy, eagerly. " It was only what you might have expected him to do : it was only what he had a right to do by the code most of us live by, but he, too, feels that it was a mistake. Or perhaps I ought to say that he feels it was n't as right as it seemed to him at the time."

" Well, that's a step," admitted Jasper. And he added, " He did me a beastly injury."

"And what had you done to him ? "

" I had taken my rights."

" Yes," said Dorothy, with intention.

" Do you mean that they were not my rights ? He had given them to me himself."

"No, I don't mean that," said she quietly. Her assent maddened him more than any denial could have done. It gave him a feeling of helplessness absolutely singular in his experience.

" Oh, I know what you mean," he retorted bitterly. " You mean that you despise me ! " Philip's words came back to her, and she wondered how she had ever borne to hear them from him, and allowed him to go from her feeling that what he said was true.

" No," she said gently.

" It's the same thing. I don't thank you for the difference. But you *shall* think differently of me ! " He rose
quickly and stood before her. " Listen. I have passed
three days face to face with death since we met last. Perhaps I am not the same man you have known in all
respects." His husky, inadequate voice gave the statement
meaning; almost gave it reality. " Would you believe me
changed if I were to say so ? " He looked closely at her.

" I don't know," she said, looking up at him doubtfully. A new light came into her eyes. " Such things do
change a man."

" You imply a doubt whether they would change me.
But you shall believe it," he said fiercely. " I will go on
to Maverick to-day and withdraw from the suit against my
father which is to come on to-morrow, I will give up to
my brother the share in the ranch which my father claims
for him."

" You will ! " exclaimed she. " Oh, I shall be glad for
your father." Her eyes left him musingly, in a happy look.

" And for me ? "

She glanced inquiringly at him. She brought herself
back to the consideration of his relation to his proposal
with an effort. " Oh, I shall be very glad for you, too, of
course."

His face fell. " Is that what you mean? " he asked. " Is
that all you mean ? "

" I shall feel it is good of you—from your point of view ;
yes, very good."

He bit his lip. It was hardly this measured approbation
that he had sought. She saw the defeated look on his face,
and with a movement of compassion and self-accusal, she
rose, holding out her hand to him. " I shall think better of
you, if that is what you mean. It is generous ; it is right."

He held her hand firmly, searching her eyes with a piercing gaze. "How much better?" he asked.

She withdrew her hand. "What do you mean?" she asked, in confusion.

"I am ready to do all that there is to do to show my sincerity."

"Yes," assented she bewildered; "that is true."

"Will you do nothing for me?"

"What do you wish?"

"Believe in me again." He stooped over her.

"I will. I do." She withdrew herself from him a little, vaguely alarmed by his manner.

"You know very well what I wish, Dorothy. Believe in me as you used to."

"I can't do that," she said, looking into his eyes unfalteringly. Her breath came quickly.

"Would it be such a miracle, then?"

She nodded.

"Ah," cried he, "you can work it for *him!*"

"It is not the same," she stammered.

"No," he rejoined, "it is not the same. It should be much more difficult. He won you from me through this mine."

"Oh, don't say it," begged Dorothy.

"—— and he has not scorned to take a more material profit from that villainy. What is he giving up? You made that the test a little while ago. By that measure do I show so badly?"

"He will pay you the money," she said desperately.

"Perhaps. I don't know. It would n't be unlike him, you must own, if he did n't. But can he give me back what else he has taken from me?"

"What?" she asked in a half whisper, though she knew what he must say.

" *You!* Can he pay that debt ? Can he give you back to me ?" Dorothy dropped her eyes. He took her hand and bent over her tenderly. She seemed suddenly stricken powerless; she could prevent nothing. "It is only you who can pay that debt for him," he said.

His weakened voice had a winning note in its ineffectiveness. For the space of an instant, while she stood there arraigning Philip, as he meant her to, and liking his own surrender as he had hoped, something in her—an effect of nerves rather than of impulses, even the most trivial,—responded to him. The plea was ingenious ; it addressed itself with overwhelming force to a whole side of her nature ; for a moment she felt as if she was about to be carried off her feet—toward what she knew not. Not away from Philip, certainly ; but at least toward the man by her side. She felt the dangerous stirrings of pity at her heart. But a moment later she glanced up and saw him watching her, and another thought came into her mind.

Then she spoke. "It does not seem to me a debt ; but if it were, you must know that I could not pay it," she said, steadily.

A look of bitter disappointment crossed his countenance.

"Do you mean that ?" he asked, scanning her face.

"Yes."

"Yet you expect me to pay my debt," he said bitingly, "—what you regard as mine: You expect me to restore to my father and to him !" It was a question, though he put it forth as a statement.

"I expect nothing. You wish that for yourself, do you not ?"

Jasper smiled sardonically. "Do you suppose that I can wish for anything apart from my wish for you. You don't know how I love you—you have never known. Say that we may be again as we once were, and you will see what I would be strong enough for. You could do what you would with me."

Her eyes blazed with sudden intelligence. "Do you mean to say—do you dare to say," she asked shakenly, "that you would only do what you have been proposing to do, if—that you would not do it unless—— Oh! Oh! And you offered it as a *bribe!* Oh, go, go!"

He caught her hands, and prisoning them in his, looked down steadfastly into her eyes, with a long, intent, hungry look. An expression of acute misery came over his face. "Ah," he cried desperately, "now you *do* despise me!"

She lowered her eyes. She did not answer. He dashed his hand to his face, and without a word walked quickly away from her side, and out into the roadway before the hotel, with the uncertain steps of a sick man.

Dorothy stood where he had left her. She heard his retreating steps, but did not look round. Her eyes were fixed on the rosy summit of the peak. As she looked the sun suddenly went down. A chill was borne to her through the air, and she started. She perceived that she must have been standing so a long time. She put her hand to her face. There were tears in her eyes, too. She saw her father coming toward the hotel from the direction opposite to that which Jasper had taken. A chill went through her for another reason.

CHAPTER XXXIV

MARGARET stood in the window of her sitting-room at the Centropolis House, which commanded a view of the arrival platform of the railway, and exchanged signals with Deed as he alighted from his train, on his return from Piñon. She saw Philip follow him, with their hand luggage, and as he set it down on the platform, he too glanced up at her window, and catching her eye, waved his hat toward her, with a smile of greeting. Then Vertner seized upon them, and she saw him going through the hopeless struggle to tell them only so much of the truth as he thought they would like ; with a beating heart she saw her husband pressing, insisting, and finally pinning him, and Vertner going through the stages of impotent yielding, burlesquing his helplessness with desperate gestures. She saw her husband cowed and dazed, as she had feared, by his news, and saw Philip fall upon Vertner with questions; then it was Vertner who took the initiative, and he forcibly pulled into the conference the conductor of the train, who was passing them, left them for a moment to dash into the hotel, bestirred himself, bustled about, and finally pushed Philip on the train again, handed his valise up to him, and waved a gay and cheering hand to him, as the train pulled out of the station. Deed, when he had seen the last of the train, turned and challenged Vertner again, and they talked soberly for some moments.

They were palpitating moments to Margaret. Since Dorothy had so suddenly left Maverick with her father, she had been in a distracted state. It seemed as if she was almost to blame for it, as if she could have prevented it if she had not gone at Mrs. Felton's invitation for a long drive, on that day, to Loredano; and returned only to find them both gone, leaving no trace save a confused and hurried note from Dorothy, which told her nothing. She quailed before the thought of what this failure of his hope must be to her husband.

She heard his quick step in the passage and ran to admit him. When she had kissed him she searched his face, and withdrew herself from his embrace in alarm, recognizing the set look of resolve she remembered from the fatal day on which he had left her to go and right himself with Jasper.

He went to the window, while she watched him anxiously, and cast a glance up and down the track. Then he dropped restlessly into a seat, and fixed his eyes dejectedly on the carpet. She took a seat opposite him; when he glanced up she was shocked by his haggard and desperate face. Again she saw in it that look of a man whose fight is done.

"I've got to stop this," he said briefly.

"What, James?"

"The whole of it. Have things been going so well with us for the last six months that I need say? You know what's happened?"

She nodded, with her eyes intent upon him.

"She's gone; Jasper's with her; I've failed. That's the end of it. I say I've got to stop it."

"Oh I shall be glad—glad!" she whispered, trying to trust him because she had learned that lesson, but inwardly filled with anguishing doubt.

"I've been a fool. Since Jasper paid us his visit at Mineral Springs I've known that; you showed it to me; and instead of owning up on the spot, and doing what was left to redeem you and me from the consequences of my folly, I've been blundering on since, trying to deny it to myself, and trying hard to believe that I could invent some new way to whip the devil around the stump, and avoid what I—what

I didn't want to do," he ended huskily. "It would have worked if it had only been a question of myself, or you : I dare say I could have found obstinacy and pride and reckless selfishness enough for that." He sighed. "But Philip makes all the difference!"

"Yes," said Margaret, still in a whisper.

"Even with him, I thought I could help him to dodge the penalty; I thought I could hoax, or blind or buy off fate in his case. But Jasper has got in his blow in return already; the infernal business of give and take has begun. The boy has got to repeat my experience, unless—unless—— ! He's paid; he's restored; it makes no difference. There is a sore underneath. We must cure that first. My fault is so hopelessly mixed up with his that nothing he can do can really help him. It's I who have to do !"

"But what, James?" cried Margaret in an alarm she could no longer hide. "But what?"

He returned her frightened look with a tender one. "Jasper's suit against me comes on to-morrow."

"Yes," she assented breathlessly.

"If it is decided in my favour the fight merely shifts; it doesn't end. If it's decided against me, am I likely to bear it well? Do you think I could resist striking back? That is the way it has been with me; that is the way it *will* be with me. It's endless. Ah, Margaret, we know that—don't we? Resistance can't stop it; it piles it up. And if that is true for us, how much more it will be true for Philip! The fight must be between brothers, there, with none of the habit of forbearance on either side that makes certain things impossible between father and son! I can't see him marching helplessly into that miserable maze, and involving an innocent girl as I involved you, and him. I can't. I've got to stop it."

"But how? Fighting only makes it worse. You say so yourself," she said tentatively.

He stared into her eyes a moment.

" I'm not going to fight," he said. He drew a long breath as he rose. She got up and came to him and slipping her arm in his, looked up into his face. He glanced down at her; his eyes gleamed with the exaltation of his resolve. "I'm going to surrender."

A joyous light dawned in her eyes.

" Do you mean that you will give him back the ranch,— that you will restore everything as it was before, before—?"

" Before I took what belonged to me? Yes, Margaret, I'm going to try your remedy, whatever you like to call it. I've used up all my own. Don't think I like it. I loathe it. But I'm going to do it. I shall sell the 'Lady Bountiful' as soon as Spring opens, and buy the range back from Snell at once (it will be easy enough—this bluffing suit of Jasper's frightens him, though his title is perfectly good); and I shall let Jasper know immediately—before the trial."

" Oh, James!" she murmured, clutching his arm, and looking up into his face, lovingly, admiringly, happily.

"Don't praise it, Margaret," he cried, turning hastily from her shining look, as from something to which he had no claim, " or I sha'n't have the heart to do it. And God knows I don't want to do it." He walked away from her to the window, and went on with his back to her. " It's right; you needn't say it; I know it. It's right, and it's the only thing to do, just as it was the only thing to do in the beginning. I see the folly and error of fighting evil, fast enough, if that's what you want me to see—the way to conquer it is to yield to it, to give it more than it asks." He turned toward her with his hands in his pockets. "The mistaken way is to strike back, and to that mistake there is no end. I've learned that. But it's hard, and if I knew a decent way to dodge it I should n't be a hero about it. Don't imagine it."

For answer to this she simply put her arms about his neck, and drew his lips to hers.

" You are hero enough for me!" she said.

CHAPTER XXXV.

DOROTHY drew back a pace as her father came up to her on the piazza, while Jasper walked away in the other direction. Maurice was smiling, and wiping his brow with one hand ; in the other he held his parson's wide-awake.

" It's warm walking," he said. " Who was it who just left you ? I thought his back looked like Jasper's."

" It *was* Mr. Deed," she said, trying to find her voice.

" Ah, well, he will be coming back then. But I'm sorry you did not keep him."

" He is not coming back," said Dorothy, in the same still, controlled voice. " I want to ask you something, father," she added with an effort.

He looked at her inquiringly.

" Well, my dear, what is it ? " He turned half about, pursuing Jasper's retreating figure absently. " I'm sorry you did not keep him," he said.

" Listen, father." She laid a hand on his arm, and he looked around at her, surprised by her tone. " Did you borrow a large sum from him—from this Mr. Deed ? "

He started.

" He has been telling you that ? " exclaimed he.

She went on, intent upon her purpose. " Is it true ? "

He bit his lip. " Yes, it's true."

" And did you make Philip take his brother's mine to pay that debt for you, when—when—— ? "

He gazed at her sternly ; he seized her wrist. " What is the matter with you, Dorothy ? Are you mad ? Don't let one of your impulsive ideas get the better of you! They make you absurd; they are very young."

"Is it true?" she repeated in a dry, estranged voice.

"No," returned he doggedly, "of course it is n't true."

"But you took the money from him to pay *him?*"

He released his hold on her wrist, and shuffled his hands into his pockets. He shrugged his shoulders.

She stared at him irresolutely. "Will you answer me, father?" A cold terror crept about her heart. "Did you?"

He forced his vagrant eye to face her. "Excuse me, Dorothy. There are matters which I have always reserved to myself. They are not a part of your province. Please understand that this is one of them."

She put this away with a gesture. "Answer me, please, father," she said coldly. "Did you?"

"Yes, if you must know," he jerked out at last. "But——"

Her face grew very white and rigid. "That is all I want to know," she said. She clutched the work in her hands against her breast, and went quickly past him, and into the hotel.

She rose early the next morning, and taking her breakfast in her room, to avoid meeting her father (it must come, but she did not feel strong enough for it yet), she walked out in the early morning sunshine to the Garden of the Gods. As she went through the splendid gateway, the two towering masses of rock caught up her thought to the level of their lonely summits; they seemed to swim up there in the air, in the isolation of a serene and immemorial past; they made human troubles appear small and fleeting. She walked on, finding a kind of medicine in the sweet, stimulating air, and the bright sunshine.

In the first moments of her humiliation she had thought that she must seek refuge from her father somewhere; and Margaret had occurred to her as a resource. Her shame for him and for herself seemed in the beginning a feeling she could never face by his side. Their life together was too

close to leave an opening for compromise; if she was to
remain with him she knew that it must be as his daughter,
with all that the word had meant for her since her mother's
death ; and she did not see how that could be ; it implied
a perfect trust and understanding between them which no
longer existed. But she had seen immediately that she
could not go away from him even for the moment; her permanent feeling of loyalty, which she had never allowed to
falter, would not suffer it ; if she could find it in her heart
to leave him upon one impulse, she saw that she must
straightway return to him upon another. The protecting,
almost motherly instinct which had taught her the thousand
cares for his happiness that had so long compassed him
about, would not let her forego her place by his side. Her
eyes were opened (even if they were not so widely opened
as she supposed), and she seemed to be seeing her father
through a new and loathly medium which distorted all that
she had trusted and loved in him; but the love and trust
were actually stronger than all newer feelings. She saw this
almost at first, and afterward it was borne in upon her ; she
took strength from the belief to face the prospect of the
days lived by his side which seemed now to stretch in a
dismal procession far into an unlovely future.

She had thought of going to Margaret at first, as I have
said, but that resort presented difficulties even if she had
been resolved to go somewhere, or to some one. She could
not tell her about her father ; and if she could she was not
sure that Margaret, with all her fineness of perception in
certain directions, would understand.

No, it was not Margaret for whom something in her
seemed to cry out. She felt bruised, disheartened, dis-
illusioned ; she longed to lean herself on a different kind of
strength. She perceived, in a moment, that she was thinking of Philip ; and, the moment after, faced the fact with all
its consequences, without disquiet. She saw him suddenly

as her only refuge ; and rejoiced, after a tremulous thought,
in seeing him so.

His blundering force—not sharpened to a point, like his
brother's, but so sure, large, restful—seemed to her, as her
heart went out to him in the exile to which she had condemned him, the most excellent thing in the world. She
wondered where he was ; she had said that she would see
him ; he would have come back with his father to Maverick.
But when he found her gone, which way would he turn?
The thought came to her that he would fancy she had fled
from Maverick, of her own motion, to avoid the consequences
of her rash yielding to his father's entreaty ; it was suddenly
intolerable to her that he should think that, and she thought
she would walk on through the Garden of the Gods to
Manitou, and send a telegram to Beatrice at Maverick to
say where she was ; she had promised her that much, and
had not kept her promise because her father, for his own
reasons, had asked her not to.

The unquestioning obedience which had gone with her
unquestioning trust was broken down by her new vision of
her father, and the knowledge that he would not wish a
thing was not the final hindrance it had seemed yesterday.
She quickened her pace believing for a moment that her
strong desire that Philip should not think what she
fancied him thinking alone controlled her ; but the need for
him—the need for his strength, his unconscious manliness,
for that open-air quality in him which seemed to annul difficulties and anxieties, for his wholesomeness and genuineness,
came over her in an irresistible flood.   And when she had
recognized this she did not deny its meaning to herself in
any way ; she knew that it was he whom she wished ; and
not for any reason but one obvious and sufficient one.

She had imagined, altogether afresh, while she lay awake
during the night, the persuading causes which had led him
to the act that had separated them, and saw her father in

them all. In her passionate wish to exculpate Philip she perhaps implicated her father, in fancy, more deeply than she could have alleged any solid warrant for. But, indeed, in the strenuous swing to the opposite point of view which had been operated within her with the swiftness and certainty of her woman's processes, she now found it as abundantly easy to discover excuses for him as she had before found it abundantly hard. And the knowledge that her father had injured him in injuring her was not the reason it should have been for wishing that she might never have to face him again. On the contrary.

The rattle of a horse's hoofs echoed behind her on the hard road along which she was walking, and she turned and saw Philip coming toward her. He reined in his horse, as he came near. Her limbs trembled under her, and she experienced an inconsequent impulse to flight; but she walked on until his voice behind her brought her to a halt, and she forced herself to turn and look toward him. He raised his sombrero as he drew in his animal by her side, and with the same motion threw himself off, and stood beside her. He put out his hand silently, and she slipped hers into his waiting clasp, shyly and limply at first, and then, as her little hand was swallowed up in the embrace of his big one, and she felt him bending over her inquiringly, anxiously, tenderly, she surrendered it to him, wholly, giving back his firm grip with her own quick, warm, vigorous clasp. Then she looked up at him, and read the suffering through which she had caused him to pass in the drawn lines of his strong, browned, honest face.

" Your father told me I should find you here," he said.

"Yes," she answered, dropping her eyes.

" You are not angry with me for coming ?"

She glanced up at him again, her eyes filling perilously, helplessly. In that flashing gaze he saw himself forgiven, and blessed. He took her in his arms.

"But you must tell me something first," she said some moments later, when they had settled everything.

"How much I love you?" He shook his head, with a smile. "I can't."

"No, no. This is something serious."

"Ah!" returned he, prolonging the intonation.

"Oh, you know what I mean," she cried, answering the laughing look in his eyes. "This is a different kind of seriousness. I want to ask you something."

"Well?" inquired he, trying to be as sober as the occasion appeared to demand.

"How much did my father have to do with—with what you did?"

It was a dangerous moment. He temporized, as was his habit. "How—your father?' 'he asked. "I don't understand, Dorothy."

"Oh, yes, you do. I know that he had something to do with it. He has owned that to me. It is shameful; but I must ask you. I can't let you go on, I can't go on myself, not knowing what his actual share was in—in what you did."

"But you have forgiven me. What difference can anything else make?"

"Does it make no difference if he really did what I have been accusing you of—and did it without even the courage to do it for himself? Does it make no difference if he did it, in fact, and chose you—*you*, Philip, to do it for him: that it's his wrong and that he's let me make you suffer for it? No, if that's true, we have wronged you too deeply. I couldn't—"

"Don't say it, Dorothy! You are mad. The wrong, whatever it was, was all mine."

"My father profited by it. You found a large sum for him. I know that. How can I know that he did not instigate it?" she asked desperately.

He did not answer for a moment. He felt himself halted. For a single instant he felt a kind of impatience stealing upon his easy-going nature ; but surely he could grant her this last barrier against full and actual surrender, this little withholding of herself from him. She doubtless took it for a sincere objection. The reflection lent him a patience which taught him a defence stronger in its weakness than any other could have been in its strength. "Rubbish, Dorothy!" he said. "Rubbish! No one had anything to do with what I did, except myself—unless it was some devil in me. Your father was entirely outside of the matter, and the money you are thinking of was paid back to Jasper long ago."

"Oh, was it? I am so glad!"

"Well, I was glad to pay it," he rejoined soberly. He heaved a deep sigh of relief as she turned away, and forgave himself for so much of untruth as there was in his statement about her father's complicity, as he caught sight of the glad smile on her face, and remembered how hard it would be to say exactly what the truth was about that. He knew that she could not always rest content with this ; but for the moment it served, and if it came to another moment he hoped to be strong enough for it.

"He must pay you," she said.

"Who?"

"Papa. It is his debt. Doubly his."

"Of course," assented Philip unfalteringly, turning the sharp corner with the quick command of resource which this conversation was teaching him. "I have his notes : he is to pay me interest on them, and take them up as fast as he has the money." He said this without smiling, though a humorous memory of a long list of such arrangements made by himself on his own behalf mingled in his mind with the absurdity of the idea that Maurice would redeem his obligations. "It is simply transferring a debt from a hard creditor to an easy one," he said.

She wondered if he did not see how this, which looked so innocent in his phrase, had involved her—how the transaction had simply used her : how she had been bandied about in it by her father like a negotiable security. She did not blame Philip for his share in it ; she felt sure—too sure—of the absolute generosity of his motives ; but she turned scarlet with a new sense of shame for her father.

"And you will let him pay you ? "

His candid, good-natured eyes did not quail, as she clung on him studying his face.

"Let him ! I'll sue him if you like ! " retorted he fondly. And it occurred to him that this might not be from every point of view an event without its rewards. The talk which he had had with Maurice before coming on to her had made several things plain to him ; none of them increased his fondness for Maurice.

Dorothy had to laugh. "You need n't do that," she said. They turned their faces toward Colorado Springs, and walked on through the rock-strewn park—as empty at this hour as that other park in which they had lately parted so definitely, so finally. They found a number of things to say to each other which it would not be fair to repeat. Philip led his horse with his arm through the bridle, and Dorothy retraced by his side the steps she had lately taken alone.

The shining of the sun had seemed very good to her a few moments before ; but it was a dull radiance compared to that which fell upon them as they walked together—walking, as she felt, into a new life, into an unexplored but happy future, into a future made up out of the most airy but the most substantial materials : a future guided and guarded by love.

She told him that she knew she could not guess how she had made him suffer ; but if anything could teach her it would be her own suffering in giving him that pain. It was foolish to talk of that ; but how were they to be properly happy if they did not let themselves remember a time when they had n't been ?

But they were, in fact, too happy in having found each

other again by any means to study very minutely the process by which they had re-discovered that they were necessary to each other. Only Philip must sometimes say, for mere uneasiness in his restoration to her trust,

"You'd better say again that you forgive me. Or perhaps you'd better say you don't. If you say you do, it makes me happy of course ; but that isn't the point. You'd better harden your heart for your own sake."

She merely smiled at him.

"Dorothy," he went on more seriously, "I'm really all that you thought me. Your pardon is heaven to me ; one must have known the other thing to know the sweetness of your trust; but I mustn't abuse it. I did exactly what you said : I took the 'Little Cipher' from Jasper knowing it to be his by all the laws that make right, right, and wrong, wrong for men anywhere ; and I saw long ago how it was all you said and more than you said as it touched you and me and our love. You'd better take back your forgiveness."

She shook her head. "I can't take back what I never gave. If I were to forgive you, I should have to judge first ; and "— with a little lift of her eyes—"I can't judge you Philip— any more." And then, in a moment, to turn him from this difficult subject, "How did you leave your father ?"she asked.

"Ah, it's to *him* I owe you !" he cried. "He never said it ; he merely brought me your message. But I know it well enough. It's from him you've taken a picturesque version of the facts which enables you to think well of me. If you had known him, Dorothy, you would have been on your guard ; you would have understood that he never sees quite straight; he sees too heartily, too warmly and too hot-headedly to be a safe witness—especially where he cares. He cares so much—that splendid, downright father of mine!"

"Oh, he's good ! I have been so sorry for him. It was being sorry for him that first helped me to be a little sorry for you, you know."

"Yes, I know," he answered vaguely to her roguish smile, rather than to her words (it is difficult to confine one's replies altogether to the theme of actual discourse in these situations; there are interruptions). He added in a moment, 'You couldn't have minded about me for any one else's sake so safely. It is always safe to do a thing because you like father."

"Oh, I don't know for whose sake I sent that message," she declared ambiguously. She flashed a look at him, and challenged his smile with, "I didn't say it was for yours."

"No," laughed Philip.

"No; I think it was for my own," she assured herself. "I wanted to make sure that I had been right!"

She joined in his smile. "Well, you're sure now," he said.

"Am I? But now you see I don't know whether I am right to be sure." They could laugh at anything and they laughed at this.

"That you were wrong?" queried he. "No, I shouldn't like you to be sure of that. You were altogether in the right, Dorothy," he told her more seriously. "Your only mistake is in pardoning me. Take it back while there is time!"

"I'll see about it," rejoined she with a baffling glance at him which temporarily put an end to the discussion. "But how did you find us? How did you know where we were?" she asked suddenly, as she disengaged herself. This simple question had not occurred to either of them hitherto.

"Why, I didn't find you exactly; I partly stumbled on you. But the finding, such as it was, is Vertner's. His acquaintance with the whole fraternity of railway conductors was a blessing for once. One of them remembered that you had travelled with him this far. After that I had to hunt you up,—or rather your father, and he sent me on."

"It wasn't fair of the conductor to tell," she remarked.

"No," said Philip, with equal seriousness, "that's what I thought."

Nonsense like this floated on the current of their mood, and they welcomed it as a defence against more serious things. There was so much to be said between them that by a common impulse they avoided trying to say any of it, except as they said it in the interchange of silent glances. They seemed to themselves to have plenty of time before them: they best realized their happiness for the moment through a sense of the leisure which allowed them to feel that they could play with it.

Long silences fell between them, and they would walk on, hearing no sound but their own footsteps, and those of the horse following them; and at these times they let the sunshine, the gay, brisk, bright morning, which seemed made for them, and the massive beauty of the park, express their bliss for them in their various voices. But they had to talk, too, and they spoke a good deal, in a fragmentary, unserious way, of their future; they speculated luxuriously about it, they made and unmade plans, they warned each other affectionately that neither must build too much on the virtue and solidity of the other's character in scheming this life together. But they said they would be constant and that must be their sure armour against all doubts and differences—the certainty that they were all in all to each other. They owned soberly the differences of character existing between them, but they agreed that it was largely these which had drawn them together, and they promised each other to respect them always, if for no other reason; they said that they should rejoice in them.

Philip told her that he should not even be jealous of her having all the sense in the family; every one had been telling him, since he had been old enough to make mistakes, that what he needed was a "balance-wheel"; he should have one now, and nothing could be more useless than a balance-wheel that kept quiet. He said he should be rid, now, of the left-handed compliment that he had excellent "works," but no contrivance for keeping them in running order, and making them perform their functions. It appeared that their functions would be brilliant if the lack were supplied. Now they should see ! If they were n't it would be her fault.

" Oh, I sha'n't be strict with you, if that's what you are hoping for," she declared. " I've had enough of that."

" But I have n't. It's the only thing for me. I shall never be of any use without it. And you must remember I 've got to earn our living. When you see that, perhaps sternness will come easier to you."

" I do n't know. Shall I never have a holiday ? "

" Well, you 'll have to spend a good deal of your time forgiving me for the daily assortment of folly and reckless. ness. You might lay off for that."

" Ah, that's all very well. But, as Mr. Vertner says, ' Where do I come in ? ' "

" Dear old Vertner ! " exclaimed Philip in the overflow of his liking for the world. " What a first-rate, unprincipled, warm-hearted, loyal good fellow he is ! He would n't like your not coming in handsomely. But where do n't you come in ? I do n't see but you 've got your work cut out for you."

" My work—yes ! But my pleasure. How about that ? If I'm to spend all my time correcting your faults, how shall I ever find a moment to enjoy them."

" Enjoy them ? "

" Well, of course I like them. How should I like you if I did n't ? "

" Yes," admitted Philip, meditatively, " they do cover most of the territory in sight."

She laid a silencing hand on his lips. " Hush ! " she said. " It is I who am all faults. You will find it all you can do to get along with me."

He stopped short in the road along which they were going, and took her in his arms. He looked down into her face for a long moment tenderly.

" I 'll risk it ! " he said.

CHAPTER XXXVI

"WELL, that's over!" exclaimed Vertner, as he opened the door of their house for his wife, one afternoon a month later, and followed her in. "I must say I don't feel like coming back home and settling down to the old humdrum routine after an event like this. Can't we have some champagne?"

"In the middle of the afternoon?"

"No, I suppose not. But I feel the need of some excitement. Perhaps we have reached the climax, though. They looked very happy going away, didn't they?"

Beatrice seated herself provisionally in her wedding finery, stooping first to pick up one of Edward's toys from the floor. They had drifted into the room in which Margaret had borne to see Deed go from her in anger on another wedding day. The iron pyrites still winked from the "what-not"; the Navajo blanket continued to do duty as a *portière*; the rag carpet was on the floor, the stained glass window, through which the sun was shining at the moment, continued to take itself without seriousness.

"Yes," said Beatrice, smoothing her silk thoughtfully, with long, ruminating fingers, "they did look very happy going away. Do you suppose they will be able to keep it up?"

Vertner hovered restlessly about, without sitting down. 'What makes you think they won't?" he asked.

" I didn't say they wouldn't. I was only wondering."

Vertner sighed and gave an absent touch to the lavender tie of festal effect, which he had worn in honour of the occasion.

" It's a large field for speculation—any marriage," he said. " Perhaps this is a little extra large. But then they're both extra nice. I guess it will go."

" You wouldn't say that——? " began Beatrice doubtfully.

" Yes, I would. There are a lot of things of that kind that I could say; but there are answers to all of them. Yes," he repeated meditatively, after a moment, " all of them. You see they are interested in each other. They won't get tired of each other's conversation right away, and by the time they begin to,—well, I shouldn't wonder if Dorothy were a little older."

" Oh ! " gasped Mrs. Vertner, as if she had been surprised in a covert thought. " Do you think that, too, Ned ? "

" I *have* thought it ; but only at moments. In the other moments,——"

" Well ? "

" I've thought that Phil might be something of a trial to a woman at any age."

" I don't believe you think any such thing," declared his wife promptly. " Why, there's something almost likeable even about his faults."

" Yes. Have you noticed that is· what every one says ? I say it myself, and I stick to it. But hasn't it occurred to you that in some situations—like a wife's, for example— a man's faults can't be the perennial joy that they are to an impartial outsider like you, who doesn't have to breakfast with them ? "

" Oh, I know, Ned. But Philip is so good ! "

"Ah, now you've hit it! He's a good fellow: that's exactly what he is—the best! And if his need to be a good fellow sometimes makes him a good fellow at some one else's expense, why that's only what you mean by his faults being likeable. If he has the sense to avoid being some time or other a good fellow at his wife's expense—or what she will think her expense: that's the real trouble—I don't see why she shouldn't continue to admire him for the manly and charming fellow he is, to the end of the chapter. She starts in with one great advantage: she is acquainted with him."

"And with another," added the practical Beatrice, "—— that they are not to live with her father."

"Yes; that's almost the pleasantest thing about the marriage—that it sets her free of her father." He seated himself in the chair before the fire where he sat in the evenings to read the Denver papers, and, after piling on a couple of logs, stretched out his feet cosily to the crackling blaze. "I don't see any harm in his new field of labour being $60 or $70 to the Eastward. I should n't be sorry to see the fare raised—if I could always be sure of a pass. I believe you 'll see great changes in her : she will be just as nice, but differently nice. Come to think of it she will *have* to be rather nice to really be worthy of Phil. That little piece of business of his at Piñon just before his father found him, and he went down to Colorado Springs to look her up, is the kind of thing that might help a woman to like him exclusively for his virtues—if she knew about it."

"You mean his selling the 'Pay Ore' to pay Jasper back $5,000 when he found that those Ryan people had opened a paying vein in his own mine? Yes, that was strong in him."

"Strong! Well, if you'd ever opened a true fissure vein that showed all the symptoms of making an income of $3,000 a month for you, for four or five years to come, and

had sold your claim to raise ready money, you would think
it strong. It's the sort of thing to make any one who
ever owned a mine think Phil about right. When I remember that, I have to believe that if they are not happy
it will be her fault. Think of the rascal never having told
her about it ! "

" Oh, I shouldn't wonder if she had a good many things
to learn."

" About her father—yes. But she'll never learn them
from him. And Maurice's being so far away will prevent
the question from coming up, I hope, for her sake. Talk
about aproposity ! "—this was one of Vertner's words—
" what do you say to Maurice finding that position in New
York ! I always said he had a manner. Now, he's found
a place where he can use it. To be assistant rector of a
fashionable city congregation, where the people demand a
certain distinction, and don't haggle too much about the
salary they give for it, or the sincerity they get back for it,
is a position in which Maurice can't help shining if he tries.
A place like that, where too much earnestness would imply
a criticism on the congregation and be in a man's way,
would have been a great thing for him if it had come to him
younger; he might never have found himself out. And
even as it is—(if he can keep the place—if this story does n't
rise to plague him), imagine his parish visits ! He will
raise them to the dignity of a career. And how he *will*
manage the music ! "

" I don't care," said Beatrice, coming over and standing
near him by the fire, with her elbow on the mantel. " I'm
sorry for him. Did you see him this afternoon, after the
service, when Dorothy said goodbye to him in the vestry ?
He really cares for her ; I shall always say that for him."

" Oh, don't tell me that he has his good points,"
retorted Vertner, rising. " I'm his consistent admirer.

Have n't I praised him since the first day I saw him? I hope I know what is due to an editor who has had the discretion to relieve me of an inconvenient reputation, and does n't mind leaving his money in the business."

" I wish you'd give up that wretched paper, Ned !"

" Why, the Salvation Army people were around yesterday suggesting that very idea. I think I will."

" Yes; I suppose they are afraid of its influence," said Beatrice.

Her husband stared at her for a moment; then he snatched her down upon his knee with a howl of delight.

" Yes; that's it," he agreed. " They are frightened at the way I'm spreading churchly ideas among my two hundred and thirty-four subscribers. They want to buy me off !"

" No, but seriously, Ned ? "

" Well, they want a paper of their own, under another name, and they see that the *Kalendar* has the plant, and all that ready for them. They heard that I knew when I had had enough, and they made me an offer."

" And you've accepted it ? "

" Yes; at a loss of a hundred thousand dollars."

" Absurd ! "

" Didn't I expect to make that out of the paper when I started it ? "

" I suppose so," admitted Beatrice with a smile.

" Well, then ! " challenged her husband. " And that isn't the only thing I've lost, either. I've lost my confidence in human nature. I supposed you could *give* people anything."

" And can't you ? "

" Not the *Kalendar*, with Rev. George Maurice as editor. Heigho ! I was sorry Deed was so cold to him."

" Oh, I think he feels very sore about Mr. Maurice's connection with what Philip did—with that matter of Jasper's mine."

" Don't call it Jasper's mine, please, Trix."

" But what shall I call it ?　It *is* his mine, isn't it ? "

" Well, it's become so—by a fluke ; but it isn't ladylike to press the point."

He regarded her with a quizzical smile, and Beatrice burst into a little rejoicing laugh.　"You are trying to set me a standard for Dorothy's behaviour, I think," she said.

"If she falls below the standard I shall punish you for it.　I don't mind letting you know that.　Well, I don't care," he declared warmly, after a moment.　" It would be mean to take a man back, and forgive him handsomely, and persuade him that there was a new deal, and then to twit him at appropriate moments about the old hand, in the face of it."

"Of course it would," assented Beatrice with equal warmth, " but Dorothy isn't like that."

" No ; women are," returned Vertner reflectively ; " but probably Dorothy isn't.　It's really a kind of generosity that has made her hard with him, when you come to think of it ; I shouldn't wonder if she knew how to be at least as generous in forgiving as in condemning.　I guess we can trust her.　But it would be a temptation for some women—living next door to the subject of discussion."

" Yes, yes, Ned, but you will see.　To Dorothy that mine in sight from her door will be like a sacred pledge—a guarantee, if you can think she needs one.　His having done that—his having sold the mine to meet that debt to Jasper, and then having taken the position of superintendent of his own mine under the new owners——"

" Yes, it does rather force her to cast a benevolent eye on the ' Little Cipher ' as a part of the view from their cabin window.　But it will make it embarrassing for Jasper if he should want to look after the ' Little Cipher ' himself when the Ryans' lease is up, won't it ? "

" Oh, Jasper!" exclaimed Beatrice impatiently, "I don't care about Jasper!" She drew off her long white wedding gloves, and, rising from his knee, began slowly to smooth them out upon the mantel.

"Ah!" exclaimed her husband from the window, "that's the limitation of your sex—your not caring about Jasper. You have to like people to be interested in them. Where's your miscellaneous human interest?" he asked, turning upon her.

"It isn't centred in Jasper," replied Beatrice with a smile.

"Do you mean to say that the spectacle of that successful young man's first defeat doesn't move you?"

"Oh, I enjoyed *that* on Mr. Deed's account!"

"I should hope you did! If I were Deed and had a friend who didn't enjoy that up to the hilt, I'd disown him. It was sublime."

"It was effective," admitted Beatrice.

"Effective? It was a ten-strike. It bowled Jasper out. And it was the only thing that could have done it. At a casual glance—that is to say, at a fool glance—it looks weak. When you come to your senses you see how weak it was. If I had enough of that sort of weakness I'd take a contract to twist the earth backwards!"

"You needn't do that, Ned, to prove that Mr. Deed did the best and bravest thing. I'm ready enough to admit that anything that humiliates Jasper as much as that must have a good deal of some kind of force."

"Ah yes," cried Vertner, in sober joy; "it did weary him, didn't it! Taken with Dorothy's dismissal, it seems as if it might also save you the trouble of disliking him. My word for it, he is disliking himself."

"And yet he has the ranch back; he is to have it under his sole charge for the rest of the partnership term;—he has all that he has claimed."

"Yes, yes," assented Vertner heartily, with emphatic nods of his small, shrewd, blonde head; "that's just the pesky part of it.   He was safe against every chance but that; and if it had happened to be anybody but Deed, he would have been safer against that chance than any.   But it did happen to be Deed, you see.   Jasper had a perfect position.   The incalculable has happened and left him with no position at all.   It makes the poor fellow feel foolish."

"But I don't believe that was Mr. Deed's object."

"No, and that's the other pretty and excellent point about it.   He has accomplished exactly what he has been after from the beginning, by giving it up and turning his back on it."

"Yes, I suppose he has won, as we should say.   But now he doesn't seem to care.   He seems to have got past that."

"Ah," cried Vertner, as he seated himself in his chair before the fire, and held out his hands contentedly to the blaze, "that *is* winning!   It's a good thing to win. But I shouldn't wonder if the best thing was not to need to win."

RICHARD CLAY AND SONS, LIMITED, LONDON AND BUNGAY.

THE MANXMAN

By HALL CAINE

In One Volume, price 6s.

The Times.—'With the exception of *The Scapegoat*, this is unquestionably the finest and most dramatic of Mr. Hall Caine's novels . . . *The Manxman* goes very straight to the roots of human passion and emotion. It is a remarkable book, throbbing with human interest.'

The Guardian.—'A story of exceptional power and thorough originality. The greater portion of it is like a Greek tragic drama, in the intensity of its interest, and the depth of its overshadowing gloom. . . . But this tragedy is merely a telling background for a series of brilliant sketches of men and manners, of old-world customs, and forgotten ways of speech which still linger in the Isle of Man.'

The Standard.—'A singularly powerful and picturesque piece of work, extraordinarily dramatic. . . . Taken altogether, *The Manxman* cannot fail to enhance Mr. Hall Caine's reputation. It is a most powerful book.'

The Morning Post.—'If possible, Mr. Hall Caine's work, *The Manxman*, is more marked by passion, power, and brilliant local colouring than its predecessors. . . . It has a grandeur as well as strength, and the picturesque features and customs of a delightful country are vividly painted.'

The World.—'Over and above the absorbing interest of the story, which never flags, the book is full of strength, of vivid character sketches, and powerful word-painting, all told with a force and knowledge of local colour.'

The Queen.—'*The Manxman* is undoubtedly one of the most remarkable books of the century. It will be read and re-read, and take its place in the literary inheritance of the English-speaking nations.'

The St. James's Gazette.—'*The Manxman* is a contribution to literature, and the most fastidious critic would give in exchange for it a wilderness of that deciduous trash which our publishers call fiction. . . . It is not possible to part from *The Manxman* with anything but a warm tribute of approval.' —EDMUND GOSSE.

The Christian World.—'There is a great fascination in being present, as it were, at the birth of a classic ; and a classic undoubtedly *The Manxman* is . . . He who reads *The Manxman* feels that he is reading a book which will be read and re-read by very many thousands with human tears and human laughter.'

Mr. T. P. O'Connor, in the 'Sun.'—'This is a very fine and great story—one of the finest and greatest of our time. . . . Mr. Hall Caine reaches heights which are attained only by the greatest masters of fiction. . . . I think of the great French writer, Stendhal, at the same moment as the great English writer. . . . In short, you feel what Mr. Howells said of Tolstoi, "This is not like life ; it is life." . . . He belongs to that small minority of the Great Elect of Literature.'

The Scotsman.—'It is not too much to say that it is the most powerful story that has been written in the present generation. . . . The love of Pete, his simple-mindedness, his sufferings when he has lost Kate, are painted with a master-hand. . . . It is a work of genius.'

LONDON : WILLIAM HEINEMANN, 21 BEDFORD STREET, W.C.

THE BONDMAN

By HALL CAINE

With a Photogravure Portrait of the Author.

In One Volume, price 6s.

Mr. Gladstone.—'*The Bondman* is a work of which I recognise the freshness, vigour, and sustained interest, no less than its integrity of aim.'

The Times.—'It is impossible to deny originality and rude power to this saga, impossible not to admire its forceful directness, and the colossal grandeur of its leading characters.'

The Academy.—'The language of *The Bondman* is full of nervous, graphic, and poetical English; its interest never flags, and its situations and descriptions are magnificent. It is a splendid novel.'

The Speaker.—'This is the best book that Mr. Hall Caine has yet written, and it reaches a level to which fiction very rarely attains. . . . We are, in fact, so loth to let such good work be degraded by the title of "novel" that we are almost tempted to consider its claim to rank as a prose epic.'

The Scotsman.—'Mr. Hall Caine has in this work placed himself beyond the front rank of the novelists of the day. He has produced a story which, for the ingenuity of its plot, for its literary excellence, for its delineations of human passions, and for its intensely powerful dramatic scenes, is distinctly ahead of all the fictional literature of our time, and fit to rank with the most powerful fictional writing of the past century.'

The Athenæum.—'Crowded with incidents.'

The Observer.—'Many of the descriptions are picturesque and powerful. . . . As fine in their way as anything in modern literature.'

The Liverpool Mercury.—'A story which will be read, not by his contemporaries alone, but by later generations, so long as its chief features—high emotion, deep passion, exquisite poetry, and true pathos—have power to delight and to touch the heart.'

The Pall Mall Gazette.—'It is the product of a strenuous and sustained imaginative effort far beyond the power of any every-day story-teller.'

The Scots Observer.—'In none of his previous works has he approached the splendour of idealism which flows through *The Bondman*.'

The Manchester Guardian.—'A remarkable story, painted with vigour and brilliant effect.'

The St. James's Gazette.—'A striking and highly dramatic piece of fiction.'

The Literary World.—'The book abounds in pages of great force and beauty, and there is a touch of almost Homeric power in its massive and grand simplicity.'

The Liverpool Post.—'Graphic, dramatic, pathetic, heroic, full of detail, crowded with incident and inspired by a noble purpose.'

The Yorkshire Post.—'A book of lasting interest.'

LONDON: WILLIAM HEINEMANN, 21 BEDFORD STREET, W.C.

THE SCAPEGOAT

By HALL CAINE

In One Volume, price 6s.

Mr. Gladstone writes:—'I congratulate you upon *The Scapegoat* as a work of art, and especially upon the noble and skilfully drawn character of Israel.'

Mr. Walter Besant, in 'The Author.'—'Nearly every year there stands out a head and shoulders above its companions one work which promises to make the year memorable. This year a promise of lasting vitality is distinctly made by Mr. Hall Caine's *Scapegoat*. It is a great book, great in conception and in execution; a strong book, strong in situation and in character; and a human book, human in its pathos, its terror, and its passion.'

The Times.—'In our judgment it excels in dramatic force all the Author's previous efforts. For grace and touching pathos Naomi is a character which any romancist in the world might be proud to have created, and the tale of her parents' despair and hopes, and of her own development, confers upon *The Scapegoat* a distinction which is matchless of its kind.'

The Guardian.—'Mr. Hall Caine is undoubtedly master of a style which is peculiarly his own. He is in a way a Rembrandt among novelists. His figures, striking and powerful rather than beautiful, stand out, with the ruggedness of their features developed and accentuated, from a background of the deepest gloom. . . . Every sentence contains a thought, and every word of it is balanced and arranged to accumulate the intensity of its force.'

The Athenæum.—'It is a delightful story to read.'

The Academy.—'Israel ben Oliel is the third of a series of the most profoundly conceived characters in modern fiction.'

The Saturday Review.—'This is the best novel which Mr. Caine has yet produced.'

The Literary World.—'The lifelike renderings of the varied situations, the gradual changes in a noble character, hardened and lowered by the world's cruel usage, and returning at last to its original grandeur, can only be fully appreciated by a perusal of the book as a whole.'

The Anti-Jacobin.—'It is, in truth, a romance of fine poetic quality. Israel Ben Oliel, the central figure of the tale, is sculptured rather than drawn: a character of grand outline. A nobler piece of prose than the death of Ruth we have seldom met with.'

The Scotsman.—'The new story will rank with Mr. Hall Caine's previous productions. Nay, it will in some respects rank above them. It will take its place by the side of the Hebrew histories in the Apocrypha. It is nobly and manfully written. It stirs the blood and kindles the imagination.'

The Scottish Leader.—'*The Scapegoat* is a masterpiece.'

Truth.—'Mr. Hall Caine has been winning his way slowly, but surely, and securely, I think also, to fame. You must by all means read his absorbing Moorish romance, *The Scapegoat*.'

The Jewish World.—'Only one who had studied Moses could have drawn that grand portrait of Israel ben Oliel.'

LONDON: WILLIAM HEINEMANN, 21 BEDFORD STREET, W.C.

THE HEAVENLY TWINS

By SARAH GRAND

In One Volume, price 6s.

The Athenæum.—'It is so full of interest, and the characters are so eccentrically humorous yet true, that one feels inclined to pardon all its faults, and give oneself up to unreserved enjoyment of it. . . . The twins Angelica and Diavolo, young barbarians, utterly devoid of all respect, conventionality, or decency, are among the most delightful and amusing children in fiction.'

The Academy.—'The adventures of Diavolo and Angelica—the "heavenly twins"—are delightfully funny. No more original children were ever put into a book. Their audacity, unmanageableness, and genius for mischief—in none of which qualities, as they are here shown, is there any taint of vice—are refreshing; and it is impossible not to follow, with very keen interest, the progress of these youngsters.'

The Daily Telegraph.—'Everybody ought to read it, for it is an inexhaustible source of refreshing and highly stimulating entertainment.'

The World.—'There is much powerful and some beautiful writing in this strange book.'

The Westminster Gazette.—'Sarah Grand . . . has put enough observation, humour, and thought into this book to furnish forth half-a-dozen ordinary novels.'

Punch.—'The Twins themselves are a creation : the epithet "Heavenly" for these two mischievous little fiends is admirable.'

The Queen.—'There is a touch of real genius in *The Heavenly Twins.*'

The Guardian.—'Exceptionally brilliant in dialogue, and dealing with modern society life, this book has a purpose—to draw out and emancipate women.'

The Lady.—'Apart from its more serious interest, the book should take high rank on its literary merits alone. Its pages are brimful of good things, and more than one passage, notably the episode of "The Boy and the Tenor," is a poem complete in itself, and worthy of separate publication.'

The Manchester Examiner.—'As surely as *Tess of the d'Urbervilles* swept all before it last year, so surely has Sarah Grand's *Heavenly Twins* provoked the greatest attention and comment this season. It is a most daringly original work. . . . Sarah Grand is a notable Woman's Righter, but her book is the one asked for at Mudie's, suburban, and seaside libraries, and discussed at every hotel table in the kingdom. The episode of the "Tenor and the Boy" is of rare beauty, and is singularly delicate and at the same time un-English in treatment.'

The New York Critic.—'It is written in an epigrammatic style, and, besides its cleverness, has the great charm of freshness, enthusiasm, and poetic feeling.'

LONDON : WILLIAM HEINEMANN, 21 BEDFORD STREET, W.C.

IDEALA

A STUDY FROM LIFE

By SARAH GRAND

In One Volume, price 6s.

The Morning Post.—'Sarah Grand's *Ideala*. . . . A clever book in itself, is especially interesting when read in the light of her later works. Standing alone, it is remarkable as the outcome of an earnest mind seeking in good faith the solution of a difficult and ever present problem. . . . *Ideala* is original and somewhat daring. . . . The story is in many ways delightful and thought-suggesting.'

The Literary World.—'When Sarah Grand came before the public in 1888 with *Ideala*, she consciously and firmly laid her finger on one of the keynotes of the age. . . . We welcome an edition that will place this minute and careful study of an interesting question within reach of a wider circle of readers.'

The Liverpool Mercury.—'The book is a wonderful one—an evangel for the fair sex, and at once an inspiration and a comforting companion, to which thoughtful womanhood will recur again and again.'

The Glasgow Herald.—'*Ideala* has attained the honour of a fifth edition. . . . The stir created by *The Heavenly Twins*, the more recent work by the same authoress, Madame Sarah Grand, would justify this step. *Ideala* can, however, stand on its own merits.'

The Yorkshire Post.—'As a psychological study the book cannot fail to be of interest to many readers.'

The Birmingham Gazette.—'Madame Sarah Grand thoroughly deserves her success. Ideala, the heroine, is a splendid conception, and her opinions are noble. . . . The book is not one to be forgotten.'

The Woman's Herald.—'One naturally wishes to know something of the woman for whose sake Lord Downe remained a bachelor. It must be confessed that at first *Ideala* is a little disappointing. She is strikingly original. . . . As the story advances one forgets these peculiarities, and can find little but sympathy and admiration for the many noble qualities of a very complex character.'

The Englishman.—'Madame Sarah Grand's work is far from being a common work. Ideala is a clever young woman of great capabilities and noble purposes. . . . The orginality of the book does not lie in the plot, but in the authoress's power to see and to describe the finer shades of a character which is erratic and impetuous, but above all things truly womanly.'

LONDON : WILLIAM HEINEMANN· 21 BEDFORD STREET, W.C.

OUR MANIFOLD NATURE

By SARAH GRAND

In One Volume, price 6s.

The Daily Telegraph.—'Six stories by the gifted writer who still chooses to be known to the public at large by the pseudonym of "Sarah Grand." In regard to them it is sufficient to say that they display all the qualities, stylistic, humorous, and pathetic, that have placed the author of *Ideala* and *The Heavenly Twins* in the very front rank of contemporary novelists.'

The Globe.—'Brief studies of character, sympathetic, and suggesting that "Sarah Grand" can do something more than startle by her unconventionality and boldness.'

The Ladies' Pictorial.—'If the volume does not achieve even greater popularity than Sarah Grand's former works, it will be a proof that fashion, and not intrinsic merit, has a great deal to do with the success of a book.'

The Pall Mall Gazette.—'All are eminently entertaining.'

The Spectator.—'Insight into, and general sympathy with widely differing phases of humanity, coupled with power to reproduce what is seen, with vivid distinct strokes, that rivet the attention, are qualifications for work of the kind contained in *Our Manifold Nature* which Sarah Grand evidently possesses in a high degree. . . . All these studies, male and female alike, are marked by humour, pathos, fidelity to life, and power to recognise in human nature the frequent recurrence of some apparently incongruous and remote trait, which, when at last it becomes visible, helps to a comprehension of what might otherwise be inexplicable.'

The Speaker.—'In *Our Manifold Nature* Sarah Grand is seen at her best. How good that is can only be known by those who read for themselves this admirable little volume. In freshness of conception and originality of treatment these stories are delightful, full of force and piquancy, whilst the studies of character are carried out with equal firmness and delicacy.'

The Guardian.—'*Our Manifold Nature* is a clever book. Sarah Grand has the power of touching common things, which, if it fails to make them "rise to touch the spheres," renders them exceedingly interesting.'

The Morning Post.—'Unstinted praise is deserved by the Irish story, "Boomellen," a tale remarkable both for power and pathos.'

The Court Journal.—*Our Manifold Nature* is simply full of good things, and it is essentially a book to buy as well as to read.'

The Birmingham Gazette.—'Mrs. Grand has genuine power. She analyses keenly. . . . Her humour is good, and her delineation of character one of her strongest points. The book is one to be read, studied, and acted upon.'

LONDON: WILLIAM HEINEMANN, 21 BEDFORD STREET, W.C.

THE EBB-TIDE

By ROBERT LOUIS STEVENSON

AND

LLOYD OSBOURNE

In One Volume, price 6s.

The Times.—'This is a novel of sensation. But the episodes and incidents, although thrilling enough, are consistently subordinated to sensationalism of character. . . . There is just enough of the coral reef and the palm groves, of cerulean sky and pellucid water, to indicate rather than to present the local colouring. Yet when he dashes in a sketch it is done to perfection. . . . We see the scene vividly unrolled before us.'

The Daily Telegraph.—'The story is full of strong scenes, depicted with a somewhat lavish use of violet pigments, such as, perhaps, the stirring situations demand. Here and there, however, are purple patches, in which Mr. Stevenson shows all his cunning literary art—the description of the coral island, for instance. . . . Some intensely graphic and dramatic pages delineate the struggle which causes, and a final scene . . . concludes this strange fragment from the wild life of the South Sea.'

The St. James's Gazette.—'The book takes your imagination and attention captive from the first chapter—nay, from the first paragraph—and it does not set them free till the last word has been read.'

The Standard.—'Mr. Stevenson gives such vitality to his characters, and so clear an outlook upon the strange quarter of the world to which he takes us, that when we reach the end of the story, we come back to civilisation with a start of surprise, and a moment's difficulty in realising that we have not been actually away from it.'

The Daily Chronicle.—'We are swept along without a pause on the current of the animated and vigorous narrative. Each incident and adventure is told with that incomparable keenness of vision which is Mr. Stevenson's greatest charm as a story-teller.'

The Pall Mall Gazette.—'It is brilliantly invented, and it is not less brilliantly told. There is not a dull sentence in the whole run of it. And the style is fresh, alert, full of surprises—in fact, is very good latter-day Stevenson indeed.'

The World.—'It is amazingly clever, full of that extraordinary knowledge of human nature which makes certain creations of Mr. Stevenson's pen far more real to us than persons we have met in the flesh. Grisly the book undoubtedly is, with a strength and a vigour of description hardly to be matched in the language. . . . But it is just because the book is so extraordinarily good that it ought to be better, ought to be more of a serious whole than a mere brilliant display of fireworks, though each firework display has more genius in it than is to be found in ninety-nine out of every hundred books supposed to contain that rare quality.'

The Morning Post.—'Boldly conceived, probing some of the darkest depths of the human soul, the tale has a vigour and breadth of touch which have been surpassed in none of Mr. Stevenson's previous works. . . . We do not, of course, know how much Mr. Osbourne has contributed to the tale, but there is no chapter in it which any author need be unwilling to acknowledge, or which is wanting in vivid interest.'

LONDON: WILLIAM HEINEMANN, 21 BEDFORD STREET, W.C.

A VICTIM OF GOOD LUCK

By W. E. NORRIS

In One Volume, price 6s.

The Speaker.—'*A Victim of Good Luck* is one of those breezy stories of his in which the reader finds himself moving in good society, among men or women who are neither better nor worse than average humanity, but who always show good manners and good breeding. . . . Suffice it to say that the story is as readable as any we have yet had from the same pen.'

The Daily Telegraph.—'*A Victim of Good Luck* is one of the brightest novels of the year, which cannot but enhance its gifted author's well-deserved fame and popularity.'

The World.—'Here is Mr. Norris in his best form again, giving us an impossible story with such imperturbable composure, such quiet humour, easy polish, and irresistible persuasiveness, that he makes us read *A Victim of Good Luck* right through with eager interest and unflagging amusement without being aware, until we regretfully reach the end, that it is just a farcical comedy in two delightful volumes.'

The Daily Chronicle.—'It has not a dull page from first to last. Any one with normal health and taste can read a book like this with real pleasure.'

The Globe.—'Mr. W. E. Norris is a writer who always keeps us on good terms with ourselves. We can pick up or lay down his books at will, but they are so pleasant in style and equable in tone that we do not usually lay them down till we have mastered them; *A Victim of Good Luck* is a more agreeable novel than most of this author's.'

The Westminster Gazette.—'*A Victim of Good Luck* is in Mr. Norris's best vein, which means that it is urbane, delicate, lively, and flavoured with a high quality of refined humour. Altogether a most refreshing book, and we take it as a pleasant reminder that Mr. Norris is still very near his highwater mark.'

The Spectator.—'Mr. Norris displays to the full his general command of narrative expedients which are at once happily invented and yet quite natural —which seem to belong to their place in the book, just as a keystone belongs to its place in the arch. . . . The brightest and cleverest book which Mr. Norris has given us since he wrote *The Rogue*.'

The Saturday Review.—'Novels which are neither dull, unwholesome, morbid, nor disagreeable, are so rare in these days, that *A Victim of Good Luck* . . . ought to find a place in a book-box filled for the most part with light literature. . . . We think it will increase the reputation of an already very popular author.'

The Scotsman.—'*A Victim of Good Luck*, like others of this author's books, depends little on incident and much on the conception and drawing of character, on clever yet natural conversation, and on the working out, with masterly ease, of a novel problem of right and inclination.'

LONDON: WILLIAM HEINEMANN, 21 BEDFORD STREET, W.C.

THE COUNTESS RADNA

By W. E. NORRIS

In One Volume, price 6s.

The Times.—'He is a remarkably even writer. And this novel is almost as good a medium as any other for studying the delicacy and dexterity of his workmanship.'

The National Observer.—'Interesting and well written, as all Mr. Norris's stories are.'

The Morning Post.—'The fidelity of his portraiture is remarkable, and it has rarely appeared to so much advantage as in this brilliant novel.'

The Saturday Review.—'*The Countess Radna*, which its author not unjustly describes as "an unpretending tale," avoids, by the grace of its style and the pleasant accuracy of its characterisation, any suspicion of boredom.'

The Daily News.—'*The Countess Radna* contains many of the qualities that make a story by this writer welcome to the critic. It is caustic in style, the character drawing is clear, the talk natural; the pages are strewn with good things worth quoting.'

The Speaker.—'In style, skill in construction, and general "go," it is worth a dozen ordinary novels.'

The Academy.—'As a whole, the book is decidedly well written, while it is undeniably interesting. It is bright and wholesome : the work in fact of a gentleman and a man who knows the world about which he writes.'

Black and White.—'The novel, like all Mr. Norris's work is an excessively clever piece of work, and the author never for a moment allows his grasp of his plot and his characters to slacken.'

The Gentlewoman.—'Mr. Norris is a practised hand at his craft. He can write bright dialogue and clear English, too.

The Literary World.—'His last novel, *The Countess Radna*, is an excellent sample of his style. The plot is simple enough. But the story holds the attention and insists upon being read ; and it is scarcely possible to say anything more favourable of a work of fiction.'

The Scotsman.—'The story, in which there is more than a spice of modern life romance, is an excellent study of the problem of mixed marriage. The book is one of good healthy reading, and reveals a fine broad view of life and human nature.'

The Glasgow Herald.—'This is an unusually fresh and well-written story. The tone is thoroughly healthy ; and Mr. Norris, without being in the least old-fashioned, manages to get along without the aid of pessimism, psychology, naturalism, or what is known as frank treatment of the relations between the sexes.'

The Westminster Gazette.—'Mr. Norris writes throughout with much liveliness and force, saying now and then something that is worth remembering. And he sketches his minor characters with a firm touch.'

LONDON : WILLIAM HEINEMANN, 21 BEDFORD STREET, W.C.

CHILDREN OF THE GHETTO

A Study of a Peculiar People

By I. ZANGWILL

In One Volume, price 6s.

The Times.—'From whatever point of view we regard it, it is a remarkable book.'

The Athenæum.—'The chief interest of the book lies in the wonderful description of the Whitechapel Jews. The vividness and force with which Mr. Zangwill brings before us the strange and uncouth characters with which he has peopled his book are truly admirable. . . . Admirers of Mr. Zangwill's fecund wit will not fail to find flashes of it in these pages.'

The Daily Chronicle.—'Altogether we are not aware of any such minute, graphic, and seemingly faithful picture of the Israel of nineteenth century London. . . . The book has taken hold of us.'

The Spectator.—'Esther Ansell, Raphael Leon, Mrs. Henry Goldsmith, Reb Shemuel, and the rest, are living creations.'

The Speaker.—'A strong and remarkable book.'

The National Observer.—'To ignore this book is not to know the East End Jew.'

The Guardian.—'A novel such as only our own day could produce. A masterly study of a complicated psychological problem in which every factor is handled with such astonishing dexterity and intelligence that again and again we are tempted to think a really good book has come into our hands.'

The Graphic.—'Absolutely fascinating. Teaches how closely akin are laughter and tears.'

Black and White.—'A moving panorama of Jewish life, full of truth, full of sympathy, vivid in the setting forth, and occasionally most brilliant. Such a book as this has the germs of a dozen novels. A book to read, to keep, to ponder over, to remember.'

W. Archer in 'The World.'—'The most powerful and fascinating book I have read for many a long day.'

Land and Water.—'The most wonderful multi-coloured and brilliant description. Dickens has never drawn characters of more abiding individuality. An exceeding beautiful chapter is the honeymoon of the Hyams. Charles Kingsley in one of his books makes for something of the same sort. But his idea is not half so tender and faithful, nor his handling anything like so delicate and natural.'

Andrew Lang in 'Longman's Magazine.'—'Almost every kind of reader will find *Children of the Ghetto* interesting.'

T. P. O'Connor in 'The Weekly Sun.'—'Apart altogether from its great artistic merits, from its clear portraits, its subtle and skilful analysis of character, its pathos and its humour, this book has, in my mind, an immense interest as a record of a generation that has passed and of struggles that are yet going on.'

The Manchester Guardian.—'The best Jewish novel ever written.'

LONDON: WILLIAM HEINEMANN, 21 BEDFORD STREET, W.C.

THE KING OF SCHNORRERS

Grotesques and Fantasies

By I. ZANGWILL

With over Ninety Illustrations by PHIL MAY and Others

In One Volume, price 6s.

The Athenæum.—'Several of Mr. Zangwill's contemporary Ghetto characters have already become almost classical; but in *The King of Schnorrers* he goes back to the Jewish community of the eighteenth century for the hero of his principal story; and he is indeed a stupendous hero . . . anyhow, he is well named the king of beggars. The i'lustrations, by Phil May, add greatly to the attraction of the book.'

The Saturday Review.—'Mr. Zangwill has created a new figure in fiction, and a new type of humour. The entire series of adventures is a triumphant progress. . . . Humour of a rich and active character pervades the delightful history of Manasses. Mr. Zangwill's book is altogether very good reading. It is also very cleverly illustrated by Phil May and other artists.'

The Literary World.—'Of Mr. Zangwill's versatility there is ample proof in this new volume of stories. . . . More noticeable and welcome to us, as well as more characteristic of the author, are the fresh additions he has made to his long series of studies of Jewish life.'

The St. James's Gazette.—'*The King of Schnorrers* is a very fascinating story. Mr. Zangwill returns to the Ghetto, and gives us a quaint old-world picture as a most appropriate setting for his picturesque hero, the beggar-king. . . . Good as the story of the arch-schnorrer is, there is perhaps an even better "Yiddish" tale in this book. This is "Flutter-Duck." . . . Let us call attention to the excellence, as mere realistic vivid description, of the picture of the room and atmosphere and conditions in which Flutter-Duck and her circle dwelt; there is something of Dickens in this.'

The Daily Telegraph.—'*The King of Schnorrers*, like *Children of the Ghetto*, depicts the habits and characteristics of Israel in London with painstaking elaborateness and apparent verisimilitude. *The King of Schnorrers* is a character-sketch which deals with the manners and customs of native and foreign Jews as they "lived and had their being" in the London of a century and a quarter ago.'

The Daily Chronicle.—'It is a beautiful story. *The King of Schnorrers* is that great rarity—an entirely new thing, that is as good as it is new.'

The Glasgow Herald.—'On the whole, the book does justice to Mr. Zangwill's rapidly-growing reputation, and the character of Manasseh ought to live.'

The World.—'The exuberant and even occasionally overpowering humour of Mr. Zangwill is at his highest mark in his new volume, *The King of Schnorrers*.'

LONDON: WILLIAM HEINEMANN, 21 BEDFORD STREET, W.C.

THE PREMIER AND THE PAINTER

By I. ZANGWILL and LOUIS COWEN

In One Volume, price 6s.

The Cambridge (University) Review.—'That the book will have readers in a future generation we do not doubt, for there is much in it that is of lasting merit.'

The Graphic.—'It might be worth the while of some industrious and capable person with plenty of leisure to reproduce in a volume of reasonable size the epigrams and other good things witty and serious which *The Premier and the Painter* contains. There are plenty of them, and many are worth noting and remembering.'

St. James's Gazette.—'The satire hits all round with much impartiality; while one striking situation succeeds another till the reader is altogether dazzled. The story is full of life and "go" and brightness, and will well repay perusal.'

The Athenæum.—'In spite of its close print and its five hundred pages *The Premier and the Painter* is not very difficult to read. To speak of it, however, is difficult. It is the sort of book that demands yet defies quotation for one thing; and for another it is the sort of book the description of which as "very clever" is at once inevitable and inadequate. In some ways it is original enough to be a law unto itself, and withal as attractive in its whimsical, wrong-headed way, as at times it is tantalising, bewildering, even tedious. The theme is politics and politicians, and the treatment, while for the most part satirical and prosaic, is often touched with sentiment, and sometimes even with a fantastic kind of poetry. The several episodes of the story are wildly fanciful in themselves and are clumsily connected; but the streak of humorous cynicism which shows through all of them is both curious and pleasing. Again, it has to be claimed for the author that—as is shown to admiration by his presentation of the excellent Mrs. Dawe and her cook-shop—he is capable, when he pleases, of insight and observation of a high order, and therewith of a masterly sobriety of tone. But he cannot be depended upon for the length of a single page; he seeks his effects and his material when and where he pleases. In some respects his method is not, perhaps, altogether unlike Lord Beaconsfield's. To our thinking, however, he is strong enough to go alone, and to go far.'

The World.—'Undeniably clever, though with a somewhat mixed and eccentric cleverness.'

The Morning Post.—'The story is described as a "fantastic romance," and, indeed, fantasy reigns supreme from the first to the last of its pages. It relates the history of our time with humour and well-aimed sarcasm. All the most prominent characters of the day, whether political or otherwise, come in for notice. The identity of the leading politicians is but thinly veiled, while many celebrities appear *in propriâ personâ*. Both the "Premier" and "Painter" now and again find themselves in the most critical situations. Certainly this is not a story that he who runs may read, but it is cleverly original, and often lightened by bright flashes of wit.'

LONDON: WILLIAM HEINEMANN, 21 BEDFORD STREET, W.C.

THE POTTER'S THUMB

By FLORA ANNIE STEEL

In One Volume, price 6s.

The Pall Mall Budget.—'For this week the only novel worth mentioning is Mrs. Steel's *The Potter's Thumb*. Her admirable *From the Five Rivers*, since it dealt with native Indian life, was naturally compared with Mr. Kipling's stories. In *The Potter's Thumb* the charm which came from the freshness of them still remains. Almost every character is convincing, and some of them excellent to a degree.'

The Globe.—'This is a brilliant story—a story that fascinates, tingling with life, steeped in sympathy with all that is best and saddest.'

The Manchester Guardian.—'The impression left upon one after reading *The Potter's Thumb* is that a new literary artist, of very great and unusual gifts, has arisen. . . . In short, Mrs. Steel must be congratulated upon having achieved a very genuine and amply deserved success.'

The Glasgow Herald.—'A clever story which, in many respects, brings India very near to its readers. The novel is certainly one interesting alike to the Anglo-Indian and to those untravelled travellers who make their only voyages in novelists' romantic company.'

The Scotsman.—'It is a capital story, full of variety and movement, which brings with great vividness before the reader one of the phases of Anglo-Indian life. Mrs. Steel writes forcibly and sympathetically, and much of the charm of the picture which she draws lies in the force with which she brings out the contrast between the Asiatic and European world. *The Potter's Thumb* is very good reading, with its mingling of the tragedy and comedy of life. Its evil woman *par excellence* . . . is a finished study.'

The Westminster Gazette.—'A very powerful and tragic story. Mrs. Steel gives us again, but with greater elaboration than before, one of those strong, vivid, and subtle pictures of Indian life which we have learnt to expect from her. To a reader who has not been in India her books seem to get deeper below the native crust, and to have more of the instinct for the Oriental than almost anything that has been written in this time.'

The Leeds Mercury.—'*The Potter's Thumb* is a powerful story of the mystical kind, and one which makes an instant appeal to the imagination of the reader. . . . There is an intensity of vision in this story which is as remarkable as it is rare, and the book, in its vivid and fascinating revelations of life, and some of its limitations, is at once brilliant and, in the deepest and therefore least demonstrative sense, impassioned.'

The National Observer.—'A romance of East and West, in which the glamour, intrigue, and superstition of India are cunningly interwoven and artfully contrasted with the bright and changeable aspects of modern European society. "Love stories," as Mr. Andrew Lang once observed, "are best done by women"; and Mrs. Steel's treatment of Rose Tweedie's love affair with Lewis Gordon is a brilliant instance in point. So sane and delightful an episode is rare in fiction now-a-days.'

LONDON: WILLIAM HEINEMANN, 21 BEDFORD STREET, W.C.

FROM THE FIVE RIVERS

By FLORA ANNIE STEEL

In One Volume, price 6s.

The Times.—'Time was when these sketches of native Punjabi society would have been considered a curiosity in literature. They are sufficiently remarkable, even in these days, when interest in the "dumb millions" of India is thoroughly alive, and writers, great and small, vie in ministering to it. They are the more notable as being the work of a woman. Mrs. Steel has evidently been brought into close contact with the domestic life of all classes, Hindu and Mahomedan, in city and village, and has steeped herself in their customs and superstitions. . . . Mrs. Steel's book is of exceptional merit and freshness.'

Vanity Fair.—'Stories of the Punjaub—evidently the work of one who has an intimate knowledge of, and a kindly sympathy for, its people. It is to be hoped that this is not the last book of Indian stories that Mrs. Steel will give us.'

The Spectator.—'Merit, graphic force, and excellent local colouring are conspicuous in Mrs. Steel's *From the Five Rivers*, and the short stories of which the volume is composed are evidently the work of a lady who knows what she is writing about.'

The Glasgow Herald.—'This is a collection of sketches of Hindu life, full for the most part of brilliant colouring and cleverly wrought in dialect. The writer evidently knows her subject, and she writes about it with unusual skill.'

The North British Daily Mail.—'In at least two of the sketches in Mrs. Steel's book we have a thoroughly descriptive delineation of life in Indian, or rather, Hindoo, villages. "Ganesh Chunel" is little short of a masterpiece, and the same might be said of "Shah Sujah's Mouse." In both we are made the spectator of the conditions of existence in rural India. The stories are told with an art that conceals the art of story-telling.'

The Athenæum.—'They possess this great merit, that they reflect the habits, modes of life, and ideas of the middle and lower classes of the population of Northern India better than do systematic and more pretentious works.'

The Leeds Mercury.—'By no means a book to neglect. . . . It is written with brains. . . . Mrs. Steel understands the life which she describes, and she has sufficient literary art to describe it uncommonly well. These short stories of Indian life are, in fact, quite above the average of stories long or short. . . . There is originality, insight, sympathy, and a certain dramatic instinct in the portrayal of character about the book.'

The Globe.—'She puts before us the natives of our Empire in the East as they live and move and speak, with their pitiful superstitions, their strange fancies, their melancholy ignorance of what poses with us for knowledge and civilisation, their doubt of the new ways, the new laws, the new people. "Shah Sujah's Mouse," the gem of the collection—a touching tale of unreasoning fidelity towards an English "Sinny Baba"—is a tiny bit of perfect writing.'

LONDON : WILLIAM HEINEMANN, 21 BEDFORD STREET, W.C.

www.ingramcontent.com/pod-product-compliance
Lightning Source LLC
Chambersburg PA
CBHW022020110726
47901CB00006B/1598